Bubba and the Missing Woman

By

C.L. Bevill

D1521624

Note to readers: This is the third book in a series. The first novel is *Bubba and the Dead Woman.* The second is *Bubba and the 12 Deadly Days of Christmas.* Ideally, the novels should be read in sequence. Otherwise your brain might explode. (Not really.)

Table of Contents

Chapter One – Bubba and the Missing Woman 5
Chapter Two – Bubba and the Search for the Missing Woman 16
Chapter Three - Bubba and the Gut-Wrenching Feeling of Frustration 28
Chapter Four - Bubba Meets Willodean's Family and Not in a Good Way 40
Chapter Five – Bubba and the Hunt.....................53
Chapter Six - Bubba Wants to Take Something Apart With His Bare Fists...............................68
Chapter Seven - Bubba Makes a Tremendous Decision..82
Chapter Eight – Bubba Does Dallas.....................96
Chapter Nine – Bubba's on the Hunt Again.......108
Chapter Ten - Bubba and the Vision of Brownie's Sterling Moment Or Brownie Meets Matt Lauer121
Chapter Eleven – Bubba Gets Busted 133
Chapter Twelve - Bubba Gets Incarcerated for The First Time in *This* Novel and Boy Howdy it Ain't But Half Over......................................146
Chapter Thirteen - In the Land of Blind People, Bubba is the Least Crazy 158
Chapter Fourteen – Bubba and Inevitability....173
Chapter Fifteen – Bubba Goes to Prison.............186
Chapter Sixteen – Bubba Does Dallas Again.....199
Chapter Seventeen - Bubba Hits a Brick Wall, The PSS Blows Chunks Again, and Then Some Other Stuff Happens..214
Chapter Eighteen – Bubba and the Crime Lord227
Chapter Nineteen – Bubba Gets a Clue 241
Chapter Twenty – The Return of Bubba.............255
Chapter Twenty-One – Bubba's Got Something268

Chapter Twenty-Two – Bubba Yells, "Damn the Torpedoes!" 284
Chapter Twenty-Three – Bubba and Sheriff John Do a Thang 296
Chapter Twenty-Four – So What Happened to Willodean? 305
Epilogue - I Ain't Giving Nothing Away with the Chapter Title So You'll Just Have to Read It......323
Author's Note................................332
About the Author............................334
Other Novels by C.L. Bevill 335

Chapter One

Bubba and the Missing Woman

Thursday, December 29th

Bubba Nathanial Snoddy prayed that he wouldn't find *another* dead body.

He especially didn't want to find another woman's dead body. In fact, Bubba prayed that he wouldn't find a particular woman's dead body. Certainly, he didn't want to find *any* dead body, but he really didn't want to find *her* dead body. He wanted to find *her* alive. Maybe concussed from a car wreck. Possibly weak from blood loss. But alive. Alive and kicking and screaming at him for stealing her official county vehicle. Maybe shouting at him because they hadn't managed to make it to their very first date.

That would be good. Undoubtedly, that would be the best of the worst case scenarios that danced through his frantic brain. Perhaps someone had seen the accident, and the woman had been picked up by a Good Samaritan. Possibly someone, the Good Samaritan, had taken her to the hospital since there was blood on the steering wheel and on the door. Someone had been hurt in the wreck. With sickening conviction, it had doubtlessly been the missing woman.

"Call the hospital," Bubba said urgently to Sheriff John Headrick. Both men appeared somewhat out of place standing next to the smashed sheriff's department vehicle. They towered over the SUV. Bubba was six feet four inches and restlessly imperative as he continued to peer around them.

Sheriff John, as he was known to his constituents,

was an inch taller and sometimes known to wear boots with a one-inch heel to raise him even higher over those that would test his legal officiality. His gaze was no less agitated as he systematically scanned the horizon for any sign of movement.

Both men were anxious to do *something*, but they were at a loss as to exactly what the something was supposed to be.

"The hospital," Sheriff John repeated numbly. His voice was similar to the sound of granite as it was ground through a rock crusher. Not many days past he had been hanged by the neck from an ancient oak tree by a demented killer. His tracheotomy and wretched red marks were still healing and blatantly obvious.

"Maybe she got there somehow," Bubba said. He gestured at the blood on the steering wheel. He wanted to say that it was possible. He wanted to shout it at Sheriff John because everything else was too heart-wrenching to consider. It was something that he had to grasp at in order to make his guts cease their endless twisting.

"Maybe," Sheriff John grated.

Doubt stained his face. His steely gray eyes squinted as he took a rasping breath. He keyed his shoulder mike and spoke with the dispatcher. Bubba began to look over the ground, methodically searching for drops of blood or any other evidence that might indicate where the woman had gone. He walked carefully because Sheriff John had said something that made his insides congeal like cold grease in a cheap diner.

Sheriff John had said, *"Don't touch anything else, Bubba. It's a crime scene now."*

"Crime scene," Bubba had repeated with irritation. *"It's a car wreck. We need to call folks in to look for her. She could be injured and stumbling around."*

6

The scene of the car wreck was the culmination of a horrendous holiday week. Four days earlier, Bubba had discovered a dead man in a Santa/nativity scene in front of city hall. Then another woman had been viciously murdered with a Santa Claus-themed cheese knife. Bubba had ascertained that his mother, Miz Demetrice Snoddy, was somehow involved.

The intended victims had received letters from the Christmas Killer ambiguously warning them of their impending murders in an ugly and gruesome manner. Miz Demetrice had been notified that she would be last for her alleged sins, like a dreadful cherry on top.

Sheriff John had been involved as well and was the third victim to be targeted, but Bubba had gotten the better of the situation. He'd saved Sheriff John from the hanging and scared a whole tribe of fainting goats in the process.

That hadn't stopped the Pegramville Chief of Police, Joe Kimple, from throwing Bubba's proverbial tushy into jail for the day. It had taken the sworn testimonies of both Sheriff John and his wife, Darla, who had both been drugged by the Christmas Killer, to get Bubba out of the pokey.

With more than a little assistance from the woman who was presently missing, Bubba had been released. *She* believed in Bubba. She pressed his side. She let him come with her to investigate a lead. She had even told him she was interested in him and that she wanted him to know it *before* he was wholly cleared of any wrongdoing.

Of course, Bubba had messed up by stealing her official car earlier in the day. It had dawned on Bubba that he knew something that the Christmas Killer knew, and he didn't have the time to convince the woman of his certainty. So he stole the Bronco, albeit for a good reason. In the process, he'd managed to get to two innocent women before they died of smoke inhalation in a fire the Christmas Killer had set.

Again, Big Joe Kimple had been front and present for the inconvenient part of the denouement. Bubba still couldn't believe Big Joe actually looked at Bubba's left index finger when Bubba asked him to do so. Consequently, it would have seemed wrong *not* to knock him out with a roundhouse punch. So Bubba obliged.

Bubba had to stop to think if Big Joe somehow bought his way into being Pegramville's Chief of Police. Or had he simply waited for everyone else qualified to die out?

Then Bubba had rushed to the Snoddy Mansion where the Christmas Killer was intent on more mayhem and killing. Fortuitously, Miz Demetrice had been locked up by Big Joe under suspicion of the murders the Pegramville Chief of Police had been earlier attempting to pin on Bubba. Unfortunately, that left Bubba's maiden aunt, Caressa; his grasping cousin, Fudge; Fudge's capricious spouse, Virtna; Miz Adelia Cedarbloom, a family friend and house keeper; Brownie, Fudge and Virtna's only Satanic offspring; and his beloved Basset hound, Precious, to face the wrath of the vindictive Christmas Killer.

"She's not at the hospital," Sheriff John said in that harsh voice, concluding his conversation with the dispatcher. "Ain't at the clinic neither." He hesitated and his voice cracked a little before he went on, "You said she was going to tell you about her problems."

Bubba ran a hand through his dark brown hair and his cornflower blue eyes were wild. "She said something about a bad relationship," he muttered. He turned to Sheriff John. "We can get Lewis Robson's hounds out here." He gestured at the sun pushing down on the trees in the distance. "Sun's going down. Temperature is gonna be in the forties tonight. But there's a freeze tomorrow night. We cain't let her be all alone out here."

Sheriff John put his hand on Bubba's shoulder. "Boy," he said, "I think maybe she ain't out there. I think maybe someone took her. I think they followed her and saw an opportunity to crash her vehicle with theirs."

"And maybe some idiot who hit her SUV took her to the doctor," Bubba snarled. "Just maybe it ain't the way you're seeing it." His voice broke as he looked around again. There was a shrill sound of a siren in the distance rapidly approaching them. "Maybe they ain't reached the hospital yet."

Sheriff John frowned although his face was already grim. "Girl left Dallas P.D. because a fella was stalking her. Came down here for a fresh start. She tole me all about it. I wouldn't tell you exceptin' you need knowing."

Bubba's head snapped around. Fire burned in those blue eyes. His face stilled into rock. "A stalker," he repeated.

It made him think of a time where the missing woman jumped when some booming clamor startled her. They'd been talking, Bubba and the missing woman, talking about something he couldn't quite recall. It had probably been more important than he'd ever imagined. Then something had happened.

There had been a sudden noise from down the street. A man had been dumping his trash into a dumpster, loudly banging the heavy can against the metal of the larger container. The woman had jumped a mile, and for a split moment, she looked scared. The normally unflappable woman had an expression of fear in her lovely green eyes. The thought that had gone through Bubba's head was, *Something's frightened her badly.*

And what had the woman said at the cemetery the night they first kissed? She said, *"I have a...history with a bad relationship. It's part of the reason why I moved to Pegram County. One day I'll need to tell you about it."*

But the woman hadn't had a chance to tell him. Bubba abruptly realized that they had shared their first kiss only the day before.

Yesterday, I kissed Willodean Gray. It was the best kiss I ever had. A hundred on a scale of ten, and I ain't exaggerating. It rocked me like a San Francisco earthquake. And today, she's as absent as snow in a Texas winter.

It was also the day the Christmas Killer had been captured. Bubba had charged into the Snoddy Mansion and found that he didn't actually know who the killer was. But the killer hadn't hesitated in confessing all and sundry.

Once the killer's family had lived in Pegramville. The killer's father had been part of a charitable association, the same one which all the victims and intended victims had belonged. The killer's father embezzled money for Christmas gifts for his children, too ashamed to admit that he was bankrupt. Miz Demetrice was the one who was outraged the man stole from homeless orphans.

The man, Matthew Roquemore, went to prison where he belonged. When he had been released, he committed suicide. Matthew's wife and children moved away from Pegramville, but the daughter of the man, LaNell Roquemore, grew into Nancy Musgrave. Nancy, a psychotic social worker, held a grudge. A murderous grudge. And she had been ready to collect on the perceived debt of injustice.

As Nancy had been about to commit more insidious murders, Bubba's cousin-once-removed, a little hellion of a boy named Brownie, charged to the rescue, zapping Nancy with a homemade stun gun.

Bubba would have smiled wryly, but he had other things on his mind.

The air had barely been cleared in the Snoddy Mansion about the real Christmas Killer's identity when Bubba comprehended Deputy Willodean Gray was ominously absent. Sheriff John ascertained the location of her replacement vehicle by the GPS tracking device inside it, and they had found the wrecked SUV.

Without Willodean, alone on an isolated road, with little to indicate what occurred.

The roads were empty. The siren still wailed in the distance. A flock of starlings launched from the fields opposite the woods. Their cawing protest was directed at nothing at all.

"How do you know?" Bubba asked slowly.

Sheriff John took his Stetson hat off his head and ran his fingers through sweat-soaked steel gray hair the same color as his eyes. "How do I know what, Bubba?"

"How do you know *this*," Bubba waved at the wreck, "is from the fella who was stalking Willodean?"

Sheriff John touched the bandages at his throat. He was going to speak with a rasp for the rest of his life. But he was going to have the rest of his life, and it was primarily due to the younger man with the haunted expression standing next to him. Bubba had been framed before, and there were folks in Pegramville, hell, in Pegram County, who believed in him. One was his own mother, Miz Demetrice. Another was Willodean Gray. Sheriff John had initially been skeptical. Bubba had been in his jail how many times?

That's a whole mess of smoke without any fire.

There was a pool going on when Bubba would next walk through the Pegram County Jail's doors. Tee Gearheart, the benevolent Pegram County Jailor, held the monies until the exact time and date could be formally established. Even Sheriff John had thrown in a $20, and he knew personally that Miz Demetrice had snatched up the entire month of February.

"If a car plowed into the side of her official vehicle, then why ain't there radiator fluid?" Bubba asked. "Any car that hit hers would have hit it front ways. There would have been damage to it. Oil leaking, coolant, too. Bits of bumper." His eyes flew over the asphalt. "I don't see nothing like that."

Sheriff John's eyes snapped downward, looking for what Bubba had suggested. It was a decent notion. It didn't do anything to disprove what he thought happened. Someone had planned to take Willodean Gray by force. There was little chance of that occurring around the Pegram County Sheriff's Department, and Willodean frequently had a loaded sidearm strapped to her side. So how did a stalker get her all to himself?

Her apartment? Maybe. Most folks knew Willodean was a crack shot at the range. She even shot better than Sheriff John, and he hardly ever missed a vexatious squirrel.

A man waited for an opportunity and planned. A sneaky man schemed. Oft times, Willodean was alone on patrols. If a fella waited for that, he might know where she was going. He might be listening on the police band. There wasn't a law against folks owning a police band radio. Lots of people listened to the police band for gossip, amusement, and sheer persnicketiness.

If a man knew she was coming alone, then a fella could be in the right place with the right kind of vehicle.

If that same fella managed to stun Willodean, then she wouldn't be apt to shoot him. "Did he reverse into her?" Sheriff John pondered aloud.

Bubba froze. The Pegram County official unit had been pushed almost off the side of the farm road. From a distance, it might appear as though it was simply parked there. There were a thousand typical reasons for a Pegram County Sheriff's Deputy to be parked along a county road. People wouldn't pay much attention until it sat there too long.

Turning slowly, Bubba judged the area. A hundred feet from where they stood, a turn-out meandered into the forest. Ruts disappeared into the growth. The path might go off to some fishing hole along Sturgis Creek. It might lead to someone's deer stand. It could go nowhere at all. Mentally, he could see someone parked there.

Waiting. Sheriff John's thoughts paralleled Bubba's. *A big truck? The kind with the reinforced corners to avoid typical bangs and dings as it went along its daily bizness.*

The distant sirens neared as Sheriff John and Bubba walked toward the turn-out. They could see marks on the asphalt where tires had been pushed sideways. There were little bits of red and white plastic from someone's lights. There was a section of a metal emblem that had been torn away. Bubba nudged it with a foot while Sheriff John made a grumbling noise.

"Dodge," Bubba said. He would know. His tortured face turned to Sheriff John. "How did she know she was being stalked again?"

The unsaid question was more disturbing. *Why hadn't she told me about her stalker?*

Bubba kept the thought to himself. He knew the answer. Willodean was a sheriff's deputy, and she didn't want the protectiveness that occurred when a big bubba like Bubba decided that they were meant to be.

She hadn't liked it much when he shoved her out of the way when an irate Army officer once took a swing at Bubba. She hadn't cared for it a damn bit when she realized he stole her official vehicle in part to protect her from a mad-dawg killer. Oh, the sanctioned version was that Bubba hadn't had time to explain it to Willodean. The unsaid portion was that he preferred she stay at the sheriff's department and fume at him from over the police band in relative safety.

Willodean had thought that she could take care of business herself.

But she's a little bit of a woman, he frowned. He turned his head so that he could see the open door of the wrecked SUV. He couldn't see the blood there from where he stood, but he knew it was there. *And she's hurt.*

"The letters started again," Sheriff John said, his voice like a great crackling hunk of hailstone during tornado season. "That no-account had done found her again. Just like he done before."

Two Pegramville Police Department vehicles wheeled to a stop beside Sheriff John's county car. Big Joe emerged from one and looked around. His beady eyes focused on the wrecked sheriff's deputy SUV. "Where the hellfire is Gray?" he bellowed. "Did ya'll call an ambulance?"

A Pegramville Police officer named Haynes, a man not overly talented in the way of thinking, stepped from the other car. "Hey, Chief," he called to Big Joe. "George Bufford just called. One of his tow trucks got stolt sometime last night."

Bubba once worked for George Bufford at Bufford's Gas and Grocery convenience store at the bottom of the exit ramp from Interstate 38. George Bufford wasn't a particularly nice man. He was having an affair with his secretary, Rosa Granado, and his wife was suing him for divorce on account of the fact that he was a pure-D butthead. Bubba didn't know much about that specific legal precedence but more power to Mrs. Bufford.

Bufford's Gas and Grocery was also a 24/7 garage, although most folks didn't take their cars there after eight at night. Bufford's also had two tow trucks. One only worked about half the time because George was too cheap to have his mechanics do regular maintenance on it. The other was a ten-year-old...Dodge. Melvin Wetmore, a mechanic at Bufford's, habitually left the keys in the tow trucks.

Bubba said flatly to Sheriff John, "Bet it was the Dodge."

Sheriff John nodded. Despite the fact that the Christmas Killer had just been apprehended, even if it had been by a ten-year-old Boy Scout, the day was getting more and more dismal.

Bubba was more than inclined to agree. "Call the hospital again," he said dully. "Maybe we're wrong."

But they weren't wrong.

Willodean was gone.

Chapter Two

Bubba and the Search for the Missing Woman

Thursday, December 29th

Brownie Snoddy was fairly happy at the state of affairs. He had shown the adults of the Snoddy household that he was large and in charge. There had been a *situation,* and Brownie had been the one to improvise, adapt, and overcome. That had been the mantra of his mother's father, who had been a U.S. Marine for twenty-three years. Papa Derryberry had ever been spouting awesome Marine sayings that Brownie longed to emulate. Papa also called Army and Navy Troops "Citified pansies who are dumber than a box of hair." But Brownie wouldn't tell Cousin Bubba that because Brownie knew that Bubba had once been in the Army. So had his Great-uncle Elgin, but pretty much no one talked about Elgin. *Except when Aunt Demetrice said she used a grenade to kill Great-uncle Elgin. And that don't make sense because she also said she shot him with a spear gun. How do you kill someone with* both *a grenade and a spear gun? How does an old lady like Auntie D. get a grenade and a spear gun? Then Miz Adelia said Uncle E. had a heart attack...*

The boy's thoughts snapped back to the present. The evil perpetrator, Nancy Musgrave, was being loaded into an ambulance. She was handcuffed to the side of the stretcher, and she was stridently mouthing several invectives at anyone who came close to her. Brownie marveled at the older woman's inventiveness. He hadn't heard some of the four-lettered phrases, and he was sure that his fellow Boy Scouts would need to be educated on their colorfulness. After all, a Boy Scout needed to share his knowledge with his comrades in arms. *Wouldn't be right to keep those to myself,* he reasoned thoughtfully.

Brownie looked around. Bubba had made tracks with the Sheriff, off to look for someone else. The paramedics had already loaded the Pegramville Police Officer that Big Joe zapped with Brownie's homemade stun gun into another ambulance. But the ambulance hadn't departed, and the rear doors were still open. The two paramedics were working on the police officer.

Golly, his legs are still *twitching. Have to make a note of that in my research journal.*

Brownie's mother and father stood near Fudge's truck talking quietly. Virtna said something about "properly redressed" and "monetary compensation." Miz Adelia passed out cups of coffee to the dozen other officials wandering around the property. Aunt Caressa sat on the veranda fanning herself with a newspaper and shaking her head. Wallie, the construction contractor who was rebuilding Bubba's house, sat on the back of his truck avidly watching the goings on. After all, it wasn't every day that someone got to watch a killer nabbed by the likes of the Snoddys. The three former patients of Nancy Musgrave had been herded into a tight circle by a young sheriff's department deputy. All three appeared distinctly uncomfortable with the law's proximity. The one calling himself Jesus Christ, and Brownie knew that the man was really crazy and not really the son of God, lectured the deputy on the difference between violence and pacifism.

What's that mean?

But something else concerned Brownie. *Where's the media?* he thought with ostensive irritation. He wanted to shout out his participation in the capture of the Christmas Killer. Hey, he had personally saved-how many people had he saved? Brownie broke out his fingers.

There's Ma, Pa, Aunty Caressa, Miz Adelia, and why ain't she giving me another one of them cinnamon rolls? Bubba, too. The three loonies. Do they count? Brownie considered. *Heck yes, they count.* They were certainly going to count when he told the newspaper about his heroism in tedious detail. *That's...*Brownie frowned, *How many people is it?* He needed a pen and paper.

Precious could be heard baying from inside the mansion. Miz Adelia had locked the dog up after the Basset hound tried to bite a chunk out of Big Joe's leg.

Didn't lock me *up.* Brownie thought about that and scowled. *I should leave the part out about biting a policeman when I talk to the newspapers. And I saved Precious, too. Dogs count. Yessiree Billy-Bob Johnson with a cherry on top.*

Two things especially annoyed Brownie. One was the already mentioned dearth of news representatives. Two, Big Joe had confiscated Brownie's stun gun. The police chief handed it over to one of the deputies and scuttled off in his car to parts unknown. Another police officer in another vehicle followed him up the highway lickity-split. Something else was going on that no one was going to share with Brownie.

Brownie scraped his feet on the earth. No one paid attention to him, except one of the loonies. He didn't remember her name, but she wore three sweaters and appeared as mousy as Mickey's real life counterparts. She also had a habit of talking funny.

From about twenty feet away she cast him a skeptical glance and said loudly, "Thou saucy, mud-mettled hempseed."

A pout stitched Brownie's eyebrows together. He suspected that he had just been insulted. He stuck his tongue out at the loony, but she one-upped him when she returned the tongue extension and crossed her eyes in addition. Brownie couldn't think of a better face to pull, so he glowered instead.

In any case, he had bigger fish to fry. He needed a piece of paper and a pen. Jotting down a few notes about what had happened would present better to the local newspeople. He looked around irately. He had personally captured the Christmas Killer. *Where are the fardle-barping news people?*

The police weren't happy about letting folks back into the mansion, so Brownie wasn't going to get paper from there. He cast his eyes on Wallie. The construction man had been helpful when a killer was threatening his folks, but previously, Wallie had taken exception to Brownie messing with his tools. There had been several specific and nonspecific threats mentioned. He couldn't quite understand how Wallie would make Brownie sing "fall-set-o."

The thought made Brownie all the more determined to find a piece of paper so that he could add that to his notes. A boy, almost a man, needed to know how to make someone else sing "fall-set-o." If a grown man like Wallie, who was fairly buff and somewhat intimidating, used it as a threat, it was almost unquestionably a threat to be reckoned with and thus worth knowing.

Focus, Brownie, he told himself. Suddenly, he brightened. *Well, hey. All the po-lice just done gone inside and left their cars all open.* Three police officers and one sheriff's deputy had just tromped inside the Snoddy Mansion for an impromptu get-together. He could see them huddled inside the door, speaking in low voices, glancing around to see if anyone was listening to them.

Brownie sidled over to the nearest police vehicle.

Well, look at that, he thought triumphantly, *a piece of paper. Also, my stun gun.*

•

Miz Demetrice Snoddy was incarcerated in the Pegramville City Jail. It wasn't nearly as fun as the county jail. They had two sections. One was for the fellas. One much smaller one was for the gals. The female jailor named Barnheart apparently had the sense of humor of an igneous crystallization of ancient magma with ketchup on top. Probably less than that. She didn't understand Miz Demetrice's need to quote from Gandhi or from Dr. Martin Luther King, Jr. She also didn't understand that Miz Demetrice had a need to share legal advice with the prostitute who had been in the jail since the evening before or that Miz Demetrice felt compelled to share skin preservation tips with Jailor Barnheart.

"Exfoliation, dear," Miz Demetrice announced snidely, not exactly proud of the unpremeditated and underhanded insult. "That's the key to avoiding those wretched crow's feet around your eyes."

"Well, you've got stars around your eyes," Jailor Barnheart said in retaliation.

"My great-nephew has a way with a Sharpie marker," Miz Demetrice responded snippily. Brownie had gotten very colorful with the permanent markers, and Miz Demetrice hadn't gotten all of the markings off from around her eyes.

Permanent markers are very...well, permanent.

One of the dispatchers wandered back to talk to Miz Demetrice. Mary Lou Treadwell was typically the receptionist and dispatcher for the Pegram County Sheriff's Department, but the two law enforcement agencies were often forced to share assets in the impoverished city and county. Mary Lou was apt to gossip and enjoyed the recent excitement as much as the next nascent blabbermouth.

Of course, Miz Demetrice couldn't rightly speak against the art of gossiping. If one didn't chinwag, then one probably didn't get to speak for weeks. After all, folks could only watch so much television and read so many books. Rumormongering was next to a national pastime in the city of Pegramville and very nearly a religion in Pegram County.

Mary Lou said, "Hey, Miz Demetrice."

Mary Lou looked the Snoddy matriarch over and thought that she appeared fairly perky for a woman accused of attempted murder and worse. But then Mary Lou knew in her heart of hearts Miz Demetrice was only capable of murdering her own belated husband, Elgin. Allegedly, he had died of a heart attack while fairly young, but it had been insinuated that he had been poisoned, shot, electrocuted, and stabbed with a pair of spiffy Manolo Blahniks. *Or was that on* The Real Housewives of Beverly Hills? *Hell, if Miz D. done kilt everyone who ticked her off, Pegramville would be a population of one.*

Miz Demetrice looked up from the bunk. She was relaxed and fairly comfortable, but the jail didn't provide pillows or blankets. It was something she'd have to bring up at the next city council meeting. Even accused criminals need a little creature comfort. Feather pillows, a rum shot followed by a vermouth mixer, and perhaps a portable fan because the jail was on the warm side.

"Mary Lou," Miz Demetrice said. Indeed, she would have gotten up and offered to shake hands or something equally appropriate in the realms of etiquette, but she was at a loss as to what would be the proper thing under the circumstances. Possibly, she could write a tome on proper jailhouse protocol. After all, it was getting to be a regular family tradition.

Mary Lou brushed some scarlet red hair away from her face. She was the type of girl who enjoyed a decent plastic surgeon and the amazing variations supplied by the cosmetic industry. In fact, her husband was said to be very pleased with Mary Lou's recent D-sized additions, and Mary Lou was said to be looking well-worn in the mornings when she appeared for her work shift.

"Did you hear, Miz D.?"

"Hear what?" Truth be told, Miz Demetrice had heard many things. The prostitute in the cell next to her was a wishing well full of inane information and that was despite the fact that Miz Demetrice had declined to throw in a coin. Her name was Gigi, and she was new in town, working her way from Baton Rouge to St. Louis via the back roads and other roads not typically traveled. Gigi talked nonstop until Miz Demetrice had been forced to mention that there were security cameras in the hallways of the jail recording *everything*. It was only a little white lie but Miz D. was right tired of listening to the enthusiastic Gigi speak on subjects as varied as oral techniques, to the adorable color of her toenails especially when they were lifted above her head.

"Well." Mary Lou licked her lip in anticipation of imparting serious gossip. She didn't have a lot of time after all. "The other guy called in sick for his shift, *again*, and I got to pull a double, so I'm gonna have to run right quickly. So after Big Joe arrested you, Bubba stole Deputy Gray's county car."

Miz Demetrice made a muffled noise, but Mary Lou went on regardless. "He went to Lou Lou Vandygriff's house and found it on fire. Big Joe said it was Bubba who done set the fire, but Willodean was arguing with him something fierce and all. So Bubba rescued Miz Lou Lou and that caregiver gal, too."

And I'm locked away in here, Miz Demetrice thought sourly.

"I wasn't on duty then," Mary Lou said without hesitation. "But Arlette Formica was, and she tolt me just about everything. Bubba rescued those gals and then plumb decked Big Joe. Laid him out like a piece of beef on a butcher's block."

Miz Demetrice nodded solemnly. If there was ever a list of police officers who deserved to be plumb decked, certainly Big Joe figured prominently at the top. She noticed Gigi had sidled over to the bars and was raptly attending Mary Lou's words.   Mary Lou actively demonstrated Bubba's blow to the chief of police with a powerful right hook that decimated all of the air in her vicinity.

"Ooo," Gigi marveled.

"So Bubba stolt Deputy Gray's vehicle again," Mary Lou said. "Arlette said he knew where the Christmas Killer was." She paused to scratch at the side of a D cup. "There was something about drugs being used on folks, too. Psycho-something-or-others. I don't recollect the name." She laughed. "If it ain't Percocet or a birth control pill, I wouldn't know much about it."

I suppose I can't escape now, Miz Demetrice lamented. *I could rip parts of my shirt off and stuff my ears so that I wouldn't have to listen to the little chit. But then Mary Lou might take it the wrong way. And why in the name of God's green earth is Lou Lou Vandygriff's house being burned down?*

Clarity came to Miz Demetrice a moment later. Lou Lou Vandygriff had been the secretary of the Pegramville Historical Society Board, the same board that had Matthew Roquemore sent to jail. *If Miz Lou Lou was targeted, then it was because she knew something. But Miz Lou Lou's in the advanced stages of Alzheimer's disease, and she pretty much knew next to little about what had happened five minutes before.*

"And Bubba said the Christmas Killer was at the Snoddy Mansion," Mary Lou went on.

Miz Demetrice perked right up.

"Ooo, oh," Gigi said, "*the Christmas Killer.* I read about him." She gnawed on a red and green striped fingernail. "But on account I didn't get a letter I weren't real concerned."

Mary Lou was getting into the story telling. She waited for Gigi to finish and ascertained that Miz Demetrice was about to impatiently demand that she complete the tale.

Mary Lou said, "So he went to the Snoddy Mansion to save everyone's bacon. I reckon he knew that you were here, but the rest of the family was there. Your sister, Miz Adelia, your nephew, and his family, that poor little boy."

That poor little boy *probably ground up the Christmas Killer's heart in a blender and drank it as an aperitif.*

"There was something about a white van," Mary Lou continued.

White van? White van? Like the white van seen at the Boomer's goat farm after someone tried to make Sheriff John's neck look like one of those long-necked gals from Africa, except without all the fancy rings? Miz Demetrice frowned. *Like a white van from...a place that had access to psycho-something-or-other drugs? Like...*

"Deputy Gray even got on the police band herself," Mary Lou added. "Arlette said she sounded like she rightly cared for Bubba. Arlette said something about the two of them being married, but that ain't right?" She scowled. "I would have been invited."

"Rumors, dear," Miz Demetrice said more gently than she felt.

"Oh," Mary Lou said, only slightly mollified. "You *will* invite me?"

"Of course, dear," Miz Demetrice agreed. She would probably invite everyone in the county in sheer gratitude of the nuptials. Heavens, she might even invite the Lutherans. "You too, Gigi."

"Oh, thank you, Miz Demetrice," Gigi said gratefully. "Most folks don't think much about a gal like me being near their kinfolk. But a girl's got to do what a girl's got to do. Don't the bible say something about whoring being next to something or other?"

"*Cameras*," Miz Demetrice mouthed to Gigi and pointed heavenward. Gigi winced and shut her mouth. But Miz Demetrice did make a mental note to check her bible on prostitution references. One never knew when it might come in handy.

"Mary Lou, dear," Miz Demetrice prompted encouragingly. Outwardly her façade was peaceful but inwardly she had a strong urge to grasp Mary Lou by the hair and bang her head against the bars until she finished the story.

"Oh, yes," Mary Lou said. "Well, Bubba rushed over you all's place and found...*the loonies*." Apparently, the name had caught on. Bubba should be proud of himself.

"What loonies?" Gigi asked.

"Mayor John Leroy, Jr. has a program whereby he uses patients from a local mental institute for work-study," Mary Lou repeated obediently.

Miz Demetrice was certain that Mary Lou had memorized that for some reason. Mayor Leroy was already in the process of covering his less-than-honorable tuckus.

"Three of them were assisting with the Pegramville Christmas Festival," Mary Lou finished as if from rote.

"You mean ya'll have crazy people working out in the public?" Gigi said with disdain. Seemingly, prostitution was acceptable and insanity was not.

"Poor misunderstood folks with mental challenges, dear," Miz Demetrice said tactfully. "Do go on, Mary Lou. I'm all atwitter and at my age, that isn't likely to be a good thing."

"I don't know exactly what occurred," Mary Lou said tentatively. "I heard that Bubba's all right though," she added quickly when she correctly read Miz Demetrice's expression. "Fine and dandy, and he ain't even under arrest." She considered it for a moment. "Well, he *was* under arrest, but then someone said Big Joe changed his mind."

"And the Christmas Killer?" Miz Demetrice snapped.

"Well, they said they caught someone," Mary Lou trailed off. "Actually, there was some debate about that. One officer said the little boy caught the Christmas Killer."

"Brownie?" Miz Demetrice said doubtfully. "Brownie caught the Christmas Killer?" *Quite probably Brownie found the Loch Ness Monster, as well and was keeping it in a goldfish bowl.*

"Who's Brownie?" Gigi asked confused. "Who would name their kid after a dessert?"

"It's all real confusing," Mary Lou said with a glance at Gigi. "And is Brownie named after a *brownie*?"

"It's a family name," Miz Demetrice said shortly. "The Snoddys have a long history of...eccentric family names."

Gigi laughed. "And I thought my family wasn't able to catch catfish in a coffee cup."

"You've no idea," Miz Demetrice muttered.

Silence ensued for a moment. In the distance they could hear someone clanging the bars, and a siren briefly came to life.

"So who was the killer?" Gigi asked, as if she would know the person.

Mary Lou said excitedly, "It's either Jesus Christ or Nancy Musgrave. Those silly oss-i-fers cain't make up their minds."

"*Jesus Christ* kilt someone?" Gigi asked incredulously.

"It's one of the mental patients who thinks he's Jesus Christ," Miz Demetrice interjected impatiently. *Jesus isn't really a killer. He's just a poor misunderstood soul with an attraction for stealing hemorrhoid cream and underarm deodorant.*

She had to stop and think about the other one. It made more sense if one disregarded the fact that Miz Demetrice didn't yet understand the motivation. *Nancy Musgrave, the social worker, is a serial killer with an odd affinity for murdering people with Christmas related implementations?*

Sighing heavily, she didn't know why it had happened or what Nancy's reasons might have been. Nancy had obviously been connected to the man from the Pegramville Historical Society Board who had been incarcerated years before.

His daughter? A deranged relative? But a social worker? *Doesn't that paint a wretched picture about our societal outreach programs? How is a pitiable misbegotten individual going to receive any kind of help when his social worker is Charles Manson's understudy? Really.*

Chapter Three

Bubba and the Gut-Wrenching Feeling of Frustration

Friday, December 30th

Bubba was tired of standing around.

The sun had set. A passel of law enforcement congregated around Deputy Willodean Gray's wrecked county car. Sheriff John had obtained a map of the area and tried to institute a grid search. Someone had brought out bottled water and sandwiches from a Pegramville hoagie shop and passed them out. The food had tasted like ashes in Bubba's mouth, but he had forced it down his throat because he knew he was going to need the energy it would supply.

Word had trickled back that Nancy Musgrave was locked in the county jail and the county prosecutor was having her transferred to a woman's prison because of the infamy of the case. The local jail wasn't set up for women ordinarily, and the state offered to house Nancy for the interim.

Furthermore, the news was out about the missing sheriff's deputy. The media had descended in droves on the site. Bubba could see no fewer than five separate vans parked beyond an unofficial line two deputies patrolled. Individuals had shoulder-held cameras pointed in the sheriff's direction and were following as if they had fixed onto him with laser sights. Sheriff John had called in for reinforcements. A Texas State Trooper's car had pulled up earlier. Also, there was, and Bubba wasn't certain because he couldn't recall if he'd ever met one before, an FBI agent in a dark suit with a sanctioned high-and-tight haircut. The Fed wandered around, attempting to appear official.

A group of local officers had come to speak with Bubba again. Sheriff John had led the charge questioning Bubba, but the older man already knew what Bubba knew, and the questions were lackluster and repetitive.

Mildly surprised that his mother hadn't appeared, Bubba realized there was every chance that Big Joe hadn't gotten around to releasing Miz Demetrice from the city jail. *The jerk.*

There was also every chance that Miz Demetrice had taken control of the facility and was lying in siege until she could force the government to bend to her will. Free ice cream and socialized medicine was only the tip of her particular iceberg.

Bubba was getting tired of being tired. No one was doing anything. For some reason, Sheriff John was certain Willodean had been snatched by a mysterious individual. The magic word "kidnapping" and the extra-special addition of "sheriff's deputy" seemed to have thrown an extra Jamaican hot pepper into the gumbo. The city was involved. The county was involved. The state was involved. The Feds were involved. The media was involved. The Girl Scouts might have been involved, but Bubba hadn't yet seen them.

Bubba didn't feel involved. He felt as if he was standing around, mired in mud, while Willodean was somewhere hurting, possibly bleeding, and needing help.

Oh, things were being accomplished. In the back of Bubba's mind he had to acknowledge the effort being made. Officers of all sorts were spread out asking residents along this road if they had seen anything. They had been tasked to fan out and knock at every door within a mile. Then they would reconnoiter and take on the next few miles.

Bubba had heard Sheriff John put out a bulletin about the Dodge tow truck which would promptly appear in every police station in Texas. There was a photograph of a non-smiling Willodean peering out of the same bulletin. Sheriff John had taken a few precious minutes to personally call Willodean's family in Dallas. In a few more minutes, Bubba knew that Sheriff John would be talking to the news. The older man adjusted his shirt and brushed the dirt off of it in preparation of being on camera. Gravelly voiced, with a bandage still on his neck from an attack from the Christmas Killer, he was prepping for the ritualized sacrifice of speaking to reporters. He was going to get the word out about the missing sheriff's deputy. People would know she needed help, and if a soul did see her, then they needed to do their duty.

Bubba couldn't fault Sheriff John for being held back by technicality and legal procedures. It was the same as being stuck in a field of the thickest goo without a branch or a rope in sight.

Bubba spared a moment for Willodean's family. Previously, he hadn't thought about them, and it made his stomach knot up. It had to be a thousand times more hellish for them. They had next to little knowledge about what had occurred. Had they known about Willodean's stalker? Had they supported her move to the boonies in order to protect her? *Protected her just about as well as I did.*

Bubba said a dirty word, and a nearby officer flinched. Bubba turned to the man, who was someone he didn't recognize, as well as a Texas State Trooper. "You got a cell phone I kin borrow?"

The trooper stared at Bubba. Bubba noticeably wasn't law enforcement, so the man plainly didn't know what to make of him. Clearly, he wasn't exactly a suspect either, but neither was he being included in the planning session occurring not thirty feet away. Consequently, the trooper shrugged and pulled out a Droid.

Bubba stared at the phone that appeared tiny in his hand. The trooper sighed and showed him how to turn it on. Then he showed Bubba how to unlock it by running the tip of his index finger over the little lock icon and moving it sideways. Finally, he showed Bubba how to dial a number.

"These things get more complicated every time I pick one up," Bubba muttered, thinking longingly of Sheriff John's wife's unsophisticated model. The phone rang on the other end, and after a few minutes, Miz Adelia picked up. "It's me, Miz Adelia," he said curtly.

"Oh, thank the Lord," Miz Adelia said. "Bubba, these folks won't say a lick about nothing, and your mama ain't home yet."

"Mama will get out as soon as Big Joe gets around to it," he said quickly. "Ain't gonna harm her overly."

"But what about the other poor souls in the jail?" Miz Adelia said, only half joking. Bubba could hear Precious, his dog, bark in the background to be let outside and knew that he didn't have to ask about her.

"Look in Ma's rolodex and call Lewis Robson," Bubba instructed. "Tell him to meet me out where all the circus is occurring on Shorely's farm road. Cain't miss all the happenings."

"But that's rightly close where my cousin goes to-"

"Yes, I know about your cousin, and I'll try my best to avoid that area," Bubba said before Miz Adelia could say anything about her cousin Ralph's illegal pot patch set in the middle of Sturgis Woods.

The Cedarblooms weren't terribly criminal, but Miz Adelia's mother was dealing with a late-stage cancer.

Ralph had kindly hopped into the affair by volunteering to supply medicinal marijuana to Charlene Cedarbloom. The fact that marijuana was not legally medicinal in the state of Texas, was not properly addressed by any of the Cedarblooms. Nor was the matter that Ralph made a tidy profit selling the remainder of his crop to third parties.

Bubba could have called Lew Robson directly about his hounds, but he knew that Charlene Cedarbloom was in rapid decline. He didn't want to see Ralph arrested any more than Newt Durley's relatives, who had an active still further back in the Sturgis Woods. The fact that their booze was only illegal because they didn't care to apply for a license to sell it, was beside the point. Durleys had grown up with alcohol and illegality, and Newt and his brothers were proudly carrying on the tradition. Newt frequently celebrated the tradition in the jail while sobering up from the potent mix made in the forest.

"What's wrong?" Miz Adelia snapped. "It ain't Ralph's little bit of maryjane, that's certain."

"Willodean Gray is missing," Bubba said solemnly. Saying the words didn't make anything better. In fact, it made it worse. Saying the words aloud made it seem as though it was acceptable. "We need to search the...Sturgis Woods for her."

Hint. Hint. Wink. Hint.

Miz Adelia was silent for a moment. She was taking in information. She didn't waste time with asking what had happened to the beauteous deputy.

"You'll need something of hers for the hounds to scent," she said instead. "I'll need to make some phone calls."

The silent message was, if Ralph Cedarbloom needed to haul his sit-upon out to the woods and clean up, then he best do so in a hasty manner and thank you very much for the information, Bubba.

Bubba brought his head up and saw the state officer watching him.

"Something that belongs to her?"

He could have hit himself. Perhaps there was something inside the wrecked SUV that the hounds could scent, but the crime scene technologists were still working on it. The fact that their presence had been called for made Bubba's heart descend into the pit of his stomach like the fancy ball dropping in Times Square on New Year's Eve.

No one was saying, "It'll be all right, Bubba." As a matter of fact, the message was the opposite. "It *ain't* gonna be all right, Bubba," was the dispatch he was getting, and there wasn't a damn thing he could do right now. Futhermore, it was becoming, "And things are rapidly getting so grave that you're going to have to lick a cat's behind to get the god-awful taste of fear and distress out of your mouth."

The night was full and dark beyond the lights of the police car. No one could see anything to do a search. The moon hid behind clouds, and even the few stars that were visible seemed gloomy and disinclined to be of assistance.

Willodean wasn't a runaway, and someone had likely stolen a Dodge tow truck to bring her to a stop. Sheriff John wasn't going to like Bubba's interference, but he was so damned tired of waiting. It was a case of do-something-or-he-would-go-insane.

"Bubba?" Miz Adelia said gently. "Ain't your fault, boy. You wouldn't do nothing to hurt that gal."

But I didn't do anything to help her.

Bubba heard the plastic of the phone crack in his hand and the trooper said, "Cra-ap," under his breath.

I stole her car. She had to take another one to get out to the Snoddy Mansion. She might have been with me...instead of-

"Bubba Nathanial Snoddy!" Miz Adelia yelled, and the noise from the Droid sounded a little off. Bubba pulled the phone away from his ear and comprehended that pieces of the phone were falling away. "Don't you dare blame yourself!" Miz Adelia finished.

Perhaps she had pulled out her handy book of things to say to a person who is feeling things he doesn't care to admit. God knew there had to be such a book out there about Bubba. Miz Adelia and his mother probably shared it upon occasion.

Bubba cautiously brought the phone back to his ear. He was actually holding it together with his oversized ham hocks. Amazingly, it was still working for the moment. "Tell Lew to meet us out here at first light. Before that if he can. I'll cover his fees."

"Bubba, you sound awfully strange," Miz Adelia croaked. She might not have been croaking; the phone was not working very well.

"I'll get something that belonged to Willodean for the hounds," Bubba gritted out. He would have to get it from her home. Even though he had never been inside, he knew where she lived. Sheriff John would have access or know a way to get in. Bubba knew how to gain access if the sheriff didn't. "Tell Ralph I said hey."

"Um," Miz Adelia croaked. "Sure, I reckon."

"Tell Lew first light, hear?"

Bubba pulled the phone away from his ear again. He looked down at it as he pressed the "end call" button on the little screen. "Fancy phone," he said regretfully to the trooper. *It was a fancy phone. Not so much anymore.*

The trooper looked down at the phone with dismay. "It gets the Internet and it's 4G," he said slowly. "I can

Tweet and Facebook whenever I feel like it."

He can do what? Tweet? Facebook? What the frick are those? Bubba glowered and tried to give the Droid back to the officer while more bits fell off. It made an abnormal whistling noise, and smoke started pouring from one side.

"I don't think it's supposed to do that," the trooper said dismally.

"Sorry," Bubba offered. "Ifin you'll give me your information I'll send you a check for it." He sighed. "It hasn't been the best of weeks for me. I've also got to pay back someone for the damage I did to a car I borrowed."

The trooper stared. "You damaged the sheriff's county car you borrowed?" He whistled. "*You're* Bubba Snoddy, and I heard all about that."

"No, it was *another* car that I borrowed," Bubba said slowly. "I asked permission first. But there was a herd of fainting goats and the sheriff was hanging from the Christ Tree, so I couldn't very well take it slowly."

"Of course not," the trooper said strangely. He cautiously put the Droid on the ground, and several people paused to watch it catch fire. Finally, one of the Pegramville City Police Officers took a fire extinguisher from his vehicle and put the fire out with two strong puffs of chemical spray.

The fire reminded Bubba that he hadn't asked about anyone else. There was Lou Lou Vandygriff who had been in a fire the previous day. Along with her was Mattie Longbow, who was Miz Lou Lou's caregiver. Both women had been drugged by Nancy Musgrave. He hadn't spared either of them a thought after he had seen Willodean's empty vehicle.

Miz Beatrice Smothermon's funeral had been set for the previous day, as well. It must have been a truly empty church with a quarter of the population locked up, being threatened by a murderer, or missing. And Bubba's mother, Miz Demetrice, was still in jail.

Ma will be fine.

Sheriff John stepped up beside Bubba and stared down at the remnants of the Droid that had just been annihilated. "What did that phone do to you, Bubba?"

"I said I was sorry," Bubba muttered. The trooper had meandered off into a group of other troopers and was casting frequent, odd looks over his shoulder at Bubba. "Hell, I'll do car repairs on his personal vehicle for six months if that's what it takes." *After* they found Willodean.

"Statie said you called in someone about their hounds," Sheriff John said.

Bubba looked down at Sheriff John's toes. "They look protected enough under those heavy boots you wear," Bubba said.

"What?"

"Ifin I stepped on them big toes of yours."

"Ifin..."

"You got a key to Willodean's home?" Bubba said.

"Boy, you change subjects faster than a fart blowing in a windstorm." Sheriff John grimaced and pulled at the bandage on his neck.

"You hear anything about Miz Lou Lou and Miz Mattie?" Bubba asked, eying the bandage.

"Doc Goodjoint kept them in for smoke inhalation. But I heard the old lady gave the hospital staff hell on a pogo stick. And Mattie's family already picked the gal up." Sheriff John sighed. "They're fine and Miz Lou Lou's family is already planning a good place for her to recuperate."

"Good," Bubba said. "I ain't goin' to apologize for calling in Lew Robson. You would have done it, just a little later."

"Yeah, it was on my short list." Sheriff John looked down at the decimated phone again. "I need to round up about a hundred folks to do a search of the area and the forest here. I'm calling in the police academy students from Dallas, Houston, and Shreveport. We cain't do it before the 2nd of January."

Dread coalesced through Bubba's soul. The 2nd was three days away. A person could die of dehydration in three to five days. Without liquid, an injured woman could...

"Christ," Bubba swore. It was half a curse and half a prayer.

"Hounds are a good call," Sheriff John grated. "Lewis Robson's dogs can track a pickle through a cucumber patch."

It was in the forties, and everyone was wearing coats, but Bubba wiped sweat from his hand with an impatient hand. Sometime after midnight, someone had passed him a sweat shirt with the letters "PPD" on the back. It was a tight fit, but it had kept him from shivering.

"What else can happen?" Sheriff John said mostly to himself. "One guy called in sick. I got one in the hospital with a broken leg. Gray's missing. We need all the help we can get. I don't got time to be noble about this, Bubba. I got to take what I can get."

"I need something for Lew from her place," Bubba said gruffly.

Sheriff John's craggy face was grim. "I-I," he stammered for a moment.

Bubba looked at the ground. No one, least of all Bubba, wanted to face what might be the inevitable conclusion. "Let me get a shirt she wore or something, John. You don't think she's here, but we have to know for certain."

"Take my vehicle," Sheriff John said. "Gray's keys are in the center console. Go right there and bring something back. I think Lewis Robson likes the items in a paper bag, so make sure you get a bag before you pick up...her clothing."

"Yeah," Bubba agreed faintly. He didn't want the hounds to mix up the scents if he handled the clothing with bare hands. His hands were filthy with smoke and dirt and everything else he'd handled in the last sixteen hours of the day.

One of the reporters wanted to jump in front of Bubba's face but he cast her such a frightening expression that the solitary woman peeped like a chicken and stepped back without protesting.

Bubba drove through Pegramville and thought about how empty it was in the early morning. A rusting Suzuki Samurai nearly drove into him as Bubba went through a four-way stop. A man with a startled expression eyeballed Bubba through the windshield, watching as he drove the sheriff's department vehicle past him. He probably thought Bubba had stolen another car.

After a few minutes, Bubba reached his destination. Willodean lived in a duplex. She rented from Judge Stenson Posey's sister. In one side lived three college students. The other side was Willodean's. Bubba parked on the street, pulling in diagonally. There was no driveway for the entry side of the duplex. Cars were haphazard on the street leaving only a half of a spot for him to park within. He figured that if someone was going to complain they could get in line.

It took Bubba a minute to find the keys from the center console of the SUV. There were several. Fortunately, one set was neatly labeled "Gray." He took another moment to look at Willodean's home. He was supposed to be here last night. It would have been his first time at her residence. There was a neat walkway lined with flower beds that had been put to sleep for the winter. The walkway split into two directions leading to the separate doors of the duplex. The students' side had a keg sitting on the porch and a black brassiere hanging from an otherwise empty flag pole.

There was a swing on Willodean's porch. A set of bronze wind chimes dangled from the porch rafters. He could picture her sitting there with her lovely black hair moving in the breeze, listening to the music of the chimes. He took a moment to collect her mail from the box. She had been just as busy as he had been this week. She'd been trying to protect him and helping out in the sheriff's absence. The mail had piled up.

Unlocking the door, he pushed it open as he tidied the stack of envelopes and junk mail in his hand. It made Bubba think of the letters that Sheriff John had mentioned. *"The letters started again,"* is what Sheriff John had specifically said. *"Girl left Dallas P.D. because a fella was stalking her. Came down here for a fresh start. She tole me all about it. I wouldn't tell you exceptin' you need knowing."*

Thinking about a strange man scaring the indomitable Willodean Gray made the hole in Bubba's gut begin burning anew. The boiling belly intensified when someone put the barrel of a very large gun to the side of his temple and said, "If you move, I will blow a hole in your head so large, Bigfoot could crawl through it and think it was roomy."

What else could Bubba say? "I ain't moving."

Chapter Four

Bubba Meets Willodean's Family and Not in a Good Way

Friday, December 30th

Directly in front of Bubba there was a small living area decorated in shades of reds and browns. Willodean owned a comfy-looking leather couch with hand-crocheted throws draped over the sides. A painting hung on the wall of a misty landscape, a twilight tossed evening on a distant mountain. Bubba would have thought that Willodean's living room looked very inviting, except that there were two women in front of the couch pointing guns at him. Another person standing to his left had a weapon up to his temple. A fourth, a man dressed in a ragged t-shirt and old jeans entered the opposite end of the room, peering in from a small kitchen. The man observed the situation rather blandly and blinked.

It was a long minute before anyone else spoke.

Bubba said, "Can I put Willodean's mail on the coffee table?"

"Don't move," said the voice behind the gun at his head.

Bubba perceived that it was a third woman although he didn't dare turn his head to look. Instead he got an eyeful of the three people in front of him. One woman was as short as Willodean with hair as black as hers. Her face was gently rounded and a bulky t-shirt couldn't disguise she was prone to plumpness. Her eyes glittered coldly at him as she adjusted her aim.

The other one was a little taller with reddish hair. She was as trim as Willodean with similar green eyes. Both were older than Bubba, in their early thirties. The man standing in the kitchen door was older than all of them. His hair was brown streaked with gray and his blue eyes contemplative, as he studied the situation.

Comprehension was slow to Bubba. He would have chalked it up to stress and fatigue if he'd thought about it for a moment. Eventually, he added two and two and came up with sixty-four and a half.

Sheriff John had called Willodean's parents. These people were in Willodean's home. These folks were her relatives. The two women in front of him were her sisters. The man in the kitchen was her father.

And who was the one with the cold steel prodding his forehead, threatening to lower his IQ by about a thousand points? The heart-stopping voice had been that of a woman. He shifted his eyes to the left and leaned his head just a little, so he could see her. The gun pressed a little harder for a moment, but both of Bubba's hands were completely visible.

She was a little different from the other women in front of him. In fact, she was almost a foot taller than Willodean. Her hair was just as black as Willodean's. Some of her genes had clearly been dominant. But Willodean and the sisters hadn't gotten the height from her. Her green eyes spit fire at him not unlike a Tommy gun from a cheesy forties movie with Jimmy Cagney. The tall woman was also dressed in a police uniform. Bubba couldn't see the badge well enough to determine what police department she was part of, but he was thinking it was likely Dallas.

A thought occurred to him. Bubba didn't know for certain, but he came to the conclusion that Willodean was the baby of the family. And the baby's family had come rip-roaring to the rescue. There was her father. Her sisters, and...

"Pleased to meetcha, Mrs. Gray," Bubba said numbly.

•

Bubba still stood at the door. These people were Willodean's family, and they all appeared as though they could take out a Bowie knife and carve holes in his abdomen without undue strain or moral doubt. That was, with the exception of the father, who looked like he could throw a heavy book at Bubba's cranium and not think about it twice.

"You're Bubba Snoddy," Willodean's mother said. It was a frosty voice full of suspicion and condescension.

One of the sisters nodded. "Bubba Snoddy," she confirmed. She was looking at the identification from the wallet she had plucked from his back pocket. She'd also taken the stack of mail from his hand and thrown it willy-nilly on the coffee table. "He's got a fishing license, a library card, and a Blockbuster membership. There's a photo of a Basset hound." The last was pronounced with mild distaste. It might have been that she didn't like dogs, or it might have been that he had a photograph of his dog in his wallet. Either one.

"There's about twenty-three dollars in there, too," Bubba added.

He was at a loss. He was also in a hurry. Willodean's mother and sisters had grudgingly put their weapons away, but they were all glaring at him as if he had been caught in the act of something despicable. The father had retreated into the kitchen where he was making coffee.

"No condoms," the sister with the wallet said suspiciously or not so suspiciously.

Is the lack of condoms good or bad? Bubba wasn't sure.

The other sister had a strange expression on her face. "You're *Bubba Snoddy*," she repeated. "Jesus, Wills didn't say you were a freaking giant."

Well, I'm only six foot four- and wait, did she say that Willodean talked about me...to her sister? About me?

"Yeah, well, that doesn't explain why he's here," Willodean's mother snapped. "Or why he has her keys. And what do you know about her being missing?"

"I need a paper bag," Bubba said tightly. "I don't have time to explain anything to ya'll. I need something that Willodean...wore recently."

It wasn't the right thing to say. All three women froze. The oldest one's hand twitched toward her weapon again. Willodean's father made an incoherent noise from the kitchen. For an endless moment no one moved. The man in the kitchen soundlessly returned to the door between the rooms and studied Bubba with disconcerting scrutiny.

"Oh, Jesus," Bubba said.

He wasn't a talkative man and words usually got stuck in his throat. He didn't know what to say to Willodean's family. He didn't want to tell them why he needed something that she had recently worn. He suspected that Willodean's mother might already know. She was law enforcement and possibly the two sisters were as well, considering the sidearms that they had so capably held against him.

"I'll look in the kitchen for a bag," Willodean's father said slowly. "My name is Evan Gray, young man. And the lady with the largest firearm is Willodean's mother, Celestine. Anora is the black-haired one and Hattie, the one with the auburn hair. We came down to help."

Bubba thanked God for Evan Gray. No one wanted to say the actual words indicating the severity of Bubba's errand.

"I've got a gun and a shovel," Celestine said warningly.

"Sheriff John Headrick called you about Willodean,"

Bubba said instead of rising to the bait.

Evan nodded. "Early this morning. We were on the road an hour later."

"I don't know what he told you," Bubba added. The unspoken part was that he was utterly unsure about what he could tell them without breaking their collective hearts.

"Willodean's official vehicle was discovered wrecked yesterday evening," Celestine said, and even Bubba could tell the older woman was holding on by the tips of ragged fingernails as she slid down the precipice. "There was...blood that might indicate that Wills was hurt in the wreck."

Bubba noticed that Celestine wasn't calling it an accident. It indicated that she knew about the stalker. It revealed that Willodean's mother was desperately worried about her child. It made Bubba sicker than he already was.

"They've done a search of the area," Bubba said slowly. "Ain't much there to show what happened."

A bit of wreckage. A Dodge emblem. The appearance of someone who was waiting for an opportunity. That specific farm road was the way most people would go if they were going to the Snoddy Mansion. There were other ways, but it was the most direct. If a fella knew that someone was going over to the Snoddy's place, then that same fella could sit there in the pull-out and wait.

"Nothing?" Hattie said wrenchingly. She put her hand over her mouth and gasped, "God. Nothing at all?" The undeclared part was, "*No sign of Willodean?*"

Celestine stared at Bubba. "Ev," she said, her voice neutral. "Did you find a paper bag?"

Evan held up a lunch bag.

"Bubba here needs something Wills wore. Maybe

her uniform t-shirt or something from her dirty clothes basket. Don't touch the shirt with your hands, Ev. Use the paper bag to pick it up." Celestine's voice broke a little.

"There's some rubber gloves in here," Evan said carefully. "They haven't been opened. I'll use those."

Evan turned away and Bubba heard the rattle of the plastic as he did what he said he was going to do.

Anora said with a half choke, "You've got a cadaver dog here?"

Bubba swallowed. "No. Hounds. They'll scent Willodean and…"

"Why is *he* here?" a new voice demanded.

Bubba looked up and saw a young girl glaring at him from the door to the kitchen. She was about eight years old and had similar features to the Grays. Dressed in a gray t-shirt that said "Police" and jeans, she folded her little arms over her chest and cast her most determined stinky eye upon Bubba.

"Who is he?" she went on. "Is he a perp? I'm tired of hiding out in the bedroom. I can handle a little action just like the rest of you."

"This is my daughter, Janie," Anora said tersely. "Janie, this is someone who's come to help with Auntie Wills."

Janie looked Bubba up and down as if she clearly found him lacking. Her little arms didn't unfold. "He's not a boy in blue. I think he looks like a street thug. A convict. A felon. *An outlaw*. Yeah. He's up to something. You can tell by the look in his eyes."

Celestine sighed. "You've been letting her hang around the station house too much, Anora."

Anora shrugged. "Didn't hurt any of us, Ma. The loo is all right with it."

"I like Lieutenant Andrews," Janie said without

looking away from Bubba.

The eight-year-old had cold little eyes. Mistrustful eyes focused in on Bubba like he had a target painted on his forehead. "He lets me drink coffee. Chink. Chink. Where's Auntie Wills?"

"We don't know yet, sweetie," Anora said.

"And why is *he* here instead of the real popo?" Janie insisted.

Celestine looked distrustfully at Bubba again. "It's a good question."

"They're busy at the...scene," Bubba said.

How did he say to Willodean's family that Sheriff John was at an impasse? How could he say that they weren't going to actually search the area for days? Well, dammit, he couldn't. Not to Willodean's family.

There was an awkward silence. "We'll follow you out there," Celestine announced.

Oh, that'll be peachy.

Bubba would have groaned, but he thought that the three women would pull out large, pointy guns and methodically shoot him. He didn't know if the eight-year-old had a sidearm, but she probably knew how to use one.

Sheriff John is going to kill me when he sees them. Ifin these gals don't beat him to the punch.

"But he's a civvie," Janie protested. "If he's not Johnny Law, then he's a suspect, and he knows too much." She looked as though she would pull over a handy spotlight to blind Bubba while she adroitly interrogated him.

"His name is Bubba Snoddy," Anora said to her daughter.

"Bubba?" Janie repeated. "But Bubba is the name on the..."

"Hush!" Evan had returned with the paper bag in his

46

hand and put his other hand on Janie's shoulder. "That's none of your concern."

What? My name is on what?

Bubba cogitated for a moment but he was too tired, too concerned about Willodean to focus on what Janie said. Time wasn't slowing down for anyone or anything.

"Follow me out," he said brusquely, "but I'm leaving now." He cast an eye on the draped windows. Through the inch-wide crack in the drapes he could see the sun was about to peep over the horizon with ferocious declaration.

Bubba didn't want the Grays trailing him out to the place where Willodean's lonesome official vehicle was still sitting with blood inside, but he couldn't see how he could stop them.

Sheriff John will just have to turn on the charm, Bubba concluded.

•

Lewis Robson was unloading his hounds when Bubba parked Sheriff John's county car. Lew spared Bubba a brief look and brushed off two reporters who were hurling questions into his ear. The hounds were slobbering over the reporters' shoes, and one of the reporters was wiping his hands on his slacks.

Bubba jumped out of the vehicle and glanced over his shoulder. Two cars had followed him. A gaggle of Grays streamed out. Bubba didn't wait. He assumed Celestine could locate Sheriff John all by herself and give him the unadulterated hell the sheriff didn't really need.

Holding the paper bag with Willodean's clothing, Bubba went to Lew Robson. "Hey, Lew."

Lew was a good ol' boy and a member of the Real-Men-Don't-Need-to-Talk demographic. He held three hounds by leashes and waited patiently for Bubba. Lew nodded at Bubba and spat a mouthful of tobacco juice at the ground. A reporter adeptly dodged it. The man was probably used to avoiding all types of nasty things. Bubba glared at the reporter who was probably used to that, too.

The man barked, "Are the dogs being used for locating a deceased individual?"

"Ain't *dogs*," Lew said vehemently, motivated by the fact that his hounds were being called merely dogs. Dogs were *common* animals. His canine associates were more than merely dogs. Unquestionably, they were elevated to royalty in his determination.

The reporter appeared confused. "They look like dogs to me."

"They're *hounds*," Lew snapped.

He had a long, craggy face that could have been anywhere from thirty to fifty, weatherworn skin, and striking blue eyes that sparkled when he was enjoying himself. Most of the time Lew spent with his hounds, was time that Lew enjoyed. But even Bubba knew Lew wasn't going to be thrilled if they hunted a woman's dead body. For a man who owned and trained animals to track, he was remarkably weak-stomached at the thought of any living creature being harmed.

Not that Bubba wanted to find a dead woman again. *Please, God*, he prayed silently, *not Willodean*.

"Go away," Bubba said to the reporter who had asked the question about the hounds hunting down a deceased person. The other reporter correctly gauged Bubba's temperament and headed for greener pastures.

"This is a free country," the first man said fervently. "I've got First Amendment rights. The U.S. Constitution says..."

"You're interfering," Bubba said coldly. "I'll bend your camera into a pretzel and shove the bits where the sun don't shine ifin you don't stop."

"I'll complain to the…"

The man froze when Bubba took a step forward. Bubba was significantly taller than the reporter, and the reporter took the higher moral ground containing a modicum of safety. "Did you get that?" he snarled to the camera man.

Bubba handed the paper bag to Lew. "It's *her* shirt," he said.

Lew's face fell a little. "Right sorry, Bubba," he said. "Do what I can."

"I know. Don't know if the county will pay for your time, Lew," Bubba said. "I'll cover it."

"Oh, Bubba," Lew said. Clearly, he wanted to say something else but he shrugged. "Ain't gonna take your money," he muttered at last. He took a moment to spit again, aiming for one of the reporter's shoes this time. The reporter dexterously avoided it with an avid curse.

Sheriff John motioned to various police officers where he wanted them. Bubba saw Celestine had ignored the yellow tape. She made her way to the sheriff and tapped his shoulder. Bubba took a moment to feel sorry for the sheriff as they sized each other up.

Lew got his hounds in order. He issued sharp instructions as he held them by their leads.

Janie, the eight-year-old would-be police officer and Nazi storm trooper, wandered over and studied the animals with a critical eye. "You're going to look for my auntie?" she said, and suddenly, her bravado fled.

Lew shrugged uncertainly.

"What kind of hounds are they?" she asked.

Lew nodded approvingly at the use of the word "hounds." He pointed. "Duffy, over there, is a Bluetick coonhound. She's got the tan spots over her eyes and the mottled black and white. In the right light she looks properly blue."

Bubba blinked. Apparently, in order to get Lew to speak, all one had to do was to ask about his hounds.

"Then there's Franklin G." Lew pointed again. "He's a Treeing Walker coonhound."

"He looks like a big beagle," Janie said.

"Sorta. Sorta," Lew said agreeably. "That other gal is Maggie. She's a Black and Tan."

Lew began to work with the dogs while Janie watched. He brushed them with his hands and talked to them softly, gearing them up for the strenuous activity to follow.

Bubba glanced over at Sheriff John. The older man had been circled by Celestine Gray and her two daughters. He was gesturing. Celestine was gesturing, as well. Hattie was gesturing in concert with her mother. Anora had her hands on her hips and looked as if she wanted to gesture. Evan Gray stood in the background, ready to do backup gesturing. Bubba couldn't fault the Gray family. They were concerned about Willodean. Moreover, they were obviously used to being folks of action. It reminded Bubba of himself. Standing around went against his grain.

Movements out of the corner of his eye made Bubba turn his head. People were showing up at the yellow caution tape. Several of them were neighbors and people from Pegramville. Naturally, they were curious as to what was happening that had all the police in a shillyshally.

Alice and Ruby Mercer perched on a tree stump watching avidly. Even though it was early in the morning, they passed a bag of chocolate covered raisins between them. The older sisters were active participants in Miz Demetrice's gambling ring and fervent gossips. This was crucial nourishment for the act of nattering.

Probably having withdrawal symptoms, Bubba thought unkindly.

Billie Jo, Bubba couldn't think of her last name, chatted with a sheriff's deputy along the line of tape. She was the night clerk at Bufford's Gas and Grocery and loved to play bingo at the Methodist Church. Bubba couldn't comprehend why she would be standing at the side of the road, in the middle of Pegram County, watching goings-on that rightly had nothing to do with her.

Roy and Maude Chance congregated loudly with the media. It fit since they were the owners, editors, and chief bottle-washers of the Pegram Herald.

Foot Johnson stood with Lloyd Goshorn. Foot was the janitor at the county building, and Lloyd was a general handyman and town eccentric.

Although, ain't too many folks in this area who aren't eccentric, Bubba supposed.

Lloyd briefly glared at Bubba, and Bubba recalled that he had almost run the handyman down the other night.

I missed. I did. And Lloyd keeps telling taller and taller tales about Snoddy Mansion and all the gold supposedly buried there, so he's right fortunate I did miss. He's also telling tales about Willodean and me.

Bubba cut the thought right in half with a slice of a sharp mental knife. He didn't want to go there at the moment.

Bubba's eyes continued to study the bystanders. Mark Evans chatted with Mike Holmgreen nearby. Mark still had a cast on his hand from his stint as a process server. Mark had also worked at Bufford's Gas and Grocery before quitting precipitously on the same night Bubba found the dead body of his ex-fiancée.

Mike Holmgreen was a local eighteen-year-old who

had tried to burn down the high school because he had been failing algebra. Lately, he'd been running around town attempting to catch something interesting on his smart phone using the camcorder feature. He'd caught Big Joe and his merry men doing the fandango on Bubba's head the previous week, and the thirty seconds of digital had gone viral on YouTube.

Whatever that means.

There was Robert Daughtry, a recent hire at the Pegram County Sheriff's Department, talking to Patsy. Patsy was Sheriff John's secretary. She had an affinity for Neil Diamond, although she was only in her early twenties. Nadine Clack, the town's librarian, lurked behind them, visibly eavesdropping as she tilted her head to hear better.

Bubba blinked. Robert Daughtry had an odd expression on his face as Bubba stared at him. He abruptly grasped that Robert was the man in the car he'd seen previously in the morning. His had been the lone car out in the early dawn. Startled, he had stared as Bubba drove the county car on his way to Willodean's place. Seeing Bubba in the driver's seat of an official vehicle would be enough to startle most residents of Pegramville. Bubba typically rode in the back, handcuffed.

Is there anyone who ain't here? Bubba thought irately. His stomach lurched again as he answered himself.

Willodean ain't here. Dumbass.

Chapter Five

Bubba and the Hunt

Friday, December 30th

It was the little girl named Janie who peremptorily yanked Bubba out of his miserable doldrums. "I bet Ma and Gran didn't even search you properly," she said condescendingly from beside him.

Bubba glanced down at the child. She looked a little like her mother. Her hair was black, and her eyes were the same green. It was a strong family trait. Bubba knew that he wouldn't mind having a child with the same green eyes, and his heart pretty much curled into a twisty knot.

"Why would they need to?" Bubba asked calmly.

He didn't feel calm. He wanted to bellow at Lew to hurry the hell up. He wanted to pound on Sheriff John for wasting time trying to explain anything to Celestine Gray. He wanted to pick up the table someone had set up nearby with coffee and donuts and throw it across the road.

"You're a *perp*," Janie pronounced carefully. The word perp came out as if it were the contemptible thing in existence. God forbid anyone should be a *perp*. "You were in Auntie Wills' apartment. You were probably coming to remove evidence. That's called tampering. You should have cuffs on you."

"Do you read police manuals at night instead of regular books?" Bubba asked cordially.

"Why, yes," Janie said with surprise. "How did you know that?"

"Just a lucky guess," he said.

"We *know* you killed Willodean," the little girl said

coldly, staring at him with those probing would-be cop eyes.

"Jesus!" Bubba said violently and curtly. "Don't say that. She ain't dead."

Janie jumped back. She gazed at Bubba. Sheriff John, Celestine Gray, and her two daughters had all stopped talking and stared at them.

Anora said nimbly, "Stop that, Janie. It only works when you're a real police officer."

Janie muttered derisively under her breath. Bubba only caught part of it. "...*Just as good as a real one.*"

"Listen, kid," Bubba said, casting a selective glare at Lew, silently imploring the man to hurry up with his hounds. "I don't know where Willodean is. I wish to God I did. That man over there with the hounds is going to try to figure out ifin we can follow her. I hope that we can find her right quickly." His voice felt strained and he added, "I-", but he couldn't bring himself to finish, and the words died away.

Janie's mouth opened as she looked up at Bubba's distraught expression. Eventually, her features cleared into an expression of surprise. "You love her," she said.

Bubba's first thought was to protest. Real men don't tell eight-year-old nieces that they love their aunties. *Besides which, do I?* He tightened his lips and turned away from Janie's flabbergasted and self-satisfied expression. He needed more coffee if he was going to make it through the day. Maybe a couple of gallons of it.

Oh, to perdition with it, just put a coffee IV in me.

•

Thirty minutes later, Sheriff John was ready with all the combined law enforcement officers. Lew Robson finally allowed his hounds to scent Willodean's clothing. The three animals picked up the scent and began to hunt, dragging Lew behind them. They were noiseless, and the whispered words of the crowd that had gathered filtered into anxious silence.

Sheriff John trailed behind with several officers following.

The Gray family had been relegated to a position behind the yellow tape. Bubba could all but see the steam pouring out of Celestine's ears. She had wanted to participate in the action. All of her family had wanted to do so, but Sheriff John had put his foot down. He'd threatened them with time in jail if they didn't desist. In fact, Sheriff John had given Bubba the same spiel. But Bubba wasn't going to have any of it. He directed a very explicit look at Sheriff John, and the older man shrugged impatiently.

The alpha hound, the Black and Tan coonhound, set her nose down and began to track. All three animals began near the wrecked SUV. They spread out with heads low and swept the area. Almost immediately, Maggie locked on her mark. The two other hounds followed her lead. She circled once, with Lew whispering encouraging words. "Good girl," he said. "Track, Maggie. Track."

Lew let Maggie loose as she fixated on the hunt. She went back and forth, her nose actively seeking out the objective spoor. Her head came up a little and she glanced back at Lew. The other hounds trailed after her.

Bubba had seen hounds hunting before. Lew Robson was one of the best trainers around. He lived, breathed, and ate with his hounds. He also won dozens of awards, and his breeding pairs were in much demand. Bubba had helped him out a few years before, and Lew had given him a Basset hound puppy in thanks. Bubba's beloved dog, Precious, was the best pet he'd ever had.

It made him think guiltily of Precious. The poor dog

had been left at the Snoddy Mansion all day and all night. He knew that Miz Adelia would take care of her, but the dog was likely frantic at the absence of her beloved master. Or she was getting an overabundance of dogly treats from Brownie and would throw up on Bubba's bed later.

But there were other more important things on Bubba's mind.

The Black and Tan moved down the road to the north. *Dog's going to go into the forest,* Bubba thought. *Or maybe into the fields. Going to follow a zigzag pattern. Maybe we can find her before-*

But Maggie went down a straight line. She trotted along the side of the road. Her nose was in the air, not on the ground, and Bubba knew what that meant. The scent she was tracking was in the air and not on the ground. The animal's nose didn't waver as she followed. Willodean had gotten into a vehicle. The vehicle had driven north.

The hounds led the way. Lew followed the hounds. Law enforcement followed Lew. Bubba followed the law enforcement.

As the animals worked, the sky filled with dark clouds, and Bubba cursed viciously. Even Sheriff John raised his eyebrows at the language Bubba used. Lew efficiently withdrew a rain poncho from his backpack and put it on.

The rain started with a little sprinkle. Lew's face turned grim. The rain began to let loose, and soon rivulets poured along the shoulders of the road.

The hounds managed to track the scent for nearly two miles as it went down the farm roads. Lew tripped once. Sheriff John had to stop to take a breather before he trotted to catch up.

Bubba could see a news van driving behind the

larger group from a hundred yards back. Behind the news van was Celestine in one of the cars they had brought.

As the rain began to let up, the trail came to the freeway. The hounds fished around frantically, unmistakably finding nothing. After another thirty minutes of casting about, Lew Robson paused to give his animals water. He looked across at Bubba and sadly shook his head.

Bubba sat down on the side of the road and put his head into his large hands.

•

As Miz Demetrice was led down the hallway of the city jail, Gigi the prostitute said prosaically, "Robert Earl Keen says in a song, 'The road goes on forever, and the party never ends.'"

The older woman nodded solemnly. "It's a good way of thinking, dear. You should probably stop what you're doing for a living before someone hurts you."

Gigi shrugged. "It's a job."

"There are jobs, and there are *jobs*," Miz Demetrice advised gravely.

Gigi appeared confused.

Jailor Barnheart, the woman without a sense of humor, said brusquely, "Come on, Miz Snoddy. Big Joe said you're free and clear."

"Do you like to gamble?" Miz Demetrice asked the jailor.

"I play the lotto," Barnheart said amicably. "I ain't never won more than ten dollars."

"Possibly you'd enjoy poker," Miz Demetrice suggested as they returned her belongings to her. She took a moment to pat her face with powder from the compact in her purse.

"Possibly," Jailor Barnheart said doubtfully while

Miz Demetrice signed three forms and initialed two others. "I don't rightly think much of poker. My mama said it was very nearly a sin."

"My goodness," Miz Demetrice said, examining one form carefully, "do they really need to ascertain that?"

"Yes'm," Jailor Barnheart said. "Prisoner security is very important. You weren't injured in any fashion, were you?"

"I broke a fingernail," Miz Demetrice said coolly. "Could be a terrible thing. When the skin's torn like that, all kinds of germs are apt to get in, and well, I heard tell about this flesh-eating virus that loves places where lots of unclean folks are to be found." Her voice lowered to a movie villain level. *"Flesh...eating..."*

"A fingernail," Jailor Barnheart repeated. She looked at the sheet of paper. "I don't think there's a box for that."

"Perhaps the *other* box," Miz Demetrice suggested. She pointed with the finger that had the broken nail. The lacquered nail hung loosely. A line of blood was visible where the quick had torn.

"Oh, I'll have to check with my supervisor," Jailor Barnheart said fretfully. "Broken nails can turn into infections and abscesses and the like. Could be bad. Should we call the doc in to take a look at it before you leave? I don't want anyone to think we mistreated Miz Demetrice Snoddy in our jail. Oh, no, no."

Miz Demetrice straightened her jacket with a satisfied smile. The jacket was primrose pink and correctly appropriate for a chilled December day. The matching shirt and skirt were not-so-appropriately wrinkled from a night in the pokey. *The cooler, the slam, the icebox, hoosegow.* She brushed lint from her shoulder. *Although they need pillows and blankets, it was the best night of sleep I've had for weeks. But now*

I've got to go get filled in on what's happening with Nancy Musgrave.

She cheerfully left Jailor Barnheart agonizing about a potential lawsuit and strode outside. When she pulled her cell phone out of her purse, she found that she had just enough juice to call the Snoddy Mansion. Miz Adelia told her what was occurring without pause, and Miz Demetrice hung up without acknowledging it.

The Christmas Killer had been apprehended, but something else dreadful had happened.

Miz Demetrice caught sight of the Pegramville Fire Chief, Ted Andrews, loading bags into the back of his official vehicle. She stopped to ask him for a ride and he nodded. It turned out that he was headed out to the crime scene to drop off essentials for the law enforcement officials there.

Ted Andrews was a man in his fifties and fairly cordial to Miz Demetrice when she had caught sight of him loading essentials in the rear of the Suburban. "Glad to see you're out of the slammer, Miz D.," he said. "Knowed you dint kill no one. Don't reckon how anyone could see you trying to hang Sheriff John." He chuckled.

"Glad to see you're able to give me a lift," Miz Demetrice said.

How could anyone think I killed anyone, except my late, not-so-beloved husband and that was by throwing him into a volcano. The semantics of getting Elgin to the volcano were particularly troublesome, but that's neither here nor there.

"That little itty-bitty gal has been missing since yesterday," Ted said as he drove.

"Do they know what happened?" Miz Demetrice asked.

Willodean Gray was an enthusiastic partaker in her weekly poker games. She was a vivacious young woman with bright eyes, and Bubba had been pursuing her with a single-minded slowness that his mother thought might hurt him. The last week had proven that Willodean was more than interested in her only child, but the last week had also been an ordeal.

Miz Demetrice had been threatened by the Christmas Killer, and Bubba had taken that as a challenge to his manliness. Certainly, he had saved Sheriff John from slowly strangling to death, but he hadn't saved Steve Killebrew or Beatrice Smothermon. The deaths were the fault of the Christmas Killer and no one else's, but Bubba had a way of taking on blame.

And Willodean missing? Oh, Lord Jesus Christ, and all the angels above, Bubba would be tied into a hundred Gordian knots. Bless his heart.

"There was a car wreck," Ted said as Miz Demetrice cogitated. "That cute little deputy is missing. Folks seem to think she hit her head and wandered off in a daze."

"That doesn't sound like Willodean," Miz Demetrice offered. *The Willodean Gray I know would have kicked the car's ass into oblivion.* "And was it a one-car accident?"

"Don't rightly know," Ted said. "Sheriff John's got all kinds of people out there. City po-lice. County po-lice. State po-lice. Might even be Fish and Game folks there, too." He frowned. "You don't reckon it could be worse than just this gal missing, do you? They caught that killer at ya'll's place but..."

Miz Demetrice bit her lip. *Could the Christmas Killer have killed Willodean before going out to the Snoddy Mansion?*

"No, I 'spect not," Ted said after a moment, answering the silent question in Miz Demetrice's head. "Bubba went and rescued the two gals at the house fire.

60

Me and the boys put that out, and the deputy was still on the wire when Bubba hightailed it out to your place. That little boy, what's he, your great-nephew, came on a few minutes later and said Bubba had tole him to call in that the killer was out there. So the killer cain't have gotten to that perty little gal." He sighed. "Folks falling over dead left and right around here. Makes me think we're living in a cemetery." He checked his mirrors as if corpses would suddenly appear in order to back up his conjecture.

Willodean went missing after Bubba went out to the Snoddy Mansion?

Miz Demetrice was perplexed. She was also worried. If she knew her son, and she thought that she did rather well, then he would have stayed up all night looking for Willodean. There were only so many places a young woman could go, and Willodean was a fine, upstanding member of law enforcement. Certainly, she joined in the weekly Pokerama, but everyone knew that was less than truly criminal. The fact that she had illegally allowed Bubba and Miz Demetrice to paw through some of Sheriff John's papers, was purely for the sake of swiftly identifying a killer and the killer's potential victims. After all, some wrongs *do* add up to make a right.

"They haven't found anything yet," she mused.

"Not as though I've heard," Ted said. He patted his police radio mounted on the dashboard. "And there's plenty of stuff being said on the radio. Just a little blood in her vehicle." He glanced at Miz Demetrice. He'd heard about Bubba's fascination with the deputy. He'd even heard that they were married with thirty-six bridesmaids and groomsmen in attendance, but he also knew about Pegramville's rumor mill. *There couldn't have been thirty-six. Maybe ten. And everyone knew the*

Goodyear Blimp didn't do weddings. Did it?

"Not enough blood to make her anything but injured of course."

"Of course," Miz Demetrice murmured. *Oh, Willodean. Where are you, dear? Oh, poor Bubba. He must be devastated.*

"Lew Robson came out with his hounds," Ted continued unthinkingly. "Last I heard they was headed for the freeway." He turned on his windshield wipers. "Crap, er, I mean, carp. It's starting to rain. I know we're having a drought, but this is the last thing the sheriff needs right now."

Miz Demetrice peered out the front glass. The dribbles progressively got heavier. The temperature was dropping rapidly along with the onslaught of the poor weather. A young woman was out there somewhere, with some kind of injury, in this miserable weather.

The older woman frowned grimly. "You've got some rain gear, Ted?" she asked politely.

They pulled up to a conflagration of vehicles, people scrambling for shelter, and diehard reporters determined to get a story through rain or shine.

"Sure, I got rain gear," Ted said. "Don't use it much. Fires don't do much in a heavy rain."

After putting on the Fire Chief's rain poncho, Miz Demetrice disregarded the vinyl pants because they would have dragged by about a foot and a half. Miz Demetrice proceeded to cajole and bully a harried Mike Holmgreen into giving her ride to find Bubba and the others.

The eighteen-year-old Mike, would-be arsonist and viral-media artist, gave in rancorously. "Granny says you cheat at poker," Mike said accusingly to Miz Demetrice as if that might cow the older woman. They piled into a beat-up Ford Mustang with another boy driving.

Miz Demetrice dimly recognized the young man as the one who had been lately a process server. "Had another surgery, Mr. Evans?" she asked politely. She still remembered the bad things that the inimitable Mark Evans had said about her to Bubba, despite the fact that he'd never met her previously.

"Yes, ma'am," Mark said nervously. "Almost done with them. Plus, that fella who stomped on my hand went to jail for six months. And the fella I worked for, Mr. Minnieweather, well, his insurance paid for all the medical costs plus living for the next year. I'm going to all the college classes I want. I write with the good hand anyway." He'd heard things about Miz Demetrice, too. Cheating at poker was the least objectionable of the things he'd heard.

Miz Demetrice looked down her nose at Mark. "I'm sure that's admirable," she said and didn't mean it at all.

"The po-lice ain't going to get upset with us?" Mike asked from the cramped back seat.

"Not overly," Miz Demetrice said. It wasn't meant to be reassuring. "And did you know your Granny likes to crumble Cheetos over ice cream and pour cheap wine over the top of it? It's quite gruesome to watch."

Mike stared at the back of Miz Demetrice's head from the rear seat. Grannies weren't supposed to do things like that. And older ladies weren't supposed to fight back so viciously either. "What else goes on at those poker games?" he asked uneasily.

Miz Demetrice turned and glared icily at Mike. "Things," she said, "that are best not discussed in public places." She smiled evilly. "*Terrible, awful, horrendous things.*"

"Let's just go get you where the po-lice are," Mark

said fearfully.

•

Miz Demetrice found Bubba sitting in a puddle of mud with his head held in his hands and his eyes firmly closed. She looked around. Sheriff John argued with the taciturn Lew Robson. Other officers milled about. A news van parked a hundred yards back. A cameraman was filming but it was half-heartedly. Another car sat nearby. The three women sitting in it watched apprehensively. Everyone was soaking wet with the exception of Lew, who had his bright yellow slicker on.

Lew's hounds were lying in the thick grass on the shoulder. He'd obviously rewarded them because all three hounds had toys clamped in their jaws. The Black and Tan had a floppy, pink, man-shaped doll in her mouth and happily chewed on it. The Bluetick had a rawhide chew and gleefully gnawed it to more manageable pieces. The Treeing Walker coonhound had a well-masticated Garfield doll and growled at it as he tossed it about. Apparently, the plush cat was meant to be taught a lesson.

The three women watching from the car keenly observed Miz Demetrice as she got out of the antique Mustang. They also watched as Mark Evans and Mike Holmgreen correctly interpreted an especially nasty glare from Sheriff John. Mark put the Mustang in gear with a grinding noise and abruptly reversed until he could safely turn around.

Miz Demetrice stood by the side of the road and studied Bubba. Her first urge was to throw herself at her only child and comfort him in the way that only a mother could do. But Bubba didn't need that at the moment. He needed something more and something she was unsure that she could give to him.

While Miz Demetrice thought about it, she saw Mike

pointing his cell phone at the group while Mark reversed down the road. Mark's Mustang hydroplaned on the wet road, and the car went into the ditch. A moment later the wheels roared as he tried to pull back on the asphalt, but he was high-centered. One of the police officers groaned audibly and slogged back to help them.

Miz Demetrice's gaze next went to the car with the three women inside it. The driver was in her fifties and stared at Miz Demetrice as if she could see inside her brain. She was also wearing a police officer's uniform. *If she's a police officer, then what is she doing in the civilian car?*

A thought occurred to Miz Demetrice. She stared at the women in the car. Willodean had talked about her family. There was a history of law enforcement in the clan. *That is Willodean's mother. A police sergeant from Dallas. Those other two are her sisters. They've been called because...Sheriff John thought they needed to know.*

The two women stared at each other for a long moment. Miz Demetrice, in the oversized rain gear, and Celestine Gray, from the inside of her car. Two mothers caught up in the scheme of something much bigger than the two of them. Two titans were about to fight the good fight. They judged each other minutely and then grudgingly approved each other.

Finally, Miz Demetrice turned to Bubba and set her shoulders in a fashion that WWE wrestlers would have approved. *This might be very ugly. It might very well need to get ugly.*

"Boy," she said imperiously, "what in the name of Jehoshaphat's jumper cables are you doing sitting in the mud on the side of the road?"

Bubba slowly lifted his head. His weary face and

bloodshot eyes gazed at his mother. There was still a bump on his head from being stomped on by the Pegramville City Police the previous week. Somehow he'd managed to remove the remnants of the Sharpie markers that Brownie had used to draw on his face. Not that it mattered to his overall appearance at that particular moment. He appeared ten years older than he actually was.

"Ma," he said flatly, "I don't reckon you shot your way out of jail with a gun carved out of soap."

"Big Joe finally came to his senses," Miz Demetrice said, staring down at her son. On the inside she wanted to hug him and yank on his ear for this flagrant hopelessness he was displaying. "Of course, that isn't to imply he owns the sense God gave a turnip."

Bubba looked at the mud he was sitting in. He looked at Lew Robson who was shaking his head at Sheriff John.

"Hounds tracked Willodean here," Bubba said gruffly. "Then it started to pour. Lew tried but the scent is gone."

"Nancy Musgrave couldn't have done this," Miz Demetrice said peremptorily. "She set the fire at Lou Lou Vandygriff's with the loonies in tow. Then she went to the Snoddy Mansion to catch us. She didn't know you were with...Willodean. She didn't know I was incarcerated."

Bubba's head turned downward again. "Ifin Nancy had done it, at least we would know something."

Miz Demetrice wanted to wail. Many times over the years she had wanted to wail, but it wasn't done. She hadn't been born a Snoddy, but she was a Snoddy now all the same. And Snoddys don't wail when the going gets tough. Her shoulders straightened and she said deliberately, "Boy, just because the hounds don't have a scent doesn't mean you just up and give up."

His head shot back up, and he glared at his mother. Blatantly, Bubba wanted to argue. He was sick and desolately tired, and hope had taken a bus, followed by a train, and then an airplane to parts unknown. There didn't seem to be a return ticket. Slowly, he came to his feet and towered over his mother. She looked like a child with the oversized, rain poncho draped over her. Cornflower blue eyes stared meaningfully at him.

"Willodean wouldn't want you to give up." Miz Demetrice blasted her remaining salvo at him.

Bubba's large chest heaved once. He took a deep breath and exhaled. He took another one. He nodded shortly and slowly looked around. If Muhammad couldn't go to the mountain, then the mountain would go to Muhammad. There was another way, and he had to figure out what it was.

Chapter Six

Bubba Wants to Take Something Apart With His Bare
Fists

Friday, December 30th – Saturday, December 31st

Bubba had been shoved into his bathroom with two instructions from Miz Demetrice, "Get clean, and get some shuteye." Despite the fact that he thought he wouldn't be able to go to sleep, he set his alarm for three hours later. After showering, he lay down on his bed and was snoring within sixty seconds.

In due course, Precious nudged open the bedroom door with her prodigious nose and examined the situation from a dogly perspective. She sniffed Bubba's size-12 shoes and immediately interpreted the scents of smoke, dirt, and other dogs. She curled her canine lip and snorted. Her human had been *consorting* with other animals while she had been locked in a bedroom. Additionally, the human known as Miz Adelia had only given Precious *three* doggy treats instead of her minimum requirement of five. And the little human known as Brownie, had come in to play with her for only a few minutes before hastily disappearing. Someone else had been bellowing the boy's name in a manner that connoted trouble in store for the young man. Then Brownie had promptly vanished.

Everyone else was stiff legged and irritable. The entire mansion smelt of strangers. *Stinky, weird strangers.* It was similar to the twice-yearly opening of the mansion for visitors who liked to make odd cooing noises and touch walls. And horrendously, Precious was not permitted to mark over the new scents with her own unmistakable scent, which denoted that this was *her* territory.

Bad things were happening. Typically, her human didn't sleep during the daytime. When he was home, his primary duties were playing with Precious and scratching behind her long, long, long ears. Unfortunately, these important details were interspersed with dressing, bathing, sleeping, and doing chores for the human known alternatively as Ma or Miz Demetrice or even sometimes Why, me, Lord?

Precious scratched at the offensive shoes and dogmatically kicked them under the bed where they would offend her less. Later she would carry them down to the kitchen and prod open the back door and bury them by the oleanders near the decorative reindeer horns she had recently been forced to wear.

Bubba snorted. Precious lifted her head and approached slowly. Mostly, her human smelled of soap and water. But one of his large hands hung off the bed, nearly touching the floor. She sniffed cautiously. There was still a hint of strange dogs. Consequently, she licked it off. Then she licked the hand some more to ensure complete compliance with her doggish standards.

Bubba murmured and said, "What in the name of Ozymandias's legs?" Then he shifted again, and the hanging hand absently scratched at Precious's jaw.

The dog pulled away for a moment. *I'm not that easy. You smell like other dogs. I don't forgive you. Where were you? I was locked in a room. There were bad people here I needed to bite. You suck.*

Precious looked around for something to chew to show her severe displeasure. She could rend it into minute, soggy pieces to exhibit her discontent. Bubba's hand searched for a moment and found her. One clever finger discovered the place just behind her ear that made one of her legs bounce with joy.

"Who's a good widdle-wubby-dubby dog?" Bubba slurred.

Not me. I'm not a good widdle anything. Precious told her vigorous leg to stand down, but Bubba kept at the spot behind her ear, and unexpectedly, the other leg began to twitch in time with the scratching. She tried to turn her head away but couldn't quite contain herself. *You're not my human anymore. I hate your guts. OH, scratch there, HARDER!* She abruptly gave up. *Oh, I love you desperately!*

•

Miz Demetrice peeped in and saw that Precious had managed to clamber onto the bed and was resting her distinctive nose and ears across Bubba's back. The Basset hound briefly opened her brown eyes and stared at the woman with sleepy regard.

Miz Demetrice took a moment to pull a blanket over both man and dog. She turned off his alarm clock, went back to the door, and cracked the door to Bubba's bedroom so that Precious could scratch it open if she so desired. She went downstairs for a little stimulation. If she wasn't mistaken it was caffeine o'clock. Although she had gotten a decent night's rest in the jail despite Gigi's enthusiastic description of what an "Around the World" entailed, she still needed to stay alert and active for the sake of her son.

All was not well in the Snoddy Mansion. There had been a murderer inside, and she had aggressively threatened all the inhabitants. Fudge and Virtna were on the verge of fleeing, although that wouldn't have bothered Miz Demetrice overly, but both were making noises as if they were owed compensation for their suffering. Truly, the pair of Snoddys had their good points, but they were few and far between.

Brownie was animated to the point of rushing up and down the stairs in boundless spurts of energy. He had buzzed around the mansion so much, that Miz Adelia had checked his chocolate milk for coffee. As it turned out, it was merely the excitement of actually apprehending an infamous murderer.

Big Joe had called about Brownie's stun gun and said that it had disappeared from one of the squad cars. The officers recollected that Brownie had been lurking around all the official vehicles for hours. Brownie had also complained bitterly that the stun gun had been a science project made for Boy Scouts and entirely his possession. He had even borrowed his mother's Droid to check on the legal status of owning stun guns in the state of Texas.

Despite the question of legality, Fudge had bellowed so loudly that the huge, foyer chandelier had rattled. But Brownie had vanished into the ether. Sort of like Willodean, but she was well aware that the boy would reappear once the dinner bell was rung.

Only God knew when Willodean would reappear, Miz Demetrice thought calmly.

She went into the kitchen and made a pot of coffee. Miz Adelia had vanished, but Miz Demetrice knew that the housekeeper was coordinating with her cousin Ralph about the pot patch down by Sturgis Creek. Ralph was trying to save his bacon by covering up all clues to his horticultural side-business. Because it was winter, there wasn't a crop presently growing, but the evidence was strewn over a half acre of creek-fed bottomland. Unfortunately for Ralph, there wasn't a bit of equipment that didn't have his fingerprints all over it or the Cedarbloom name stenciled across the back. And Ralph couldn't very well claim that all that farming equipment had been recently stolen.

Aunt Caressa wandered in and helped herself to the coffee. "Well, dearest," she said to Miz Demetrice, "your holidays surely are exciting. It hasn't been this interesting since you put an Arizona Bark scorpion down Elgin's pants that one Christmas Eve."

"*Good times,*" Miz Demetrice murmured.

"It should be an interesting newsletter this year," Aunt Caressa remarked.

"Murderers, evildoers, greedy relatives, and missing folks, oh my," Miz Demetrice said. "And I went to jail, too." She considered. "Although it was far from the first time. That jail needs a fresh coat of paint and a jailor who can smile just a mite." She considered again. "But Bubba has to have the all-time Snoddy record for being in and out of jails during a calendar year."

They sat at the kitchen table and looked out the window facing the wide side yard. Brownie had re-emerged from his self-imposed isolation and chased something through the yard. "I believe that boy saved our lives," Aunt Caressa said with amazement.

Miz Demetrice sighed as she looked at Brownie. "With a stun gun? Really?"

Aunt Caressa held her hands in the air two feet apart in a demonstration of size. "That woman's handgun was this big. The bullets would have made holes the size of grapefruits."

"That's a big gun," Miz Demetrice admitted. She had several weapons around the house to include shotguns, rifles, pistols, and muzzle loaders. There were a few knives, including a bayonet from WWII and a switchblade that had been acquired during a particularly memorable poker game in San Francisco. However, she didn't have a handgun that was as large as Aunt Caressa indicated.

"What about this missing gal?" Aunt Caressa asked

as she raised her cup to her lips and then sipped with a pinky held out.

"The sheriff's deputy," Miz Demetrice looked out the window. Brownie had an axe and attempted to run while holding it over his head. He was also whooping like a Visigoth in full-frontal attack. She would have been alarmed, but she didn't see anything else that was warm-blooded in his immediate vicinity.

"That's the one that Bubba is sweet upon," Aunt Caressa said sadly.

"Indeed," Miz Demetrice agreed. "The hounds lost her scent at the freeway. Girl could be halfway across these lesser 48 states by now. My God, she could be north of the Mason-Dixon Line."

Aunt Caressa frowned. Being north of the Mason-Dixon Line could be a fate worse than death. "Folks don't just kidnap sheriff's deputies."

"Someone did," Miz Demetrice said.

"Bubba shore likes that gal," Aunt Caressa said wistfully.

"Bubba said something about Willodean having a stalker," Miz Demetrice said.

"A stalker?" Aunt Caressa repeated as if she was unfamiliar with the word.

"You know, someone who follows you around, sends you cards, dead flowers, and turns up unwanted," Miz Demetrice said.

"Oh, you mean kind of a like a Republican," Aunt Caressa concluded.

Miz Demetrice smiled grimly. "This fella is someone who wanted Willodean, and Willodean didn't want him. Followed her to Pegramville."

The two older women considered their coffees for a long moment, and Aunt Caressa said, "I reckon Miss Willodean should have shot him then." She stirred the coffee although it was well stirred already. "Seeing as how she carries around a gun and all."

"That would have been ideal," Miz Demetrice agreed. "But alas."

"Should have shot him and drug him halfway inside the doorway," Aunt Caressa said firmly. "That's a legal defense in Texas."

"I'll try to remember that," Miz Demetrice affirmed. One never knew when an absolute standard would come into play. Especially of late, with dead bodies seeming to appear everywhere. It was kind of like bluebonnets in the spring on the sides of the highways, except the bodies didn't look pretty, and they didn't smell good neither.

Please, Lord, she prayed silently, *not one more. Not Willodean.*

•

Bubba woke up late. It was dark outside and in. A weight rested across his stomach, and there was a whining canine complaint as Bubba moved. Aching muscles protested. It didn't seem like he had done much the previous day and night, but patently he had exerted himself more than he'd thought. There was a brief moment of forgetfulness. Nothing was in his head, and it felt relaxing and redeeming.

Then he remembered, and he wasn't relaxed anymore and nothing had been redeemed.

Willodean. Willodean was gone. And he'd slept the day away like a damned fool. He cast a glance at his alarm clock and saw that it was past midnight. Willodean had been missing for coming up on forty-eight hours, and even a Luddite like Bubba had heard that if the police didn't find a missing person within forty-eight hours, they were unlikely to find that person at all.

Or did that saying only pertain to finding a murderer?

Bubba shook his head. He didn't want to think about murderers and Willodean Gray in the same sentence. That was unbearable. He took a breath and took a moment to scratch Precious as she wallowed on his bed. The dog was happy to take up all the warmth that her master had vacated.

He spent a little time in the bathroom and got dressed. He put on a warm shirt and heavy blue jeans. He put on a thick pair of socks and covered them with the most comfortable work boots that he had. He found his largest flashlight; it was a Maglite that held four D batteries. He retrieved a coat, suspecting he was going to be outside quite a bit.

Because his brain was no longer half dead with fatigue, it occurred to him that Lew Robson's hounds could have gotten an older scent from Willodean. She drove that road every day, and she had been down it the same day and the night before. He hadn't thought of it when Lew's hounds were tracking, but it hadn't rained for two weeks and the dryness could preserve the scents.

Willodean could still be in the forest or the fields. If Sheriff John hadn't searched there yet, then Bubba would. Every damnable inch by himself if he had to, in the middle of the night and in the cold, too. "Precious," he said to his dog, "come on, girl. We've got places to go and things to look at." Precious's head perked right up.

Miz Demetrice waited downstairs. She had a coat on, as well, and she was holding a spotlight. She also held out a thermos of coffee for him. Her expression was grim as she prepared to face his wrath at her actions.

"Folks have been searching all day," she said. "And you needed the sleep."

Bubba took the coffee. She reached into a pocket and handed him an energy bar. His lips twitched as he realized how prepared his mother was.

"I know, Ma," he finally said, holding back the minute bit of anger he felt at the fact that she had deliberately turned off his alarm. "You coming with us?"

"Of course, boy," Miz Demetrice looked at him incredulously. "Willodean's my friend. And Snoddys look after their friends."

•

The wrecked SUV was gone. It had been towed away by the sheriff's department. Spotlights set up by the police illuminated the scene. Remnants of yellow tape fluttered in a cool night breeze. Two county cars were parked at the scene, and one news van reposed at the closest spot that it could without the occupants being arrested for interference. Two other civilian cars were parked nearby.

Bubba grimaced. Miz Demetrice said an ugly word. Precious woofed softly. She didn't know what was going on, but she was involved and that meant everything was all gravy.

"That's her family?" Miz Demetrice said.

One of Willodean's sisters stood by the yellow caution tape and watched Bubba pull up in the old, green Chevy truck. The other sister was absent. She was probably staying at a local motel with her eight-year-old would-be police detective. "That gal over there is one of her sisters," Bubba said.

Bubba climbed out and allowed Precious to follow. He grabbed the Maglite and observed Willodean's sister, Hattie, straighten as she recognized him.

Two deputies gazed at Bubba without much change in their expressions. There was a generator rumbling nearby, and three spotlights still operated, leaving yellow pools of light spilling over the asphalt and the withered winter grasses on the sides of the road. One of the deputies glanced at a map that was taped to a nearby table. He saw that another table still held lukewarm coffee and a half-dozen, plastic-wrapped sandwiches.

One of the deputies was Steve Simms. Simms was someone who Bubba had dealt with in the past. The man thought a lot about his badge and liked to give out speeding tickets at a certain blind spot just outside Pegramville. He favored tourists with out-of-state plates. Bubba thought Simms must be itching with a need to ticket out-of-towners. Since there was a cluster of folks from all over who had come to see what happened when a murderer was on the loose, Simms was missing out on the revenue.

Once the word had leaked out about the Christmas Killer and the odd manner in which Steve Killebrew and Beatrice Smothermon had been murdered, the media poured in.

The attempt on Sheriff John had added fuel to the flames. Now a beautiful sheriff's deputy was missing. Non-Pegramville residents were abounding, and poor Simms was stuck here without access to a radar gun and a fresh pad of tickets.

"Bubba," Simms said warily, "you ain't supposed to be here."

Bubba didn't have an answer for that. So he said instead, "Just tell me where they haven't searched yet, Simms."

Simms made an agitated noise. He didn't like Bubba. Bubba had a perverse tendency to be arrested, even if most of the time it turned out that he hadn't done anything wrong. And then there was Willodean Gray and the fact that she was connected to Bubba. No one knew what had happened to her, and although Simms didn't think that Bubba Snoddy would do anything bad to Willodean, he couldn't completely discount the other man.

Bubba gestured to the table with the map. Hattie moved closer, deftly avoiding the yellow tape. Miz Demetrice and Precious drifted in for prime eavesdropping range. Precious spared a brief growl for Simms.

Simms glared at the dog and then pointed to the map. "These grids have been searched. Look, you can start over here by Sturgis Creek, but officers will be going behind you."

That was a benign warning. *Don't mess with evidence. Don't try to hide anything. We're watching you.*

Bubba didn't care much. There was a reason to search, and this was the second night that Willodean would have spent out in the cold, if indeed she was out here. He spared a glance at his mother. "You up for this, Ma?"

"I could do a little walking through the woods," Miz Demetrice allowed. She held up the spotlight. "Maybe we could find...something." She didn't know what words to use. She wanted to find Willodean alive as much as Bubba did, but as the hours had crawled past, hope was fading fast.

Hattie said, "My parents are in these segments." She pointed.

"I assume your ma still has a gun," Bubba said shortly. He sighed, "Ma, this is Hattie Gray. She's Willodean's older sister. Miz Gray, this is my mother, Demetrice Snoddy. She's right fond of Willodean and wants to help in any way she can."

Hattie shook Miz Demetrice's hand. "Wills talks

about you, Miz Demetrice. She said you're a real trip."

Bubba cleared his throat. "I'm going, Ma. You need to stay with me or stay here. I cain't be looking for you lost in the woods, too."

"He's a tad cranky," Miz Demetrice said to Hattie as Bubba turned away.

•

Bubba, Miz Demetrice, and Precious discovered a disintegrating pile of construction junk dumped in the forest just off the farm road. They found a rusting 1963 ½ Ford Galaxie with an armadillo living in it. There was a farmhouse that was leaning against two trees with a floor that had completely rotted away. Bubba pointed out where Ralph Cedarbloom's pot patch had been to his mother, although it was obvious that *something* had been there. The area had been utterly cleaned out. There wasn't anything left and someone had raked the earth with a brush hog just to be on the safe side.

"The po-lice are going to wonder about this," Miz Demetrice sighed.

"They'll figure it out," Bubba snapped.

They walked and searched until well after noon. Bubba recognized that Miz Demetrice was beyond dog-tired and took her back to the mansion. He returned and found dozens of Pegramville residents ready to search for Willodean Gray.

•

Hours later, every grid had been checked. The Grays had collapsed in their cars. Hattie rested her head on Anora's shoulder. Janie stared out at the woods; her little face was full of desolation. Celestine was grimly silent. Evan's face was shattered.

Bubba stood alone beside the map staring at it. Every grid square had been crossed out. Sheriff John was having a powwow with Big Joe, a state trooper, and the man Bubba thought might be a Fed.

Precious rolled in the dead grass on the side of the road and made noises that indicated she was hungry.

When Sheriff John turned away from the other men, Bubba was waiting. "Bubba," Sheriff John said tiredly. He scratched at the bandage at his throat, and his voice sounded hoarser than ever. Bubba decided that the older man hadn't gotten more than a few hours of sleep in the previous two days.

"What do you know about her stalker?" Bubba asked.

Sheriff John snorted. "Ain't much to tell," he said. But Bubba knew the older man was lying.

"I kin just ask her mama," Bubba threatened.

Sheriff John's eyes narrowed. "Why don't you pour salt on it, too, I reckon?"

"Look, John," Bubba said as he shrugged his weary shoulders, "I figure that we cain't find Willodean. But maybe we can find the man who took her."

"Leave it to the po-lice," Sheriff John advised. "We're working on it." He studied Bubba's face and added, "Working damned hard, too."

Bubba watched Sheriff John walk away. He tamped down the fury he felt. Fury wasn't going to do Willodean an ounce of next-to-nothing. He took a moment to throw a sandwich to Precious. Precious jumped on the sandwich and immediately stripped the roast beef from the bread via the swallowing-whole method.

"What do I know?" Bubba muttered. *Some fella had made Willodean unhappy. She had been so unhappy that she'd upped and moved to Pegramville. She didn't seem predominantly unhappy in Pegram County. She'd been, no strike that, she is interested in me. But she's been jumpy. Why? Because this fella popped up again?*

80

Precious devoured the cheese with heartfelt intensity. Then she gulped down the bread. She burped contentedly and then farted. Finally, the dog looked around and pretended that none of that had actually happened.

Because she got letters from this guy. Letters. Bubba's thoughts came back to visiting her home for a piece of her clothing. There had been mail in her box. There was more mail on her coffee table.

Bubba knew what he was going to do, and it didn't involve banging his head against the nearest, convenient brick wall.

Chapter Seven

Bubba Makes a Tremendous Decision

*Saturday, December 31*st

Bubba approached Willodean's duplex again. Dread churned massive holes in his intestines. If the truth be told, he didn't want to read the letters that she'd received. In fact, he thought it was probable that the letters were no longer at her place. She could have taken them to work. After all, she had told Sheriff John about them. Wouldn't the police want to keep the letters as some kind of record of a crime?

An errant thought gave him a pause. Did Willodean's family know about the stalker? Celestine was a Dallas Police Department Officer. He'd seen the sergeant's stripes on her shoulder. One of the daughters, Anora, let her daughter hang out around the precinct house too much, so she was likely one, too. The other daughter talked in a similar manner and was right handy with the large gun that she'd pointed at Bubba. That was indicative of Hattie being on the force, as well. Was the whole family PD?

Not Evan Gray. Not eight-year-old Janie. Well, he amended silently, *not yet for the kid.*

Bubba sighed and set his thoughts back to where they needed to be. Willodean hadn't talked about her family much. She had discussed them with Miz Demetrice, but they'd had a little more time for conversation while playing excessive hands of Texas Hold 'Em.

Not so much conversation for Bubba. He had dragged his heels, thinking about his first love, his ex-fiancée, Melissa Dearman nee Connor. She hadn't been a good choice seeing as how she had slept with their commanding officer and then later married him. Neither had the woman he dated before Willodean had come around. Lurlene Grady, aka Donna Hyatt, had set Bubba up for Melissa's murder. Choosing women wasn't Bubba's strong suit, and the awareness had made him as skittish as a virgin in a prison rodeo. Consequently, he'd intentionally been slow about courting Willodean Gray.

The previous week had upped his schedule. Willodean had shown in several ways how much she cared for him, the least of which had been the brain-numbing kiss at the cemetery.

Kisses, Bubba thought with a teensy-tiny ray of something called fondness. It gave him a brief warm feeling that was like a beam of light burst forth from the heavens. *Not just one.*

The unhurried sluggishness of his pursuit made him feel something other than boiling rage at her disappearance. Regret. Utter regret that he'd missed spending time with Willodean. The feeling made him sick.

Staring at Willodean's little porch, he thought that it didn't look any different in the middle of the afternoon. The swing was swaying a little in the breeze. The bronze wind chimes played an accompaniment. She should have been sitting there, ready to say something sassy to him.

Swinging his gaze to the other porch of the duplex, he noticed that the black brassiere was gone; instead, there was a pair of Smurf covered jockey shorts hanging from the flag pole. *I got a pair just like those.*

Unreserved resolve set in. Bubba didn't have Sheriff John's keys today. But he did have a need to look at the letters Willodean had received. *Read the letters. Find a clue to the man's identity and whereabouts. Find the stalker. Find Willodean.* It was a mantra that he could live with...for the moment.

The door of the duplex opened, and a girl with blond hair in dreadlocks peered out at him. She looked at him and then out toward the old, green Chevy with the Basset hound sticking her head out the window. "Hey," she said, "you're the guy who came looking for Mark Evans in my psych class. I remember your dog, too."

Bubba recalled the girl. She worked for Edward Minnieweather serving papers to folks in the Pegram County area. She had been wearing a Jim Morrison t-shirt then, and now she was wearing a Led Zeppelin one. *And nothing else.* Bubba's eyes instantly went up to the roof of the duplex.

"Yeah," he said. *Nice new roof. The trim was just painted.* "Found him, too. In the hospital. Didn't have much to say neither."

"Well, that guy he served beat the bloody hell out of him," the girl said with a wry smile. "I talked to Mark last week. He just got another surgery on his hand, and he made up all of his psych work. I can't believe he got a B in that class. To get a B, I would have sucked- well, I would have bent over backwards, and well, that doesn't sound any better does it?"

Bubba wasn't sure if it sounded any better, so he kept wisely mum on the subject. "Do you know the lady who lives there?" He pointed at Willodean's door.

"Sure, Willy," the girl said. "She's the bacon. But she's cool. She said if she smelled something wafting over, she would ignore it as long as it was in proportion to the situation." She nodded firmly. "That's kew-ell."

"KIKI!" a voice bellowed from inside.

The girl glanced over her shoulder and then looked back at Bubba. "I heard your truck and thought it was the pizza guy." Her bright blue eyes looked him up and down, determining that he didn't have a pizza box in his immediate possession. "Guess not."

"Do you have a key to Willodean's place?" Bubba asked.

The girl, whose name was in fact, Kiki, studied Bubba. "You were with the cop that day you were looking for Mark." She pursed her lips. "You had handcuffs on, and you had more bruises and bumps than Mike Tyson after a fight. Was it you that Mark tried to serve?" She shook her head and answered her own question. "No, it was that really big guy, Gollihugh." She looked at Bubba again. "Of course, you're a *big* fella, but that Gollihugh is supposed to be like seven feet tall."

"Dan Gollihugh *is* seven feet tall," Bubba said. "Bad temper, too. If Minnieweather sends you out to serve him, you might want to take a pass. Getting legal papers makes Dan as mad as a mosquito in a mannequin factory."

"Most of the kids who work for Minnieweather kind of figured that out," Kiki said with an amused nod.

"KIKI!" the voice bellowed again. "IS THE PIZZA HERE? I got the munchies wicked bad!"

"NO!" she bellowed back. The breeze blew a little harder, and the Led Zeppelin t-shirt fluttered in a way that showed just about everything and then some.

Bubba's eyes went back to the roof. His own mother had, for some bizarre reason, recently told him something about feminine hair removal, and here was an example that was practically winking at him. One type was called a Brazilian wax, and one type was called a Hollywood wax. Kiki had one or the other, but he couldn't remember which one was which. Furthermore, he didn't care to ask her what the difference was. Even thinking about it made red flags appear on his cheeks.

"Why do you want a key for Willy's place?" Kiki asked curiously. She smoothed down the shirt over her thighs, and Bubba sighed with relief.

"She's missing," Bubba said shortly.

Kiki frowned. "Missing? I saw her on…Wednesday. She borrowed our grill. She had a date, and they wanted to barbeque." Her eyes examined Bubba's contorted features. "That was you, wasn't it? For the date?"

Bubba nodded. He couldn't get past the lump in his throat. "There was a car wreck out toward the Snoddy Mansion. Her county car was pushed to the side of the road. We've been searching all night."

"And the folks who were here yesterday," Kiki said, "they're her family, right?"

Bubba nodded again. "They're out searching, too."

"Shit, I'm sorry," Kiki said. "Willy is good peeps. Even for a popo." She shrugged. "But she never gave us a key. Hell, *I* wouldn't give us a key."

Bubba sighed. It had been a long shot. He could look under Willodean's welcome mat and under the flower pots, but Willodean wasn't the type to hide keys in obvious places; hence, the set of keys that she had given Sheriff John. "Thanks anyway," he said and turned toward the other side of the duplex.

Kiki smiled at him and shut the door behind her.

Maybe there's a window cracked or maybe the door will fly open by itself when my foot hits it in just the right place. Bubba smiled grimly. He'd fix the door himself, but he needed to look at those letters.

The other door opened again. Kiki was triumphantly holding up a Hello Kitty keychain. By all rights, the keychain should have been glittering in the sunlight like a disco ball but it wasn't.

"I forgot," she announced cheerfully. "The guy who lived here before Willy gave this to me." She trotted out sans underwear and handed it to Bubba. "Bet Willy didn't change the locks. Of course, she doesn't really know that she can trust us. We would never rip off a sheriff's deputy. Besides Willy is too Cool-and-the-Gang to mess with. My other roommate would sell his soul to get with her."

Bubba made a growling sound in response to her statement.

Kiki laughed and dreadlocks went flying. "Oh, calm yourself, big fella. Willy said she was interested in one guy and one guy only, so who could that be, I wonder." She twirled and went back inside, and Bubba inadvertently got a glimpse of rounded pink cheeks. It made *his* cheeks turn red again. He wasn't sure about the color of his *other* cheeks.

Before another second had passed, Kiki stuck her head back out the door. "If you need more people to search, let me know. I'll Tweet it so the whole world hears. My name is Kiki Rutkowski. I'm all over the Net."

"Oh-kay," Bubba agreed doubtfully. Kiki vanished again.

Bubba got inside Willodean's house before Kiki could return outside. *Does that girl understand that she doesn't have underwear on?*

Shaking his head, Bubba looked around. He went through Willodean's mail lying on the coffee table. He searched through a small desk in a smaller bedroom. He looked through her garbage. He balked at her bedroom door. One day he was going to have to explain to someone that he had illegally broken into Willodean's house. It was a similar reason to why he had stolen Willodean's official county car, but it was still illegal.

Bubba's moral code allowed for such. It was okay to

hit Big Joe because Bubba knew that his family might be in mortal danger, and Big Joe wasn't going to just let Bubba up and go. It was all right to commit a criminality when the higher moral ground needed to be taken. Accordingly, it was acceptable to break into Willodean's home. But later on, he would have to expound on why that was all right to Willodean herself. He hoped that she understood, but Bubba knew that it was a decision he would repeat over and over again if necessary.

But Willodean's bedroom was her sanctuary. Crossing that precise line was like traveling the road to Ickyville. Besides, he didn't think that she would keep a stalker's letters in her bedroom. He looked at the nicely organized room with a large bed, two night stands, and a rocking chair.

For a long moment, Bubba couldn't confine his curiosity.

Clearly, she favored maroon and gold in her bedroom. The bed had been made with a silk, maroon comforter that had probably been rumpled by Janie. Near the head of the bed, gold pillows were lined up next to ones that had been hand stitched with homey sayings. "A stitch in time saved nine" was emblazoned on one. "Never say never" was on another. A third one said, "In God we trust, and all others we run through the NCIC."

A hefty sigh coursed through Bubba's big body. He inhaled and thought he could smell her unique fragrance. Then his eyes settled on the isolated box sitting on the end of the bed. It was a hat box, and he recognized the maker. The Stetson logo was prominent. The red ribbon attached to the top was more prominent.

Bubba's eyebrows knitted together in a frown. He

stepped across the doorway and touched the box. It was new, and the logo shined brightly. There was a tag attached to the ribbon. He took a moment to turn it over. Janie's words came back to him, *"Bubba. But Bubba is the name on the..."* Then her grandfather had shushed her.

The tag said, "To Bubba. From Willodean." She hadn't put any Xes on it, but it wasn't necessary.

Last Sunday, Bubba had lost his Stetson hat to a mob of disconcerted city police officers just before one of them had kicked him, leaving the bump on his forehead. The hat had been trampled and lost to a couple dozen impertinent feet. Bubba had other hats, but he surely liked that one. In all the excitement and fuss of what had happened afterwards, he'd forgotten about it.

But Willodean hadn't.

Bubba's big heart pretty much turned over in his chest. It might have broken in two, but there wasn't anyone else there to hear the crack, so it was hard to really say.

•

It was a long time later that he let himself out of Willodean's home and locked the door behind him. He stood on the little porch and stared at the Hello Kitty keychain. He was about to turn to retrace his steps to the other side of the duplex, when the mailbox caught his eye.

It took Bubba a moment to figure out what the day of the week was and knew that the mail had been delivered. He flipped the box's lid open and withdrew a sheaf of letters. One was an electric bill. Another was a credit card application. A third one was a card from Hattie Gray. The fourth one had careful block lettering on it and no return address.

He opened Willodean's door again and put her mail

on the coffee table with the rest. Then he picked up the fourth envelope and opened it without compunction. What the letter said made him want to crush the paper into a ball, throw it to the ground, and stomp on it.

Ifin that's what Willodean's been dealing with, then no wonder she's flappable, he thought with a surge of anger coursing through him. *Ker-ist.* Bubba fingered the envelope, knowing he was getting his prints all over it. He hadn't considered he should take it directly to Sheriff John. It was likely Sheriff John had the other letters. The question that resulted as Bubba's mind worked was, *Does Sheriff John need this one, too? Did I mess up by opening it?*

The postmark said Dallas, Texas and was dated the 28th. Dallas was only a few hours' drive away. This was sincere evidence. *If the worst was to happen...*Bubba closed his eyes, and his lips became a flattened grim line of pain, *then Sheriff John is going to need this.*

Bubba locked up Willodean's house again and took the letter to a nearby 7-Eleven. There he made a copy of the letter and the envelope, while Precious bayed from the cab of the truck, indignant that she hadn't been allowed out again. Finally, he dropped off the envelope and letter at the Pegram County Sheriff's Department.

Robert Daughtry was sitting at the receptionist's desk. His dirty, blonde hair was rumpled, and his shirt was askew, but Bubba didn't hold it against him. The man stared at Bubba as if Bubba had grown a set of horns. Bubba would have checked, but he was certain his horns hadn't come in yet. Instead, Bubba put the original letter and envelope on the desk.

"Give this to Sheriff John," Bubba said. He was briefly reminded that Robert had been out at the place where Willodean had vanished from, watching avidly like a couple dozen other Pegram County residents.

He'd been talking to Patsy, Sheriff John's secretary, and Nadine Clack, the librarian with Ben Franklin glasses, had been unashamedly eavesdropping.

Robert's eyes dropped to the letter and the envelope. "What's th-th-that?"

"Something Sheriff John needs to look at concerning Willodean Gray," Bubba said. "I touched it, so my fingerprints are all over the envelope, but I guess that's water under the bridge and over the dam, too."

"I-I-I," Robert stuttered as he looked back up at Bubba.

Bubba figured that his towering over the desk was making the poor man nervous so he stepped back. "It was in her mail," he added helpfully. "Tell Sheriff John I'll call in to check with Miz Demetrice now and again, but I don't have a cell phone and ain't likely to sprout one soonest."

"I-I-I- what?"

Bubba stared at the man. Robert Daughtry was older than Bubba and seemed a mite intimidated. *Probably because I was accused of several murders and in jail about a half-dozen times, and now I look like I could chew up nails and spit out barbed wire fence. Hell, I'd make Rambo go a tick past apprehensive.*

"Just give it to Sheriff John," Bubba said as gently as he could. "I'll be calling him."

Robert gawked at Bubba as he turned to depart.

Bubba was a little surprised that someone hadn't arrested him for something or other. After all, he didn't usually come to the sheriff's department unless he was in handcuffs. Well honestly, it felt a little odd.

•

The Snoddy Mansion was aflutter with activity. Fudge and Virtna were packing to leave. Fudge was gleefully speaking to Miz Demetrice as he collected a few of Brownie's toys from varied locales. "Shore 'nuff, Auntie D., it's been right interesting being here."

Bubba paused at the door to one of the largest living rooms. He cast an eye over his shoulder as Virtna carried a suitcase out the door. It didn't appear as though the suitcase had an excess of questionable objects contained within it. But the Louisiana Snoddys were clever. Fudge's truck was probably loaded to capacity.

Bubba didn't feel like dealing with it. His mother was more than capable. He briefly looked at Miz Demetrice. She was absently listening to Fudge as she sipped a glass of merlot. It was somewhat early in the day, but seeing as Miz Demetrice didn't have a prescription for Valium; the merlot seemed an acceptable substitute.

"Ain't had this much excitement since Pa got arrested for robbing that bank," Fudge went on blithely. "Pa was a dumbass, but I believe he had a good heart."

Bubba's Uncle Beauregard, Fudge's father, had been a dumbass. He'd robbed the bank located next to a police station at lunch hour. As soon as he had pulled out his unloaded weapon, ten police officers were drawing down on him. He'd been fortunate that he hadn't been shot on the spot. He hadn't been so fortunate in jail because he'd died years later still on the inside.

"And well, Brownie caught a murderer," Fudge said proudly, "with a stun gun he made from his own hands. That's something else."

"Something else," Miz Demetrice agreed doubtfully and looked cautiously around for Brownie.

"I cain't believe the calls we've gotten," Fudge said.

Virtna brushed past Bubba and added, "We've set up a Facebook page for Brownie. He's got over a hundred thousand friends."

Fudge picked up something that looked like it was once a toy train. It had been chewed on or burned. Possibly both. He examined it uncertainly and then tossed it into a bag.

Precious nosed against Bubba's legs, and he reached down to scratch behind her ears. She took it in stride and then played hard to get. Turning her nose away, she trotted to the Christmas tree that was still in the corner and hid behind it.

Brownie came ripping through and abruptly stopped next to Bubba. "Say, Cousin Bubba," the boy said to him. Bubba looked down and wondered if he could introduce Brownie to Janie, the would-be-Joe Friday. *That would be really interesting. Could be fireworks.*

"Yeah, boy," Bubba said warily.

"I'm sorry about your friend being missing and all," Brownie said sincerely.

Bubba ruffled Brownie's hair. "Thanks, boy." He would have added that everything would be all right, but Bubba wasn't certain about that.

"Pa says I can come back in the summertime," Brownie revealed gleefully. "I'll bet she's back by then. Maybe for Spring Break, too."

Miz Demetrice cast Bubba a pained stare that denoted his forthcoming doom, and Bubba shrugged. *What could the boy do then?* He considered. *Probably destroy city hall. Maybe make a bomb for fun. Won't be boring.*

Fudge and Virtna finished with expressive flair. Fudge grasped Miz Demetrice in his arms and hugged her. The older woman peeped while Virtna nodded approvingly.

Speedy hugs were transferred all around. Bubba

saw that Miz Adelia peeked in and quickly absconded in what he could only assume was abject terror of being touched by Brownie. Aunt Caressa stuck her head in and promptly fled to Outer Mongolia.

Fudge paused to solidly punch Bubba in his shoulder. Bubba staggered and then absently rubbed his arm. "Hope they find that gal real soon," Fudge said firmly. "But we've got a plane to catch. Ain't been on a plane since that trip to Las Vegas and well, you know, they won't let me in Nevada no more. Dang."

Bubba took a moment to wonder where Fudge and his family were taking a plane to and why was the pair so happy. The answers weren't immediately forthcoming, so Bubba let it go. Other things were lurking in the depths of his brain and crawling out to viciously poke him in the back of his eyeballs.

Brownie let a tear leak out of his eye as he captured an obviously reluctant Precious behind the Christmas tree and imparted a needy squeeze to the struggling canine.

Miz Demetrice and Bubba watched the trio drive off in Fudge's truck. Bubba shook his head; his mind was on other things completely. He spared his mother a glance. Miz Demetrice seemed tired.

"Going out to look in the morning again," she said. "Got the entire Pokerama group and their families coming. Also got the church, the police auxiliary, and the entire Loyal Order of the Moose."

Bubba nodded. "There's a gal who lives next to Willodean. Her name is Kiki Rutkowski. She's a college student and said she'd help search ifin you were to call her."

Miz Demetrice said, "Good. The more the better."

"Going to Dallas," he said pithily.

"Got people coming from two counties away and the

entire high school band and- say, what?"

"Willodean ain't out there," Bubba stated. "But there's a fella who knows where she's at."

Miz Demetrice stood still. "This fella is in Dallas?"

"I reckon," Bubba said, and the tone of his voice made his mother shudder.

"What will you do, Bubba dear?"

"I aim to persuade this man to tell me where Willodean is," Bubba vowed. "One way or the other."

Chapter Eight

Bubba Does Dallas

Saturday, December 31st – Sunday, January 1st

Bubba drove into Dallas city limits about nine p.m. The city was lit up, and he could see all of its twinkling beauty. The skyline sparkled against the night sky. Reunion Tower was the most recognizable with its ball top standing off to one side. It was a solitary Christmas ball glittering with lights alongside a sea of velvet blackness. The Bank of America Plaza Building was the next most outstanding with its impressive lines of green neon lights streaking down its edges. There were other standout buildings like the J.P. Chase with its keyhole shape at the top, the Trammel Crow Center with its pyramidal glass top, and Fountain Place with its glass green prism shape. He was also familiar with the older buildings with historical notes abounding, although they didn't dominate the horizon: The Cathedral Santuario de Guadalupe, which was part of the first Catholic parish in Dallas County and the Old Red Courthouse, which was presently a museum that celebrated Downtown Dallas's greatest historical events. In comparison, the nearby Texas School Book Repository was a pinpoint in history known primarily for being the vantage point of an unbalanced assassin.

It was a stunning place to be certain, but Bubba wasn't captivated. At the moment, Dallas was just a place to discover where Willodean Gray was to be found.

Finding a cheap place to stay wasn't hard. The first hotel didn't care for dogs. The second hotel was less picky. Bubba could see why when he opened his room's

96

door with a rusting key that was older than he was. It was clean but beyond ratty. The brownish rug was tattered and repaired with uneven stitches of orange yarn. The tables had cigarette burns on the tops. The suppleness of the bed was similar to a very flat rock.

Bubba looked around as Precious sniffed precariously. She finally settled her gaze fully upon him and tilted her head as if saying, "What in the wide world of sports are we doing in this dive?"

Then the fireworks started.

Really, there were fireworks. Bubba and Precious went outside and found that the languishing downtown hotel had a prime view of the New Year's fireworks presented by the City of Dallas. Precious didn't care for the noise and hid between Bubba's legs with her paws over her ears and eyes.

Gradually, it dawned on Bubba that it was New Year's Eve.

Other people wandered out into the streets to watch.

"Hey," a man said to Bubba. Bubba looked at the man. He was in his thirties and smelled strongly of tobacco. His brown eyes were friendly enough, and he looked at Precious curiously. "Nice Basset hound."

Precious grunted. She knew when she was being discussed, but the loudness of the exploding fireworks was making her nervous. She whined and hid her eyes again.

"Thanks," Bubba said.

He watched the show from the street in front of the hotel. The locale provided an easy vista for the explosions as they burst forth from a setup near the Trinity River.

"Looking for work?" the man said.

"Looking for someone," Bubba said curtly.

"Oh?" the man glanced around. "Who's that?"

"Looking for a gal," Bubba said.

"My name's Bam Bam," the man said. "I kin...hook...you...up." In between pauses the man's hands moved in elaborate poses until they stopped in front of his chest and waited for Bubba's response. The index and pinkie fingers of both hands were pointing inward as if saying that Bam Bam was indeed, the man.

Bubba scrutinized Bam Bam. "Your mama a Flintstones fan?"

"Hahaha," Bam Bam said. "I know a girl who can rock your world. Her name is Gummi Worm. She's phat." There were more hand gestures. Bubba wondered if the man was signaling for a plane to land on a carrier, but there wasn't a carrier within 300 miles of the Dallas/Fort Worth Metroplex.

Bubba blinked as he comprehended the words. "Not that kind of gal."

Bam Bam nodded understandingly. "Then you want a *gal*." More hand gestures ensued.

A little uncertain, Bubba shrugged. "A specific gal."

"I know a little she-male who will make you squeal," Bam Bam said confidently. "Just...like...that." There were a few more expansive hand gestures.

"I think we're misunderstanding each other," Bubba said. "This woman is missing. She's got black hair and green eyes and a saucy mouth. She's *very* important. I'm looking for her."

"Oh," Bam Bam said solemnly. He reached into a pocket and produced a business card. He snapped it sharply as he presented it to Bubba. "My card, my man, if you change your mind. Hope you find yo homegirl."

Bubba took the card, and a fresh batch of fireworks started up. He looked at the card. It said, "Bam Bam Jones: entrepreneur". Below the name was a cell phone number. He sighed and stuck the card in a pocket.

Bam Bam deftly moved onto the next man standing alone on the sidewalk. "Yo," he said cheerfully. "That's a kicking shirt. You new in town?"

Bubba herded Precious back inside before the dog lost her mind. The fireworks died away after thirty minutes, and Bubba lay on the bed. He didn't think he'd be able to sleep wondering where Willodean slept. However, the next thing he knew Precious scratched at the door, and light billowed in from a narrow window.

Half staggering, Bubba let Precious out and followed her. He was still dressed in the clothing he'd worn the day before. She already had the know of the building and went down the stairs, past the front desk, to the main entrance without pause. A few seedy-looking individuals hung out in the decrepit lobby and studied Bubba calculatingly. "Hey, ya'll," he said.

They stared at him.

"Bad night, huh?" he added after their continued silence. He let Precious outside. She gleefully discovered the nearest patch of grass and made it her own. Bubba waited and thought about his plan.

Now that he was in Dallas, he was at a loss. He had a copy of a letter and an envelope. He had a postmark with a date and a zip code. But he didn't know who the stalker was, and he didn't know how to find out.

I went off half-cocked.

Normally he would ask Willodean's family. But her family was still in Pegram County looking for Willodean. He needed information. Then he remembered it was Sunday. *Sunday, the first day of January of a brand new year. Willodean's been missing for three whole days. Three days in the cold. Alone, frightened...*

Bubba got himself organized and showered. He made certain Precious ate some kibble. He took his truck and found a store that sold prepaid phones. Ostensibly, and despite what he'd said to Robert Daughtry, he *was* going to sprout a cell phone soonest. He paid for it and returned to the hotel to charge the thing. While it charged, he made himself a list on the hotel's stationary.

The top of the list read:

1. Find Willodean

Whereupon he put the pen down because he couldn't think of anything else to add.

Duh, Bubba told himself silently.

Precious pawed at the brownish carpet. Something else brownish endeavored to evade her. She'd found an errant mouse and was trying to corral the poor creature. "You got any suggestions, Precious?" he asked in a calmer tone than he actually felt.

Precious glanced at her master and woofed softly. She returned her attention to the mouse. The mouse squeaked and hauled ass for a hole in the wall.

"Where do I get information?"

The library. But the library's closed until tomorrow. I could go to where she used to work, but I don't know that. I could call her parents and ask them for information, but I don't know that they would tell me anything, and do I really want to twist the knife in their guts?

Bubba had a decidedly strong urge to throw a table against a wall, although it wasn't the wall's fault. *And ain't the table's neither.*

The phone was half charged when Bubba ran out of patience and called his mother. Miz Demetrice's cell phone immediately rolled over to voicemail. Another call to the Snoddy Mansion confirmed that his mother was out searching the area near where Willodean's wrecked vehicle had been found. Bubba left his new cell phone number with Miz Adelia.

Bubba felt worse than useless. He could be searching the bottomlands near Sturgis Creek. But somewhere, somehow, Bubba knew Willodean Gray wasn't there. The certainty might have come from John Headrick's horrified conviction about Willodean's disappearance. The certainty might have come from the haunted expression of her father's face and the cold realization of her mother's. The certainty might have come from reading that wretched letter that Willodean had received.

Or it might have been as simple as the fact that Willodean wouldn't voluntarily vanish.

Precious let the mouse go and came to brush her nose against Bubba's leg. He absently petted her. She nudged his leg. He met her eyes because his head hung down as he sat in the rickety chair next to the wobbly table.

The dog stared at him with her sad brown eyes. She seemed to say, "Why are you moping again? Do I have to do everything? I've got enough on my plate without having to do humans' work, too. For love of Saint Bernard, just figure out who can help you right now. Lord have mercy. Doesn't a dog do enough without having to play psychiatrist to her human?" There was a preeminent pause. "And give me a bleeping Milk-Bone while you're at it."

A thought occurred to Bubba. He wasn't the only one who wanted to help. There were others. The girl with the dreadlocks offered to help. She said something about the Internet, and even a technophobe like Bubba knew that the Internet had all kinds of information galore.

It took him three minutes to remember Kiki's last

101

name. It took him another minute to get an actual operator to give him her number. On the fifth minute, he was speaking to her.

"Dammit," she said into the phone. "I got the worst mofo hangover in existence and I don't like my phone ringing before- hey, it's after twelve. I guess you're saved because we had to get up anyway to go do valuable community service. Who is this anyway?"

"Bubba Snoddy," he said.

"Bubba," she said. "Okay. Bubba. Big fella. Looking for Willy. I haven't seen her. And someone called us about searching, so we're headed out to help search in a couple of hours. Is there any news?"

"She's still missing," Bubba said.

"Damn," Kiki said.

"You can help me," Bubba went on quickly.

"Okay, how?"

"I need some information about her. Something happened to her in Dallas, and I don't have access to a computer."

"Okay," Kiki said again.

He heard her moving around on the other end of the line.

"I'm turning on my laptop. It's gonna take a minute to boot, and then we'll see what we can see."

Bubba waited. He really liked that Kiki wasn't asking all kinds of questions that Bubba wouldn't even know how to begin to answer. Like "Why aren't the police doing this?" and "Why aren't you searching for Willy yourself?" and "Why can't you go use an Internet café?"

Finally, Kiki said, "Okay. Browser's up. Let's go. Let me put her name in the search engine and see. It's Willodean. Funky name."

There was an urge to beat his chest with his fists and

yell, "Hurry the hell up," but it was an unproductive feeling, and Bubba controlled himself.

"39,000 results," Kiki said. "Can we narrow that down?"

Bubba figured that she wasn't speaking to him and said nothing.

"We'll add Texas," Kiki decided. "Oh, that's better. Hey, she's not on Facebook. Who's not on Facebook? Got to get that girl into the 21st century."

"I'm not on Facebook," Bubba said.

"You, I understand," Kiki laughed. "Do you know how to use a computer?"

"I know how to turn one on," Bubba said. "I use one at the garage all the time."

Many of the cars he worked on required a specialized software program to diagnose its ailments. It was usually a matter of plugging one end of a wire to the car and the other end to a portable unit. Whereupon the unit would tell him what computer component would need to be replaced or kicked.

Thank God, the old, green Chevy is too primitive to need that. And hey, I used a computer in college. Several. There was the Dell that I dropped on the floor. The HP that got thrown across the room. And what was that one that I spilled beer on? Anyway...

"Okay, there's a Willodean Gray Realty in Houston. That's not her. That lady looks like she's ninety years old." Kiki paused. Someone said something in the background. "Okay, *forty* years old. That's one of my roommates talking in my other ear. He's assisting."

"Willodean Gray graduated from Ferris High School in...1938," Kiki muttered. "So *not* her."

Bubba shrugged impatiently.

"And here we go," Kiki said triumphantly. She was silent for a moment. The voice in the background said something sharp. "Yeah, I see that, Dougie."

"What is it?" Bubba couldn't help himself.

"A year ago, Dallas Police Department Patrol Officer Willodean Gray was assaulted by a man while she was on patrol." Kiki's voice trailed off. "She was hurt badly enough to have spent a week in a local hospital. Jesus."

Bubba's voice was icy as he replied. "What was the man's name?"

"Hang on, the article is a little spacy," Kiki said. "Yesterday they said something about Willy being stalked. You think this guy is the same guy that wrecked her car?"

"Maybe."

"All right. His name is Howell Le Beau."

Bubba wrote the name under the single item of his list. He asked Kiki to spell it for him twice. "Can you get an address for this man, Le Beau?"

"Find a person search engine," Kiki said immediately. "You're not going to kill him, are you? Would that make me an accessory? Dougie, you're in pre-law, would that make me an accessory?"

"I'm not going to kill him," Bubba said before Dougie could say anything.

"That's good, even if he might deserve it." Kiki fell silent for a moment. "Still reading here. Looks like he stalked her for months. She had a restraining order on him and everything. Well shit, he beat the holy hell out of her." She fell silent for a moment. "I guess I shouldn't have said that."

She hit that nail on the head. Bubba didn't want to think about anyone beating the holy hell out of Willodean Gray. She was petite, and although he'd seen she could handle herself, he could well imagine some taller, hulking man getting the best of her.

Rage percolated up from deep inside him. He could

also well imagine wrapping his hands around the neck of a man he'd never met.

"There's another name here," Kiki said rapidly. "Charles Park was the detective in charge of the case. There's a quote from him about domestic violence."

"Domestic violence," Bubba repeated doubtfully.

"Looks like Willy had a very brief relationship with the man," Kiki said defensively. She correctly perceived his disbelieving tone. "And that doesn't make any difference. If she said no, then she said no. It shouldn't make any difference to you either."

"It doesn't," Bubba said. "I just...don't like to think of her hurt like that."

"That's understandable," Kiki responded mollifyingly. "This guy, Charles Park, is in the Assaults Unit, and his phone number is included in case any witnesses want to step forward."

"What happened to Howell Le Beau?" Bubba asked after he took down the name and phone number of the investigating officer. *Is it possible the man who'd attacked Willodean was still in jail?*

"Hold on," Kiki said. Bubba heard clicking as she typed on the laptop. "There are several articles about Howell Le Beau. Hmm."

Dougie said something in the background.

"Yes, Dougie, I know that's totally unfabulous. Peeps shouldn't be able to make deals like that," Kiki said. "This guy, Le Beau, made a deal with the prosecutor. He agreed to six months in, plus fines, plus all of Willy's bills, and a shitload of therapy sessions." Kiki blew out air noisily. "That sucks the big, fat purple wang."

"This man, this Howell Le Beau is out of prison now?" Bubba said slowly.

Kiki sighed. "Looking at the dates, yes. He could have- what's that, Dougie?" Dougie said something, and

Kiki said to Bubba, "He could have been out of jail early for good behavior, too. The prisons are overcrowded, and they release people early who behave."

The little throwaway cell phone made a distinct cracking sound as Bubba's hand flexed. He recalled the state trooper's ruined phone and forced himself to relax his hand.

"Is there an address for Howell Le Beau?"

"Let me look," Kiki said. After a minute she said, "No Howell Le Beau, but there's only four Lebeaus in the Dallas/Fort Worth area. That's without the space in between Le and Beau. I bet you can call all of them and ask if Howell is available. You could pretend to be an old high school buddy."

"Give me the names and numbers," Bubba said.

Kiki did that and added, "Be easier if you just get a smart phone. You can hook up with the Internet from there. It's also got tons of apps that you can use. I bet Willy's connected."

Bubba didn't know how to reply to that. He didn't know anything about Willodean's preference on cellular phones. He wouldn't mind learning, but first he had to find her and find her alive.

An ice-cold uncertainty trickled through his veins.

"Thank you," he said to Kiki.

Kiki didn't immediately respond. "I wish I could tell you something better," she said finally. "You should go see the police investigator and get the 4-1-1 on the Howell Le Beau thing. Maybe they're already looking for this dude."

Not fast enough to suit me.

"Anyway, call me back if you need the information ninja again," Kiki said. "I'll keep my phone with me, even when we're out searching today."

Bubba would have told Kiki that cell phone towers

were few and far between in the Sturgis Woods, but she'd already disconnected.

Folding the piece of paper up to tuck into a pocket, Bubba paused to scratch behind Precious's ear. He deliberated about what he should do next. He found a moldering phone book in a nightstand drawer to look for the official address of Dallas investigator.

But a knock at his door interrupted him.

Chapter Nine

Bubba is On the Hunt Again

Sunday, January 1st

Bam Bam Jones stood there with a cheerful grin on his face. He wore a Dallas Cowboys jersey and white leather pants with purple calf-high boots. One of his hands was at chest level with two fingers pointed to his immediate left. The other hand was just below the first hand with two fingers pointed to his immediate right. The convoluted hand positions emphasized the twinkling diamond and gold rings he wore.

"The doorman didn't announce you," Bubba said.

What's with all the hand gestures? Maybe he's got some kind of weird muscle disease.

The other man looked confused for a moment. "There ain't be a doorman on this place, brotha."

Precious sniffed Bam Bam from between Bubba's legs.

"There's that cute little girl," Bam Bam said as he extended fingers downward for Precious to smell. Precious took a step forward and sniffed cautiously. She allowed the other man to scratch her head and behind her ears. She knew when a human was present to adore a canine goddess.

"I'm a little busy," Bubba said. He patted his pocket. He had his list. He patted another pocket. There was the little disposable cell phone. He would have brought a charger with him except the old, green Chevy truck didn't have a place to plug it in anyway.

"As we all are," Bam Bam replied cheerfully. "I was thinking about your sitch and I got a lady you gots to meet."

"What I've gots to do is to go find a police investigator," Bubba said.

"Jump back!" Bam Bam said forcefully. "The 5-0 ain't going to he'p you. You gots to go to the right peoples. This lady is a *psychic*." He put his index fingers to his temples as if he was the psychic and was having a vision. "She sees things. *Knows* things."

"A psychic," Bubba said thoughtfully. "I don't hold truck with such."

"Think about it," Bam Bam said, pointing rapidly at Bubba and then back at himself. He made a fist, hit his chest three times, and pointed at Bubba. "You got my card?"

Bubba nodded.

"Bring a picture of yo homegirl and my homegirl will hook it up phat." Bam Bam grinned. He had a surplus of white teeth that might make a shark jealous. He rambled down the hall singing a song about a girl's excessively large backside. His hands were jerking and contracting in time with the song.

Precious peered dubiously around the corner at the man.

Bubba went back into his room and took out the entire phone book again. He needed the reference material. He'd put it back. *Eventually.*

It turned out that the central division of the Dallas Police Department was only six blocks from his hotel. Parking the truck in a massive lot next to the Dallas Police Department, he got out. He left Precious in the truck with the windows open and instructions to eat anyone who came near the vehicle. Precious appeared doubtful.

Going inside the main entrance Bubba found the front desk. He had to compete with several people for the sergeant's time.

When Bubba managed to get a question in, the sergeant only paused to take a note. "Yeah, it's the *first* of January. Ain't many investigators in. But I'll check."

Bubba sat next to a man who held a handkerchief over a cut on his forehead. A drip of blood meandered down the side of his nose. On the other side, a woman who looked asleep leaned on Bubba as soon as he sat down. She turned to him and put her head on his shoulder and let her hands wander freely. Bubba kept busy trying to extricate himself.

The octopus-handed woman on Bubba's left still strove to snuggle up to him when the police investigator finally appeared an eternity later. He was an Asian-American in his early thirties. His hair was black, his eyes a weary brown, and he was leanly proportioned. Bubba watched as he looked around, and the desk sergeant pointed at Bubba.

Bubba extracted himself from the woman. She murmured, "Oh, but you're *so* cuddly," and turned to her other side to molest the man there.

"You're Bubba Snoddy?" the investigator asked. He wore a long sleeved white dress shirt with a ratty black tie and business-casual khaki pants. His gold shield hung around his neck from a chain. Part of the identification tag that was under the shield said, "ark," so Bubba went with the conclusion this was Charles Park.

Bubba nodded and stuck his hand out. The investigator stared at Bubba for a long moment and then at his large hand. Finally, he reached out and shook it like it was a bomb about to explode. "I'm Charles Park," he said.

"I reckon you're a busy man, working on a Sunday and a holiday," Bubba said as amicably as he could. He surely didn't want to piss a man off right in the first minute of meeting him. Of course, that would hardly be the first time to do so for Bubba.

"Crime never stops," Park said wryly. "Follow me. We'll talk in back."

Park led Bubba into a labyrinth of offices and cubicles. Both uniformed and plain-clothed officers seemingly meandered about on their various businesses. Their ultimate destination was a cubicle in a sea of other cubicles.

Entering the cubicle, Park pointed at a chair. "I called Sergeant Gray," Park said bluntly as he watched Bubba sit down.

"Okay," Bubba said. He assumed Sergeant Gray was likely Celestine, Willodean's mother. He wasn't sure what Celestine would have to say to another police officer about him, but it probably wasn't anything positive. Nevertheless, Bubba didn't have a lot to lose in the situation. His mind went blank for a moment.

Do so have something to lose, kaka brains. Don't forget that.

"You know about Willodean." Bubba plowed right ahead. He didn't care to waste time anyway.

"I also spoke to Sheriff Headrick. Deputy Gray's disappearance is all over the news," Park said neutrally. "As a former member of the Dallas Police Department, we are naturally concerned about her wellbeing."

"That's good," Bubba said. He disliked the company line being toted out to placate the intruding family/friend/someone unidentifiable who wanted to know about their progress even though the deputy hadn't vanished in *their* precinct. "Then you're looking into this fella, Le Beau, am I right?"

Park frowned down at Bubba. His thin face glowered for a moment as he attempted to put on a poker face. The investigator didn't know that Bubba had a lifetime of experience with poker faces, especially that of his own mother's, who was undoubtedly a distinguished expert in the field of poker faces. "Pegram County Sheriff's Department hasn't asked for our assistance yet. They've got enough to worry about," he said slowly. "How did you know Le Beau's name?"

"You don't know where this guy is," Bubba said just as slowly. It wasn't a question. He watched a muscle in the other man's cheek twitch in response. "But you *have* checked on Le Beau, right." The last wasn't a question either.

Park finally sat down at his desk chair. "You're a friend of Deputy Gray's? Did she talk about Le Beau?"

The former was an interesting question. Bubba wanted to be more than Willodean's friend, but there was more at stake here. He didn't want to squander precious minutes explaining to another law enforcement official how critical events had become.

"We were supposed to go on our first date last Thursday," Bubba said carefully.

Park finally managed to contort his face into neutrality. Despite that, Bubba could tell Park was surprised. "Sergeant Gray didn't say anything about that," he said.

"Not sure ifin Willodean told her. Don't reckon I told her."

"Why not?"

"The Grays are in a lot of pain right now," Bubba said gently. "Didn't see the need to put more on them."

"Why would that give them more pain?"

"I didn't know why before, but Willodean hadn't been dating anyone for a long time. It wasn't my place to tell them otherwise." Bubba warily organized the words in his head. "Besides, at the time I spoke with the Grays, I was in a hurry."

Park rattled his fingers on the desk. "Why were you in a hurry?"

"I went to her home to collect a piece of clothing for the hounds to scent," Bubba said, a little less carefully.

Bubba knew that Park was looking at him suspiciously, and he wasn't happy about it. If Bubba had given it more thought, he should have realized that would be the result. In the world of police officers, everyone was a potential wrongdoer. Even Willodean displayed that attitude upon occasion. As a person who was inordinately interested in Willodean, Bubba was a person of interest to the police.

"I wanted to get it back to the site as soon as I could. There was blood on the steering wheel of her vehicle, and she could have been out there injured. That's why I was in a hurry."

"Christ," Park said. He glanced at a framed photograph on his desk. Bubba saw that it was a very small baby who was unhappy to have been photographed. Her little wrinkled face screamed rawly into the camera.

Park studied the picture for a moment before continuing, "I hate to think of what those people are going through right now. I've got a baby daughter. She doesn't sleep through the night yet, and I expect I'm going to lose a lot of sleep through the years to come over her. And worse, I guess since you've come knocking on this door, the hounds didn't produce any results."

"Nope," Bubba said. "Have you checked out this man, Le Beau?"

"I've got calls into his parole officer," Park said. "Man hasn't called me back yet."

"Perhaps a *personal* visit," Bubba suggested, tamping down angry impatience.

"You don't sound as much of a redneck as I was led to believe," Park remarked.

"There's rednecks and there's *rednecks*," Bubba explained without rancor. "This parole officer work on Sundays?"

"Don't give up, do you?"

"You said you have a daughter," Bubba said brusquely. "What if she was missing? What if you had to wait on someone to 'call' you back? What if you could do something and do it, now? Would you take time to ask me questions about my motives?"

"They're still searching for Deputy Gray. I caught Sheriff Headrick out at the site. He said you're an interested party and don't have any reason to harm the woman. But get this straight. There's no proof of a crime being committed other than a hit-and-run. No one knows what happened to Deputy Gray, and you don't need to be jumping to conclusions.

"I don't have any authority to do anything to Howell Le Beau except ask him questions." Park sighed. "I need to call my wife, and then we'll take a trip down to south Dallas. I don't suppose you'd go and wait in your hotel room."

Bubba stared at Charles Park.

"I didn't think so," Park said sullenly. "You'll come with me, and you'll wait in the car. You'll do what I say or you'll go to county lockup."

"Sheriff John ask you to take me along?" Bubba asked perceptively.

Park drummed his fingers on the desk again. "He said you wouldn't- how did he put it? Roll over like a mangy cur in the mud. Yeah, that was it. Then he suggested that it would be better to keep an eye on you."

•

114

First, they went to the regional office of the Dallas Parole Office to find out where Le Beau's parole officer was located. Precious rode in the back of the unmarked Ford Crown Victoria. Park muttered bad things about the dog. That was followed by sneezing, and he abruptly lowered all of the windows. "I'm allergic to pet dander," he announced snidely.

"Now that's a damn shame," Bubba said insincerely. "Hey, I don't think I ever rode in the *front* of one of these. It ain't bad."

Park sneezed again and actively dug through his pockets. He extracted a pill from one of his pockets. "Allegra," he explained. He washed it down with a cup of cold coffee that he'd brought with him. He paused to glare over his shoulder at the Basset hound.

Once they found the DPO regional office, they had to dig up an assistant regional director and explain why Park wanted Le Beau's parole officer's home address and phone number. The assistant director was less than thrilled but gave up the information.

Park dry swallowed another Allegra pill while he entered the address into his GPS. He pulled out a cell phone and called the parole officer's home number.

Even Bubba heard the abrupt answer on the other end.

"Joe's Mortuary! You stab 'em and we slab 'em!" someone answered, nearly shouting, and hysterical giggles broke out in the background.

"Guillermo Sanchez, please," Park said politely. Bubba controlled an urge to yank the cell phone out of the investigator's hand and bellow for the parole officer's immediate attendance.

There was a loud bang that clearly came through the cell's speaker. Someone said, "Shit! Don't drop it! Hey, Gui! It's for-"

Silence ensued. Park checked the phone's screen. "They either hung up or the call dropped."

"Call again," Bubba said flatly.

Park rolled his eyes. Then he hit the appropriate keys. Bubba could hear that the connection went through, and the phone rang once. There was, "Roadkill Café! You kill it, we grill it!" followed by more manic giggles.

"Can I speak with Guillermo Sanchez- and shit, they hung up again!" Park said and hit the end button on his cell phone.

"Let's go to his house," Bubba suggested insistently.

The investigator looked at the GPS and began to drive to the parole officer's house. After ten minutes, Park stopped sneezing, and Precious stopped baying. Bubba stopped scowling at his watch. Five minutes after that, they pulled up in front of the ranch house that was the Sanchez's domicile.

There were cars parked in every conceivable spot nearest to the house. A Dodge truck was parked crookedly on the lawn. A low-rider Chevy quietly competed with a sparkling BMW. A Harley-Davidson Sportster sat next to a Ducati. Children charged across the front yard in an unmitigated mass of squealing youthfulness. Three adults lounged on the front porch drinking bottles of beer while observing the chaos.

"Ah, a *party*," Park said understandingly.

Bubba shrugged. When he climbed out of the car after Park, the investigator shot him a dirty look. He said sardonically, "You won't say anything, am I right? I don't care if you're the Jolly Green Giant. I've got cuffs that will fit you and the means to get you into them."

"Ho, ho, ho," Bubba said darkly.

"As long as we're on the same sheet of music," Park smiled with pure ice. "The dog stays in the car."

116

Precious woofed in protest.

They found Guillermo Sanchez in the backyard gleefully downing Jell-O shooters with four other men. The five men were loosely supervising a smoking grill. The men, all dark haired and brown eyed with similar familial appearances, paused to critically examine the new arrivals.

The largest one, six feet tall and three hundred pounds, waved his small paper cup at them and said, "Cheezit, *the cops*." He wore an apron that said "Who you calling bitch, BITCH?" on it. "Were we too loud? What neighbor didn't I invite?"

Another man waved a spatula at Bubba. "He doesn't look like a cop. He looks like...he blocked out the sun." The remainder of the men collapsed into frenzied giggles.

The man with the apron abruptly stopped giggling and put down the cup of Jell-O as he stared at Park. "Crap, I know you, don't I?"

Park nodded. "Charles Park, DPD Assaults Unit."

"Gui," another man drunkenly grabbed the large man's arm. "Did you assault someone? How come you didn't tell us? That's got to go in the family newsletter. Maybe he smeared a Democrat," he said hopefully to one of the others.

"Shut up, Enrique," Guillermo snapped. "It's work."

There was a portable phone sitting on the table next to the grill. It rang, and one of Guillermo's brothers snatched it up and punched the button while yelling, "Oriental Massage! We rub you right!" The others broke out in braying whinnies.

"Sorry," Guillermo said to Park and Bubba. He said to one of the men, "Hey, Tino, watch the steaks, man. I'll be back."

One of his brothers adjusted his sunglasses and did a

lousy Arnold Schwarzenegger imitation, "I'll beee baaaaaack."

Hyper giggles followed them as the large man led them inside the patio doors. They walked past a group of women discussing the merits of types of birth control. One paused to glare at Guillermo.

"Not again, Gui," she said. "This is a holiday and a family event. Can't you leave work at *work*?"

"I turned off my cell phone, baby," Guillermo replied penitently. He glanced at Park and Bubba. "It has to be important. Right, *muy importante*?" His eyes pleaded with them for understanding.

"It's very important, ma'am," Park said.

"Urgent," Bubba added.

"Right," the woman, who Bubba thought was Guillermo's wife, said suspiciously.

"Seriously, baby, this is my cousin from my mother's side," Guillermo added to the woman. He paused to wrap a hefty arm around Park.

Park winced.

"You know how wild Mama's side of the family is."

"Haha," the woman replied.

Guillermo took them to a small room that was his home office. He had to kick two teenage boys off his computer. "*Christo*, what am I going to do with you boys? Didn't I say no more surfing on my computer?"

One boy slithered off before Guillermo could catch him, but the large man caught the other one by the arm before the boy could punch anymore buttons on the keyboard. With his other hand, Guillermo turned the screen toward him. "Anime porn? Are you kidding me? Mondo, we're going to talk in a few minutes, and you better not disappear. Make sure your brother is there, too."

Guillermo sort of flung the boy at the door. The

teenager fled into the hallway. The big man shrugged at Park and Bubba, saying, "Kids. I need to change my password again."

He looked them over. "I guess you want to know about one of my parolees, huh? Which one of the shitheads did something?"

"Le Beau," Park said.

Guillermo's features crinkled like a Chinese Shar-Pei. "Got time to sit down?"

"No," Bubba said immediately.

The parole officer shrugged. "I need downtime, too, you know. I can't babysit all those little bastards all the time. They report to me, and then I make sure they're doing what they need to be doing. Le Beau's been working at a construction firm, and his bosses got no complaints about him. He reports in once a week. Everything's been fine. No arrests. No bitching. He's been seeing his shrink regularly."

"I'm going to need his home and work addresses," Park said. He pulled a little pad from his left front, chest pocket and prepared to write. "It wasn't listed on his file. And he's not in the book."

"Dammit." Guillermo sat down heavily in the same chair his son had been sitting in and shuddered at what was still on his monitor. "I'm going to have to steam clean my computer and this frigging chair. Those little punks have just gotten on my last nerve." One hand waved at the computer. "I didn't even know you could get this. Who animates porn?"

"What does Le Beau say about Willodean Gray?" Bubba said, intensely tired of the subject of teenagers and Internet porn.

"What did I tell you?" Park said to Bubba.

Bubba shrugged unremorsefully.

Guillermo tapped on keys and looked up.

"Willodean Gray?" he repeated. "The same thing those animals always say about their victims. They're sorry. They wish they hadn't done it. They wish they could turn the clock back. Their mamas beat them when they were kids. It's pretty much the same for Le Beau." He scratched his chin. "But I was hoping Le Beau was working past that."

"Did Le Beau recently threaten Deputy Gray?" Park asked.

"I would have reported that immediately," Guillermo said tiredly. "I completely respect the officers who take down these pieces of crap, and I would never shrug something like that off." He paused to take a breath. "That being said, Le Beau's got issues. But he's been on the straight and narrow. I'm surprised that's he's gone off the rez." He stopped to consider the statement. "If he has."

Guillermo gave them the two addresses and a single telephone number he possessed. He walked them out to their car. Several of the children actively petted Precious as she drooled down the side of the Crown Vic.

Park backed the car up when Bubba heard Guillermo Sanchez yelling for his two teenaged sons. "MONDO! JUAN! We've got something to talk about, you little turds!"

"I wonder if girls surf for porn," Park pondered.

Forty-five minutes later, they stood at the home address Guillermo had given them. It was an empty lot enclosed by chain link fence. According to the clerk of the hole-in-the-wall grocery store five hundred feet away, the building had been torn down the week before.

Chapter Ten

Bubba and the Vision of Brownie's Sterling Moment
Or
Brownie Meets Matt Lauer

Monday, January 2nd

Bubba slept restlessly that night. A mental calendar appeared in his head as if it had neon backlighting it. The days kept getting crossed off by ruby red, neon Xes. First were the 29th of December and the 30th, and the 31st concluded December. The calendar flipped to January and the 1st was immediately Xed out.

Four days. Four damn days. Goddammit.

He sat up in the bed not dissimilar to a slab of granite and wiped the sweat from his brow. The room wasn't warm, but he was drenched from the horrifying pictures that coursed through his head when his eyes closed. Precious protested the abrupt movement, in a dogly fashion from the foot of the bed, as he got up.

Glancing out the window Bubba thought about his game plan.

Talk to Le Beau's employers. See if the man is at work. Rip him into pieces until he fesses up with what happened.

Bubba frowned at the window. The little opening of the curtain revealed it was still dark outside although the little digital clock said seven a.m. He wasn't frowning at the fact that it was still dark. He was frowning because an unwanted, errant thought had come trickling into his head.

What if Howell Le Beau doesn't come back to work?

Another unwanted thought came to him. It was a resonation of something his mother had said.

Willodean wouldn't want you to give up. So what if Le Beau doesn't come back? He immediately answered himself. *Find him. He cain't hide. He can hide but not forever.*

After a shower in the smallest bathroom in existence, Bubba went out and waited at the construction company where Le Beau was supposed to be employed. He spent the time throwing a ball for his dog and making sure she had water and some kibble. Three hours later, he checked the door and discovered that a sign announced the company was closed until the 4th of January.

Bubba considered calling Investigator Charles Park but remembered the last thing the man had told him the day before. *"Don't go out looking for Le Beau by yourself. If you do, it will be considered interfering in official Dallas Police business and I will arrest you."*

Wasting another hour calling the phone numbers of the people named Lebeau in the Dallas/Fort Worth Metroplex, Bubba paused about noon to find something to eat. A pancake house near the county courthouse looked busy, so he stopped there. He ordered coffee and a meal for himself. Precious had to wait in the truck with the windows down. She didn't mind much. She had a hard time waiting for something to happen, so she sprawled over the bench seat with four paws pointing heavenward, snoring like a freight train.

Bubba sat at the counter and absently ate while he watched a large plasma screen television prominently displayed behind the extensive counter. The sandwich was hot and the coffee didn't taste horrible and the news seemed benevolently mild, so it was all win-win. At least it was for that moment in time. When he finished, the waitress zipped past and energetically freshened his coffee.

While staring into the black liquid in his cup, it dawned on Bubba that the crowded restaurant had suddenly gone very quiet. There was an air of expectation. He looked around and saw that they were all staring at the plasma screen television. Someone said, "Hey, turn that up."

A waitress used a remote to raise the volume, and Bubba glanced at the television. He blinked and glanced back, taking in what happened on the big screen. The ribbon on the bottom of the scene announced this was a replay of something that had happened earlier in the day. It was just as clear that many of the people in the restaurant had heard about it and wanted to see it for themselves.

"Just wait," one man said.

"I saw this earlier, and it's funny as hell," another one said.

Matt Lauer sat on a perky couch speaking into the camera. His glasses perched on the end of his nose as he checked his notes. "Today," he said, looking back into the camera's eye, "we have the young man from Louisiana who bravely fought off a killer."

There was a quick shot of co-news anchor Ann Curry. She sat nearby at another station, waiting patiently. She looked over to her left and smiled. "And his parents as well. All in the studio today."

Matt nodded indulgently; he was obviously happy that such an attention-grabbing human interest story was appearing on *The Today Show*. "Here is Brownie Snoddy and his parents, Fudge," Matt's voice cracked a little at pronouncing the names, "and Virtna. Those are certainly interesting names, aren't they, Ann?" He adjusted his suit lapel while he waited for Ann to respond.

Ann, apparently more on her game and probably

had heard the names of the guests before Matt, smiled again. *"Interesting* names for *interesting* people."

The scene turned to Brownie, who sat in-between Virtna and Fudge. Sitting on an adjacent couch, all three were gussied up as if going to Sunday church. Fudge wore an ill-fitting blue suit with a yellow shirt and a dilapidated tie that appeared as though it might strangle him. Virtna sported a peach silk dress that clashed with her red hair. Her hair was scraped back with a peach-colored bow that wouldn't look out of place on top of a large present. Brownie donned his Boy Scout uniform, every award in its proper place. His pants were neatly ironed, and the creases were visible. Bubba couldn't help but note that there wasn't anything left of the arrow-pierced heart on Virtna's forehead. Furthermore, Fudge's Sharpie-generated "I fart" had disappeared under pancake makeup.

Brownie held an inconspicuous shoe box in his lap that bounced with the boy's every movement. He wasn't just excited to be on national television; he was thrilled to death. In a moment he was going to get up and start doing cartwheels across the set. Then he was probably going to beseech Ann Curry to do some with him.

Bubba, watching with the cup of coffee in his hand, would have been impressed to discover if Ann Curry could do cartwheels in her smart suit.

"Can you tell us what happened?" Matt Lauer asked Brownie.

"That pesky Nancy Musgrave was threatening my folks," Brownie said loudly.

He determinedly waved his little hands. His face was intent. This was a serious story meant to be told in a grave manner. There could be no absurdity involved.

"My cousin, Bubba, told me the Christmas Killer was

inside the house, about to do something wicked-bad-awful to my ma and pa, and I cain't allow something like that."

Matt shook his head. "No, of course not. Very brave of you."

Bubba nodded. He allowed that that had been pretty much how it had been.

Brownie nodded fiercely. "Cousin Bubba went in, and I knew he was trying to distract that terrible woman. You know, she didn't think much of kids. Wasn't even polite to me while I was chasing the dog."

"The dog?" Matt repeated.

"Precious," Brownie said. "She's Bubba's Basset hound. The best hound ever."

"Okay," Matt agreed.

Bubba thought that Matt probably owned a poodle, or God forbid, a cat.

"Well, Bubba went in first. I called the po-lice on the po-lice radio. Bubba had done stole Miz Willodean's ve-hick-el and there it was, just waiting for it to be used." Brownie paused to glance at his parents. "I dint have a cell phone. Ma says I ain't old enough yet." It sounded like an oft-used accusation.

"Your cousin *stole* the police vehicle?" Matt nodded as he spoke.

I did steal it. Bubba forced a lump down his throat. *That was the last time I saw Willodean. But...*his thoughts faded into dismal uncertainty as the camera's angle came back to Brownie.

"And the lady on the other end, well, she was right surprised *I* was talking to her," Brownie said. "But I told her, 'The Christmas Killer is at the Snoddy Mansion, and we needs the po-lice right quickly.' She told me that they was a-comin' but I knew it would take too long."

A close-up shot of Brownie followed. His eyes were

coolly resolved. The story was about to come to its exciting climax. The entire restaurant was silently expectant, hanging onto the ten-year-old's every word.

Brownie went on, "I decided I would sneak into the mansion and try to hear what was going on. There weren't no gunshots, you know, so I reckoned that the Christmas Killer hadn't gotten very far with his or her evil plan. At that time, I dint know it was Nancy Musgrave. Bubba had told me that the Christmas Killer was inside. Well, I knew for certain it wasn't Ma or Pa. It wasn't Aunt Caressa; she snores like cats was throwing up hairballs, you know. It wasn't Miz Adelia; you wouldn't believe what she said she would do to me ifin I came into her kitchen again."

"I might," Matt murmured.

"So that left Nancy Musgrave and the three loonies," Brownie said and then immediately said, "Oww," when his mother elbowed him sharply in the ribs. "What?"

"Those poor, insane people aren't to be called 'loonies'," Virtna chastised.

"Then what do you call them?" Brownie demanded. "*You* called them, 'loonies'."

Virtna smiled grimly at the camera, noticeably aware of its ever-present scrutiny. "We don't call them that," she gritted. Fudge opened his mouth but closed it quick. It occurred to Bubba that Fudge's face changed to the color of bone and he visibly shook. Evidently, he had stage fright. Possibly, he was hung over. Probably, he was both.

Virtna added, "We call them something respectful. They're folks after all, just in a bad way."

Bubba glanced around the restaurant. Everyone who could see, hear, or smell watched in a manner that would indicate they were completely entranced.

"Okay, then," Brownie snarled. "So it had to be

Nancy Musgrave or one of the three..."

"Mentally challenged individuals," Matt suggested.

"Yeah, that, what he said," Brownie said with a quick glare at his mother. "And they was all inside, sitting at the dining room table. La de dah."

"All those people at the dining room table," Matt said questioningly.

Virtna interjected, "It's a large table. Probably from the nineteenth century. Could pre-date the Civil War."

Brownie glared at his mother again. *He* was supposed to be telling the story. Matt smiled and patted the couch next to him. Brownie crossed over so quickly that his form was a blur. Settling down beside Matt Lauer, he put the shoebox between them. He had a captive audience for his exhaustive tale of murder and the heroic kicking of a bad gal's tushie. He looked from Matt to the camera. Unmistakably, the ten-year-old was a natural for the camera.

Brownie said, "She was telling them all about how she had done it, and why, too."

Matt appeared just as entranced as the people inside the restaurant. There was a quick shot of Ann Curry, who held a cup halfway to her mouth. She rested on the edge of her seat, captivated with anticipation of what the child was going to say next. "The Christmas Killer said why she had done it?" Matt asked.

"Oh, yes," Brownie nodded. "Revenge." The word was drawn out as if it were a sword. "Reeee-veeeeennnnggeeee." "Something about her pa and Christmas and green ribbons and something about the his-ter-i-cal board."

"Historical board," Virtna corrected from off camera.

"Right," Brownie agreed, a little less enthusiastically. From a ten-year-old's perspective, it was all stuff loosely understood and hardly applicable to the current situation of being on national television. Moreover, it hardly compared to sitting next to Matt Lauer as if they were best buddies.

Don't take a nap around the little pain in the ass. God forbid he has a Sharpie available.

"Nancy Musgrave sent out letters to everyone," Brownie added. "Like she was warning them that she was coming to get them. Had everyone real upset-like. Even Miz Demetrice, who's my great-aunt, was mighty upset, and she could scare a haint up a thorn tree."

"Brownie!" Virtna snapped.

"It's what Daddy said."

"Fudge!" Virtna said.

"I ain't said it *on* camera, dammit," Fudge said. The camera's view went to them. Fudge was pulling at his ugly tie. Virtna's face was turning the same color as her hair. Brownie cleared his throat imperiously, wanting the attention back on him.

"Well, this woman, this Nancy Musgrave," Brownie spoke again and the camera's angle went back to him as he sat next to Matt, "she decided that she was going to kill every one of them. That's what the sheriff said. But Bubba and Miz Willodean and I think, Miz Demetrice figured it out before she could get to the next folks. Bubba saved the sheriff's life, you know."

Bubba took a drink of coffee and used the cup to salute Brownie's image on the oversized plasma screen television.

"So Nancy Musgrave came to get Bubba at the mansion," Brownie said. "She was a-sittin' at the table, with all my kinfolk, and the loon-, I mean, mentally somethinged people, and pointing a big gun at them." His hands spread out wide to indicate the size of the weapon.

The camera focused briefly on the width between

Brownie's hands.

"That's a pretty big gun," Matt said.

"A fifty caliber pistol," Fudge said knowingly. The camera snapped to him as he held his hands apart in the same distance as Brownie had. Then they began to spread. After a few seconds, the alleged weapon was as large as a cannon. No one protested at the evident fabrication. As Brownie began to speak again, the camera's view went back to him.

"Well, I snuck up," Brownie said cunningly. "I had the stun gun I made in Boy Scouts," he added. "I knew if I could get up to her, I could use it on her."

"Stun gun," Matt repeated. The tone of his voice hinted at laughter tinged with a morsel of disbelief.

Brownie's eyebrows shot together as he registered the amused tone of Matt Lauer's voice. "You bet. I spent the better part of a month making that sucker and I tested it on..." his voice trailed off as his head turned toward his parents. "Well, I tested it on a dummy at the karate school."

Right, Bubba thought. *And the dummy wasn't made up of stuffing and leather.*

There was another brief camera shot of Virtna and Fudge. Virtna's face was no longer the color of her hair. Instead it was the shade of a ripe beefeater tomato. She knew what Brownie had done.

The camera went back to Brownie as he considered whether he should run or not. The publicity and attention to the situation won out. He went on, "Nancy Musgrave talked about Christmas flowers and something about using them on the folks she done killed and such.

"Cousin Bubba tried to get closer to her so he could jump her, but she was watching them all too closely. I swear to Jesus above that she was 'bout to shoot them all, starting with Bubba, but them loonies-" there was an abrupt noise from Virtna.

"Um, special folks, I mean, they done gave me away."

Matt leaned toward Brownie. "And that's when you-"

Brownie interrupted. It was his story and even Matt Lauer wasn't going to take it away.

"She was turning around, swinging that big, bad boy gun in my direction." He took a moment to mimic Nancy Musgrave's actions using his hand with index finger pointed out as the large weapon in question. "That's when I reached out and zapped her with my stun gun."

A moment of anticlimactic silence in the studio was replicated in the restaurant. No silverware clinked. No liquids slurped. Bubba was pretty sure that no one was even breathing. In a few moments someone was going to keel over because they didn't have any oxygen.

Matt suddenly chuckled. "Really, it really shocked her enough to knock her down?"

It was clear to everyone listening that Matt was dubious about something a Boy Scout had made from scratch.

Bubba thought, *You don't know* that *kid very well, now do you?*

Brownie glowered. He reached for the shoebox. "Got it right here," he announced.

Matt blinked. He laughed again. The laugh had that same hint of disbelief. He glanced at the audience as if silently asking them, "Do you believe this kid?" He looked at Ann Curry. "Well, I would sure like to see that, wouldn't you, Ann?"

Bubba sighed. *Oh, Matt Lauer* shouldn't *have said that.*

On the screen, Brownie flicked the lid off the box and

yanked out the stun gun. As it had before, the little black device appeared fairly innocuous. Bubba shook his head derisively.

Why did the police return that *to him?*

Brownie, still the stun gun connoisseur of smoothness and precision, flipped the little switch with one finger and efficiently pressed the little leads to Matt's hand. Matt still looked at Ann Curry and his expression was, at that moment, tolerant and tickled. The next moment, all of his features began to twitch spasmodically. His glasses fell off his face and disappeared from view. Making a noise that sounded like a combination of a grunt, a burp, and a fart, he abruptly fell onto the floor in between the couch and the coffee table.

Shocked silence ensued. Someone in the restaurant spit coffee out through their nose. Someone else said, "Wait for it."

Understandably, the camera crew didn't know exactly what to do. A shocked gasp erupted that Bubba knew came from Virtna. One of the cameras focused on Matt Lauer's convulsing foot sticking out from behind the coffee table. Abruptly, the camera's view briefly focused on Brownie, who was spinning the stun gun in his hand like an outlaw with a 19th century revolver. The smug look on the boy's face said everything. The camera went to Ann Curry, who was perceptibly tongue-tied.

She leaned forward a little and looked over the coffee table at Matt Lauer, and then her face tilted toward Brownie, who still twirled the stun gun in his hand. Her lovely mouth opened, and for a moment there was nothing. Then as Brownie looked at her expectantly, she said, "Don't tase me, bro?"

The entire restaurant roared with laughter.

Bubba sighed again.

Chapter Eleven

Bubba Gets Busted

Monday, January 2nd

Bubba pretty much ran out of ideas. Eventually, his thoughts came barreling back to Howell Le Beau's parole officer, Guillermo Sanchez. Guillermo was supposed to be on top of Le Beau and all over keeping the man in line. Bubba had an inkling that parole officers were overburdened, but in this case, his interest was paramount. Whatever Guillermo knew might help find Willodean.

After paying for his lunch and listening to the restaurant's customers natter about Brownie and Matt Lauer, Bubba found his way back to the regional Dallas Parole Office. He spoke to three clerks and one receptionist before someone deigned to call Guillermo's office phone. Guillermo strolled down to the lobby a few minutes later.

The large Hispanic man dressed in business casual – Dallas style. He wore a black Guayabera shirt with four pockets embroidered with little lines of flowers. Black pants and black Crocs completed his ensemble. Grasping a tall travel mug of a steaming substance, he also appeared hung over. His eyes were bloodshot, and he looked like he was ready for a nap or some Pepto-Bismol, either one.

"Ah, *Christo*," he said when he saw Bubba. "You again." He cast a sharp look at the receptionist. "Can't you tell me who it is when someone comes to see me? Then I can pretend that I'm not here or have an emergency somewhere else?"

"Wasn't one of your parolees," the receptionist said

with a shrug and went back to painting her nails purple.

"Come on," Guillermo said. "We'll talk in my office. I don't have long. I have to do two home inspections and one work follow-up. One of the homes is a guy who likes to eat road kill. He seriously goes around looking for road kill and brings it home so he can use it. He puts it in his freezer and uses a ton of Febreze. It's totally gross, but he's cut way down on his spending." He paused to think about it. "But he probably blows it on air fresheners." He steadily drank from the travel cup until every drop had been consumed.

Bubba followed Guillermo to a small office. One framed diploma and several pictures of a very large family decorated the walls.

"Aie," Guillermo murmured, staring sadly at his empty cup. "I need some more caffeine. You wouldn't believe how much alcohol we drank this weekend." He looked at Bubba. "Well, maybe you would. You were there for a little while. My family, they get together once or twice a year. This year, obviously, in Dallas for Christmas.

"We ate tamales until they came out of our ears. We had turkey enchiladas. We had pumpkin empanadas that melted in your mouth. And beer and rum, and Aunt Maria made this Christmas punch that lit your insides on fire. I think the back bathroom is probably broken forever."

He sat down forcefully in his chair and waved at a straight-back chair next to his desk. "But you don't want to hear about that."

Bubba sat down and thought about what he wanted. The most important thought was that Guillermo was under the impression Bubba was someone Guillermo thought he was *supposed* to talk with. What was going to happen when Charles Park found out what Bubba was doing?

The answer came fast and cynical. *Who cares what Park thinks if this leads to Willodean?*

"This woman is missing," Bubba said slowly. "Her name is Willodean Gray. She's a fine person."

Guillermo nodded. He pulled a file folder out of the leaning tower of other file folders. He opened it and started running a finger down the first sheet. Bubba could see there was a Polaroid photograph stapled to the side. The man pictured was in his late twenties with a buzz cut and a tired expression. Bubba looked hard. He wanted to remember that man, especially if he got a chance to set his eyes directly upon him.

"I've never met her, but I've talked with her on the telephone. When Le Beau got out of the joint, I got in touch with the deputy and tried to keep her abreast of what I could." Guillermo rubbed his face tiredly as he spoke. "I'm not sure how much I should share with you."

"Finding her quickly is the most important thing right now," Bubba said with urgency.

"It's just that Le Beau isn't my average bob. Sometimes we call the parolees 'bobs.' They come and go and bob their heads to just about everything we say. 'Yes, sir, I've got a job,' they say. 'Yes, sir, I haven't been drinking,' they say. 'Yes, sir, I've been doing my program,' they say. All the time nodding their heads up and down. Like a bobble head doll. Most of the time they should be shaking their heads instead."

Bubba wanted to say a nasty word but he gritted his teeth and waited for Guillermo to finish saying what he needed to say. It had always been Bubba's observation that people would keep talking and talking if a fella encouraged them to go on. Unfortunately, it was also Bubba's observation that he wasn't a patient fella when it came to imperative situations.

"Yeah, Le Beau was infatuated with the deputy, only then she was a patrol officer," Guillermo went on. "He knew her patrol area. Knew her phone numbers. Had her address. Followed her around like a dog.

"They dated, what, one time, and I guess she was smart enough to realize that Le Beau was a burrito short of a combination platter. Only saw him the one time. But Le Beau has a history of fixating on pretty, young women. So he started writing letters to her."

Bubba pulled the copy of the letter and envelope out of his pocket. He unfolded it and handed it to Guillermo. Guillermo examined it with a sour expression. He noticed the date on the post mark on the envelope. "Shit and shinola," he commented. "The day before."

Guillermo pushed the letter away and then abruptly dragged it back. " 'I'm watching out for you,' " he read. " 'I hope for forgiveness.' "

Bubba didn't need to hear it again. "Same type of letters?"

"Yes, the same." Guillermo's lips flattened into white lines. "Le Beau had to know that he was going to get nicked for this." He tapped the letter. "But it's not really a threat."

"Not a threat?" Bubba was incredulous. "He's sending her letters saying he's watching her. Sounds like a proper threat to me."

The other man looked up. His head tilted as he considered Bubba's vehement tone. "You sound a little too concerned, *compadre*. What's your interest in all this?"

"Getting Willodean back safe and sound," Bubba snapped. "Making sure she isn't lying somewhere in a ditch needing help."

"And no one is happy about the fact that Le Beau

wrote more letters to the deputy and that his address of residence is no longer in existence," Guillermo stated. "If it makes a difference, I checked his home residence two weeks ago. That same residence. There was some construction work going on then, but the residents hadn't moved out. I asked Le Beau about it, and he said they were doing renovations to the place and that he was looking for a new place to live."

"He didn't want to tell you he'd been evicted," Bubba guessed. He tried very hard to keep the embittered tone out of his voice. He wanted information from Guillermo Sanchez, not to antagonize him.

"One of the stipulations of being paroled is to have a stable environment to live in," Guillermo said as if from rote.

"What about his family?"

"His mother is in a retirement home and he's got a brother who doesn't want to have anything to do with him." Guillermo pushed the letter and envelope back to Bubba. "Le Beau's got involved in his church. He volunteers at a soup kitchen. He's making regular retributory payments.

"And let's get this straight. Le Beau was convicted on *stalking* charges. He agreed not to have any further contact with Willodean Gray. He was sentenced to the max on a third degree felony, ten years. He served six months and was released on conditional parole. Most importantly, he's been a model parolee."

Bubba was muddled. *What about the assault and the week Willodean spent in the hospital?* "That's it? Just the stalking charges?"

A furrow stitched Guillermo's black eyebrows together. "There was initially some question about the assault on Willodean Gray, but that was completely cleared up." He tapped the desk. "The Penal Code is very clear about stalking perquisites in relation to what constitutes a crime."

Confusion made Bubba a little sluggish. "What do you mean, the assault was cleared up?"

Guillermo's face fell. "I don't believe I got your name," he stated. His glower intensified. "Park didn't say anything about you when he called first thing this morning. He was asking the same things as you. Where is Le Beau's family? Where else might Le Beau be located? But you, you didn't show me a badge. You didn't even say what your name is."

"Bubba Snoddy," Bubba said promptly. He realized he wasn't going to get any more information from Guillermo Sanchez. Probably the parole officer wouldn't speak to him again, ever.

"Snoddy. Snoddy. Snoddy? That sounds awfully familiar. Isn't that the name of the kid who did that thing to that host of the talk show this morning?" Guillermo paused and then asked, "And you work with Park?" It was a question that wasn't exactly a question. It was sort of like an accusation. *Do you? Do you* really?

To lie or not to lie. Oh, dear. Ma would be flicking the back of my head with her thumb and index finger right now, even while she figured out how to get the parole officer to talk.

"Park allowed me to tag along," Bubba said carefully.

That's the truth. Go with it.

"Uh-huh," Guillermo said.

"So how about those addresses and Le Beau's church, too," Bubba announced quickly.

Before Guillermo figures out that I ain't any kind of po-lice man.

But as Bubba stared at the other man, he knew it was too late.

"You can get them from Park," Guillermo said

138

shortly. He snapped shut the folder on his desk. "I'll walk you out."

Bubba wisely kept his mouth shut, and Guillermo Sanchez didn't say anything else. As Bubba followed him out, he thought he could see a little steam being emitted from Guillermo's ears. The parole officer knew very well he'd been had.

When they got outside, Park was leaning against his unmarked Crown Victoria parked in a no-parking zone. The investigator had his arms across his chest and an intense scowl twisting his face.

Guillermo shook his head. "Dammit, I'm a fool," he cursed himself. Then he hit Bubba's arm in rebuke. "You're not even on the force? *Estupido.*"

"Did Bubba *say* that he was a police officer?" Park demanded as he pulled away from the car and walked closer.

The parole officer shrugged and then shook his head. "No, he never said that. He just didn't know what he should have known." He glared at Park. "It's *your* fault anyway. He was with you at my house. I mean, he was *with* you. You didn't say he wasn't one of you. You didn't say anything about him." He waved his hands expressively. "I wouldn't have told him anything if I'd known he wasn't with you." He glanced back at Bubba. "Looks like a bubba, doesn't he? I should have known. DPD doesn't have anyone this damned tall."

Charles Park and his finely featured face turned to look at Bubba. Bubba aimed to pretend he was innocent. It was a little hard.

So Bubba went with confrontational instead. "Did you talk to Le Beau's boss?"

Park glowered harder. "What did I tell you?"

"Maybe his co-workers?"

Guillermo whistled. "What, is this guy a relative of

the deputy's?"

"Man, that sheriff told me to keep an eye on you," Park said to himself. Then to Bubba he said, "Are you going to behave?"

"Are you going to talk with Le Beau's mother and brother?" Bubba shoved, gleefully going with the oh-the-hell-with-it-let's-piss-everyone-off method.

"And he's got copies of a letter from Le Beau to the deputy," Guillermo inserted.

Park stepped closer to Bubba. "Where did you get a copy of a letter from Le Beau?"

"It was in her mailbox," Bubba said. "Can you understand that the Pegram County Sheriff is searching all over the area where her vehicle was found?"

"And why shouldn't he?" Park asked.

"That's what I thought, too," Bubba snapped. "But these damned letters popped up, and I found out that Willodean fled Dallas to get away from the little piece of dog poop, that one," he gestured at Guillermo, "seems to think is incapable of doing Willodean any harm."

"Hey," Guillermo protested. There was a howl from the parking lot that seemed to indicate Precious had heard something she didn't like either.

People trickled past giving the three men and their raised voices a wide berth.

"Le Beau is the one we need to find so we can find Willodean," Bubba gritted, hating to say the obvious. "He's the one with the strongest reason to have kidnapped Willodean."

"Who said anything about the deputy being kidnapped?" Guillermo asked. "I thought it was a car wreck, and she might still be in the area. That county's got all kinds of crap raining down from the skies. There was that girl who was looking for Confederate gold and then the woman who wanted to murder the entire board that had her father convicted of a crime. Then the missing deputy. Sheesh."

"And the other vehicle just vanished into thin air," Bubba snarled. "At the very same time that Howell Le Beau just happens to be missing. This is a man who beat the crap out of her, who writes creepy letters to her, and you're all like, 'He goes to church and pays his bills on time.' Have you lost your ever freaking minds?"

"We're looking into Le Beau," Park said. "The law works the way that the law is supposed to work."

"The law fucking SUCKS!" Bubba bellowed, finally losing the tenuous grasp on his temper.

Park nodded calmly. "Okay, enough of this," he said. He took a step toward Bubba and one of his hands landed on Bubba's wrist.

Bubba said, "What?"

Bubba was aware that Park effortlessly twisted his arm and Bubba was forced into a turn. Never mind that Park probably weighed eighty pounds less than Bubba. An abrupt pressure against one of Bubba's legs resulted and Park twisted again. His lean limbs compelled Bubba's exactly where he wanted the other man to go.

A long moment of weightlessness occurred as Bubba looked over at Guillermo Sanchez. Guillermo's mouth opened and gaped like a teenager at his first porn movie. The word that came from the parole officer's mouth was, "Duhhhh-*aaaaa*-mmmmm-nnnnn."

Time slowed to a series of incremental movements.

Bubba became air borne and not in a military fashion. An incredibly concentrated expression shaped Park's face. His hands deftly moved the much larger man into the position that he required. Bubba turned in the air and tried to put his hands out to catch himself, but his hands were restrained by one of Park's hands. Park's other hand planted itself in the center of Bubba's back and punched him into the grass of the ground next to the sidewalk they'd been standing upon. Bubba came down hard, and the earth shuddered. One of his shoulders took the brunt of the collision. His face went sideways, and one cheek took the rest of the impact. The remainder of his large body followed and then bounced once.

As Bubba's face ground halfway in the dirt and grass, he couldn't see exactly what Park was doing. But Bubba knew from the sudden debilitating weight Park had straightaway come down on top of him. The investigator's knee dug into Bubba's lower back and almost immediately the click-click-snap of handcuffs could be heard as his wrists were secured behind him.

All Bubba could do was gasp for breath and wonder how the smaller man had gotten him subdued so damned quick.

Time caught up, and he heard Guillermo say, "*Pendejo* got suhh-*lammed*."

Park let up a little, and Bubba got some air. "Told you what was going to happen," the investigator said. "Bet you thought the little guy couldn't do it to you." He wasn't even breathing hard.

"I was wrong," Bubba wheezed.

Park chuckled and recited Bubba's Miranda Rights. Then he searched him and relieved him of several items to include the folded-up copy of the letter. He spent a moment reading the letter before placing it on the ground in a neat little pile with all the other items that he'd taken from Bubba.

A moment later Park helped Bubba to his feet and escorted him to his Crown Victoria. "Wait," Bubba gasped. "What about my dog?"

"No dogs in lockup," Park snarled. Then he sneezed violently. "Ah, there I go just thinking about your damn dog."

"Cain't just leave my dog out here," Bubba said. "And what about Willodean? Are you going to look for her? You cain't lock me up, dammit. I didn't do anything- well, I didn't do much wrong."

"Interference with public duties concerning a peace officer is the charge. And you can tell it to the judge," Park said.

"Hey, Guillermo," Bubba yelled over his shoulder as Park opened the door to the back of the unmarked police car. "Bet your kids like dogs, right?"

Guillermo followed them reluctantly. "Yeah?"

"Go take care of my dog," Bubba said. "Park, would ya'll give him my keys? They're on the ground with the rest of the other stuff." Park grudgingly plucked the keys off the ground and tossed them to Guillermo, who looked at them as if he held a spider.

"I'll lock up your truck, too," Guillermo said hesitantly.

Park shut the Crown Vic's door before Bubba could answer. As the investigator returned to retrieve the pile of items that he'd plucked from Bubba's pockets, he watched Guillermo go over to the old, green Chevy and pet Precious's head. The Basset hound wasn't happy, but she knew when someone appreciated a good animal.

Bubba attempted to talk when Park got into the vehicle, but the investigator wasn't saying anything.

"I'm not sorry," Bubba said. "This woman is important. If it was your daughter or your wife, you would understand."

"You've tried that tack before," Park said. "I get that Deputy Gray is important. But you're trampling all over other people's rights. We'll question Le Beau. We'll find out what he knows. But we do it in the right manner.

143

The legal manner. That's all there is."

Bubba settled down for a moment. "If she's dead and it turns out that we could have prevented it, then you'll be partially responsible." His voice was an icy breeze.

Park rattled his fingers over the steering wheel. "I warned you, Bubba," he said after a long minute. "I warned you that the law is in effect because that's the way this country is run. There's no evidence that Le Beau had anything to do with Deputy Gray's disappearance. As a matter of fact, you've got less than an assumption. This letter isn't signed, and I imagine you put your fingerprints all over the original. Which, by the way, is where?"

"I gave it to Sheriff John," Bubba said. *Well, I left it with the receptionist with instructions to give it to Sheriff John. Close enough for government work.*

"Uh-huh," Park muttered. "But you made a copy."

"I wanted to see if I could connect the postmark with Le Beau," Bubba explained.

"And you didn't feel like you should mention it to me," Park went on.

Bubba didn't say anything else because he knew he was wrong. He'd also known that law enforcement wouldn't have allowed him to help if he'd mentioned the letter.

Park pulled up into the Dallas County Jail's unloading zone.

"County," Bubba mused. "It's been a while since I've been here."

"What?" Park barked.

"Oh, just contemplating," Bubba said dismally. He'd been hoisted with his own petard, and now he was going to have to deal with it. *But it isn't about just me, is it?* asked a nasty little interior voice.

"Can we just get this over?"

Chapter Twelve

Bubba Gets Incarcerated for the First Time in *This* Novel
and Boy Howdy it Ain't But Half Over

Monday, January 2nd – Tuesday, January 3rd

There wasn't a friendly jailor named Tee Gearheart in the Dallas County Jail who wanted to discuss the size of his child's genitalia. There wasn't a fine selection of cells to choose from so as to get the best view. There wasn't anyone to trade wry commentary with and therefore pass the day in a rapid manner. There were, however, several very large and capable men who directed Bubba through the process of booking while keeping their hands close to their batons and mace.

Charles Park appeared twice during the procedure and complained about paperwork.

The second time Park arrived, Bubba was handcuffed to a fixed set of seats while the remainder of the detainees watched the early news on a television attached to the ceiling.

"They're going to keep you overnight, and you'll see someone in the morning," Park told Bubba. "I have to fill out five forms in triplicate for this, and I'm not happy."

"You're still looking for Le Beau," Bubba said taciturnly, not impressed with the amount of paperwork Park was going to fill out.

"Yes, I'm still looking for him," Park said shortly. "I got a BOLO on him, and Sanchez is working on the violation of his parole terms. He'll probably go back to Huntsville within a few weeks."

A mental door slammed inside Bubba's head. "But you'll make a deal with him about Willodean?"

Park sighed. "Bubba, you might want to prepare yourself for the worst."

"It's been four days, no, five if you count today," Bubba said. Even he didn't recognize the granite-like finality of his tone. "Five isn't too long. She could still be alive. She's strong. She's a fighter."

Park's face was grim. The investigator didn't believe in the remote possibility. He thought Willodean's remains might be found one day, a pile of bones strewn over some remote landscape by a hunter looking for a five-point buck. It would take weeks to get dental work comparisons and the identity confirmed.

"Get some rest tonight," Park advised. "It quiets down after ten p.m. Most of the detainees don't cause a lot of trouble, and besides, you're big enough they won't mess with you."

After being booked, which included fingerprints and pictures, Bubba was allowed a phone call, which meant leaving a message on his mother's cell phone. He was placed in a holding cell with several other men. Most of them wanted to keep to themselves, but one grinned happily at Bubba in recognition.

Bubba nodded at the jailor when he removed the handcuffs and locked the doors. Then he turned to the grinner. "Bam Bam," he said. "Fancy meeting you here."

"My brotha," Bam Bam said. He rose up and bumped fists with Bubba. His hands started convoluted movements as he spoke. "I be here on account there was a plain-clothes individual who did not appreciate my entrepreneurial status." He bumped his chest three times with a closed fist and then pointed in the direction of the jailors.

Bubba nodded. "Yeah, I ticked one of those off, too."

Bam Bam shooed a man off a bench and motioned to Bubba. "Sit, my man. It be a whole long time before a

147

judge can see you. One of the C.O.'s will let you know when it's getting close."

"C.O.?"

"Correctional officer," Bam Bam explained. "Whole 'nother language in here. And hey, didn't I tole you that you couldn't trust the 5-0?"

"I think you said they wouldn't help me," Bubba corrected as he sat down. He was tired. He'd skipped dinner, and he didn't think the jailors would be bringing chow anytime soon. He needed to think about what he was going to do to get out of jail. The daunting truth was he wasn't going to be able to help Willodean while being locked up, and he should have been thinking about *that* before he'd lost his temper.

"Still missing yo homegirl?" Bam Bam asked conversationally.

"Yeah, she's still missing," Bubba said.

"Where you looked?"

"Everywhere I could," Bubba answered on a sad note.

"You check her cell phone?"

"Cell phone?"

"Sure. Most cells got GPS on 'em," Bam Bam said as he examined his fingernails. He wore a Lakers jersey with red leather pants and a lime green pair of Nike Zoom Hyperdunk shoes. (Bubba only knew what they were because Brownie pointed them out in a magazine and mentioned that they cost much more than his mother would fork out in a given month. Brownie had allowed as to how he was enamored of those particular shoes and was in the market for ideas on how to raise his allowance. Bubba allowed as to how Brownie was not permitted to mug little old ladies and/or rob banks, and the two went on to other topics of discussion.)

"That's a good idea," Bubba said. If Willodean had

her cell phone on her, then they would know where she was located. But a thought came to him. Cell phones died without being charged. There wasn't a lot of coverage near Sturgis Woods, as he had warned Kiki of the dreadlocks. Still it was a good thought. Bubba hoped that Sheriff John had already thought of it because the Dallas County Jail wasn't going to give him a second call.

"I watches the Discovery Channel," Bam Bam shared. "They gots lots of shows about criminal investigations. Never know when a fella needs a little *in-for-maaa-cee-on.*"

"Ain't that the truth?" one of the other detainees said bitterly. "I got nailed for jaywalking."

"Jaywalking?" another detainee asked with apparent skepticism.

"Well, there was something about assaulting the police officer, too," the first detainee admitted with a red-faced sneer. "He was being a jackass. So I kicked him in the knee. I had my steel tipped boots on, so a bone got broke. Obviously, I was entrapped."

"*Rookies,*" Bam Bam said. He leaned over to Bubba. "Don't never confess what you done in here. These little rooks will come back in three to six months at your trial as witnesses for the prosecution and say you copped to *everything.* They'll say you robbed a nun at gunpoint in front of a group of Catholic school girls. You even be D.B. Cooper, too."

The first detainee heard that and hastily amended his story. "I'm not saying I kicked the cop. But he was kicked by someone. Someone with steel tipped boots. Yeah, that's it. Who's D.B. Cooper?"

"So what happened to your girl?" Bam Bam asked.

"There was a car wreck and she vanished," Bubba said shortly.

Bam Bam took that in.   "Sheeee-it," he said. "Vanished. Just like that?"

"Just like that."

"Try her cell phone," Bam Bam counseled. "Maybe it he'ps. Maybe it don't. Worth a shot."

Bubba shrugged.   He was going to give it a shot when he got out of the jail. He might shoot some other things, too.

"They search for this girl?" Bam Bam asked.

"Searched all over," Bubba said.

"This about that *girl* down south of the Big D?" Bam Bam asked as his eyebrows furrowed. Comprehension cleared his frown away.   "Got *all* kinds of peoples looking for that girl on account of who she be."

"Probably the same one."

"She be a..." Bam Bam paused and warily looked at the other detainees.   "Well, she be something I don't wants to say in here, am I right?"

"You're right."   Bubba thought Bam Bam was trying to say that he knew that Willodean was a sheriff's deputy but that he didn't want the others to know. Why, Bubba wasn't sure, but he went with it.

Bam Bam sat back, and his eyes ran over Bubba's large form. "But you ain't."

"I ain't," Bubba agreed.

I ain't what? A sheriff's deputy? No, I'm not. I'm a big, dumb sonuvabitch, right now. Sorry, Ma.

"You is one crazy-ass cracker," Bam Bam said, and to Bubba it sounded like a compliment. The man leaned in closer to Bubba. "It's okay," he whispered. "I gots a cousin who's a patrolman for the state of Alabama. He pays his taxes on time, and he don't he'p a brotha out when he gots a speeding ticket in Mobile. Ain't that some freaky shit?"

"Freaky," Bubba replied.

"So what you doing up here?" Bam Bam looked around as if he could see the entirety of the city of Dallas. "That girl didn't disappear up here. You think she's here somewheres?"

"I think a man who might have taken her is here," Bubba said, and his voice was all icy fury again.

"Man like that," Bam Bam said reasonably, "ain't gots no reason to be on the street."

"They called him a *stalker*," Bubba remarked. He didn't have an idea why he was sharing with a man named Bam Bam except that it seemed like it made sense to talk it out. Bubba's mind was on Howell Le Beau. If Bubba had to be locked up, he wasn't going to stop thinking about the circumstances. Possibly he could come up with a better plan to find the man who might very well have taken Willodean.

"A stalker," Bam Bam said with evident fury. "I knows lots of homegirls who has men who don't know the meaning of the word 'no'. A woman's got a right to say no. Man just has to understand not every girl wants to be with him. You remember that girl I tole you about? Gummi Worm? She had a fella like that. Be all, 'You with me now, babe,' and she was all like, 'I don't think so.' "

Bam Bam's hands began to fluctuate wildly again, emphasizing parts of his dialogue that he felt strongly about.

"Girl had to take him down with pepper spray and dude was all, 'What for you do that, girl?' The 5-0 had to take his sorry ass to the hospital to check out his eyeballs." He finished with a chuckle. "Pepper spray made him cry big green boogers down his chin."

"What makes a fella do that?" Bubba asked. *Understand the man? Understand what he did with Willodean. Maybe. What else have I got right now?*

151

"Dunno," Bam Bam said. "Wicked bad crazy fucks, them is. Word, my brotha." He snapped his wrist in time with what he was saying.

"They're obsessed," one of the other detainees said. It was the man who'd been nicked for jaywalking and possibly some other stuff he didn't think was worth mentioning. "Stalkers are sometimes psychotic or nonpsychotic, depending on pre-existing diagnoses."

The holding cell quieted, and everyone stared at the man. He shrugged painfully.

"It was on *E!* last night," he said defensively. "They had a two-hour special on Hollywood actors and actresses who were stalked. Talked to family members and shrinks and the whole nine yards. Should have stayed home and watched all of it," he added in a furious undertone.

"Stalker dude got a shrink?" Bam Bam asked Bubba.

"You mean the man I'm looking for?" Bubba said.

Bam Bam nodded.

"Yeah, the parole officer said something about one." Bubba cogitated. "But a therapist ain't gonna speak to me. I'll be lucky if the po-lice don't drive me to the county line and drop me off while waving a shotgun at my butt."

"Where's your dog?" Bam Bam asked suddenly, looking around as if the Basset hound would appear out of nothingness.

"Parole officer's got her," Bubba said.

"That's some freaky shit, too," Bam Bam said earnestly.

Don't therapists have to warn folks if their patients threaten someone? Bubba considered what he knew about psychology. He'd taken the one class as an elective. What did Bubba remember?

Babies like pooping. Sometimes a cigar is just a cigar.

Kids develop cognitive thinking about the age of thirteen. What else?

"Did you hear about that Tom-Cruise-crazy shit that happened on the news show this morning?" one of the detainees asked. "Never would have believed that, if I hadn't seen it."

"That news guy drooled down the side of his cheek," someone else said.

"And the kid laughed his ass off," another one side. Everyone giggled except Bubba.

Bubba was thinking, *Who do I know that will tell me about stalkers and crazy people?*

"And that other news girl is all like, 'Don't tase me, bro,'" Bam Bam chortled.

Bubba glanced around him coming back to the moment. Several men laughed about some topic Bubba had missed. He didn't really care about that. He needed to get out of the jail, and he was going to have to wait for a judge to see him. Then he was going to have to hope that his mother was on her way to Dallas to bail him out.

Speaking of crazy, I should have called Ma before I got thrown in jail. I plumb forgot. She's gonna be mad about that. She's gonna act like someone peed in her Cheerios.

Bam Bam said to the other detainees, "There was this one dumb cracker who thought he could dress up like Judy Garland and trip-trip-trap through the barrio wearing ruby slippers. I dint think they made ruby slippers in a size 13. Biggest damn shoes I ever did see. Then he be like, 'Click my heels together and say there's no place like home.'"

I need someone really special to tell me what I need to know about a stalker, Bubba decided. *I need someone who's an expert in being off the wall.*

"And there was this one girl who went to Walmart dressed in a G-string. *Only* a G-string," Bam Bam kept

153

talking jauntily.

"What's wrong with that?" one of the others asked.

"Girl be five hundred pounds heavy," Bam Bam said. "I like a big girl, but that be a really big girl. They make G-strings for girls that big? Same place as the size 13 ruby slippers, am I right, brothas?"

A light bulb popped above Bubba's head.

All of the detainees in the holding cell looked up at the electrical bulb which had suddenly detonated.

I need...a crazy person.

•

Lawyer Petrie and Miz Demetrice stood in the small courtroom while Bubba was still handcuffed to a long bar next to long rows of seats on the side.

Bubba's mother glared at him volcanically. She dressed in a lemon yellow dress holding a matching purse. Even her pumps were lemony. Somehow she'd managed to get the remainder of the Sharpie marker-drawn stars off her face and looked like the pristine Texas matron that she presented to the world at large. The only problem was her sulfuric gaze directed at Bubba, and it didn't bode well for his immediate future.

Lawyer Petrie stood next to her. The man dressed in his typical three-piece, black suit, replete with a gold fob draped from one button hole. He held a black derby in one hand in deference to the presence of the judge. The expression on his face revealed that he was mentally spending his revenue obtained from not only representing Bubba in court but having to travel from Pegram County to do so.

Bubba was tired and hungry. He hadn't gotten a good night's sleep. The men in the holding cell snored, and one clearly had a digestive tract issue of massive proportion. He wondered if Guillermo Sanchez had fed his dog. He wondered if Willodean had anything to eat.

154

He wondered if she was thinking about who was looking for her.

I am. I swear. Just as soon as I stop being stupid.

The judge finished with her paperwork and looked up. A correctional officer nudged Bubba's elbow. "That's you, Snoddy. Stand up."

Bubba stood, and the judge asked something about being responsible until the court date. Bubba strove to look solemn. "I will," he said. Then he hastily added, "Ma'am."

The judge twitched and looked back down at what was probably Bubba's arrest record. It was a large pile of papers. "I see you've been around the block, Mr. Snoddy," the judge said.

Bubba hadn't caught the judge's name. *Does she know Hizzoner Stenson Posey?* "I've been in a few jails," he allowed.

"Most of the charges were dropped," the judge said as she flicked a few pages.

"I seem to be a mite unlucky with getting arrested," Bubba added. There were a few chuckles from the courtroom's observers.

Miz Demetrice cleared her throat, and Bubba didn't need to be psychic to figure out what she thought. *Ain't helping yourself, boy.*

"Unlucky," the judge repeated.

From where Bam Bam was handcuffed on Bubba's left, he leaned in and whispered, "Good tactic. I be trying that later. Unlucky. Folks like me always be unlucky."

"I remember this case from a few months ago," the judge went on as one fingernail lifted a few pages. "They caught the two perpetrators red-handed confessing to the murders and the attempt to pin it on you."

155

"Yes, ma'am," Bubba said. *That would be Lurlene Grady and Noey Wheatfall.*

"And last week, there was the woman who wanted to kill everyone on a decades old Christmas society board? Something about her father going to jail?"

"That's what she said," Bubba stated. *That's Nancy Musgrave.*

"And now there's a sheriff's deputy missing," the judge went on. "You charged up here to Dallas looking for her?"

"Yes, ma'am," Bubba ascertained. *I charged up here to Dallas to find the man who might have done it.* He wasn't sure what else there was to say. He could have said, "Please, ma'am, I need to get out of here so I can find Willodean soonest," but he didn't think the judge with her cynical eyes would understand. As a matter of fact, those eyes looked both suspicious and ready to condemn him without recourse.

"It isn't done to interfere with a peace officer," the judge said as she slid the paperwork away from her. Her eyes settled on Bubba like a missile sighting an errant enemy tank.

"Yes, ma'am," Bubba said obediently. "It was a mistake." And in that particular moment, he felt repentant. It reflected in his words. He couldn't say anything else that was more sincere.

The judge sat back in her high-backed chair and looked at Bubba in a considering fashion. She looked as if she was...judging him. "All right then. Can you bond out, Mr. Snoddy?"

"Alfred Petrie for the defendant," Lawyer Petrie said loudly, coming to his feet.

Alfred? That's Lawyer Petrie's first name? Now that don't sound right.

"$10,000 bond," the judge pronounced and thumped

her gavel. She appeared so happy about it that she thumped the gavel again.

Miz Demetrice grunted loudly in a most unladylike way.

Lawyer Petrie coughed into his hand. "We can take care of that, Your Honor."

Bubba almost smiled, but the judge was looking at him, so he went for the grateful expression. Based on Her Honor's face, he didn't quite pull it off.

Chapter Thirteen

In the Land of Blind People,
Bubba is the Least Crazy

Tuesday, January 3rd

In order of most importance, Bubba had to pick up his dog, his truck, and his limited amount of luggage from the third-rate hotel. Miz Demetrice badgered him as he proceeded about his business, but he simply ignored her which had the effect of aggravating her further. Lawyer Petrie took the silent high ground and drove Bubba to Guillermo Sanchez's house where he retrieved Precious from Mrs. Sanchez. Precious appeared content and well-fed. Mrs. Sanchez was only mildly irritated.

"That dog *loves* bean burritos," she said in a warning manner as Precious attempted to lick Bubba to death. The fact of an animal consuming highly combustible food stuffs didn't signify well for the three-hour trip to come.

Bubba thought he could detect remnants of bean breath emitting from Precious's mouth. Mostly, Precious smelled like dog.

Then Mrs. Sanchez handed Bubba his set of keys for the Chevy truck. "Your truck is still at the DPO," she said helpfully. "Gui said you were looking for that missing girl. Stupid police don't have much sense putting you in lockup."

Miz Demetrice and Lawyer Petrie watched from Lawyer Petrie's black sedan. His mother still stared at Bubba as if she could turn him into stone with her belligerent death glare.

"Yeah," Bubba said in a subdued fashion. He knelt

and scratched Precious as she continued her tonguey assault on all of his exposed flesh. "I shouldn't have been messing with the investigator's business."

Mrs. Sanchez stared down at Bubba's face and he looked away. Truth be told, Bubba wasn't happy with himself, and he sincerely doubted that he would be happy with *anything* for some time to come.

"You like this missing girl," she said to the top of his head.

"Yes," he said simply. *Like her a lot.*

"People will understand that," Mrs. Sanchez. "Gui said you didn't hurt the investigator when he arrested you and that you could have."

Bubba remembered Charles Park's extensive array of lightning-swift moves and doubted that. One moment Bubba had been saying, "Duh," and the next he had been lying on the ground with Park snapping shut the handcuffs. Park hadn't been in the least inconvenienced by Bubba's mass.

"Keep looking," Mrs. Sanchez advised. "I'll light a candle for you and the deputy at the church today. You'll need all the help you can get."

Coming to his feet, Bubba felt a wave of shame threaten to swamp him. He'd been thinking only of himself. "Thank you, Mrs. Sanchez," he said. "And would you thank your husband for watching out for my dog. He dint have to do that after I fooled him."

"Oh, Gui thought it was funny," Mrs. Sanchez said. "Well, he did after a few hours anyway. Under the circumstances, it's understandable." She shook a warning finger at him. "*Almost.*"

Bubba got Precious into the Caddy and slid into the back seat with the dog, who wasn't done with her animalistic attentions to her master.

Giving a set of directions to Lawyer Petrie, Bubba

settled in for the ride. After a few minutes he said, "Search didn't find nothing, Ma?"

"Ifin you had called me," Miz Demetrice said icily, "then you would already know that." She had discovered that her verbal tirade wasn't getting her anywhere so she chose arctic silence as her weapon of choice.

Bubba sighed.

"Ma," he said. "I love you, but I make mistakes the same as most."

"I'd rather *you* made less," she pronounced.

Lawyer Petrie chuckled under his breath.

"Ifin I can find this man who stalked Willodean," Bubba continued, "then perhaps I can convince him to tell me where she is." He paused for effect. "Just like I told you before."

Bubba could see clearly from the back seat as Miz Demetrice's shoulders straightened and set into an iron-like configuration. Either she was about to crack, or she wouldn't speak to him for the next five days.

"I'm going back to Pegramville today," he announced.

Lawyer Petrie said, "Good. Good. I think the judge will like that just fine."

"The searches find anything at all?" Bubba asked again.

"It was discovered that Farmer Scoresby has a two-headed cat that he calls Twoface," Miz Demetrice said sourly. "There was also a cat named Mr. Freeze and one named The Riddler. Apparently Farmer Scoresby has a keenness for Batman villains."

"Did Sheriff John check Willodean's cell phone?" Bubba asked.

"Her phone is dead. Sheriff John thought of that on the second day," Miz Demetrice said, her tone a minute amount more moderate. "The last registered location was just south of Pegramville where it pinged a tower there. Sheriff thinks it was when she was on her way to the Snoddy Mansion on the day she...disappeared."

Bubba moved uncomfortably in the back seat. His hand came down on Precious's head. She rested her snout across his knee as if her master might get away if she did not weigh him down. His other hand came down on a stack of papers. He saw they were missing posters. The photograph on them was Willodean Gray. He picked one up and read the details, although he was well familiar with them.

Miz Demetrice said, "We're dropping them off with a local organization here." Bubba's gaze came up and saw that his mother turned her head and regarded him with expressive sadness.

"There's a fraternal police group that will start picketing the city with them. They're going after major intersections that are closer to Pegram County first. They're hoping that they manage to find someone who's seen something or someone."

Bubba stared at the photograph of Willodean. It was a different one than on the bulletin that Sheriff John had sent out. She smiled into the camera. Arms were draped over her shoulders. The photo had been enlarged from some family shot.

Bubba studied Willodean's likeness. Her black hair tumbled loose over her shoulders. Her green eyes sparkled. She appeared happy. She had seemed happy the evening she'd kissed him.

His lips flattened into a white line of eternal grimness. He checked his pocket and found the phone the jail had given back to him. The screen wouldn't even turn on; seemingly the brief charge hadn't been enough for the cheap unit.

"Can I borrow your phone, Ma?"

Miz Demetrice handed it back to him with only a slight reflection of outward irritation. It was a strong suggestion of how annoyed with him she was, since she didn't squabble about his time spent in the jail.

Bubba took about five minutes finding Charles Park at his desk.

Park answered with a curt, "Investigator Park."

"This is Bubba Snoddy," Bubba said.

Somehow Bubba had managed to turn on the speakerphone function of his mother's phone and he wasn't certain how to turn it off without disconnecting the call. When Park snorted everyone in the car fell silent and listened.

"That was fast," Park said. "Judge Perez doesn't usually let people out who interfere with a peace officer. She has a special place *under* the jail."

"I think she might have felt sorry for me," Bubba said. *Not really.* But the judge hadn't been completely indifferent to the story.

"Huh," Park said. "Perez must be getting soft."

"Guillermo Sanchez implied that Howell Le Beau wasn't the one who assaulted Willodean," Bubba said.

Miz Demetrice made a hoarse noise from the front of the car. Lawyer Petrie remained stalwartly silent. Precious grunted and got more comfortable.

Park didn't say anything.

"Is it true?"

"What difference does it make?" Park asked. "Le Beau was stalking Deputy Gray. No ifs, ands, or buts about it. He copped to it."

"Sometimes I drive by the sheriff's department to see if I can catch a glimpse of Willodean," Bubba said inflexibly. "Does that mean I'm stalking her?"

"It's an issue of harassment," Park said. "I'm

thinking the deputy doesn't mind if you drive by and try to catch a look-see."

"Did Le Beau assault Willodean? Did he put her into the hospital for a week?"

Miz Demetrice made another gruff sound.

"No," Park said after a lengthy hesitation. "Le Beau followed her. She made a routine stop, and the guy got the drop on her. It turns out that Le Beau probably saved her life. But Deputy Gray was unconscious for two days, and the mounted dash camera didn't show what happened. We caught that guy who assaulted her two weeks later on another routine stop. He ran a light in front of a highway patrolman halfway to El Paso. He's doing twenty to life in Huntsville."

"The news initially reported it incorrectly," Bubba said contemplatively. Kiki of the dreadlocks had probably pulled up the news articles about Willodean in chronological order.

"We didn't know until the Deputy woke up," Park said. "Doesn't make much difference. Le Beau vanishes the same day that Deputy Gray vanishes. It doesn't take much to do the math. It's my experience that coincidences are unlikely, sometimes improbable."

"And you spoke with Le Beau's employer?"

"Bubba, I hate to break it to you, but I don't have to tell you jack diddly poo," Park said with unmistakable impatience. "This kind of behavior is going to get you thrown right back in county lockup."

"I'm just trying to get a feel for this guy, Le Beau," Bubba said. "Guillermo sounds like he kind of likes the fella, like most of the fellas he deals with are scumbags, but occasionally one tries to get back on board with the rest of civilization. Like Le Beau. He was trying to get his life right."

"So Le Beau went back to writing letters to Deputy

Gray after he agreed not to have any contact with her because he was trying to do the right thing?" Park laughed.

"That letter I found sounded sorta like...an apology. I don't rightly reckon," Bubba admitted. "But I aim to find out."

"Do I have to warn you again about-"

Bubba cut him off. "Talk to you soon, Park."

As Bubba brought the phone down, Park yelled, "Dammit! Don't hang up! I'm talking-"

A large finger jabbed at the end button.

Miz Demetrice had her arm resting on the back of the bench seat and her chin thoughtfully propped on the closed fist as she stared at him. She said gently, "Willodean moved down to Pegramville after someone assaulted her."

Bubba nodded.

"My God," she muttered. "Some men are truly vile beasts. There's a very special place in hell where men like that have their testicles ripped out on a daily basis and fed to them with a roasting fork."

"Amen," Bubba agreed. *That's the Ma I know and I love.*

"If you haven't found this other man, this Le Beau, then why are you going back to Pegramville?" she asked tentatively.

"There's someone there I need to speak with."

•

Bubba had to stop once to add water to the radiator of his truck. He had to stop to add air to one of the tires and then to blow trash out of his carburetor. But he made it to Pegramville before the sun went down and the sixty-odd-year-old engine had blown itself into smithereens no matter what his mechanical skills.

His destination looked like a regular hospital.

Whitewashed walls set the backdrop for a manicured lawn that spread far and away. There weren't any fences and especially not any with concertina wire mounted on top. The parking lot was close to the front entrance, and inside a nearby gazebo, a pair of nurses smoked cigarettes and chatted affably.

There was even a handy formal sign on one side that announced the name of the facility. Bubba slowed his truck to a crawl as he looked at the sign. Satisfied he was in the right place, he parked in-between a Mercedes Benz and a Volkswagen Rabbit.

Precious scratched at the door when they stopped. Bubba let the animal out for a few minutes and then herded her back inside the truck. She whined at him but relented good-naturedly. After all, she'd had three hours of nearly nonstop Bubba attention and she was moderately content. Furthermore, the building they'd stopped at smelled odd, and she wasn't enthused enough to follow the odors inside.

There was a smaller sign at the front door, next to a bell. The visiting hours were plainly denoted. Bubba rang the bell, and the door chirped itself open a moment later without anyone asking what his business was there.

Inside was a nice-sized foyer with marble floors and seats that had been bolted to the walls. An oversized desk sat to one side with a woman sitting at it. She looked at Bubba expectantly.

"Well, great!" she enthused. "A visitor!"

"Okay," Bubba said. "I need to see someone." The direct approach was always a good way to start.

The woman was young, red haired, and seemed perpetually cheerful. She smiled up at him as he approached. Her nametag read Cybil. Next to the name she had drawn a very large happy face to specify her level of perkiness.

Cybil pushed a logbook toward him and said, "You'll need to sign in. And no *nom de plumes*. That's a joke," she added when Bubba didn't obediently smile in response.

Bubba reached for a pen and signed where she indicated. She started in on what was obviously a well-rehearsed spiel.

"There's no guns, knives, box cutters, tweezers, scissors, clippers, cuticle trimmers, darts, butchery equipment, sharp-edged objects, or any object that can be used as a lethal device allowed within the confines of the facility."

Pausing at the middle of writing Snoddy, Bubba said, "I got a buck knife."

The young woman tilted her head to one side, reminding him of Precious in one of her more harmonious moments.

"Well, of course you do. Most folks don't think about what they've got in their pockets. I like to carry around a Swiss Army knife, myself. The classic one. It's got a nail file on it. And did you know that credit cards can be filed down to make a knife? Why, the stories I can tell about the weapons that have been made here!"

Bubba finished his name in the log book and pushed it back. He wasn't certain if he was supposed to respond to her or not.

"They make knives out of spoons and old nails," Cybil went on as if he had answered her. "Plexiglas, plastic, Frito-Lay chips, and once even a crucifix. Well, we don't get too many of the hard cases anymore; they do get a little harebrained in here. There's one fella who made a radio out of ramen noodles. He says he has a daily discussion with the Angel Gabriel." Cybil tilted her head the other way. "And they make tattoo machines out of batteries and sewing needles. They use the ink out of disposable pens. I suppose they get bored since they don't get the Internet."

Bubba was unsure what he was supposed to do next. Finally he interrupted her. "So can I just-"

Cybil pointed at the double door behind her. "Straight back there. Most of them are in the dayroom. If you can't find someone then they're probably in their rooms. Oh, and you'll have to leave the buck knife. I'll give it to you when you come back out."

Pulling out the buck knife, Bubba said, "You just let people come and go?"

"Well sure, silly," Cybil chided him as she took the knife and put it into a drawer. "It's *not* a prison."

She took out a large sticker that said "Visitor", handed it to him, and motioned for him to stick it on his shirt.

Cybil pressed a button on the desk, and the doors burped open. Bubba pushed through the double doors and walked down a hallway. A few people walked past who didn't pay any attention to him at all. A woman passed by doing the tango with a partner that was a large, plush teddy bear. The bear did not appear pleased.

The dayroom was at the back of the building. Double doors opened into a spacious expanse with dozens of couches and chairs. The six-foot-tall windows allowed the setting sun's light to pour in. An array of noises from talking, music, and someone bouncing a super ball off the walls, overpowered Bubba's thoughts.

People spread out doing numerous things. A few obvious nurses and attendants in scrubs patrolled. A television blared an old episode of *Murder, She Wrote*. Two patients were loudly arguing about who did it.

"It was the gas station guy," one said.

"It was the gardener," the other one protested.

"There wasn't a gardener," the first one said.

"It was the invisible gardener," the other one replied reasonably.

"There was an invisible gardener?" asked the first one.

Other patients played chess and Chutes and Ladders. One man played a particularly vivacious game of Operation. Whenever the buzzer went off while he tried to retrieve a piece, he jumped and yelled, "Bananafanna monkey turds!"

Three patients were involved in something that appeared to be a re-creation of a famous historical event. One patient had found a hat that was similar to the one in Leutze's painting *Washington Crossing the Delaware*. He was posed with his hand on a bent knee as he stood in the "boat" that had been constructed with chairs. Another man held a flag and was seemingly battered by a nonexistent breeze. The remainder of the patients in the group had paddles made from cardboard and were steadily paddling against an imaginary icy current in order to defeat the Hessians. "Stroke, men!" General Washington boomed. "We must defeat the British and their little dogs, too!"

A nurse paused by Bubba, looking at his sticker badge, and said, "Visitor?"

"Yes," Bubba said, overwhelmed by what he saw. His mouth remained open after he replied.

The nurse chuckled. "It's always thought-provoking around here."

A voice said next to Bubba, "Thou unmuzzled, dizzy-eyed canker sore."

Bubba turned to see Thelda. Thelda had been one of Nancy Musgrave's patients. She was in undeterminable middle age, with gray hair and gray eyes, and had a keen propensity for sweaters. She wore four of them at the moment. Two were blue, one was red, and one was gray. A drip of sweat rolled down her forehead. She stood next to him and stared at the floor.

"Thelda," he said.

The nurse said, "Okay, great. I'll leave you two alone."

"But I'm not-" Bubba started to say to the nurse, but she had vanished into the group of patients intent on crossing the Delaware with General Washington.

"Harder, men! We must save America from three-eyed, three-legged purple snarflulots!"

Certainly, the Dogley Institute for Mental Well-Being wasn't exactly what Bubba had thought it would be. Considering that he had lived in Pegram County his entire life, he was amazed that he hadn't been here before.

Probably because they haven't gotten tired of me at the jail yet.

"So, Miz Thelda," he said conversationally, "how are you?"

"Thou art rightly a fawning, tardy-gated younker," she enunciated.

"Sorry about Nancy Musgrave," Bubba said.

Thelda twitched. "Thee was sincerely a hideous, shrill-gorged codpiece."

"Yeah, I reckon I didn't like her much neither," Bubba admitted. "Especially after she killed two folks that I liked quite a bit. Then she tried to kill another three, or was it four? I plain forget. And then she was going to kill me, followed by Ma. Well, I didn't think much of all of that. Of course, Brownie put a right clever end to it."

Thelda stared at the floor.

"I don't mean no disrespect, Miz Thelda," he said

politely. "But I got a problem with someone I think isn't right in the head. That deputy I like is missing, and I believe this fella has something to do with it. But I don't understand why that's so. I need to speak with an expert."

Bubba rubbed his chin and looked around to see if anyone listened. Once he had gotten to the Dogley Institute of Mental Well-Being where Nancy Musgrave, the Christmas Killer, had worked, his plan for illumination didn't seem as shrewd. The three patients that she had dragged around with her and who had half-heartedly aided in her campaign for revenge, were from here. If ever an expert on mental disabilities was to be found, then the Dogley Institute was the place to find one.

Across the room, a short, balding man in his thirties caught sight of Bubba and said loudly, "Bubba! Have you come for further heeeeaaaaling?"

The sheet that the balding man wore lofted in the air as he played a game of Twister with three other patients.

Bubba waved at the man. He had been a second patient of Nancy's who fancied himself Jesus Christ. Bubba didn't know Jesus' real name, but he did know that he liked to pontificate and steal hemorrhoid cream from the five and dime. He also didn't care for underwear, in much a similar manner as Kiki of the dreadlocks.

"Right hand, green," another patient called.

Jesus said, "The greeeen shall come unto meeee." The green circle did not come unto him, and he cursed vehemently. Twister wasn't really a good pick for a man who preferred to go commando.

"Miz Thelda," Bubba said, turning back to the mousy woman wearing four sweaters. "I'm sorry your routines got all messed up, and I'm sorry Nancy Musgrave got you all wrapped up in this mess, but I really need David Beathard."

David Beathard was Nancy Musgrave's third patient. He had several alternate personas. The one Bubba wanted was that of a psychotherapist. David might be a mental patient, but he had tons of legitimate knowledge in his head about psychology. Bubba confidently believed David Beathard could give him some valuable insight into what was going on in Howell Le Beau's brain.

"Verily," Thelda agreed. "Thee art in the corner." She pointed.

Bubba looked, but he didn't see the man who was in his thirties, dressed up like Mr. Rogers. He favored a button-down cardigan and taupe slacks to accompany his thick rimmed Buddy Holly glasses. Sometimes he puffed on a pipe that was always empty. It was all part of his therapist personality.

"Thou are truly a shag-eared mold wart," Thelda articulated fervently and turned away. Bubba stared after her for a moment, wondering what message she was undertaking to get across this time. Thelda preferred to speak in Shakespearian insults and was often frustrated that her communications weren't crystal clear.

Turning back to the dayroom, Bubba searched for David Beathard but couldn't immediately find him. A man dressed entirely in purple leaped in front of him and bellowed, "Da da DAH!"

Bubba spared the purple man a brief glance. His shirt was purple with the logo, "Nexium®", on it. His pants were purple, albeit they were jeans that had been dyed purple. His shoes had been white tennis shoes but had been painstakingly colored purple with a marker. A purple bandana was tied around the man's head and upper face, with two holes cut out for eyes. Two earnest eyes stared out at Bubba.

"Hey," Bubba said while he scanned the rest of the room for David.

"I AM the superhero, THE PURPLE SINGAPORE SLING," the man announced enthusiastically. He planted his hands on his hips and thrust out his chest in a heroic pose.

"You're purple all right," Bubba agreed. "Don't suppose you know David, do you?"

The Purple Singapore Sling waited in front of him. He took a breath and then pushed his chest out again.

Bubba sighed. "I don't need saving right now," he said politely. "Maybe later."

"Psst," The Purple Singapore Sling whispered while he maintained his gallant posture. "It's *me*, Bubba." He arched his back just a little and thrust out his chest more. "I AM the superhero, THE PURPLE SINGAPORE SLING!"

With no little amount of dismay, Bubba realized that The Purple Singapore Sling was none other than David Beathard with an all new plum-like disguise.

The Purple Singapore Sling grinned brightly at Bubba before he swung away and leaped over a couch, singing out, "I have come to SAVE the day!"

Chapter Fourteen

Bubba and Inevitability

Tuesday, January 3rd

It had been weeks but the Snoddy Mansion was finally devoid of people.

Only hints of the masses of people who had recently wandered there remained. There were remnants from the onslaught that had been Hurricane Brownie, and the police had raided the kitchen of the last cinnamon roll, leaving only sugary crumbs to mourn their passing. The hardwood floors were dirty and chairs askew. The Christmas tree was turning brown, and the needles were falling like snowflakes in a Northern blizzard.

The Louisianan Snoddys had absconded days before, headed for the bright lights of a distant media torrent. Miz Demetrice's sister, Caressa, had made tracks for Dallas, certain the air there was safer in general. Miz Adelia had thrown her hands up in despair and fled for the sanctity of her home, promising to return the following day with two of her nieces for a major overhauling of the state of cleanliness. She had stomped out to her car, saying over her shoulder with no little amount of vehemence, "We're gonna lick this calf all over again!"

Alone at last. Miz Demetrice sat on the front veranda eyeing some wood rot on one of the columns and wondering if it was too late to donate the entire mansion to some historical society that had access to lots of cash. She had returned from Dallas without her son but with a feeling of dread permeating every inch of her bones.

It was the unspoken that bothered her. Bubba was

tilting out of control. He grasped at straws, no matter how remote. Even through her anger, she could see her son's façade was like a piece of fragile glass. If anything pulled just a tad more, he might break into a thousand fractured pieces.

And all the king's horses and all the king's men couldn't put Humpty-Bubba back together again...

There had been several searches for Deputy Willodean Gray in the days since she had vanished into seeming nothingness. Lewis Robson had searched twice with his hounds. The second time was even less productive than the first because of successive rain storms since she went missing. Locals and people from as far away as Houston had come to volunteer for grid searches. They had crawled, walked, and lurched through hundreds of acres of bottomlands, swamps, and fields, all to no avail.

Examining other angles, Sheriff John pulled the GPS records for both Willodean's phone and the county car she'd been driving. Both had revealed nothing out of the ordinary.

Willodean's family presented themselves for an uncomfortable press conference in front of a dozen news affiliates and begged the public for information. Her parents were gray-faced and as brittle as Bubba appeared to be. Donations had come in from many organizations, offering a significant reward for any information about Willodean Gray's whereabouts.

Bubba stampeded up to Dallas to find the man who might be responsible and ultimately found nothing but an overnight stay in jail.

And now, what is the boy doing? Talking to someone else mysteriously. Won't share anything with his mother. That boy's gone around the bend.

Miz Demetrice grimaced.

Bubba's like a five-story building with a three-story elevator.

The ominousness of the circumstances was disparaging. Miz Demetrice knew of folks who disappeared. Most came back or were later found safe and sound. She'd never known someone like Willodean, who had just gone, leaving only a little bit of blood and a mystery that was hurting all involved.

The chilling horror of never knowing what happened to Willodean wasn't any better than the finality of locating her remains. Neither outcome was particularly welcoming.

Miz Demetrice watched the daylight fade into purple streaks across a pinkish sky. She worried about Willodean but also worried about her son. Bubba had lost more than merely Willodean, and it didn't look like the missing piece was going to come back.

The distant hum of a vehicle starting down the Snoddy Estate's extended drive made her sigh. Initially, she hoped it was Bubba returning but quickly acknowledged that it didn't sound like the capitulated rumble of the old, green truck.

When the car pulled up behind her Cadillac, she knew she had seen it before. There was enough light still to recognize her visitors. Miz Demetrice brushed off the skirt of her lemon yellow dress and stood.

The occupants wearily got out of the car and stared at her for a long moment. Finally, Willodean's mother, Celestine Gray, said, "Mrs. Snoddy."

"Come on in," Miz Demetrice said politely. "I'll make coffee."

•

There were five of them. Celestine Gray loomed over Miz Demetrice before she had condescended to sit down at the oversized table in the formal dining room.

175

Evan Gray was close to his wife's height but relatively benign in appearance. The two young women were clearly their parents' daughters and resembled Willodean as well. The fifth was an eight-year-old girl named Janie with an expansive sneer discoloring her features.

Miz Demetrice rounded up coffee, store-bought cookies and one glass of 2% milk. Cups, cream, and sugar came from the sideboard. When she put the glass of milk down in front of the eight-year-old, the girl glared at it as if it was filled with poison.

"I like coffee," Janie announced with only the scorn an eight-year-old could pull off.

One of the women who had introduced herself as Anora, who was Janie's mother, said, "And you still aren't getting any, Janie."

Janie crossed her arms over her chest and glared at the milk some more.

Miz Demetrice was reminded of a ten-year-old boy who had sat in the same chair at the great table. To be perfectly exact, Celestine Gray was sitting where Miz Adelia had said Nancy Musgrave had sat with her overgrown .50 caliber hand cannon.

"Thank you for all of your help with the searches," Evan Gray said as he took a cup of coffee from her.

Miz Demetrice served everyone and one for herself.

"The sheriff said you were responsible for half the people who were looking. He said you delivered a batch of flyers up to south Dallas," he said.

"I like Willodean," Miz Demetrice said as she added sugar and cream to her coffee. "I'm going to church tomorrow to pray for her as I'm fresh out of other ideas."

Celestine's mouth opened and then shut.

"Praying is good," Evan said hurriedly with a glance

176

at his wife. "Everything helps."

The six were quiet for a long moment. Janie took an index finger and very specifically pushed the glass of milk about two inches away from her.

"Would making it chocolate interest you, dear?" Miz Demetrice asked Janie.

Janie glowered. Obviously real eight-year-old girls didn't drink milk, much less chocolate milk. Her scowl transferred from the milk to Miz Demetrice. Miz Demetrice was an expert at receiving the hard end of a stare. She stared back until the girl looked away with a little dismayed grunt, knowing when an elder had beaten her at her own game.

"Cookies anyone?" Miz Demetrice said with a dry cheerfulness that she didn't feel. "I'm sure ya'll need all the energy you can get. They're store bought, but they're not bad. My housekeeper has a fondness for them. They're called Oatmeal Doodle Squares. They have raisins in them."

Janie brought her stare back upon Miz Demetrice. "*You* know something," she announced coldly.

Miz Demetrice was not perturbed. "As a matter of fact, I know many things. Is there a particular area to which you want to narrow that?"

"Janie!" Anora barked. Janie's chin lowered to her chest.

Celestine let out a great sigh. "Wills talked about you, Mrs. Snoddy."

Miz Demetrice turned her attention to Celestine. She wasn't wearing her police uniform. On the contrary, she had on a sweat shirt and worn jeans. Her shoes had mud on them, and the cheeks of her face were windburned from being outside for long hours in the cold of a January day.

"She called you Miz Demetrice," Celestine went on.

"Most people do around here," Miz Demetrice said in a calm tone. "You're welcome to do so."

Evan Gray appeared disconcerted to be in the Snoddy Mansion. The daughters appeared calm but anxious to be elsewhere. Janie was ready to let her ire down upon the unwary head of the first unrepentant soul she could locate.

"Is there any news about Willodean?" Miz Demetrice asked. She looked at each of them in turn. No one was sad. They were tired. They were worried.

Evan shook his head. "Nothing. We've got nothing at all."

"But I've gotten a couple of calls from Dallas," Celestine added dryly.

Miz Demetrice nodded. "About Bubba."

"Yes, about Bubba."

Taking a seat at the end of the table, Miz Demetrice paused to stir her coffee. "He's very keen to help find Willodean."

Wasn't that a way to put it?

Bubba had been trailing after Deputy Willodean Gray for months and just as he was finally about to make a move in the right direction, a rampaging killer appears and Willodean vanishes.

"We don't need his help," Janie snarled.

"Janie," Anora snapped. "If I have to tell you again, I'll take you back to Dallas tonight, and you can just go back to school tomorrow, like you should be instead of helping us."

"Mom!" Janie protested.

"And drink your milk," Anora added. "It's good for your bones."

"I can see how you might be concerned about Bubba," Miz Demetrice said, "but he only wishes for her safe return."

"Bubba is messing with police investigators," Celestine said without emotion. She cast her icy eyes upon Miz Demetrice, but the Snoddy matriarch had been stared down by much better, to include the pouting Janie. "He's interfering where he shouldn't be. He's causing problems for the people who need to be looking for my daughter."

"I'm not going to say that Bubba isn't making mistakes," Miz Demetrice said carefully. "But you cain't expect him to do nothing at all."

Celestine ground her teeth together. Miz Demetrice could hear the enamel chipping away from clear across the table.

"Willodean is important to Bubba," Miz Demetrice said. The truth was more complicated. Bubba truly liked Willodean; he might even be in love with her.

Miz Demetrice had begun to realize that it was more than just that. Something had happened on the day Willodean had gone missing, something more than her disappearance. No, it was the day before that. Bubba had gone out on Wednesday, and he had come back smiling. For a short period of time, it hadn't mattered that two old family friends had been murdered or that he was suspected in the attempted murder of Sheriff John or that his mother's life had been threatened by the same evil perpetrator. A hint of a smile remained on his face as he'd walked through the house checking windows and ensuring doors were locked.

Of course, Miz Demetrice peeked out earlier to see Bubba driving up before that, escorted by a county vehicle. He had spent quite a bit of time in close contact with the deputy and Miz Demetrice smiled to herself.

'Bout time. But how did one explain that to Willodean's mother?

Bubba was an old soul. He had strong beliefs and his

morals could make a fine dike to hold back just about any body of water. When he dated the treacherous Lurlene Grady, he hadn't made any false promises to her. His intentions had been sincere. He went out with and treated her like a lady.

So after the treachery had been revealed Bubba moved on from Lurlene Grady. When it came to Willodean Gray, he'd taken it slowly, having previously made mistakes with the feminine persuasion. Initially, Willodean hadn't shown any interest in Bubba; however, he wore her down. She had wanted to help him because she believed he was innocent.

Willodean believed in Bubba. No, she believes *in him.*

So that was what Miz Demetrice said. "Willodean believes in Bubba."

Willodean's sister, Hattie, wiped a tear from her cheek.

Evan reached out and put a hand over his wife's hand. A muscle contracted in Celestine's cheek.

"I know that if it was Bubba who was missing, I would move heaven and earth to find him," Miz Demetrice said gently. "And Bubba feels the same way about Willodean."

"Are they...?"

It was the first time that Miz Demetrice heard the tremor in Celestine's voice.

Miz Demetrice shrugged wryly. "Everyone wants to know, but no one knows but them."

"He looked like he...loves her," Janie said. Her voice was diminished from the lively, in-your-face tone it had before.

The girl toyed with the glass of milk. Half of it was gone although Miz Demetrice hadn't seen her take a drink.

"Why do you say that, baby?" Anora asked.

"When the police were all waiting for the dogs, I mean, hounds, to go searching for Auntie Wills, he looked like he was sad." Janie stared at the milk. "Real sad. Like his heart was breaking. Like Grandma looks when she thinks no one is watching her."

Hattie choked.

"I wish I could say that everything will be all right," Miz Demetrice said to Janie, "but I don't know what will happen. Only God knows."

"I've talked to *Him*," Janie said. "I don't know if *He's* listening."

Celestine covered her mouth with a trembling hand. After a moment, she reached for her grandchild's hand. "*He's* listening," Celestine told Janie. "*He* always listens."

Janie drank the rest of her milk using the hand that Celestine wasn't holding. Then she slammed the glass onto the table like it was a shot glass and the table was a bar. Then she wiped the milk mustache away with the back of her free hand. She culminated her unsavory actions by defiantly staring at the people watching her.

Her mother winced.

It was at that inopportune moment that Bubba arrived. He walked in the door of the dining room and froze. He stared at the group with an uncertain expression. His intense gaze bounced from Celestine and Janie to Miz Demetrice.

"No," he said, assuming they were there because of the worst possible outcome of Willodean's disappearance. His large hands clamped into white-knuckled fists at his sides.

Miz Demetrice stood up and said rapidly, "No, there's no news, Bubba."

His chest heaved once. After a long moment, he said, "I don't know whether to say thank God or not."

Celestine gave Janie a last squeeze and took a

moment to wipe off a bit of milk from the corner of the eight-year-old's mouth with an index finger. "That's pretty much how all of us feel," she said.

Precious scooted inside the door and paused as she took in the crowd. She snuffled once and sat down in the middle of the floor. A low whine questioned what was happening.

"Oh!" Janie said. "Another hound."

"She's a Basset hound," Bubba said.

Miz Demetrice sighed and sat back down in her chair again.

"Who's a little, precious cute girl?" Janie said as she got up to approach the dog.

Precious perked up at the sound of her name.

Bubba observed as Janie approached the hound and tentatively offered her fingers for the animal to smell.

He said in a grating voice, "Really, there ain't anything new?"

"The tip line has over five hundred messages," Evan Gray said glumly. "Most of it is trash or people who thought they saw someone who looks like Willodean, except with blonde hair or red hair or purple hair. She's in Alaska on a fishing trawler. She's in Los Angeles selling Maps to the Stars. She was on the late flight to Tokyo. The sheriff has people working on the tips."

"I hate those lines," Hattie said. "The police know that they're mostly a waste of time and manpower. But how can we not have one?"

Precious licked Janie's face and she giggled.

"You need to get the kid a dog," Celestine said.

"She wants a German shepherd," Anora said. "A real police dog. Those dogs poop piles the size of dinner plates."

"So get her something smaller," Celestine said. "Keep her out of the station house and talking to junkies

182

and prostitutes. Two weeks ago she gave me a lecture on different types of methamphetamines that she had learned from someone named 'Turtle.' "

"It'll be a great class project," Anora said weakly.

Everyone trailed off into an awkward silence.

"What's next?" Miz Demetrice asked.

"We wait," Celestine said, the grimness evident in her voice. "We wait, and we get used to waiting until we don't have to wait anymore."

"Da dah DAH!" yelled a man dressed entirely in purple as he jumped into the room.

There wasn't anyone in the room who didn't jump. Precious scrambled for the cover of the dining room table, and Janie sat back hard on her rump. Miz Demetrice dropped her coffee cup. Anora reached for her daughter. Hattie pushed back and reached for the gun strapped under her jacket. Evan jerked as his eyes got very wide.

But Celestine had her firearm out in record time and was aiming at the individual in purple who stood at the door with his arms akimbo and his chest thrust out.

Bubba yelled, "Don't shoot! He's harmless!"

Miz Demetrice eyed the spreading circle of coffee and the broken cup that had belonged to her side of the family for three generations. "That's a matter of opinion," she said.

"Harmless," the man in purple said with dubious intent.

He reached up and adjusted the purple scarf across his eyes and head. He returned his hands to his waist and puffed his chest out further.

"I'm not harmless. I am THE PURPLE SINGAPORE SLING!"

The Purple Singapore Sling eyed Celestine's Glock and laughed theatrically. "Bullets bounce off my chest!

You shouldn't bother with that."

"Bullets don't bounce off your chest, David," Bubba said, waving one hand at Celestine. "They'll bounce *through* your chest."

"Go ahead, shoot me!" The Purple Singapore Sling sang out. "I am impervious to manly weapons."

Miz Demetrice's eyes narrowed at The Purple Singapore Sling. "Is that David Beathard? Why, last week he was a psychotherapist."

"*He's* a psychotherapist?" Hattie said incredulously.

"He's not a psychotherapist either," Bubba said. "It's just one of his...personas."

"*This* is who you went to see?" Miz Demetrice demanded.

"I need to know about stalkers," Bubba defended himself. "David Beathard knows lots about psychology, and the parole officer of the man who was stalking Willodean wouldn't give me the name of his therapist."

Miz Demetrice gazed upon The Purple Singapore Sling. "But he's not exactly David Beathard today."

"You went to talk to someone crazy about Wills' stalker?" Anora asked. She looked at Hattie. "He went to a crazy person to talk about *another* crazy person."

"It's just like when Clarice Starling went to talk to Hannibal Lecter," Janie said from where she still sat on the floor staring up at The Purple Singapore Sling. She even quoted, "'Quid pro quo, Clarice.'"

"Did you let her watch that movie?" Celestine asked Anora. The horror on Celestine's face made it seem pale and lifeless.

"No!" Anora glared briefly at Janie. "She had already finished the novel when I found it under her bed last month. *Then* she watched the movie at Hattie's house. Hattie left it lying around." She flashed a glare at her sister. Hattie shrugged.

"At least she's reading at an advanced level," Evan said, resignedly.

"Seriously, my daughter is…" Celestine said and her words died as she looked at Bubba's tired face.

"Why did you bring David-I mean, The Purple Singapore Sling *here*?" Miz Demetrice asked.

"He's a superhero," Bubba said.

Celestine put her weapon away.

"He's not," Janie said. "He needs to go to the special ward at the hospital. The loo told me about it. They have these jackets you put on them so they can't do anything with their hands."

"Are they purple jackets?" The Purple Singapore Sling asked.

"I don't know," Janie answered as if that was a very good question.

"He might change back into David Beathard, psychotherapist," Bubba whispered to his mother. "Then he might be able to help me understand this Le Beau guy. And once he found out that Willodean is missing, he insisted on coming to help." Bubba glanced over his shoulder at The Purple Singapore Sling. "On account of him being a superhero and all. It turns out that he's at the institute on a voluntary basis, so he can leave any time he wants. And he wants."

"Oh," Miz Demetrice said understandingly.

She had dealt with a number of peculiar individuals in her life. After all, she had dealt with Bubba's father, who was a peculiar individual in his own right, by using a machete while he slept one night.

"Well then, Mr. Sling," she said courteously. "Would you care for some coffee and cookies?"

185

Chapter Fifteen

Bubba Goes to Prison

Wednesday, January 4th

Bubba woke up to a shower of canine slobber. Precious endeavored to comb his hair with her tongue to remind him that she was fairly peckish first thing in the morning.

A moment of blessed ignorance clouded Bubba's brain. This was followed by a second of wretched recollection. Willodean was still missing. There wasn't a sign of her stalker. The searches hadn't revealed anything. Nothing much had changed. The sun had come up, but no one was singing a chipper, choral rendition of *Happy Days are Here Again.*

Life threatened to simply go on without so much as a nod to the ignobility of it all.

The previous evening there had been a phone call from Gideon Culpepper who owned Culpepper's Garage where Bubba worked. They'd had an agreement whereby Bubba would refrain from staining the good name of Culpepper's Garage while he tried to clear up the mystery of the Christmas Killer's identity. Now that Nancy Musgrave had been apprehended, Gideon was anxious to get things back to standard operating procedure. So why wasn't Bubba back at work like a good troop?

Bubba didn't intend on going back to work for Gideon until he found Willodean, and he didn't bother returning the message.

There were other things to do, and Bubba still had some savings to live on. His situation wasn't urgent but hers was.

186

If he dared to put a time limit on the length of days or weeks he would search for Willodean, then it would be like stabbing a knife into his own back.

Calling back Gideon automatically went on the bottom of Bubba's mental checklist.

Instead he took care of personal business and showered off dog drool. Getting dressed and tromping downstairs ensued. He fed his pet while she did a little dance waiting for kibble to descend to the appropriate level for proper consumption.

Bubba got out the largest coffee mug available and filled it up with the life-saving caffeinated liquid that Miz Adelia had already made that morning. He briefly waved at Miz Adelia, who had brought relatives to help with the massive clean-up of the mansion. Apparently, the housekeeper was highly offended about how the place had been left by relatives, police, and various and sundry individuals.

He ate two still-warm cinnamon rolls and didn't think about how the taste of the rolls was off. It wasn't that the rolls weren't up to their usual standard, because they were. But nothing tasted right to Bubba.

After demolishing the hapless kibble, Precious begged for a biscuit and readily got one for her efforts. She swiftly withdrew to the darkness and sanctity beneath the kitchen table to devour her booty.

Bubba stared out the window and contemplated the tasks yet to be completed. Thus far, people had come and gone in his search.

One of those people was still wandering about the house. David Beathard, appareled in purple, told all he was there to save the day, the country, the economy, and the world, not necessarily in that order.

Miz Demetrice made phone calls in the library. She still had a few tricks up her sleeves about finding

Willodean and was trying to pull them all out. The fact that she had on a short sleeve, silk blouse was immaterial.

Jasmine, one of Miz Adelia's nieces, rushed into the kitchen and urgently ran a hand over her face. The agitated action disturbed Bubba's reverie.

"Bubba," she said, "make that man stop talking to me. I cain't get a thing done with all his yammering."

Jasmine was seventeen years old and in her last year of high school. She had saved enough money to start at Texas A&M and would be leaving the following year. She was interested in zoology and had little to no patience with people who interfered with her logical process of achieving her goals.

"Who?"

"The Purple Singing Swinger," Jasmine snarled. She pointed toward the hall.

"Da Dah DAH!" The Purple Singapore Sling called and leaped into the kitchen.

Precious woofed from under the table and withdrew further into the shadows with her biscuit bounty. The valued treat was to be protected from odd men garbed entirely in purple who might steal her dogly booty.

"David," Bubba said, "leave Jasmine alone. She doesn't need to be rescued."

The Purple Singapore Sling frowned in obvious disagreement. "She has wrinkled fingers from sticking her hands in the buckets."

"Miz Adelia has extra rubber gloves under the sink," Bubba said.

Jasmine sighed with exaggeration and retrieved a pair.

"My super senses detect the presence of *Coffea arabica*," The Purple Singapore Sling announced. "I have determined that this genus will be effective on my superhuman aspects." He found a mug and poured himself some. He added cream and three teaspoons of sugar, stirring with a gallant flourish causing some of the liquid to slosh out.

"Shouldn't he be taking some medication now?" Jasmine asked sourly.

"The Purple Singapore Sling does not need human pharmaceutical remedies," he declared. "But coffee is nice."

Jasmine narrowed her eyes at David. She narrowed her eyes at Bubba. "Aunt Adelia said you people were a few Fruit Loops short of a bowl."

Bubba shrugged.

It's probably more than a few, but who's counting?

Jasmine huffed and left the kitchen. "I got work to do," she avowed over her shoulder. "Ain't got time to mess with crazy people."

That made Bubba think of what the youngest Gray had said the night before. She had compared Bubba's going to speak with David Beathard with Clarice Starling going to see Hannibal Lecter. Bubba had read the book years before. He'd heard the movie was good, but he'd never seen it. Considering what happened in the novel, he couldn't see how they could have made it into a movie without using copious amounts of fake blood and gore.

"David," Bubba said, "don't suppose you can tell me about Willodean's stalker now?"

"I will crush the heinous fiend!" The Purple Singapore Sling stated. "I will use my super strength to smash his bones into dust."

"Nothing psychological about this guy?" Bubba asked. "Something that might help me figure out things?"

"He is an iniquitous swine who is undoubtedly up to

shades of evil!"

"And you don't want to go back to the Dogley Institute of, uh, other Superheroes?"

"Their powers are unequal to the task of locating the beautiful sheriff's deputy," David said. "I will stay with you and persevere the way only a true hero can."

"Yep," Bubba said. "That's what I kinda thought you would do."

Bubba thought about asking Dr. George Goodjoint. The elderly doctor was the town's local general practitioner and also acted as the county coroner. He had a passel of degrees mostly from fancy universities. He was also a close friend of the Snoddys.

He's also, Bubba realized, *out of town.* The doctor recently left for a two-week stay in the Caribbean. It was an annual retreat for the physician, where he combined beach bunnyism with free medical care to an island with inadequate medical care. He'd left Pegramville just after the first of the year.

Bubba was disheartened. The island didn't have any regular means of communication besides short-wave radio, and there wasn't another way that he could contact the physician.

I should have thought of Doc Goodjoint before David, er, The Purple Singapore Sling.

Bubba found his disposable cell phone on the kitchen counter where he'd left it charging the evening before. He called Kiki Rutkowski. It was easier to do so because clearly the phone remembered her number.

"Bubba," Kiki said cheerfully. Apparently, her phone recognized his phone, too. "I'm on my way to a class, dude."

"You took a psychology class, right?"

"Well, psych 101. And I got a C in it. Remember?" she said. "Anything about Willy?"

"No, I haven't heard anything," Bubba said sadly.

"Damn. Did you find the stalker guy?"

"No, he's just as gone as Willodean."

There was silence from Kiki. Then she said, "That's not good. But you know, the first report I read was wrong about him attacking Willy. Turned out that it was another guy and that Le Beau was trying to help her. Weird, huh?"

Bubba didn't waste time telling Kiki he already knew that. So he said, "I just don't know anything about stalkers. Can you help me?"

"I don't have my laptop," Kiki said. "Call me back this afternoon. I'll talk to one of the psych professors. Maybe they can offer something. That's what you want, something to pin this dude down with?"

"Anything would be helpful."

"Well, call me later." A tone sounded and she was gone.

"There are genuinely sordid and seamy individuals in the world," The Purple Singapore Sling commented. He took a drink of coffee and covetously eyed the cinnamon rolls.

Bubba put his cell phone down. "I'll say. Some of 'em don't even commit crimes."

"I will rout them out," The Purple Singapore Sling asserted. But the heroic statement was spoiled by the fact that he was attempting to stuff a roll into his mouth at the same time. The words came out as, "I wfluh rooo themph owww."

"Is there any way you can turn back into David Beathard, psychotherapist?" Bubba asked The Purple Singapore Sling. He was tired of thinking of David as The Purple Singapore Sling. Shortening the moniker to initials would be just the thing.

"But I'm a superhero," The PSS declared

triumphantly, having successfully swallowed a great chunk of cinnamon roll without requiring another person to do a Heimlich maneuver. "Beloved by man and woman alike. Able to leap a ten-story building in a single bound. Able to resist the strongest death rays shot from super villains' lairs. I can scan a man's mind with an instant's notice." He stared intently at the faint bump that remained on Bubba's forehead. "I sense you are skeptical."

"I need someone who *knows* about stalkers," Bubba said, mostly to himself.

"Well, then," The PSS replied cheerfully, "I know someone like that."

•

The Myrtlewood Unit was Texas's second largest prison for females. Well before Bubba got within visual range of the unit, he saw the signs alerting drivers they were close to a state institution and not to pick up hitchhikers. One sign had a spray-painted addition, "Especially not girls, dumbass."

"My unique powers determine that we are in the proximity of a super evil power," The PSS said as he hung his head out the window. "This human vehicle obviously has some natural dematerialized effect on my superior abilities."

Bubba glanced at David. "You look car sick."

"Car sickness," The PSS said with aplomb before he took in a gulping breath that belied the aplomb. "Pshaw. I'm not car sick-ulp."

Stopping the truck, Bubba let The PSS toss his cookies on the side of the road. Undoubtedly, they should have skipped KFC's for lunch. Three pieces of extra crispy chicken, a side of mashed potatoes and gravy, and a biscuit did not smell good coming back up and out. Fortunately Bubba had wet wipes, and The PSS felt better after that. The prison was only an hour's drive from Pegram County, but the bumping, jolting ride of the old Chevy truck was too much for The PSS's sensitivities.

"It's the presence of the super villain impacting me," The PSS defended himself.

Thirty minutes later, Bubba was talking to an officer at the visitor's center. He had his truck inspected on the way in. A dog had sniffed over it. The dog's handler wasn't happy about Precious being inside the vehicle, but there wasn't a specific rule against it. They'd been wanded by another correctional officer on the way inside the unit's visitor center. This time Bubba judiciously left his buck knife in his truck with the dog. He also left his cell phone and everything but his driver's license.

None of the correctional officers were happy about The PSS's purple mask. They asked him to remove it again and again. The PSS kept putting it back on.

"I understand your law enforcement mentality," The PSS said calmly to the last officer who asked him to remove the mask. "But I'm The Purple Singapore Sling, a superhero, and the mask conceals my alter ego. All superheroes have secret identities. It's essential."

"He's not going into the unit like that," the correctional officer said to Bubba.

There was a waiting area full of visitors. Most of them eyed The PSS as if he was a new form of alien life. The people in the waiting area probably had seen just about everything now.

They didn't live in Pegram County.

Bubba was directed to another officer who took down his name, examined his driver's license, and consulted another list.

"Huh," the officer said. "You're on the list."

"What does that mean?"

"It means the prisoner added you to a list of approved visitors," the officer said. "Mostly that prisoner has been seeing prosecutors and state-approved defense attorneys."

Bubba frowned.

The correctional officer looked at Bubba. "But then you also had someone from the governor's office call a few hours ago for a special visit. You know most folks have to wait for the weekends. Only special visitors during the weekdays."

Sometimes it was helpful that Bubba's mother had interesting connections. It turned out that the governor's wife and Miz Demetrice both enjoyed a rousing round of poker. Sometimes the state's first lady came zipping over to Thursday night Pokerama and left at dawn to return to Austin. Sometimes she even won.

The officer looked at The PSS. "Do you have a driver's license?"

The PSS appeared offended. "The Purple Singapore Sling doesn't need a driver's license. I fly."

Bubba begged to differ. He'd spent the last hour and a half with The PSS in his truck, and The PSS's breath still smelled like vomit.

The PSS squared off with the correctional officer.

"There wasn't any mention of *him* from the governor's office," the officer said.

"Yeah, well," Bubba said, "let me just speak to The Purple Singapore Sling for a moment, will you, officer?"

"Sure," the officer said.

Bubba took David aside and said, "They're afraid you'll rile up all the prisoners with your superhero-edness." Bubba nodded. *Yeah, That's it.* "Ain't many superheroes in the prison and all. Hey, you probably put half of 'em in here, am I right?"

The PSS nodded slowly. "It's true that a superhero can portray a vivid image of justice and honor."

"And the rest of the women, well, it ain't fair to let them see such an upright specimen of a hero," Bubba said, but he almost choked on his words. "Might make them go crazy with- " Bubba's voice cracked as he made himself finish the statement with a straight face " -lust."

The PSS continued to nod, rubbing his chin with his hand. "You're right, Bubba. I shall remain in here, so as not to taunt or tease the unwary inmates of this institution of rehabilitation. Those poor women couldn't stand the pressure."

The occupants of the waiting room weren't particularly enthused with The PSS's presence but The PSS occupied his time with a magazine called *Today's Prisons* as he settled in to wait.

Bubba was escorted into another area of the prison. He was searched again and his identification re-checked. Finally, he was put into a room with several seats fastened to the floor. Ten minutes later, two correctional officers escorted a handcuffed Nancy Musgrave into the room. She was directed to a seat across from Bubba, and the handcuffs were attached to the arm of the chair.

One officer said, "No funny business, huh?"

Nancy smiled at the officer. "No, sir. Not me."

"We'll be watching," the officer replied skeptically. "You've got ten minutes."

Bubba started to protest at the time limit, but he supposed he should be grateful that he'd gotten the ten minutes at all. It was the middle of the week, and Miz Demetrice had to roust the governor's office for a special phone call to the prison unit.

The two officers retreated to the far side of the room.

Bubba said, "Howdy, Miz Musgrave."

Nancy directed a cold look at Bubba. "And hello to you, as well."

It had been David Beathard's idea to have Bubba ask Nancy Musgrave about stalkers. After all, she had stalked a dozen people for years in her preparation. She had the mentality down pat. She could probably write a book. She even had the right credentials for it.

Nancy didn't look like she was suffering in prison. Her hair was loose and combed neatly. Her eyes sparkled at Bubba as she considered him. The prison wear was similar to scrubs from a hospital except the prison's name had been stenciled on the front and back of the top. She crossed one leg over the other and looked at him.

"I'd say that Ma said hey, but that wouldn't be true," Bubba said. It hadn't dawned on him until he'd reached this point that Nancy didn't have any reason to help him. Even Clarice Starling had to throw Hannibal Lecter a bone for his effort. Certainly, Bubba didn't have a bone, much less any quid pro quo.

"Do tell," Nancy said. "I was rather hoping she'd fallen down a well or something equally final, but my luck probably hasn't changed."

"No, Ma's fine."

Nancy frowned suddenly. "She's...fine." The older woman bit her lip. "They don't let us have a lot of news in here, so I haven't kept up with the headlines. I thought that- "

The lines between Bubba's eyebrows closed into a furrow. Nancy Musgrave had been expecting something else. "You thought something had happened to Ma?"

"No, I haven't heard anything," Nancy said quickly. "Just like I said."

Bubba knew Nancy had convoluted plans

concerning the twelve members of the historical society board. He'd assumed that she hadn't known that his ma would be in jail at the time Nancy had made her move to kill her off, as well as her pesky, interfering son. But had Nancy known exactly where Miz Demetrice was to be located? Had Nancy's plans been something completely different when she came calling at the Snoddy Mansion?

The inevitable question was whether Nancy had enough time to get to Willodean Gray. And Bubba knew Nancy hadn't had the time to do so. She'd been busy trying to burn up Miz Lou Lou Vandygriff and her caregiver, Mattie Longbow. Then she'd run over to the Snoddy Mansion and waited for her objective to arrive. Nancy gave her villainous soliloquy before being zapped by Brownie's homemade stun gun.

"This is about someone else," Bubba said. "The sheriff's deputy, Willodean Gray, is missing."

Nancy was unmistakably dumbfounded. "A missing sheriff's deputy? What in God's name does that have to do with me? There weren't any deputies on my list."

Her evident note of confusion made Bubba feel a teensy bit better. There was always the chance Nancy could have been involved with Willodean's car wreck in some fashion, no matter what the time frame. But only a skilled actress could imitate the surprise in her expression and voice.

"Nothing much, I reckon," Bubba said. "Willodean had a stalker."

"A stalker," Nancy repeated.

"I don't know too many folks who are expert in things psychological," Bubba said, "and furthermore, someone who knows all about stalking."

"You think I'm an expert in stalking," Nancy said blandly.

"Yes, ma'am," Bubba replied. "I'd like your opinion on how a stalker thinks."

"You think a stalker took your sheriff's deputy, and you want my help in understanding this person?" Nancy's face twisted a bit in puzzlement.

"That's it in a nutshell."

"I should be screaming at you," Nancy said. "You and that little crumbsnatcher who stunned me, too. But the shrinks here have me on three different medications. It makes me want to apologize to David Beathard about some of his meds." She shrugged. "*Almost* makes me want to apologize."

"Well, I think David would appreciate that," Bubba said.

Possibly The PSS would, too, but he's busy right now keeping a low profile from simultaneously inciting and inflaming the gals of the prison. Guess I ought not tell the Christmas Killer that particular piece of info.

Chapter Sixteen

Bubba Does Dallas Again

Wednesday, January 4th – Thursday, January 5th

Ten minutes speaking with Nancy Musgrave didn't last long. Nancy didn't really want to share pertinent information with Bubba, and Bubba didn't have anything to trade. Likewise, Bubba wasn't charming and socially adept enough to cleverly pry anything out of the antagonistic murderer.

I guess I ain't Clarice Starling, Bubba thought dejectedly.

When the guards said their time was up, Nancy said brightly, "Well, it's been educational, Bubba. Best of luck with your missing girl."

Bubba glowered. It had been a stupid idea. Nancy wouldn't have helped him because she was angry with him. He'd gotten in the middle of her murder scheme and ruined everything.

I had lots of help and I don't see her blaming all the other folks, dammit.

"I reckon I'll see you at the trial," Bubba said.

Nancy smiled as one of the officers detached the handcuffs from the chair and then re-attached them to her wrists. "Maybe. Maybe I'll plead for a deal. Tell the police where all the bodies are buried." She glanced at the sharp look of one of the correction officers. "Metaphorically speaking of course."

The correctional officers led her out of the room, and Nancy called over her shoulder, "Toodle-oo."

Bubba waited for another guard to escort him back through the halls to the visitor's center. He was searched again and his identification re-verified. Bubba looked down at the guard checking his driver's license for the umpteenth time and said, "What, do you think I switched places with one of the prisoners?"

The guard's lips twitched, and he assessed Bubba's not inconsiderable height. "There are some big girls in here."

Bubba signed out with the officer in the visitor center, and he gestured at The PSS as he went out the door. But then he paused and went back to speak to the correctional officer at the desk. This was the same man who'd said Bubba was on the list.

"Yes," the officer said curiously as he gazed up at Bubba's immense frame.

"You said I was on Nancy's list," Bubba said slowly. "You mean the governor's office added it today?"

The officer consulted a clipboard. "No, the governor's office did call today about you. That's the reason you got let in on a weekday. We only do special visits on weekdays. Attorneys. Paralegals. Social workers and the like. Not usually any family or friends. And it's not like you're her lawyer."

"I was on her list before today?"

The officer looked at the clipboard again. "From the day she walked into Myrtlewood."

"Who else is on the list?"

"Her lawyer, lawyer's assistant, a researcher, a minister, her uncle, and her brother." The officer shrugged. "Cons put down anyone who might visit on account they get bored quickly. A visitor breaks up their routine. It gets to be a big deal."

"Why me?"

The officer shrugged again. "You tell me."

Bubba thanked him and returned to where The PSS was lurking by the door. They got to the truck and let Precious out to mark a patch of nearby grass with her special essence. When they were all loaded up, Bubba said, "David, why would Nancy put me on her visitor's list?"

The PSS absently scratched Precious's head. Precious didn't seem to know the difference between a normal person and a mentally ill person, so she took the scratches with full favor.

But what's normal?

"Nancy's mental status attempts to employ various angles for revenge," The PSS said in a very psychotherapeutic manner.

Bubba looked over to see if David Beathard, psychotherapist, had returned.

Then The PSS said, "just like many a vicious, sociopathic serial villain."

Guess not.

"You spent lots of time with her," Bubba said.

"She was my social worker," The PSS said simply. "Not that a superhero really needs a social worker."

Bubba turned toward Dallas instead of Pegram County. "Guess we're going on a road trip."

"Goody," The PSS said. "I like road trips. Exceptin' we might want to stop and get some Dramamine." He looked around to see if anyone was listening. *"My alter ego gets car sick,"* he whispered so no criminal scoundrels could immorally obtain such valuable information about a superhero's weaknesses.

"Yep," Bubba said. "That sounds about right."

•

Upon reaching Dallas without fanfare from the temperamental Chevy truck, Bubba checked into the same hotel. He got The PSS a room next to his, and he even stopped at a Walmart to get a change of clothing for David. It wasn't easy finding purple clothing in the men's section. Finally, a clerk suggested that they get some larger women's wear that was in the right colors. They found an XXL purple t-shirt and some tall purple jeans that were only a little big on The PSS. Bubba didn't want to see what purple underwear The PSS had selected from the women's lingerie section.

"They have special little sequins that give my loins tremendous capabilities," The PSS told Bubba despite the fact that he really didn't want to know.

Resisting the urge to plug his ears and say repeatedly, "I'm not listening," Bubba broke out one of his few credit cards and paid for everything.

Lord, please don't let The PSS tell me what kind of superpowers his loins have.

Finally, Bubba had a free moment and called Kiki Rutkowski back.

"Dude," she said. "The bubba who's a real Bubba."

"Kiki," Bubba said. "I'm right sorry I didn't call you back earlier. I got a bit busier than a one-eyed cat watching three mouse holes."

"And let's come back to *that* later," Kiki said, enthused.

"About stalkers?"

"Boy, you don't like to stop and smell the flowers," she said chirpily, not sounding upset in the least. "Well, the prof told me some stuff. Guy thought I was talking about me and wanted me to see the campus police. Haha. He doesn't know I carry mace and brass knuckles in my tote. Let some guy try to stalk Kiki. He'd be one sorry SOB in the hospital."

Bubba sighed.

"Oh, sorry, Bubba. I get carried away. Stalkers. Stalkers. Stalkers. What did the prof tell me? I jotted down notes on my iPad. He said they don't take no for an answer. Let's see. They're OCD by nature."

"OCD?"

"Obsessive compulsive disorder. They fixate on someone or something and don't let go. Even though this guy was in prison, he was still thinking about Willy. Maybe he even manages to get more information about her. When he gets out, he's still thinking about her. Although sometimes they do move onto different targets, especially since the initial one might be out of their range of control."

"Okay. He's still writing her letters, so he found her address somehow." Bubba cogitated. "Maybe he conned it out of her family."

"They usually have above-average intelligence, which isn't a good thing for the police or the victims."

"So Le Beau's smart." Bubba didn't care for that. It meant that Le Beau was capable of saying the things that Guillermo Sanchez wanted to hear and making the parole officer think that Le Beau was attempting to straighten out his life.

"They don't usually have any other personal relationships besides the one they're trying to force on their victims," Kiki said.

"No close friends."

"They typically have low self-esteem," Kiki went on. "Because of the low self-esteem, they have a need to make up for it with a false relationship with their victim."

"Don't feel good about himself," Bubba restated.

"And they can become violent," Kiki finished reluctantly, "especially when they're thwarted."

Bubba really didn't like that. It fit with the scenario, however. Le Beau got out of prison. He played a role for a while until he found Willodean Gray, again. Then he pounced.

Figuring out how to use this information was going to be the difficult part for Bubba.

Bubba and The PSS ate at a local diner where The PSS gave superhero advice to several interested men who appeared a half step above homeless. Plainly, the diner saw its fair share of oddballs and no one called the police to intervene. Interestingly enough, the men seemed to view the superhero persona as David's "gig" and were properly impressed with his thoroughness.

Later that night, Bubba even managed to get a decent night's rest on the brick-like mattress. He only woke up once, having been dreaming about Willodean crying out for help and no one answering her.

The next morning Bubba took The PSS to the construction office where Howell Le Beau was employed. He didn't pretend to be a police officer or anything other than what he was. He didn't even attempt to get The PSS to wait in the truck with the dog.

The secretary at the construction office wouldn't tell Bubba anything about Howell Le Beau. She kept a wary eye on the two of them and offered up a simple reason for her noncompliance.

"We've gotten calls from the police already," she said dryly. The name plate on the dingy-gray metal desk said she was Edith Hanson.

Edith looked Bubba up and down with the practiced ease of someone who was used to sizing up numerous people who might be trying to pull the wool over her eyes. Then she looked The PSS up and down. "And you don't look like police officers to me."

Bubba wasn't up to clever manipulations, not that he ever relied on them. That was more his mother's shtick. Instead, he went with the down-and-dirty truth. "There's a woman missing. She's kind, clever, and beautiful. She doesn't back down from a fight, and she helps folks out who need a hand. Maybe this Le Beau's got something to do with it. Maybe he ain't. But he needs to be found."

"Le Beau hasn't come back to work," Edith said with a frown.

Bubba wasn't certain, but possibly Edith had been impressed with his descriptive detail of the lovely Willodean Gray's character.

"What do you know about Le Beau?" The PSS asked politely. "Every little nuance counts, you know, when profiling a personality."

"You know this woman personally?" Edith said to Bubba, trying to not look at The PSS. It was difficult to avoid his larger-than-life purple presence.

"Yes, I know her."

"What will you do to Le Beau if you find him?"

"I'd ask him a few questions about Willodean Gray and where she might be located," Bubba answered sincerely. It occurred to him that Edith was being rather protective of Howell Le Beau's civil rights. The secretary of a small construction company probably dealt with many, if not all of the employees. She knew Le Beau. Squeezing Edith Hanson for information was better than speaking to other construction workers who were employed alongside Le Beau.

"Hurt him?"

"I don't want to hurt anyone," Bubba also said sincerely.

The PSS was staring intently at Edith's forehead. She reached up and nervously brushed a set of bangs out of the way.

"He's freaking me out," Edith said.

"Uh, David, you're freaking her out," Bubba said to The PSS.

"I sense that she knows more that's she letting on," The PSS stated without looking away from Edith.

Edith leaned back as if the action would put The PSS

out of mental telepathic range. "What's he doing?"

"I have the power to scan men's minds," The PSS said earnestly. "Also women's." Then he added enigmatically, "*Especially* women's."

Edith shot a look at Bubba. "Is he kidding?"

Bubba shrugged. "Don't reckon so. The Purple Singapore Sling is pretty much dead serious." *So's David Beathard for that matter. Probably David's other personas, too.*

"The Purple Singapore Sling?" Edith repeated nervously. "Isn't that some kind of alcoholic drink?"

"And a superhero," The PSS declared, focusing his gaze on her forehead even more intently.

"If I was looking for Howell," Edith said quickly, leaning back further in her chair, attempting to get as far away from The PSS as she could, "I would check his church. He's very Christian. Spoke about it a lot."

Bubba glanced at The PSS. David wasn't altogether useless. *Ain't that something?*

"What church is that?"

"The First Unity Fellowship of Garland," she said hastily. "It's off I-30 to the east."

The PSS straightened up. "Thank you, madam, for your gracious assistance toward the cause of justice and fortitude."

Edith uneasily rubbed her forehead. "Yeah, don't tell Howell I told you."

•

It wasn't difficult to find the First Unity Fellowship of Garland. It was a very large, very modern eyesore planted just off the freeway. It also had three billboards that proclaimed its presence. The billboards were almost larger than the church and that wasn't saying that the church was small because it wasn't.

"Do you think that Edith told Investigator Park

about the church?" Bubba asked The PSS.

"Who's Investigator Park?" The PSS asked Bubba.

"Probably not," Bubba surmised. "Guess she didn't want to get involved with something like that. Lots of them fellas that work that site looked like they was rehabilitated members of society. Ifin she works with them regularly like, then she wouldn't want to be seen as a stool pigeon."

"The criminal justice system is geared to restore and reeducate those offenders who genuinely desire a second chance," The PSS said chidingly.

"Some of 'em, I reckon," Bubba acknowledged.

They parked in the large lot of the church and stared at the building. A huge central building dominated the area with two wings stretching out to either side. People wandered in and out occasionally, as though on schedule. It was just enough activity to indicate services were not being performed. After all, it was a Thursday and the middle of the day.

Bubba let Precious out to take care of dogly business in the form of sniffing and marking all of the recently planted trees in the parking medians. She rooted happily and gleefully spread the canine cologne.

The PSS pointed out the security cameras in the lot watching them.

"It's possible that they don't appreciate that a canine has eliminatory needs," The PSS ventured, "specifically on their property."

Or they caught sight of a masked purple man in the parking lot and aren't happy about that.

"Maybe this is a job for your alter ego," Bubba suggested. "Go undercover and all."

The PSS crossed his arms over his chest. "I'm beginning to suspect that you lack faith in my ability to contribute capably in this investigation."

"You did real good with Edith back at the construction company's office," Bubba said genuinely.

The PSS smirked. "I did, didn't I? What she was really thinking was that she wanted chocolates and needed to have her legs waxed." He gave a brief shudder as if gazing into the intricacies of the female persuasion was unsettling.

Bubba blinked. *Maybe The PSS could help out with the church. After all, ifin they were Christian like they would understand man comes in all varieties.*

A security guard met them in front before they could go inside. He was almost as tall as Bubba but lacked Bubba's width in the chest. The lack of breadth didn't stop the man from planting himself squarely in their paths.

"What's your business here?" the guard asked coldly. He stared more at The PSS than at Bubba, and Bubba figured out that he was correct. All kinds of folks got nervous around a man in a mask when it wasn't even close to Halloween.

"We're looking for some help," Bubba said honestly. It was probable that the Dallas PD had already come calling on the church about Howell Le Beau, and Bubba wanted to get a foot in the door before they said they couldn't help.

The guard gazed frankly at The PSS. "Yeah, I guess you do at that."

"I am The Purple Singapore Sling," The PSS announced boldly. He put his hands akimbo and expanded his chest accordingly. "I require assistance with an investigation into a life and death matter. As a fellow law enforcer you could be integral in aiding us and bringing a young woman back into the loving bosom of her desperate family."

"I could?" the guard said. He appeared engrossed.

"You could," Bubba agreed.

The guard thought about it. "You need the wing around back. It's marked as Entrance C. They'll hook you up."

"Much obliged," Bubba said.

The PSS gave the guard a sincere nod. "Your gracious support will be noted in the public annals for record."

"Yeah, you betcha," the guard said doubtfully. He pointed in the direction they needed to go.

Bubba and The PSS found Entrance C. It was a wing of the larger church building and a tidy little sign on the side of the door proclaimed it as "First Unity Fellowship Mental Health Outreach." Sighing, Bubba rang the bell anyway.

A young woman met them at the door. "Security called about your special needs," she said. She smiled at them. She was bright and cheerful and informed them she was a social worker and ready to help with anyone who had mental health issues. She particularly directed her benign gaze upon the man dressed entirely in purple. Moreover, she informed them the church's mental health outreach was determined on a case-by-case basis and had a sliding scale in order to facilitate assistance to every socio-economic level.

All of this information was imparted as she escorted them into a waiting room.

"We'll need to fill out some paperwork," she said and introduced herself as Neely Smith.

Thirty minutes later, Bubba had convinced Neely Smith that David Beathard wasn't an immediate threat to himself or anyone else.

"No death threats?" she asked.

"He thinks he's different people," Bubba said sotto voce.

Bubba and the social worker sat in the small waiting area as they discussed The PSS. Meanwhile, The PSS was attempting to rescue a potted plant from a darkened corner. "This calamitous shrub needs more sunlight," he proclaimed.

"I wish I was a supermodel sometimes," Neely said wistfully, "But I'm only five foot one. So if you're not here about him- " she waved at The PSS " -then why are you here?"

"Howell Le Beau," Bubba said simply.

"Can't talk about him," Neely said immediately. Her cheerful face closed off.

Bubba frowned. "Have the police called about him already?"

"No, I haven't heard from the police," Neely replied after a moment of thought.

"Do you know Howell Le Beau?"

"I cannot confirm or deny that," Neely barked.

Bubba puzzled over the answer. It wasn't exactly what he was expecting to hear.

The PSS turned to them after nudging the Wandering Jew plant into a patch of sunlight. "My superhero senses determine that the social worker knows more than she's letting on."

"Has he made any threats of suicide?" Neely asked about The PSS.

"Have you?" Bubba asked The PSS.

"Superheroes don't commit suicide," The PSS professed. "Unless we're sacrificing ourselves for the good of human kind. And that's kind of a rarity. It usually involves saving the woman we love or the universe from catastrophic disaster. That sort of thing."

"Howell Le Beau," Bubba repeated, trying to get back on point.

"I cannot divulge information about Mr. Le Beau,"

Neely said firmly.

"You have an outpatient clinic here," The PSS said thoughtfully. "I notice the building goes back significantly, leading me to believe that there is a substantial amount of working space. Is the church licensed for inpatient clinical work, as well?"

Neely frowned. "We have a small inpatient clinic for special-needs patients. Mostly they're drying out from substance abuse. We have two psychiatrists on staff and a clinical psychologist."

The PSS nodded firmly. "She can't talk about Le Beau because he's a patient here," he said astutely.

Neely's mouth opened and then snapped shut.

Wow. The PSS is better than truth serum, Bubba thought. But then he immediately glowered. It wasn't as though Bubba was getting the information that he wanted.

"But client/therapist privileges of confidentiality are somewhat obscured when it comes to psychotherapists who are not licensed," The PSS went on. "And unlicensed social workers," he added perceptively.

Bubba glanced at David. *Is David the psychotherapist back?*

"I'm almost licensed," Neely protested. "And I'm not practicing right now."

"Knowledge of mental health laws aids in the business of being a superhero," The PSS added smugly to Bubba.

"Le Beau *is* a patient at your clinic?" Bubba asked. A sinking feeling began at his chest and was pushing all of his intestines into the ground. "How long?"

Neely bit her lip. She was trying to think how she was supposed to handle this.

"A social worker can reveal the length of treatment for an individual," The PSS said gently. "There's no violation in protocol if you're not revealing why the individual is being treated."

"He's been in treatment for several months now," Neely said reluctantly. "I'd have to check the dates, but there's no question of his commitment to the course of treatment."

"Outpatient treatment," The PSS stated. "How long in inpatient treatment?"

"Since last week."

"Because he lost his place to live?" Bubba asked mildly.

"How do you- " Neely started to ask and then cut herself off. "That's part of it," she added.

"Do you know what day Le Beau came in?" Bubba insisted in a moderate tone. "It's very important."

"It's a matter of life or death," The PSS supplemented.

"Whose life?" Neely asked quickly.

"There's a woman missing," Bubba said. "The woman that Le Beau was convicted of stalking."

"Knowledge of threats against individuals is part of a therapist's obligation to divulge to the potential victim or the rightful authorities. In specific situations, clinicians are compelled to breach confidentiality in order to protect. The case that brought this to light was *Tarasoff Versus Regents of the University of California*." The PSS paused to allow Neely to grasp the information. "The young woman was murdered by a man under therapeutic treatment who had made explicit threats against her person."

Neely goggled at The PSS.

The PSS glanced at Bubba. "More useful information to use in my superhero capacity." He meaningfully tapped the side of his head with his index finger. "Knowledge is power."

"Howell's trying to work past that," Neely protested indignantly. "And he was inpatient here a full day before that sheriff's deputy disappeared. They've got checks every hour, and he certainly was present the entire time so- oh, crap." She slapped a hand over her mouth. "I can't believe I said that," she mumbled through her hand.

Bubba's heart dropped. If Neely was correct, and he had every reason to think that she was being honest in her indignation, then Howell Le Beau had nothing to do with Willodean's disappearance.

Someone else was involved, and Bubba didn't have a clue as to who the person was.

Chapter Seventeen

Bubba Hits a Brick Wall, The PSS Blows Chunks Again,
and
Then Some Other Stuff Happens

Thursday, January 5th

In the parking lot, Bubba's legs collapsed like rubber. He'd managed to herd The PSS and himself out of the First Unity Fellowship Mental Health Outreach clinic before the social worker called the police on them. Neely Smith abruptly realized that the obscure pair wasn't Joe Friday and Bill Gannon. Neither were they Perry Mason and Paul Drake. They might have been a bizarre Abbott and Costello, but all bets were off.

Bubba sank onto a grass median and put his head down.

The PSS stopped near him and didn't say anything. Finally, he touched Bubba's shoulder and murmured, "It's a good thing. We found the stalker. That's good, right?"

Bubba let out a dismayed breath. "It's good, but it ain't good."

The PSS sat down beside Bubba and spent a moment adjusting his purple mask. "It's cold today," he commented. "Wonder if I can find a purple coat that's suitable?"

Bubba wasn't aware of the temperature at the moment. But once The PSS has said something about it, all Bubba could wonder was, *Is Willodean cold right now? Does she have a jacket?*

Then self-flagellation came like a lightning bolt out

of the sky during the spring. *Stupid. Stupid. Stupid. It's not Le Beau, at all. He sent the letters, but he's practically as good as gold as to be excluded. If not Le Beau, then who? How many days has she been out there? How many days before a small woman like that dies of dehydration?*

"Oh, Jesus," he muttered.

"Why isn't it good?" The PSS enquired politely.

"Willodean went missing on Thursday, December 29th," Bubba said brokenly. "Le Beau was *here* then. No chance of mistakes, ifin that gal, Neely, is correct. I don't believe she's incorrect, but I'll tell that police investigator about Le Beau all the same. Christ, Le Beau probably mailed his letters from here."

The letter that Bubba had read popped into his head. Le Beau had written to Willodean, *"I'm watching out for you. I hope for forgiveness."* Bubba had put the worst possible connotation on the words, but it was imaginable that Le Beau had been doing exactly what Guillermo Sanchez and Neely Smith said he was doing. He was trying to rehabilitate himself.

Are the letters a way of saying sorry?

But the letters really didn't matter anymore if Le Beau had been at the inpatient program when Willodean vanished. Bubba clenched his large hands into fists and wished that he could break something.

*No, I don't want to break something. I want to break some*one. *The someone who had snatched Willodean away from the rest of the world.*

"We could go back inside and ask to speak with Le Beau," The PSS suggested. "Just to be certain."

"They ain't gonna let us," Bubba said, "and it might be a bigger waste of time than what I've already done wasted."

"You've done what you could do," The PSS said positively. "It's been a good effort."

Bubba didn't know how to respond to the man that was clearly certifiable. *Voluntary commitment? Really? No,* really?

"The police will have to confirm the man's whereabouts," The PSS commented. "But there must be other suspects."

"Some person who wanted to do something against Willodean," Bubba said slowly. "Maybe a random fella who thought she looked perty." The latter conjecture made his guts twist into tight knots of despair. A random individual would be next to impossible to trace. Ten years from now, the random individual might get apprehended in another crime where DNA evidence was extensive. In order to get out of the death penalty, someone might confess to Willodean's abduction and murder and say he threw her body in a river of which he couldn't quite recall the name or location.

"Indiscriminate kidnappings are extraordinarily rare despite extensive media exposure." The PSS thought about it. "And kidnapping police officers is even rarer."

"But they do happen," Bubba snarled.

"Mostly, abductions are committed by family members or people known to the victim," The PSS continued, a note of seriousness in his voice reaching out to Bubba.

That note of please-pay-attention-to-me made Bubba's head snap up. "What do you know, David?"

The PSS looked at the sky. "Looks like it might snow today. I hate the snow. It zaps my superhero strength. Can we go back to Walmart for a jacket? I think I saw a purple one in the women's section. It had fake fur around the neck. It also had Tinker Bell on it."

"David, you tried to warn me about Nancy," Bubba said. "I'm right sorry I didn't see it. You and Jesus Christ and Thelda. All three of you tried in your own way. I didn't see it or listen to it on account that you're, well, crazy. But I'm listening now."

"I'm not crazy," The PSS asserted forcefully. He put his hands on his waist and puffed out his chest, which was difficult considering he was still seated. "I'm a superhero."

Bubba looked away to keep himself from saying something that he would later regret. He saw the security guard coming around the corner of the building, accompanied by three other security guards. He jumped to his feet and motioned at The PSS. "Come on, David. I cain't go to jail again. They won't let me out of county for the next thirty days ifin I show my face to the judge here again."

"I like judges," The PSS said as he got to his feet and followed Bubba. "Judges like superheroes."

Bubba put his hands in the air and called to the security guards, "We're leaving."

The guards paused and watched them as they crossed over the parking lot to the old Chevy truck and clambered inside. Precious glared at the guards from the open window. She had scrambled over The PSS's lap to get to the window so that she could show them her utter disregard.

They got back on the interstate and headed into downtown Dallas. Bubba didn't have a plan to keep him focused any longer. All he had was bits and pieces of what-the-hell-am-I-doing. He had a Basset hound who enjoyed nipping first and asking questions later. His truck was on the edge of implosion because it was nearly a sexagenarian and there weren't enough stock parts in the world to make it run exactly right. His mother ran an illegal poker game when someone wasn't trying to murder her for perceived past offenses. He hadn't gotten beat up lately, but that was probably because he hadn't been standing still. No one had come digging holes on the Snoddy Estate for possibly a week or more because they were all thinking that murderers were gathering en masse, and it might not be safe with a shovel there.

And finally, Bubba had a loony riding shotgun.

Nothing made sense.

"David," Bubba said again. "Tell me what you know about Willodean's disappearance."

"My superhero powers have detected nothing of the deputy's mysterious vanishing," The PSS intoned solemnly.

"You said abductions are by folks who know the person and who are close to them," Bubba said. He narrowly avoided a Ford Pinto and received a single-fingered salute from a woman wearing a ten-gallon hat driving a Toyota Tacoma.

"People who are known to the victim," The PSS corrected.

"You're saying Willodean got kidnapped by someone known to her," Bubba phrased.

"Oh my, I think I need another Dramamine," The PSS said faintly as Bubba's truck lurched into another lane.

"Did Nancy Musgrave say anything about kidnapping Willodean Gray?" Bubba demanded.

"No," The PSS said firmly. "Nancy Musgrave did not say anything about kidnapping Willodean Gray."

Bubba thought about it. That sounded as if David was trying to tell the truth but not the *whole* truth. "Did Nancy Musgrave say anything about killing Willodean Gray?"

"Oh great balls of fire, no," The PSS said scathingly. "She wanted to kill Miz Demetrice. She wanted to kill the sheriff. She wanted to kill you, but that was later on. She wanted to kill her ex-husband, but that wasn't related to the Christmas list of killings. Her ex-husband had some issues about strippers that were very fascinating to hear about. She wanted to kill her mother for naming her LaNell Nancy Roquemore. She thought about killing her manicurist, but that was a joke, I think. Can you not swerve so much, Bubba?"

"Did Nancy even talk about Willodean?"

"No. I'm pretty sure about that, but that was while I was in one of my alter egos, and Nancy was able to subdue me with psychotropic medications." The PSS smiled grimly. "They wouldn't work now." He considered. "But possibly Dramamine has an effect on me that other human medications don't." His voice lowered to a whisper. "Like kryptonite on Superman, except it doesn't weaken me. It saves me from puking on your dog."

Precious whined and inched closer to Bubba on the bench seat.

Bubba slowed down. It was the way that The PSS had answered the question about whether Nancy had wanted to kidnap Willodean. He'd said, *"No. Nancy Musgrave did not say anything about kidnapping Willodean Gray."* If there had been a little emphasis on the words, "Willodean Gray," then the statement would mean something very different. "Did Nancy ever talk about kidnapping anyone?"

"Yes."

Bubba glanced at The PSS. He was busy hanging his head out the half-open window. The wind was whipping the tail of his scarf around. Several people riding in a yellow Chevy Camaro were goggling at him. One even had his iPhone out and was taking a picture of The PSS.

"Who?" Bubba insisted.

But The PSS immediately vomited out the window.

The Camaro instantly veered. Two other cars swerved in reaction. Bubba sighed as he heard horns honking and squealing brakes from behind him.

●

By the time they reached the bedraggled hotel, The PSS was equally bedraggled. Another trip to Walmart had involved getting replacement clothing for The PSS so he could change and they could wash the vomit covered ones. Bubba had spent the time at the Laundromat cleaning out the passenger-side of the interior of the truck.

Precious had spent the time rollicking with a beagle who had clearly escaped the confines of a local yard. The beagle fled when a middle-aged woman carrying a leash approached calling, "Here, Socrates. Here, boy. I've got treats."

The PSS laid on the floor of the Laundromat recovering from motion sickness. He answered Bubba's insistent questions with aggrieved moans of misery. The other customers of the Laundromat had congregated on the far side of the store while trying to ignore the man in the purple mask rolling around on the floor.

Two hours after their impudent visit at the First Unity Fellowship Mental Outreach, they returned to the hotel. The PSS was feeling better enough to suggest dinner. "Buffalo chicken wings," The PSS said loudly, "with ranch dip. Possibly greasy fries."

Bubba was about to demand The PSS tell him who Nancy had talked about kidnapping, when two other noteworthy things happened. He pulled into a parking place that wasn't far from the front stoop of the dilapidated hotel, and a small figure stepped off the bottom step.

Janie stood on the sidewalk, gazing at them with

impunity. She wore a little "DPD" t-shirt and jeans with Twinkle Toe shoes peeping out. She also had a jacket that looked too light for the diminishing temperature. She stared at them expectantly, and Bubba knew she had been waiting for them to arrive. Bubba looked around but didn't see anyone nearby even remotely resembling a mother figure.

"Look, it's that little girl who knows about purple straightjackets," The PSS exclaimed cheerfully. "I like smart little children." He frowned. "Except Brownie. That kid's going to kill someone. Or maybe grow up to be President." He turned to Bubba. "Did you see him on the news the other morning? There's nothing like a good tasering to a national news figure to make institutional patients laugh like loons." He paused again. "That wasn't a pun."

Bubba got out of the truck and let Precious out. The Basset hound bounded over to Janie and licked her hand. The dog had been stuck with two increasingly melancholy humans and desperately needed tactile reassurance. Janie made a cooing noise and was happy to comply.

The PSS followed and put his new purple jacket on with exaggerated flair. He adjusted the fake-fur collar and his eyes perused the area for local super villains about to strike. Instead he found people on their way home from blue-collar jobs and on their way to anywhere else and anywhere in-between.

"Janie," Bubba said as he came around the truck, "what are you doing here? This ain't the best of areas for a kid. And where's your mama? Or your granny? Or maybe a SWAT team?"

"I caught a ride with one of the patrolmen who came down to look for Auntie Wills," Janie said peremptorily. "He dropped me off at the house. Although Dad's undercover in Fort Worth, we've got all kinds of other family at home. My dad's sister, Alexa, and her kids, Dakota and Austin. Granny Redgrave, that's my dad's mother, is there, but she was drinking Muscatine wine. So I slipped out and caught the DART." The look she shot him said, "Duh, what else would I do?"

Bubba looked confused because Janie added in explanation, "Dallas Area Rapid Transit."

"Why are you here? How did you know where I was?" Bubba asked. "Where's my cell phone because I got to call your ma before your granny comes and shoots me in the head."

"Oh, tosh," Janie said. She glanced around. "You know they do drug deals in this hotel? Auntie Wills wouldn't want you to stay here."

"I could have stayed at Aunt Caressa's," Bubba said as he searched his pockets for the little disposable phone, "but it's way out of town, and since she snores like a cat throwing up hairballs, it ain't a great place to spend the night. I reckon I could have stayed there on my earlier visit, but I just didn't think of it."

"Have you seen any super villains, little girl?" The PSS interjected, evidently feeling left out.

Janie cast a grimace at The PSS, then went back to Bubba. "Grandma knows where you're at. You've got a little GPS unit in your phone. That investigator gave her the number, and the rest is pretty much conclusive." Her face was superior. One eyebrow arched smugly. "You shouldn't underestimate the police force."

Bubba had finally retrieved the phone and was gazing at it in dismay. He didn't have a clue as to what Janie was talking about. "There's a GPS in my phone?" There was a wave of bitter anger. "Stupid, cheap phone can find me, but Willodean's can't find *her*."

Janie's shoulders drooped at the grave statement.

Precious nudged her hand again and the eight-year-old bent to pet the dog. "Aren't that many cell phone towers down in Pegram County," she said shortly.

"Why are you here?" Bubba asked numbly. He didn't want to talk about the lack of cell phone towers in Pegram County. He certainly didn't want to discuss that he had found Le Beau and that Willodean's former stalker had an ironclad alibi for the time of her disappearance. He most certainly didn't want to converse about the fact that he didn't know what to do next.

"They're coming up with dead ends in Pegramville," Janie said flatly. "I heard Grandma talking about you. She didn't know if you could find out something, but there's always a shot even with you bumbling about like a big unwanted turd. I wanted to help."

"Do turds really bumble about?" The PSS asked conversationally.

Bubba stared at Janie. *Great. I've got The Purple Singapore Sling and eight-year-old detective-in-training, Janie, helping me. I don't even know the kid's last name and her ma's going to have me arrested for kidnapping her.*

"I'm going to call your ma," he said slowly. "You want to give me the number so she don't worry?"

"They won't know I'm missing for hours," Janie said confidently. "Get me up to speed on the investigation. We've got perps to shake down."

"You know, it's cold outside," The PSS said. "Cold zaps my superpowers. Makes other things shrivel up, too. Things best not discussed in front of little ears."

"He's right," Janie said. "Let's get coffee. Chink. Chink."

Bubba looked confused again so Janie added, "It's the sound cups make when you're pouring coffee."

Janie's unexpected appearance was the first noteworthy thing that happened. The second noteworthy thing took a little while longer to unfurl.

Bubba glanced around and saw a diner across the street. The diner's shopworn appearance was worse than the hotel's, and one could probably slap a saddle on a cockroach roaming there and ride it away. But on the positive side, the shop was in the open, and he thought Celestine would appreciate if he waited there with Janie instead of inside the hotel room.

Maybe Willodean's ma will only shoot one of my kneecaps instead of killing me outright.

"You can have milk," Bubba growled.

Janie rolled her eyes.

Bam Bam Jones stepped around the corner of the hotel and called, "Bubba, my brotha. Glad to see you on the out and out. We gots to get you to that psychic. She says she knows all." His hands whizzed and snapped and moved as he walked down the sidewalk. He was wearing a Saints jacket today with plain blue jeans. But his boots were knee high and made of scarlet red leather.

Abruptly, Bam Bam froze when he saw Janie. "Oh strawberry shortcake and molasses," he muttered dejectedly. "Do you know who that be?" He pointed at Janie.

"A pain in my- " Bubba started to say before Janie protested with, "Hey, watch your mouth, civilian. I know policemen, and they will take my word before yours any day of the week."

"I gotta *go*," Bam Bam said rapidly. He turned in his tracks and went back the way he'd come. He paused at the corner and called to Bubba, "Folks be looking for you, Bubba. I think maybe the po-donkey-donks came by earlier. That little gel right there been waiting awhile. Watch out for her. She bites and when you ain't done nothing to her, neither."

"You called my mother a *ho*," Janie snarled.

"I dint mean nothing by it," Bam Bam said sincerely. "Bad habit to use them words. I'll try not to do it no more."

Precious barked once and looked longingly at the doors. Apparently she was cold, too.

Bubba stared at Bam Bam's retreating figure. "What's a po-donkey-donk?"

Janie shrugged. "Another way of saying police. Probably Investigator Park looking for you. They said you've been sticking your nose in their business again." She thought about it. "Like you weren't supposed to do, but hey, if it helps find Auntie Wills, then I'm cool with it. I'll speak to the judge on your behalf. Judges love me."

"Me, too. But really, it's cold," The PSS whined.

"The diner," Bubba said. He hadn't called Charles Park either. He needed to call Park, then Anora Gray, and then his mother, not necessarily in that order.

"And there was some other peeps, too," Bam Bam's voice echoed down the street. "Best you be easing down the road, Bubba."

Bubba looked around and realized that the street had just become empty. It was downtown, and downtown was almost never empty. Furthermore, it was Thursday night, and there had been a dozen people coming and going just a few minutes previously. The entire area suddenly cleared out as if someone rang a dinner bell and a Great White shark cruised past.

The PSS looked around him and said, "I sense something bad is about to happen."

Janie blew air out through her mouth. "Let's get that coffee. I need to know what- "

A very large black Suburban screeched to a halt beside them. The doors opened, and two mean looking men pointed guns at them, while a third one simultaneously held the steering wheel and looked out for impertinent witnesses.

"*Sideways*," Janie scoffed. "They don't fire better if you put them sideways. *Gangstas*," she added derisively.

"Get in the car," one man said.

No one moved.

The man sighed. "Get in the car, or I'll shoot you in the foot and drag you in the car."

"Don't worry," The PSS said loudly and put his hands on his waist while pumping out his chest. "Bullets will bounce off my flesh."

"Ya'll mean me?" Bubba asked.

The man who'd spoken glanced at the other man. The driver said, "Hurry up. Big Mama's gonna be pissed the eff off if we don't get back before NCIS starts."

"Yeah," the first man said. "You. And oh, the hell with it. All ya'll get in."

"Cain't leave my dog."

"Oh hell no we're not taking the dog."

"Demetrius, just get them in the 'Burban. Now!"

Precious barked three times. Doors slammed. Wheels squealed. Then the street was empty again.

Getting snatched off the street was the second noteworthy thing that occurred.

Chapter Eighteen

Bubba and the Crime Lord

Thursday, January 5th

It wasn't long before they pulled into a large warehouse in an industrial section of downtown Dallas. Bubba scanned for someone who might see their predicament, but anyone who appeared as if they could help them had vanished into nothingness.

Kind of like Willodean, he thought despondently.

He was still looking when the Suburban drove right inside the warehouse, and a set of oversized garage doors automatically rattled closed behind them. There was enough light left from the setting sun to see that the entire bottom floor of the warehouse was devoid of pretty much everything except the odd box and barrel. However, there were lights coming from the opposite side. One corner of the warehouse had a mezzanine and lights coming from what looked like lampposts surrounding it.

The Suburban parked near where they'd entered the warehouse. A silver Toyota Prius already parked there, looked fairly innocuous next to the larger, more sinister-appearing Suburban.

The three men exited the vehicle and motioned to Bubba, Janie, and The PSS to do the same. Precious remained in the Suburban barking her indignation at deliberately being left behind.

Guns had vanished into pockets, and the unseen threat was enough to persuade Bubba to cooperate. Besides which it was his experience that armed strangers who kidnapped other folks in the middle of a busy downtown area, weren't going to be impressed with a six-foot-four-inch man who menacingly flexed his muscles at them. Of course, he didn't think he had ever been kidnapped before.

Might have happened when I was drunk after I found Melissa in bed with the captain, but nothing stands out.

"You're going to be in big trouble for this," Janie said defiantly to the three men. Her tone was both disparaging and interested, as if she was obliged to act insolent but found being kidnapped intriguing. The tallest one who had been the driver snorted in response.

"Yeah," The PSS agreed. He leaned toward Bubba and whispered, "I can take them as soon as I get warmer. I warned you about the cold obliterating my super strength."

"Let's just see what's going on," Bubba said.

They walked over to where the lights were, and Bubba saw an area that had been converted into a living area with an adjoining kitchen in the corner of the warehouse. The couches were leather and adorned with fake-fur throws. A large-screened LCD television near the couches played a CBS commercial. The kitchen had granite countertops, blonde oak cabinets, and stainless steel appliances.

There was a solitary individual there. The woman who was chopping vegetables on the black-and-brown-speckled granite countertop didn't exactly fit. She was short and round. Her brown eyes twinkled as she efficiently wielded a ten-inch, Santoku knife. Her short, black hair curled in a neat cap around her head. Her burnished flesh glowed with vitality. She wore a flowing purple caftan shot with streams of gold that glittered when she moved.

The PSS said, "Great, it's warm here." He rubbed his hands together and adjusted his Tinker Bell coat.

The lights that looked like lampposts weren't really.

They were outdoor patio heaters that were set up to provide warmth for the open area. Several of the heaters ringed the living/kitchen space in the corner of the warehouse. The entire area was a cloud of balmy heat.

The three men gestured at Bubba, Janie, and The PSS to move a little closer to the woman who was still actively chopping vegetables.

The woman stopped for a moment to stare at the very odd trio. She put the knife down and moved to the side to stir something in a cherry red Dutch oven cooking on the gas stove. She stirred steadily and then put the wooden spoon on a spoon rest and returned to the vegetables.

"You were supposed to return with *just* Bubba Snoddy," she said finally. Even though her words were prickly, her voice was flowing honey.

One of the three men who'd kidnapped them flinched. "They was arguing. Couldn't shoot 'em or nothing anyway."

The large woman pointed the Santoku at Janie. "*That* does not look like Bubba."

"Um, Big Mama," the second man said fretfully.

The large woman pointed the Santoku at The PSS. "*That* does not look like Bubba. I'm not sure what *that* looks like. It's a grown man wearing a purple scarf over his eyes and a Tinker Bell coat. I didn't know coats like that came in that size."

"We got it at Walmart," The PSS said proudly, puffing out his chest.

"And I reckon I hear a dog howling from your 'Burban," Big Mama went on as if The PSS hadn't spoken. "A dog ain't Bubba Snoddy neither."

"Sorry," the third man said. The driver had called him Demetrius. He hung his head a little. "They wouldn't leave the dog. And that dog looked like it was ready to cry."

Finally, Big Mama looked at Bubba. "And you *are* Bubba Snoddy. Big collard green-eating fella like you just has to be a bubba."

It wasn't a question, but Bubba nodded all the same. "I am. Can we get all this kidnapping bizness over? I got to get back to Pegramville on account of a missing gal."

Bubba was almost proud of himself. He supposed he should be nervous because the three of them had been kidnapped, but all he could manage was bothered irritability. He wanted to get back to Pegram County so he might be able to do something else for Willodean.

Something. Anything. Sooner rather than later.

"The sheriff's deputy is the missing girl," Big Mama said firmly and went to work on a batch of celery with the large knife. "All *over* the news."

"Yes, ma'am," Bubba said.

The PSS smacked his lips. "Are you making...gumbo?"

Big Mama's eyes shot up and examined The PSS. "Chicken and sausage gumbo," she said amicably. "You hungry, boy?"

"I'm a superhero," The PSS announced. "Food is energy and energy is power and wait- knowledge is power. Somehow energy becomes knowledge and it's all good. Yes, yes, I am hungry."

Big Mama sighed. "Set yourself down at the table there." She pointed at the dining room table. "The cornbread's about to come out of the oven."

Big Mama's crew gestured at the dining table and the three sat down.

"Can I have coffee?" Janie asked. "I really like coffee."

"Demetrius," Big Mama said, "get that chile some

milk. Your mama's going to be mad as hell at you."

"My ma?" Janie asked.

"No, dear, I meant Bubba's mother, Miz Demetrice," Big Mama said, "although I should have said she's already furious with him. Worried, too."

Bubba glowered. "I meant to call her."

"And what you doing with this little girl and this- " Big Mama paused to look at The PSS again " -I don't know what he is. I don't believe I've ever seen a grown man looking like that. And I know plenty of weird al hootenanny folks."

"I'm a superhero," The PSS said again. He planted his hands on his waist and intrepidly puffed out his chest even though he was sitting in a high-backed, dining room chair.

"He's very special," Big Mama concluded. She finished with the celery and went back to the Dutch oven. She stirred vigorously. "This here is the roux. The secret to a good roux is a slow even heating. You got to get it to that copper penny color. Stir. Stir. Stir."

"I guess you know Ma," Bubba ventured.

"I do," Big Mama said. "Play poker with her about every couple months, too. She's up ten thousand dollars on me. Girl be lucky at cards. Bluffs like a mutha."

"But jeez," Demetrius protested, "you get mad at me for playing a $5 quick pick at Lotto."

"Different odds, boy."

Bubba relaxed. "Ma called you today?"

"Miz Demetrice did," Big Mama affirmed. "Said you're skating on the wrong side of the ice." She waved her spoon around as if pointing at all of Texas. "And there ain't much ice in Texas."

"This woman knows Miz Demetrice," The PSS said, finally climbing on board the train of impending clarity.

Janie said, "Duh. Everyone knows Miz Demetrice.

Big Mama, too."

Demetrius put a glass of milk in front of Janie. She glared at it.

"So why not just ask me to come down and talk to you?" Bubba asked.

Big Mama started on the onions with her big knife. "I gotta reputation, boy. Big Mama doesn't *ask* nothing."

•

The gist of it was that Miz Demetrice couldn't get in touch with Bubba through his cell phone. He hadn't figured out how to access the voice messages on it, so he wasn't aware of the twenty-odd ones waiting for him. Investigator Charles Park called Miz Demetrice and Sheriff John about him. The secretary at the construction company, Edith Hanson, called Park about Bubba. The social worker at the church, Neely Smith, called the DPD about Bubba and The PSS, but especially about The PSS. Nial Sutton, owner of a yellow Chevy Camaro, called the DPD about a man dressed entirely in purple who was riding in an old, green truck on Interstate 30 and who had vomited all over his brand-new car.

Obviously, Janie's mother hadn't yet gotten the word that her daughter was mysteriously absent.

No one had called about The PSS's absence which made Bubba a little sad.

But Miz Demetrice had called her old friend, Big Mama of Dallas. Evidently, Big Mama had certain connections and quickly located Bubba. Rather her minions had located Bubba.

Big Mama explained as she constructed the gumbo. She also explained about gumbo. "I favor fresh okra. You know the slimy stuff on the inside is a thickener."

The PSS was gobbling cornbread, and Janie was daintily sipping milk. Precious had been let out of the

Suburban and was busy cadging bites from The PSS. Precious especially enjoyed cornbread.

"And you know how your mama gets," Big Mama concluded.

"I know," Bubba admitted tiredly. "I'm going back to Pegramville anyway. The Le Beau guy was a dead end."

Big Mama made a noise as she stirred the gumbo. "This just needs to simmer for a spell."

"Thank God," Demetrius said. "I'm starving."

"That's my son, Demetrius," Big Mama pointed at the young man. "Can you guess who he's named after?"

"Oh," Bubba said. "Meetcha."

"Sorry about the gun," Demetrius said lamely. The other two men were playing Blackjack on the coffee table and absently listening.

"That there is Mikael and the other one is Chi," Big Mama said, pointing at the other two men. "They're nephews." They waved and went back to Blackjack.

"Miz Demetrice *knows* Big Mama," Janie said, clearly impressed. "That's wicked bad."

"And this is the deputy's niece," Big Mama said. "Does her mother know that she's out gallivanting with ya'll?"

"No," Bubba said shortly. "I got to liking all my limbs still attached, so I'm reluctant to call her, although I don't want her worrying. Kid won't give me her phone number."

"You should call her mother," Big Mama directed sternly. "And your ma, too. Maybe his, too." She pointed at The PSS with a slotted spoon.

"My mother died on a distant world that exploded," The PSS said, reaching for more cornbread. "She put me in a special spaceship that brought me to earth. She knew that I would be stronger than humans. Bullets bounce off my flesh."

Demetrius scrutinized The PSS. "Hey, Ma, will you let me shoot him? I want to see if bullets will really bounce off."

"No!" Big Mama said. She washed her hands and dried them with a fluffy, pink towel. She poured herself a glass of merlot and sat down next to Bubba at the dining room table.

"Have some gumbo and then we'll get you down the road," Big Mama suggested. "Folks always think better on a full stomach."

"You could have said that over the phone," Janie said.

Big Mama shrugged.

"What makes you think that this Le Beau fella is a dead end?" she asked and sipped her wine.

"He's been inpatient at a mental health clinic since before the sheriff's deputy vanished," The PSS said.

Demetrius snorted. "I used that one once when- "

Big Mama cleared her throat.

"Just saying it could be faked," Demetrius added quickly.

"It's true I didn't see the proof," Bubba admitted, "but the police will make sure of it. That social worker said they had hourly checks. And there's more."

"More?" Big Mama said. Bubba frowned and she added, "Who you gonna tell? Your ma? The last time I talked to her she was talking about tying you to four horses and firing a muzzle loader into the air." She cackled. "Just like she done to your pa."

"Pa had a heart attack," Bubba said wearily.

"Okay," Big Mama said as she put her glass down. "They got hourly bed checks at this facility your guy was at and probably some other stuff, too. Cameras and all. Probably all kinds of records of his being there. If it's a reliable place, then it's a no brainer." She paused, then asked, "Who else is it gonna be?"

Bubba turned his gaze upon The PSS. The PSS hadn't answered his question about who Nancy Musgrave had been planning to kidnap. "David," Bubba said. "Tell me."

The PSS swallowed convulsively. A lump of cornbread went down awkwardly, and he thumped his chest twice. He managed to clear his esophagus and said, "Miz Demetrice, of course."

"Miz Demetrice, of course, what?" Big Mama said. "Miz Demetrice ain't gonna kidnap that girl."

"It's a real long story," Bubba said. "Did Ma tell you about the Christmas Killer?"

"The woman who wanted to get revenge for her daddy getting put in prison all those years ago," Big Mama stated. "Yep. She did mention it. Pegram County ain't had so much excitement for decades as it has this last year."

"Oh yeah," Demetrius said, "that's the place with the buried gold."

"Ain't no gold," Bubba barked. He took a breath and continued with the story about the Christmas Killer. "Well, Nancy Musgrave is the woman's name. She was a social worker with three outreach patients." He gestured at The PSS. "This is David Beathard, one of the patients. Sometimes he thinks he's a psychotherapist. She pretty much connived all of them into helping her."

"She threatened to have us put into solitary," The PSS said. "Even though I could have left, she said that with her statement the judge would commit me involuntarily. She also gave us lots of drugs."

"That's not so bad," Demetrius said.

"Not those kinds of drugs," Big Mama said.

"Too bad," Demetrius murmured.

"And Nancy also talked about her plans with her

patients," Bubba threw in.

"*Never* tell your crew all the plans," Demetrius advised gravely.

"Deniability," Janie said.

" 'Xactly," Demetrius said. He glanced at his mother. "Smart kid."

"But what David is saying is that Nancy talked about kidnapping Miz Demetrice," Bubba clarified.

"Why kidnap Miz Demetrice?" Big Mama asked.

"She was the one that Nancy blamed the most," Bubba explained. "She got the twelfth-day letter. Nancy sent letters to all her victims and potential victims. Nancy wanted Ma to watch all the others die while she had to wait for the end." He rubbed his jaw absently. "I don't remember what her letter said."

" 'On the twelfth day of Christmas, my true love gave to me, the gift of watching all the others die before me.' " The PSS appeared smug. "I helped compose it, you know."

Bubba frowned. "And there was another sentence."

" 'And if I tell, then my son will be next.' " The PSS said quickly.

"I didn't think about it before," Bubba said. "Anyone who knows Ma, knows she ain't gonna sit tight while folks are being sliced and stabbed. I guess Nancy accounted for that, too."

"Nancy was going to kidnap Miz Demetrice and hold her until all the others were dead," The PSS said somberly. "That way the one Nancy hated the most couldn't get away, couldn't be protected."

"Dah-ammm," Demetrius muttered. "That B was *all* into revenge and shit."

"Mind your language around the little girl," Big Mama snapped.

"Sorry."

"But Big Joe jumped the gun," Bubba said as he thought about it. "He just wanted to get someone in jail, and Ma was just as good as anyone."

"Big Joe is Pegramville's Chief of Police," Janie explained to Demetrius. "He's a big, dumb blowhard. He doesn't like Auntie Wills much but that's okay. Auntie Wills doesn't like him either."

Silence blew over the table like a chilly breeze.

Big Mama got up to stir the gumbo, and everyone quietly watched her.

"Ifin Nancy was going to kidnap Ma and keep her alive until all the rest was dead," Bubba said suddenly, and everyone jumped, including Big Mama, "then she had to have a place to put her."

He turned toward The PSS. "David?"

"Nancy didn't tell us that," The PSS said.

"Maybe the institute? Her house?" Bubba persisted, but The PSS shook his head.

"Oh, woman tells her crew everything and she don't say where she gonna put the gal she blamed for everything," Demetrius pooh-poohed.

The PSS shrugged sadly. "I wasn't a superhero, then."

"David," Bubba said gently, "are you sure?"

The PSS shook his head, and his eyes feasted on the cornbread again.

Janie said, "What? What are you thinking about, Bubba? That woman, Nancy Musgrave, didn't want to kidnap my auntie, so what does she have to do with her disappearance?"

"I went to the prison to talk to Nancy. I thought she could tell me something about stalkers that might help," Bubba said. "I was on her list of approved visitors."

Big Mama came back to the table. "This woman hates you, too. Am I right?"

"At the end," Bubba said, "she was just as mad at me as she was at Ma."

"And did she know about Auntie Wills and you?" Janie asked quickly.

"Hooking up with a sheriff's deputy," Demetrius crowed with his head bobbing in approval. His mother cleared her throat again and he said, "Sorry."

"Rumors run around like chickens with their heads cut off in Pegramville," Bubba said darkly. "Sure, it's possible. But we ain't even had a date yet."

"No date," Demetrius repeated doubtfully. "You ain't made a booty call with the hottie yet?"

"I was working my way up to asking her out," Bubba protested. "We were supposed to go out...last Thursday evening."

"Oh," Janie said understandingly.

"But Nancy has an alibi for the time that Willodean disappeared," Bubba said. "Hell, she was completely engaged with trying to kill me and a whole bunch of other people. David was there."

"She was *totally* occupied with attempted murder," The PSS admitted austerely.

"And her three accomplices were with her," Bubba continued.

"We were," The PSS acknowledged. "But we did try to warn you."

Big Mama's eyes rolled. "Why is this man hanging with you?"

"I thought he could help me with the psychology behind stalking," Bubba snarled. "I thought he could help me find the man who had scared Willodean so badly."

"I helped with that secretary today," The PSS dissented. "Also that social worker. Once I laid out *Tarasoff Versus Regents of the University of California,* she was a goner."

"Huh?" Demetrius said.

"It's a very interesting case by which clinicians are held accountable for imminent threats from patients to other people and from patients to themselves," The PSS explained. "Basically, it delegates that a therapist has a duty to warn when a patient has a specific threat against themselves or another person."

"I be trying to remember that," Demetrius said flatly.

Big Mama stared at The PSS. "What is he besides a mental patient? A doctor? A lawyer?"

The PSS turned to Big Mama. "A mail carrier."

"A mail carrier."

"Yes, twenty years on the job," The PSS said sadly. "People kept expecting me to go postal. That's a terrible parable for you. The fifteenth time a dog bit my ankle I threatened to parboil the schnauzer on my grill." He grimaced. "I wouldn't have done it, but the owner's kid was filming it on his smart phone, and that was the end of that career."

"So this Nancy woman never threatened your deputy?" Big Mama's attention refocused on Bubba.

"No, not even close."

"And maybe she knew that the deputy was special to you?"

"Maybe."

"That's a long shot," Demetrius said.

A confused expression settled over Bubba's face. "But Nancy was surprised when I saw her in prison."

"She was surprised to see you?" Big Mama said.

"No, surprised that something hadn't happened to Ma," Bubba said.

"They keep new prisoners segregated until they acclimatize," Big Mama said slowly. "Nancy thought something was going to happen to Miz Demetrice, and when you went in, she hadn't been able to watch the news. Hmm."

"Maybe while Nancy was killing you, someone else was supposed to kidnap Miz Demetrice," Janie suggested.

"I love the way this kid thinks," Demetrius said with a laugh.

"David," Bubba said, "is there another accomplice? One I don't know about?"

"Nancy talked to people on the phone a lot," The PSS whined. "She also upped my Thorazine level to the realm of I-forgot-most-of-that-week. It's a little cloudy."

"David," Bubba said warningly.

"I *am* a superhero now, Bubba." The PSS perked up. "If I knew where the attractive Deputy Willodean was located and who had taken her, I would have told you days ago." His face became graven with solemnity. "I swear upon my dead mother's soul as she rests upon the distant plane, XYB, in the Gamma-Omega Quadrant."

"Someone couldn't get Miz Demetrice in jail, so they took the deputy instead?" Big Mama concluded.

"If they thought that Auntie Wills was someone important to Bubba," Janie pondered, "then maybe they would have, but Auntie Wills' got a gun and she knows jujitsu."

"And it was someone who's close to your Christmas Killer," Demetrius added.

"Who's close to Nancy Musgrave?" Big Mama asked.

"She's got a brother," Bubba said. "But Nancy said that he wasn't involved. Said he worked in Dallas and has a family."

Demetrius sneered. "You believed the woman who tried to kill all ya'll? Seriously?"

Chapter Nineteen

Bubba Gets a Clue

Thursday, January 5th

"Nancy Musgrave put you on her visiting list because she thought her other accomplice kidnapped Miz Demetrice and you'd be coming to see her soon. She could torture you with it."

Big Mama's summation hit right where it hurt the most. Bubba didn't like it much because he hadn't put it together earlier; he had been completely focused on Howell Le Beau, the recognizable bad guy.

As he scowled to himself, Big Mama went on, "But her accomplice couldn't get Miz Demetrice and decided to get the deputy instead."

"But this accomplice might not want to hold her like they would have held Miz Demetrice," Janie said unhappily. Precious nuzzled her leg. "She might not be still- "

"This all be conjecture and assumptions," Demetrius said. "Ain't no evidence to show it was the Christmas Killer's brother or someone else. Could be Jack the Ripper, for all you know."

What Demetrius said wasn't much better. In some ways it was worse. If the person who had taken Willodean Gray wasn't Howell Le Beau, and it wasn't Nancy Musgrave's brother, then no one had any idea who it was. That pretty much sucked gigantic ostrich eggs.

"Big Mama," Bubba said abruptly, and he pushed the chair back as he stood up, "it's been fine meeting you, even with the kidnapping and all, but I got to go find Nancy Musgrave's brother. The sooner the better."

Big Mama took a sip from her merlot. "The DPD investigator is going to have you arrested as soon as you go back to the hotel. Throw you in the slam so hard your mama's head will bounce. It seems you might have skirted some of the instructions of the judge who released you a few days back."

A deep, black furrow crossed Bubba's brow. "Oh yeah. Guess we cain't go back to the hotel."

Big Mama put her glass down and carefully put her fingers into a steeple. "Let's get the young lady safely back to her house, and Demetrius can pick up your truck. Then you can head wherever you need go."

"I'm not going back to my house," Janie announced. "Auntie Wills needs me. I helped you put this together. And I can help more. I'll kick everyone's ass if you don't let me come."

Demetrius chuckled. "I love this kid."

"Your ma is going to be sick to death ifin she realizes that you're gone, too," Bubba said quietly to Janie. "It's okay right now because everyone is torn up and don't understand you're gone. But your ma and your granny are going to be worried senseless. Be right cruel to do that to them at this time." He hunkered down beside the young girl so that they were eye to eye. "Yes, you helped. Ain't no one gonna say you didn't. Willodean will be proud of you when we find her. I know she will. But you got to go home now and help out there as best you can."

Janie's face wrinkled. "*If* you find her." She suddenly burst into tears and launched herself at Bubba. She wrapped her thin arms around his neck and buried her face in his chest.

The PSS stood up and thumped his chest twice with a clenched fist. He said formally, "I swear I shall search for your auntie until my feet bleed and my eyes go blind."

Lifting her tear-streaked face from Bubba's chest, Janie gave The PSS an incredulous glance. "You're a crazy person, you know that?"

The PSS shrugged. "Well, even superheroes have flaws."

•

"Promise me you'll go inside and stay with your family," Bubba said to Janie thirty minutes later. The black Suburban was parked one house down from Janie's home.

"I promise," Janie said but her face was mulish. Bubba had seen the expression before. It looked a lot like her grandmother's face when she was told that she couldn't do something that she wanted to do. It even resembled Willodean's expression when Bubba thwarted her.

Janie climbed out of the Suburban. She looked at Bubba and then at Demetrius who was driving. Precious leaned out the window of the Suburban and slobbered on Janie's hand. Finally, she looked at The PSS. "I can't believe you're going to take him but not me. He's like a *perp*. He's completely ka-bonkers. You're going to need backup and he's going to be like, 'But I don't have enough purple Tinker Bell stuff to help you out,' and someone's going to shoot you in the back."

"Hey," The PSS objected, "at least I'm legal."

"Got you there, kid," Demetrius threw in.

Janie's shoulders slumped. "You better find my auntie, Bubba," she growled at him. She turned and trudged to the next house. A moment later, she opened the front door and went inside. Bubba listened. He heard a startled, "JANIE! Where have you been?" echo back to them.

"Guess they finally figured out she weren't home,"

Demetrius commented. He pulled out of the parking spot and headed toward downtown Dallas.

•

The Chevy truck seemed to be unencumbered by official individuals. Demetrius parked down the street from the hotel and the truck and waited judiciously. Bubba didn't want to wait. Demetrius held up a hand when Bubba started to speak.

Demetrius reached into the middle console and took out a small pair of binoculars. It took about a minute for him to systematically scan their surroundings.

Bubba waited for another few minutes and said, "I don't have time to mess with this, Demetrius. Let me have your Suburban and I'll- "

"Cops have come and gone," Demetrius announced. He put the binoculars back into the console. "They'll be back in the morning to pick you up."

The PSS said from the back seat, "Do you have psychic super senses, too?"

Demetrius pointed to the Chevy. "They booted your truck."

"Oh hell no!" Bubba exclaimed. "Not my truck. They might as well have put a boot on my dog."

Precious whined.

"What's a boot?" The PSS asked.

"A clamp on the wheel so that the car can't be driven," Demetrius answered. "Mostly private companies do it in Dallas. Your investigator must have some contacts."

"That foul, wretched devil incarnate!" The PSS swore.

"White folks," Demetrius said derogatorily.

All exited the Suburban and plodded over to the old, green truck. Even Precious cheerfully followed, happy to be doing something out of a vehicle.

Surveying the bright orange clamp locked in place around the rear driver's side tire, Bubba considered it carefully.

"You can take the 'Burban," Demetrius said after a moment. "Get your stuff out of the truck and- "

Bubba interrupted with, "I can take care of this."

"Do tell, country boy," Demetrius said with a sneer.

Bubba found his jack and put it under the rear axle. The scissors jack took a minute to be jacked into place, but the boot groaned as it was lifted off the ground. He handed the tire iron to Demetrius and said, "Take the spare off the side, would ya?"

Demetrius shrugged and went to town on the lug nuts.

When Bubba was satisfied the jack was secure, he unscrewed the little cap on the valve stem of the booted tire. He extracted his buck knife with an easy movement. Kneeling next to the booted tire, he opened the knife. Using the end of the blade, he pressed on the stem to let the air out of the tire.

"You think that'll work?" Demetrius said as air steadily hissed from the valve stem.

The PSS wandered up, adjusting his Tinker Bell coat as he went. He glanced at the diner. "Maybe some dinner? I bet they have a good burger. Home fries, too. After all, we missed out on the gumbo."

"We're driving soon," Bubba muttered. "Maybe you want to travel light."

"Well, a superhero does what a superhero has to do," The PSS acquiesced reluctantly.

Air continued to hiss perkily.

"The trick to this," Bubba said as if he was teaching a class, "is that the person who put it on don't put it on exactly right. As soon as I let enough air out of the tire, the edges of the boot will wiggle enough to pop right off." Ready to demonstrate the lesson, he jiggled the boot slightly. The entire mechanism sharply fell off, hitting the pavement with a loud acrimonious clank.

"I guess you been out of the woods a time or two, huh?" Demetrius was impressed. He finished with the spare and gave it a pull. It bounced twice and Bubba got to work.

He set about changing the tire with quiet efficiency. He would have to have the original one aired up quickly, but it was cheaper and timelier than waiting for a police officer to come take off the boot with a master key. Furthermore, if a police officer came to remove the boot, he would probably remove Bubba, too.

Bubba threw the formerly booted tire into the back of the truck.

"I love that," Demetrius said benignly. "I knows a guy who uses a 14-inch gas cut-off saw to take boots off. He works the private parking lots in Deep Elum about closing time. Charges $50 per car, and them folks is desperate to get those boots off so they don't have to pay no $350 instead." He pulled out a folded piece of paper from another pocket and handed it to Bubba. "This here is that guy's address in Dallas. I means the murderer's brother, not the guy with the cut-off saw."

Bubba saw that Morgan Newbrough was the name on the top of the computer-generated directions.

"How did Big Mama know- "

"Ma works things out a lot faster than the rest of us," Demetrius said. "Hope you find that deputy, Bubba. I saw her photo. Dah-ammmm, she's one fine bootylicious babe."

"She's nice, too," The PSS said.

"Need a piece?" Demetrius asked, pulling out a large pistol and offering the butt end to Bubba. "It ain't hot and you might need an edge."

Bubba stared at the weapon and then shook his head. "Naw," he muttered. "Ifin I find her, I ain't gonna need much but a little bit of mad, which I got in spades already."

"Okay then," Demetrius said. "Don't be a fool, ya'll." He grinned at them, kicked the dismantled boot onto the sidewalk, and went back to the Suburban. A moment later the big SUV passed them with a little toot of the horn.

"Get in the truck, David," Bubba said, "before a meteor lands on our heads."

•

Normally Bubba would have waited until morning before stopping at Morgan Newbrough's Dallas address. However, Willodean had been missing for seven whole days, and time seemed to be slipping away faster and faster.

"I'll be the good guy," The PSS said, "and you can be the bad guy."

"You've got a mask on, David," Bubba said gruffly.

"That's why I'm the good guy," The PSS replied. He smiled brightly as he twirled a little orange and white package around in his hands. The light from a nearby street lamp showed his pupils were distinctly dilated. "I love taking Dramamine. It makes me a little groggy and yet cures all that dratted motion sickness. And who knew it came in chewable form?"

Bubba knew because they'd stopped at a 24-hour CVS pharmacy. The PSS had misplaced the other package of Dramamine, and there was a pharmacy next to the gas station where Bubba aired up the formerly booted tire. Manifestly, the company that made Dramamine made about a million different variations, and The PSS wanted to compare all of them. At the same time.

247

What Bubba wanted was to hurry. An image of a ticking clock popped into his head and wouldn't go away.

"Why don't you wait in the truck, David?" Bubba asked. "Seeing a masked man on your porch at ten p.m. isn't really something most folks like to see."

"Really, why not?"

"They might not realize you're a superhero," Bubba said gently.

Precious barked once.

"I know you're hungry, girl," Bubba said. "We'll get something in a little while. Burgers from McDonald's?"

Precious barked again in a derogatory fashion. She put her head down on the seat and sulked.

"You could play ball with my dog," Bubba offered to The PSS.

"Really? I love to play ball with dogs," The PSS said. He threw his hands in the air excitedly. "It's much better than when they chase me. Some people just don't understand leash laws."

"Great," Bubba sighed. "Ball's in the glove box."

Bubba got out of the truck and walked up to the small house the piece of paper listed as Morgan Newbrough's home. A single, exposed light bulb from the front revealed all that it was and all that it wasn't. It was a narrow house stuck in-between other narrow houses, with a lawn that would have made a postage stamp say, "Dang."

Paint peeled in great strips off the porch's supports. The only reason paint wasn't peeling off the rest of the house was because it was constructed of red brick. One of the brass numbers attached to the side of the front door hung sideways, and the rusting mail box was ready to make an escape via falling off the wall. The mail box would have to fight its way through a slew of toys pushed off to the side.

After knocking three times, Bubba backed away so he wouldn't appear threatening. Behind him he heard The PSS saying to Precious, "Get it! Get the ball!" Precious barked sharply once. "Don't fret, dogling, I shall not use my super strength to throw the ball again!"

The nearest window was completely black one moment, and then light appeared around the edges. A silhouetted form parted the curtains and stared at Bubba. Then the curtains fluttered closed, and someone said through the closed door, "Who is it?"

"My name is Bubba Snoddy," he said, "and I'm looking for Morgan Newbrough."

Silence resulted.

The voice had been a woman's. Bubba supposed it was Morgan's wife. He didn't remember if he'd heard her name before. Nancy Musgrave had said something about Morgan the week before. He had a family. He worked at Best Buy. He lived in Dallas.

"You couldn't come in the daylight?" the voice said through the door.

"It's important."

"So is my sleep, buddy," the woman snapped.

"*Very* important," Bubba stressed.

There was a spotted-brass mail slot just under the middle of the door. A finger pushed it open, and Bubba could see the woman's mouth as she said, "People coming to my door all the fricking time now. Wanting to know about Morgan and his kookoo sister. Newspeople. The neighbors. The police. Want to know did I know what his nutcase sister did down in Pegram County. Want to know if Morgan knows about it. So I'll tell you what I told them." Her red lips compressed in anger, and then she resumed her declamation, "Morgan left months ago. He doesn't call. He doesn't send money.

I've filed for divorce. He's a shithead. And he doesn't live here."

She stopped speaking for a moment and then added, "Jesus, I'm going to need a beer to go to sleep tonight."

"Uh, right sorry about that," Bubba said politely. "You're Morgan's wife?"

"Isn't that what I just finished saying and it's gonna be ex-wife just as soon as I can."

"There's a woman missing down in Pegram County that might have something to do with this whole mess," Bubba said. "I don't want to rile you up, but is there anything you can tell me that might help?"

The finger was still holding the little brass flap open. The red lips started to move again. "I tried to have that dingwa committed. I called every-finkling-body I could think of. Nancy fooled the damned psychiatrist into thinking I was just pissed at her. She's a flipping social worker for God's sake. I mean, she knows what to say to a shrink. Ain't nobody can say I didn't try to do my part. If those stupid em-eff-ers had listened to me a year ago then no one would be dead in Pegram County, and I don't know anything about someone who's missing." After finishing her testimonial, the mouth took a deep breath of air.

"Is Morgan down in Pegram County?" Bubba persisted.

"I don't flinking know where the jackass is," the lips said fiercely. "And I can't tell you what the two of them are planning. They've been bitching about those people in Pegram County for ten years. I mean, let it go, for the love of merciful Pete. Their father stole from orphans, and Nancy still thinks that was okay because he was using the money for *their* Christmas presents. How is stealing from orphans ever okay? But no, Nancy's a few peas short of a casserole. 'It's that woman's fault. That

Demetrice Snoddy woman's fault- ' *Hey.*"

The lips stopped moving.

Bubba waited.

"You said your name is Bubba...Snoddy," the lips said.

"Yeah, Miz Demetrice is my mother."

"I didn't have anything to do with Nancy's murder plot," the lips declared.

"Lots of folks think about killing Ma," Bubba said reluctantly. "Most don't follow through. But she's still about, kicking and taking names."

"You don't sound angry," the lips commented.

"Well, I reckon you know that Nancy got caught last week."

"Yeah, I know. Didn't I just finish telling you all these people coming to my door asking questions about what Nancy was up to? The television has been playing that interview with that kid and Matt Lauer 24/7, for Jelly Belly's sake. How could I *not* know she got caught?" The lips paused to chuckle. "A stun gun. That's rich."

Bubba said carefully, "My friend disappeared the same day Nancy got caught."

"I said I've seen the news," the lips admitted. The finger tapped the side of the slot. "The news didn't say it had anything to do with Nancy."

"No one thought that it did, until today," Bubba admitted.

"What happened today?" the lips asked as if dreading the answer.

"The guy everyone thought did it, didn't."

The lips closed.

"You said Morgan has been gone for a few months," Bubba stated.

"Yeah. We were fighting about his sister again," the

251

lips said bitterly. "He packed some shit and left. A couple days later his company called him and said he was fired on account of the fact that he didn't show up. Now it's just me and my babies."

"I'm sorry about that," Bubba said.

"It's okay," the lips said. "I got a decent job. I can take care of my children without the jackass's help. I got relatives who're good to us."

Bubba thought of something he had thought about before. When he'd suspected the Newbrough siblings were behind the Christmas killings, he knew that they had to be people who was relatively new to the area. But he didn't have to go around checking everyone to see if they were Morgan Newbrough, formerly Morgan Roquemore.

"Do you have a photo of your husband?" Bubba asked. All he had to do was look at Morgan's image, and Bubba would know if the man was in Pegramville.

"Ex-husband to be," the lips retorted. "Why in seven hells do you want a picture of him?"

"I want to know if I seen him before," Bubba said honestly.

The lips sighed. "Can't help you. We moved to this house on account there was a fire in our other one. Lost everything. Photos, too. Everything we got has been donated by the church, friends, relatives, and charities. And damn, they've been good to us."

Another fire? Nancy likes fires. Had she tried to get rid of a loose end? "When did this fire happen?"

"About two months ago," the lips said. "Not too long after Morgan split."

"But this house is listed under his name," Bubba said.

"Yeah, well, it's hard to get listed under my name when he was the one who initially got all the utilities," the lips said resentfully. "That'll change when the divorce is finalized."

"This fire an accident?"

The lips pursed for a moment. Bubba wished the woman would just stand up and open the door so he could see her face, but she had no reason to trust him.

"Fire department said it was kids playing with matches," the lips said. The lips vanished and blue eyes moved down to stare through the flap's doors at him. "But you don't think that, do you? I can see it in your face."

"I think maybe Nancy tried to do you in," Bubba said. "She set fire to a storage shed and to a woman's house who was connected to the historical society board."

"The same board that put her daddy in prison," the lips reappeared and said. "Headed up by your mama."

"That's right."

"We went over to my mama's that night," the lips mused. "She had a new Disney movie for the kids." The lips went silent for a moment. "That frinking, no account, crazy-brained dingleberry."

"Your mama?"

"No, Nancy," the lips spat out.

"Do you think you might be able to find a photo of Morgan, maybe something you gave to your mama or a friend or something?"

"Maybe," the lips said. "Mama doesn't like Morgan, and mostly I give her photos of the kids and stuff. She probably used the ones of Morgan for toilet paper." The lips took a moment to curve with amusement.

But Bubba thought about another way he could find out. He also thought of someone else who might be able to give him a photo. "I appreciate your help," he said. He brought out the paper Demetrius gave to him. "I'd like to give you my cell phone number so you can tell me if you find one or maybe ifin you hear from your soon-to-be ex-husband or maybe ifin you think of something either of them might have said that could help. You got a pen?"

The lips passed a pen out to him a moment later. Bubba scrawled the number on the paper and passed the pen and paper through the slot.

The blue eyes replaced the lips again. They stared out of the slot past Bubba. Morgan's soon-to-be ex-wife said incredulously, "There's a man in a purple mask and purple clothes playing ball with a Basset hound on my front lawn."

"Yeah, well," Bubba murmured, "he's kinda my sidekick." He considered. "Or I'm his."

Chapter Twenty

The Return of the Bubba

Thursday, January 5ᵗʰ - Friday, January 6ᵗʰ

Bubba was dog-tired so they stopped at a motel fifty miles away from Dallas. Bubba figured that Charles Park wouldn't be watching the credit card of a relatively benevolent criminal such as himself so he used his Visa to pay for it. If the police came to arrest him they'd have to wake him up first.

Before retiring for the evening, Bubba made sure all superheroes and Basset hounds were fed. He followed up with attempting to figure out how to retrieve messages on his disposable phone. He would have asked The PSS for assistance, but the man fell mask-covered facedown into one of the double beds in the room and proceeded to snore just like Bubba's Aunt Caressa. Precious claimed the other bed and used feet, snout, and her butt to make a nest out of the coverlet. She took up a large percentage of the bed with her long ears and four paws spread out to all directions of the wind.

With a mournful resignation, Bubba called his mother. Miz Demetrice's phone went immediately to voicemail and he left a message. "On my way back to Pegramville, Ma," he said. "Don't got much new." He sighed. "Wish I could say there was something else." There was another significant pause. "Did you *have* to sic Big Mama on me?"

He took a shower, dried off, dressed in a t-shirt and shorts, and lay on the part of the bed that Precious wasn't using. A minute after that, the snores between the three individuals contended for the ultimate conquest of which would be loudest.

•

The morning brought a warmer Texas winter's day. The sun was out. The temperature was climbing rapidly. There wasn't a cloud in the sky.

And Willodean's still missing, was the sour acid that poured over Bubba's soul.

Bubba stood outside and contemplated how life was like a seesaw. It was up one minute and down the next. Mostly it seemed to be down, with more folks piling on the seat behind him. It wasn't a happy set of thoughts.

While Bubba waited for The PSS to complete his morning ablutions, he tried to get in touch with Sheriff John.

"P-p-pegram C-c-county Sheriff's Office," someone answered when Bubba finished dialing.

"Sheriff John, please," Bubba said. "This here is Bubba Snoddy."

"B-b-bubba S-s-snoddy," the voice repeated, kind of. It sounded like a machine gun shooting sporadically.

"Oh, Robert!" Bubba said recognizing the repetitive splutter of Robert Daughtry, the department's newest receptionist/dispatcher. "I need to speak to Sheriff John. It's right important."

"Sh-sh-sheriff isn't here," Robert stammered.

Bubba pursed his lips. "And I suspect you cain't tell me where he's at."

"Th-th-that's right."

"Okay, then take a message. Bubba called. Call him back. You got that?"

"Y-y-yeah," Robert said. "You w-w-want to leave a n-n-number?"

"Yeah," Bubba said and spouted out the disposable phone's number. "Can you tell me when you'll be speaking with him?"

"No, I c-c-can't," Robert said.

"Don't reckon Steve Simms will help me," Bubba mused.

"W-w-wouldn't think so," Robert agreed.

"Okay, add this to the message. Meet me at Forrest Roquemore's house," Bubba said. "He'll know what I'm talking about."

"F-f-forrest R-r-roquemore," Robert stuttered. Bubba thought there was a tone of amazement behind the stuttering, but he couldn't be sure.

"You need me to spell that?"

"N-n-n-n-n-no."

"Something wrong?" Bubba asked, concerned that Robert couldn't seem to get anything out.

"Y-y-you got c-c-cops from Dallas c-c-calling about you. S-s-said s-s-something about violating a judge's order. S-s-something about a b-b-boot on your tr-tr-truck."

Bubba frowned. "Maybe you should see a doctor about that stutter, Robert. I ain't one to judge, but it seems to be bothering you overly."

"F-f-f-f-fuck you," Robert said and hung up.

Bubba pulled the phone back and stared at it. "What'd I say?"

The PSS leaped out of the hotel door and yelled, "Da Dah DAH!"

Precious barked from the truck.

"Yeah, we ought to get moving," Bubba concurred.

•

Bubba stopped at the Snoddy Mansion first. Amazingly, everything appeared normal there. Miz Demetrice's Caddy was parked next to Miz Adelia's rust-spotted Ford Courier. Wallie, the construction contractor, could be seen on the second floor of the house he was building for Bubba. He directed a small crew of three men working on the roof.

Normal. Nothing was being threatened or burned, and there wasn't an avid serial killer within sight. *Normal as all get out.*

Parking his truck next to the Caddy, Bubba saw Miz Demetrice open the front door and walk onto the veranda. She crossed her little arms over her chest and settled a belligerent expression upon her face.

Bubba got out of his truck and allowed Precious to scramble down. The dog immediately began to roll in the nearby gray grasses.

The PSS got out of the passenger side and said, "This reminds me of my home planet. There was an Antebellum period before the Martians invaded. Then the world went to hell in a hand bucket. Kind of like when the Presidential elections happen here."

Miz Demetrice waited until Bubba got closer before she cried, "Bubba Nathanial Snoddy! I have raised you better than to not call your mama when you're out traipsing over Kingdom Come! Po-lice calling me up. All the newspeople wanting photographs of the Mansion where the Christmas Killer was apprehended by Brownie Snoddy. Folks tramping up and down the lane looking for God knows what."

"Sorry, Ma," Bubba said.

Precious made an abrupt sound and fled around the corner of the mansion.

The PSS said, "Bubba has been on official business and too busy with the saving of human lives to waste any time on typical communications."

Miz Demetrice paused in her glaring at Bubba to scowl at The PSS. "No one is too busy to call their mama."

"That's what Big Mama said," Bubba said darkly, "after her son kidnapped us at gunpoint."

Miz Demetrice's gaze went back to Bubba. The glare faded away into disbelief. "Oh, surely not." She covered her mouth and muffled what sounded suspiciously like a giggle. "Kidnapping? At gunpoint?"

Bubba softened slightly. "Prolly did us a favor though. That little girl, Janie, snuck off to help us and she wanted to go with us. Likely we'd be in jail now ifin it weren't for Big Mama and her son."

"Call me next time," Miz Demetrice commanded. Her cornflower blue eyes started to fill with moisture.

Bubba thought about running before the tears started to fall, but his mother went on before he could make a decision. "I was worried. You took off for the prison to talk to that dreadful woman. Didn't I call the governor's office for you? Why, yes I did. You didn't even leave a message saying what she told you. And then still I don't hear from you. Except an investigator from Dallas calling to see where you're at. Willodean's own mother knows where you're at before I know."

"She's a police sergeant, Ma," Bubba said. "She's got access to tools you don't have, like GPS trackers."

"GPS?" Miz Demetrice repeated thoughtfully. It was apparent to Bubba that his mother was filing the information away for future reference.

"Anyway, Nancy wasn't real helpful," Bubba added. "Seems to be holding things against me."

"No, I reckon she wouldn't be," Miz Demetrice murmured, "and she's quite psychotic. Or is it sociopathic? David?"

"David is only a persona," The PSS announced. "*I* am The Purple Singapore Sling."

"A Sling who needs his clothing washed," Bubba said wryly. "And I could use a change, too."

Miz Demetrice sighed and gestured at the door. "Go on then."

"My super sense of smell detects cinnamon rolls," The PSS declared.

•

By the time Precious was fed and The PSS provided with clean clothing, Bubba was running out of patience. He was perturbed that Sheriff John hadn't called back, and he was sure if he presented himself at the sheriff's department he would be straightaway arrested for something or other.   Since Robert Daughtry had mentioned that Investigator Charles Park was calling about Bubba and his lack of following through with the judge's mandates, Bubba thought going to the department would be a mistake. Sheriff John would be obligated to throw him in the clank. Steve Simms might do it just for the sheer hell of it.

And Bubba had made the mistake of telling Sheriff John where he was going.

Why *did I tell him to meet me at Forrest Roquemore's?*

"Hurry, David," Bubba said to The PSS who refused to stay at the mansion with Miz Demetrice. "We need to talk to Forrest Roquemore before Sheriff John gets there."

"What do you want with that nasty-tempered man?" Miz Demetrice demanded. "Once he called me- a very bad name on account of my being responsible for having his nephew thrown in Huntsville.   Well, I suppose I should just let that go."

"I need a photograph of Morgan Newbrough," Bubba said. He'd told his mother a smattering of what he'd surmised, but Miz Demetrice wasn't buying it. "Ifin he's around here pretending to be someone else, then I need to know."

"But why does it have to be Morgan? Why not Buck Johnson from down the street?   There's no evidence that it is Nancy's brother." Apparently, Miz Demetrice was determined to play devil's advocate.

"He left his house months before," Bubba said as he thought about what reasons he really had. "He's the only one with a big enough motive to snatch someone. Nancy had an accomplice she was expecting to kidnap you. She had to drug the loonies to make them help her. Beg pardon, David. Remember the Christmas letter she sent you? You were last. You were going to have to watch all the others die before you."

"You're really leaping to conclusions," Miz Demetrice said, and her face was sad.

"Conclusions are all I've got," Bubba suddenly snarled.

Miz Demetrice took his large hand in-between her two smaller ones. "I understand, Bubba dear. Go and see Forrest. Maybe he'll have a photograph. But here's another thought. This Morgan Newbrough's got to have a driver's license. We should ask Sheriff John to look at the photograph in their database. He's got access to that. We can also call Celestine Gray. She has that kind of access."

"But she don't know everyone in town."

The PSS frowned. "It's possible that Miz Demetrice could still be a target for Nancy's brother," he said. He turned to Miz Demetrice, "You should be extra careful."

Miz Demetrice reached around and pulled a gun from behind her. Evidently it had been tucked into her belt. She showed it to Bubba and The PSS. It was very similar to the .50 caliber hand cannon Nancy Musgrave favored. It was also something new to Bubba, who was certain she hadn't owned the gun before last week.

"Jesus, Ma," Bubba said, "that's going to dump you on your petunia ifin you fire it."

"My petunia is well padded, and I thought Nancy had

an interesting notion about oversized weapons," Miz Demetrice said as she fingered the monster pistol. "But don't worry about me. I think I will dissuade anyone from snatching me."

"I could stay and protect you myself," The PSS offered gallantly.

"Yeah," Bubba agreed hastily.

Yeah, let someone shoot The PSS while Ma went out the back. No, not really. That would be bad. Funny, but bad.

Miz Demetrice appeared alarmed. "Oh no. I'm a crack shot. You go ahead with Bubba and talk to Mr. Roquemore. Bubba will need your dauntless backup."

"Thanks, Ma," Bubba dryly said.

"Anytime, boy," Miz Demetrice returned. She pressed a quick kiss to his cheek, having to pull him down to do it.

•

Forrest Roquemore's house seemed about the same as it had the last time Bubba had seen it. It was the third house on the left as they passed the sign that said the town's name. The words Nardle – Population 67 were still featured prominently on the sign; 67 was still crossed out and 66 handpainted below it.

Roquemore's home was a shotgun house covered with brown shingles. The roof and the walls had newer shingles because bits of Hurricane Katrina had blown off earlier ones. The yard was raked dirt with only a few shrubs. Bubba recalled that Roquemore had an ongoing issue with all of his neighbors; he believed their cats defecated in his yard on purpose and that they stole his shrubberies to plant in their yards. There was a multitude of other issues to which Willodean graciously had listened. She even had diplomatically spoken to the neighbors to try to smooth over ruffled feathers.

The thought of Willodean made Bubba's stomach clench in pure agony.

"This is Nancy's great-uncle's house?" The PSS questioned.

"Didn't she take you out here?" Bubba asked as he parked on the shoulder in front of the house.

"No," The PSS said shortly. "Maybe she took David."

Bubba paused, alarmed that David Beathard was suddenly talking about himself as though he was two distinct people. "You don't remember being David?"

"Sometimes," The PSS said. "There were a lot of drugs involved last week. It's very fuzzy. There were a lot of colors. I remember watching *The Wizard of Oz* on television and I was very happy when Dorothy stepped into Oz and black and white became color."

"David, I'm going to talk to this man, Forrest," Bubba said. He wasn't certain how to respond to The PSS at the moment. "He's ninety years old and very cantankerous. I didn't see a shotgun the first time, but it's probably because the sheriff took it away from him in a previous visit. Oh yeah, Willodean said he had one that didn't work, so they probably let him keep it. He's the type to get all het up, but it's pretty much hot air. He can also be right insulting ifin he's got a mind."

"Sounds like he needs the drugs I had," The PSS said. "I can recommend a good psychiatrist. Did you know most psychotherapists have to work in conjunction with a medical doctor so as to provide the right pharmaceutical assistances to their clients/patients?"

"No, David, I did not. I'll keep it in mind for the future."

Bubba got out of the truck and brusquely commanded Precious to stay. Precious's woeful eyes glared at him as she rested her chin on the edge of the half-open window.

263

The PSS got out of the other side. Bubba sighed because he was getting tired of asking the other man to stay in the vehicle.

Oh, what the hey? That mean-tempered lech will probably like The PSS just fine.

Bubba walked up to the tiny porch and listened to it creak as he put a booted foot on it.

The PSS stepped up to the porch and stopped. Bubba raised a large fist to pound on the door when The PSS said abruptly, "My superpowers sense something is wrong."

Bubba froze in place. His fist was inches away from the door. He slowly panned around trying to see what it was that The PSS had seen. Despite David Beathard's mental issues, he wasn't a stupid person. If he said something was wrong, then it might actually be so.

The day was still clear. The sun had warmed the air up to around forty-five degrees, and it looked as though it might make it up to a balmy fifty. The neighbor's houses were quiet. There wasn't a noise around at all.

Dang, it's quiet. It's like there ain't no one about. Like a ghost town.

Bubba's head swiveled toward The PSS and registered what the other man was looking at. He wasn't staring at the skies or the ground or anywhere but at the same door upon which Bubba was about to knock. Bubba's gaze went back at the door.

It was cracked open as if someone had just walked outside and forgotten to pull it shut after them. Perhaps a little wind had nudged it open.

Remembering what Forrest Roquemore was like, Bubba didn't think the man was apt to leave his door open. He might be ninety years old, but he still had a capable brain. He knew when the police couldn't do anything to him, and he knew when a beautiful sheriff's deputy was soft-hearted enough to listen to him for a bit.

Old, cranky, greedy, and lecherous.

More importantly, a bloody handprint stained the tarnished doorknob. Bubba knew why he hadn't seen it immediately. The blood was about the same reddish color as the knob. It wasn't a lot of blood, and it had been there for a little while because the bright red color that it originally came in had darkened to a grim shade of copper.

Nothing good about this.

Bubba motioned at The PSS to move back. Then he gently pushed the door open with the tip of his boot. The view from the long hallway to the backdoor was empty of obstruction. The other door was closed, and the hallway was empty. The first room was the miniscule living room, and was the only room that Bubba had seen previously. The oversized plasma-screened television still dominated one wall. The well-used La-Z-Boy chair that was Forrest's favorite, was still planted squarely in front of the television. An old couch was crammed on the other side of the chair.

Bubba stepped into the house. It was a little dim because curtains had been pulled shut in all the windows. After his eyes adjusted to the gloom, he could see that the television had been knocked askew. There was a crack running down the middle of the screen which led to a moon crater on the bottom where something had made contact with the glass. The La-Z-Boy was moved slightly to one side. The little table at the side of the chair was overturned. There was a clear shoe print on the side of the table. A can of Coca-Cola was overturned on the rug next to the chair. A pool of cola still glistened, but the fizzing bubbles had long since faded.

"Forrest?" Bubba said. "It's Bubba Snoddy. I'm coming in to see ifin you're hurt."

There wasn't an answer, and Bubba was suddenly grateful that no one was trying to burn the building down.

The second room was a miniscule bedroom with a twin bed that dominated the area. There were stacks of magazines that barely allowed someone to get to the bed. A crackled-white armoire sat in a corner. The door was half open revealing clothes hanging inside.

The third room was a kitchen with a little bathroom tucked in one corner. Dirty dishes sat in the sink with an empty can perched on the edge. It was a testament to the Hormel Chili Forrest Roquemore must have eaten for lunch. A refrigerator with rounded corners made a muted screeching noise and burped itself into silence. A dinette set with two aluminum chairs sat on the far side. On top of the table sat a folded newspaper waiting for someone to read it.

Nothing but the living room had been disturbed as far as Bubba could tell. He peered out into the backyard, noticing that the old man's property spread out significantly. Fences opened into pasture area with a small barn. Twin ruts led through the pasture toward a wall of trees in the distance. A single donkey pawed hay from a broken bale.

Forrest Roquemore wasn't in any of the rooms, and he wasn't in the bathroom.

The PSS came up behind Bubba. "I sense someone has attacked the man you've come to see," he said mildly.

Bubba stared out the back door. Forrest didn't have a car. He'd said something about losing his vehicle and not being able to replace it. If the front door hadn't been cracked and a bloody handprint hadn't marked the door knob, Bubba would have thought the old man had stepped out for a moment.

Having a cup of coffee with the neighbors he hates so much. Right.

"You go check the 7-Eleven, David," Bubba said. "See if an old man is in there. Ask the clerk ifin they've seen Forrest Roquemore. Look in the post office, too."

The PSS nodded and went back the way he came.

Bubba checked the barn and ignored the hopeful hee-hawwwhh of the donkey. He returned to the little shotgun house and to the living room. Studying it, he could see that someone had tussled there. Something had been shoved into the plasma television and broken it. Behind the chair were a few spots of blood that Bubba hadn't seen before. The shoe print on the side of the overturned table might show that someone kicked out as they fell.

On one hand, Bubba felt horror at the fate of Forrest Roquemore. But Bubba also felt something else. If Nancy's brother wasn't in Pegram County trying to play out the macabre games she had initiated, then why would anyone try to shut up Forrest Roquemore? Forrest Roquemore couldn't possibly be connected to some unknown person who had backed into Willodean's vehicle and then kidnapped her.

What did Bubba feel? *Bitter triumph.* Although it burned like bile in his throat, it wasn't the choking essence of hopelessness and despair.

Chapter Twenty-One

Bubba's Got Something

Friday, January 6th

Standing on Forrest Roquemore's dirt lawn, Bubba called Pegram County Sheriff's Department with his cell phone. This time he immediately recognized Mary Lou Treadwell's voice.

"Miz Mary Lou," Bubba said, "this here is Bubba Snoddy."

"Bubba," Mary Lou said with excitement. "Everyone's talking about you. Boy, you bin up to something, ain't you?"

"Something," Bubba agreed.

"Sheriff John be looking for you," Mary Lou said. "Reckon you need to tell me where you're at."

"I'm at Forrest Roquemore's house," Bubba said, "just like I told Robert Daughtry I would be."

"Must have slipped his mind," Mary Lou said acidly. "Boy went off sick again. I don't believe Sheriff John is happy with that man. He calls in sick twice a week."

Snap.

"Is Sheriff John coming out here? Something's happened," Bubba said and tried to think about what suddenly bothered him.

Snap. Snap. Snap.

"What happened?" Mary Lou demanded.

"Don't rightly know, Miz Mary Lou," Bubba said. "The old man's gone as an evangelical preacher on Monday morning. There's blood on the door and Forrest's stuff is messed up proper."

Snap. Snap. Snap. Snap. Snap.

"Oh no," Mary Lou said. "Okay, I've got the sheriff on

his way. Don't go anywhere, Bubba. He's gonna need to talk with you."

Snap. Snap. Snap.

Bubba shrugged and disconnected without saying anything else. He figured that since he'd saved Sheriff John the previous week, then he still had some brownie points. (And those weren't the points connected with Brownie Snoddy.) He could talk the older man into keeping him out of jail until they could find Morgan Newbrough. That would be followed with Bubba *persuading* Morgan to tell them what had happened to Willodean Gray. When they had found Willodean, Bubba would be pleased as punch to go to jail for all of his transgressions. As a matter of fact, he would tie a bow on his body as he presented himself to the judge.

Snap.

What in the name of Sherlock Holmes' ghost is that snapping noise?

Bubba turned and saw The PSS standing close by, holding a two foot by two foot section of bubble wrap and systematically popping all the plastic bubbles.

"This is fun," The PSS said.

"Was Forrest Roquemore at the 7-Eleven or the post office?"

Snap. Snap. Snap. "No. The clerk at the 7-Eleven said that the old man was there early this morning, but he only told me after I showed him my official heroic, purple-sequined underwear."

"Bought the newspaper this morning," Bubba surmised.

"That's right and a can of Hormel Chili. With beans."

Snap.

A vein in Bubba's forehead threatened to internally combust. He had to talk it down.

It's a small piece of bubble wrap. It cain't last long.

"And the post office guy said he hadn't seen Forrest at all today," The PSS went on. *Snap. Snap.*

Bubba glanced around. Surely there was something that he could use to plug his ears with. The bubble wrap appeared promising, but he didn't think he was going to be able to pry it out of The PSS's hands.

"But he did say that he saw a small Jeep parked at Forrest's house a while ago," The PSS said and popped three bubbles in rapid deliberation. *Snap. Snap. Snap.*

Time stopped for a moment. Bubba thought his heart might have stopped.

Seriously, it can't be that easy. It can't be. And how could that possibly be the case?

"Did he mean a real Jeep or something that looked like a Jeep?" If there was one thing that Bubba knew it was cars. All kinds of cars. Big, small, foreign, domestic. Old. New. Bizarre and normal. Lots of folks called SUVs Jeeps, even though Jeep was a trademarked name.

The PSS's eyes crossed as he looked at the bubble wrap in his hands. *Snap. Snap. Snap.*

"He said a small Jeep," The PSS said. "And he gave me this bubble wrap. It might be of alien origin designed to enthrall me. Do you think the post office clerk is a super villain?"

"No, he's not a super villain, and it'll stop when you run out of bubbles," Bubba said gravely. He walked across the street and went into the post office. A very tall, very skinny man dressed in the United States Postal Service's bluish-gray garb was helping a woman open her mail box.

"You can't expect the key to bend," the clerk said benevolently. "You just put it in and turn it. Don't force it."

The woman grumbled about the cheapness of the key. "Ifin the gov'ment buys keys from the Chinese, then what do you expect?"

The door popped open, and the woman tugged out a packet of mail.

The clerk turned to Bubba, and Bubba was surprised to see that they saw eye to eye. It wasn't often that he ran into folks who were the same height. His eyes flicked down to the nametag and saw that it said Fred Funkhouse.

"Hey," Bubba said because it would have been rude to instantly demand that the civil servant tell him what kind of Jeep he'd seen at Forrest Roquemore's house. Despite the fact Bubba wanted to do just exactly that.

"Hey," Fred said. "Help ya'll?"

Bubba realized that The PSS had wandered in after him. *Snap. Snap. Snap.*

The woman at the mail box glanced at them and then sharply glanced back again. "That man's wearing a purple mask," she said as if she was reading from a weather report.

"Yes, ma'am," Bubba said. "He likes it a lot, and it don't harm no one."

Snap. Snap. Snap.

"Fred," the woman said, slamming the mail box shut. Then she had to slam it shut again because it was being contrary. "You've got to stop giving out bubble wrap."

"David here," Bubba gestured at The PSS, "said you saw a small Jeep at Forrest Roquemore's house."

Fred nodded. "About an hour ago, I reckon."

"Can you tell me what kind of Jeep it was?"

Fred nodded again. "It was a dark blue one."

"Was it a Jeep or was it something that looked like a Jeep?"

Snap.

Fred shrugged. "Guess it wasn't really a Jeep. Something that looked like a Jeep. You know, it had a

271

ragtop. Older, too. Don't think they make that kind no more."

The woman flung most of her mail into the nearest garbage can. "I saw it, too. It was a Suzuki, Fred. My brother got one of those about twenty years ago. Then they all freaked out because someone said they rolled too easy. My brother said it never gave him a problem." She sniffed at The PSS and went out the door clutching the rest of her mail in her hand.

Fred gestured. "I guess it was a Suzuki then."

A Suzuki? A Suzuki...Samurai? Really?

Bubba had seen one of those recently. And if he called Mary Lou Treadwell back, would she tell him a certain person had called in sick on the day that Willodean disappeared? If someone knew about all the secrets and not-so-secrets, it was Mary Lou at the sheriff's department. Had she told this person herself about the budding romance between Bubba and the beauteous sheriff's deputy? Had the person decided that if he couldn't get Miz Demetrice, then he would make Bubba pay with the next best thing? Had he been wasting time chasing after Howell Le Beau for the past week?

Everything fit except it didn't make sense that this person was working for the Pegram County Sheriff's Department. Even a bubba like Bubba knew the sheriff's department ran background checks on their employees. But Nancy Musgrave was smart, and it was a given that her brother was just as clever. It was possible.

Bubba went outside and looked around the teensy-weensy town of Nardle, Texas. He had called earlier in the morning and told the person he was going to Forrest Roquemore's. Forrest Roquemore had already rolled over on his great-niece, so it made sense that he might very well give up his great-nephew, too. Maybe the person rushed over to make sure Forrest didn't give anyone else up.

Damn, I'm stupid. Maybe I got that crotchety old man killed. What did Forrest know that Morgan didn't want me to know?

Two county cars pulled up behind Bubba's truck and Bubba watched Sheriff John get out of one. Deputy Steve Simms got out of the other one. Bubba crossed the road as Sheriff John approached Forrest's door.

"Stay right there, Bubba," Simms called to him.

Snap. Snap. Snap.

The PSS came up beside Bubba.

Bubba could see Sheriff John's back straighten as he examined the front door, bending to look at the door knob. Bubba hadn't closed the door because he didn't want to mess up any of the evidence. Sheriff John walked inside and Simms said, "Dallas PD cain't decide ifin they want you or not, Bubba. First there was a warrant and then that fella, Park, had it dropped. Think he felt sorry for you and all. But he did say they found that stalker guy. Actually he said *you* found him. Maybe he was throwing you a bone."

"Whoopee," Bubba said with a straight face.

"And who is *that?*" Simms asked as he looked at The PSS.

The PSS glanced away from the bubble wrap. "I am THE Purple Singapore Sling!"

"The hell you say."

"I *am,*" The PSS insisted.

"It's illegal to wear a mask," Simms said.

"Oh, put a sock in it, Simms," Bubba said. "Ain't illegal at Halloween and David ain't hurting no one."

"David? That's one of the loonies- the one who thought he was a psychotherapist," Simms said. His

273

expression displayed incredulous disbelief.

Snap. Snap.

"Well today, he's a superhero," Bubba said. "And he wants to help find Willodean Gray."

Simms' mouth opened and then shut again. As annoying as the deputy was, he couldn't think of something to dispute someone who wanted to help find the missing deputy.

Sheriff John came out, and his skin had lost most of its color. Bubba saw the bandage, which had covered his neck from a tracheotomy, was gone and only the flaming-red, half-healed wound remained. Reddish rope marks also remained about his neck. The older man had gone up against a killer and come out scarred. It would probably get him re-elected in the next round of elections.

"Do you know where the old man is, Bubba?" Sheriff John asked as he walked toward Bubba. Although the bandage had come off, his voice was still like crushed gravel.

"The place was like that when I got here," Bubba said. "I looked in the barn and round back, too. Ain't no sign of him."

Bubba wanted to get all up into Sheriff John's grill and insist they promptly go after Morgan Newbrough, but he had to convince the older man first.

Snap.

"What do you know about this?" Sheriff John asked as his steely eyed gaze took in The PSS with the bubble wrap. He might have been looking at The PSS, but Bubba knew he was talking to him.

"I wanted a photograph of Morgan Newbrough," Bubba said. He thought he might as well go for the gusto. Sheriff John liked it straight-up.

"Because?"

"His wife said he ain't been home for months and that he might be helping Nancy with all this Christmas Killer matters."

Sheriff John didn't say anything for a moment. "You think he's here and that he did something to his great-uncle?"

"Yep."

"Why didn't his wife have a photograph?" Simms asked with an obvious tone of derisiveness.

"Their house got burned down not a month after Morgan left."

"Burned like Miz Lou Lou's house? Like her shed, too?" Sheriff John made the connection. "Trying to cover up before she started on her bizness here?"

"That's what I reckon."

"And what in Hades does all this have to do with Deputy Gray's disappearance?" Sheriff John growled. "That's what you been chasing after, am I right, boy?"

"That other fella didn't do it," Bubba said.

Sheriff John's face crumpled. "Oh, damn."

"Le Beau's got an alibi. Pretty good one, too," Bubba said. The words came out stilted because he felt like a fool for chasing after Howell Le Beau and wasting precious time. "Spent his time in a mental health clinic with hourly checks. Reckon that fella, Park, will make sure of it."

"Ifin that other fella didn't do it," Simms said, "then who did?"

"David said that Nancy Musgrave talked about kidnapping Miz Demetrice," Bubba said.

Snap. Snap. Snap. "It's true. She did," The PSS admitted.

"Why in the name of roasted-molasses on a stick didn't you tell the po-lice?" Simms asked The PSS.

"No one listens to a crazy person," The PSS said with

a smile. *Snap.*

"So what?" Sheriff John said.

"Big Joe had Ma locked up instead. Made it a mite difficult to kidnap her."

"And Nancy was mad as spitting nails at you," Sheriff John said. "She tell her brother to snatch the deputy instead? That don't make sense. Ya'll hadn't even been on a date yet. And Gray didn't have nothing to do with all that historical society board bizness."

"I went to visit Nancy in prison," Bubba said. "She put me on her visitor's list from the day she got there. I think she thought I would come to ask her where my mother was, maybe to beg her to tell me. But I think what happened was that Morgan Newbrough couldn't get to my mother. And he heard about Willodean and me. So he figured that she'd be going out to the Snoddy place the same way as Ma would have been." Bubba took a deep breath. "Alternatively, maybe he even thought that Willodean had Ma in the back of the po-lice vehicle on account that Ma and Willodean get along."

"That makes more sense," Sheriff John allowed. "Deputy Gray's given all kinds of rides to Snoddys of late."

"So this Morgan fella took Deputy Gray?" Simms said. "Dang, I'm going nuttier than squirrel shit because it's starting to sound like it could have happened."

"But here's the bad part," Bubba said, "Morgan Newbrough is around here somewhere, pretending to be someone else, and I ain't exactly sure who he is."

Well, not exactly but I gotta damned good idea.

"Check with dispatch on his description from the DVM," Simms said as he reached for his shoulder mounted mike.

Bubba caught his wrist. "Cain't do that."

Simms' eyes went large and round. His hand shot up

and caught Bubba's wrist. "You want to let go of me, Bubba." His other hand touched his holstered weapon on his Sam Browne belt.

Bubba's eyes went to Sheriff John. "Ifin this guy has an in with the po-lice, he'll know we're onto him. He'll run, and we'll never know where she is. Maybe she's still alive. Maybe we can still get to her in time." He didn't want to beg but he was coming close.

Simms' hand fell away. "Use your computer, Sheriff. Ain't no one gonna know what you're looking at."

Bubba let go of Simms' wrist and said, "You sure no one can tell?"

Sheriff John nodded. They went to his county car and Sheriff John left the door open while he sat in the captain's style chair. The computer and keyboard were mounted just below eye level in the central part of the vehicle. "Got this and two others from a grant. We still need training on it, but it saves the patrols from calling dispatch for look-ups every five minutes. Let me log in."

Sheriff John tapped on keys and hummed tunelessly under his breath. "There. It should get pulled up in a few seconds."

Bubba pushed in near the door while Steve Simms wrangled for a closer position. The PSS was still playing with the bubble wrap. *Snap. Snap.*

The complete driver's license appeared on the monitor. Large enough to see from the door, the full-color photograph of the man named Morgan Newbrough materialized on the left of the screen. A man in his thirties with dark brown hair and brown eyes stared out at them.

Bubba didn't know the man.

"Shitfire damnation," he said.

Sheriff John studied the photograph on the computer screen. "Do you know him, Simms?"

Simms leaned in. "No, ain't never seen him."

"How about you, David?" Bubba said to The PSS.

The PSS sighed and peeked around the car's door at the computer screen. He stared for a moment and shook his head. "No, I've never seen that man before. David hasn't either."

"Bubba," Sheriff John said gently, "you thought that Morgan Newbrough would be someone you knew? Someone you seen around here?"

"Yeah," Bubba said. "I thought I had the little bastard nailed."

The PSS motioned for Bubba to move aside and he leaned in toward the computer. "Hmm."

"What?" Sheriff John snapped.

"Something funny about that driver's license," The PSS said.

Sheriff John's head went back to the computer screen. "What about it?"

"That man's got dark brown hair. He's got brown eyes, too."

"So?"

"The description on the license says he's got blonde hair and blue eyes," The PSS said and went back to his bubble wrap.

Bubba elbowed The PSS out of the way and leaned into the vehicle for a handier look.

"Sometimes the DVM makes mistakes," Simms said. "Folks dye their hair. Men, too. And lots of people have tinted contacts."

"David wears contacts," The PSS said knowledgably.

"Bubba," Sheriff John said slowly, "you know who Morgan Newbrough is, don't you?"

"I reckon I might."

"Well hell, boy," Sheriff John said. "Let's go get him. We'll sweat it out of him. We'll know where Gray is before you know it." His voice broke on Willodean's last name, and Bubba knew Sheriff John meant he thought they would find her remains.

Bubba stared at the image on the screen. "Somehow Morgan and Nancy managed to switch photographs on Morgan's image in the DVM. Ain't too many people can do that."

"Unlessin' you worked there," Simms said. "They didn't want to change my photograph last year because they just renewed the license. Saves money ifin you don't have any tickets or such. I didn't like the old one. Had a hunk of hair sticking up and made me look like a proper goober."

Sheriff John froze. "I know someone who worked at the DVM."

"Bet you do," Bubba said. "And he drives a Suzuki, don't he?"

Simms looked at Sheriff John and then at Bubba. "Who?"

"But it wasn't really Morgan who worked at DVM," Bubba added.

"It was the other guy who did," Sheriff John concluded. "And Nancy and Morgan targeted him? Maybe they paid him to switch the pictures? Maybe they been planning this for a long time. Setting it up."

"Nancy implied that it was years," Bubba said. "And I done upset the whole dang apple cart."

"And this other fella, the one who worked at DVM, once upon a time, just up and quit the place one day not six months ago," Sheriff John surmised. "Switched those photographs in all the right databases, maybe agreed to provide his resume for Morgan's use, and his background, too. Fella ain't married. He don't got parents left. No siblings. Moved from Atlanta last year. Has a real good record, exceptin' he fell for some line from Morgan or Nancy. Maybe they promised money or the like."

"What?" Simms asked.

"But I bet he's dead now," Bubba said with cold seeping through his bones. "Dead and buried somewhere folks ain't apt to find him and identify him anytime soon. On account of Morgan Newbrough taking his place and getting hisself hired in a new job. Not too many people about here expectin' that Morgan Newbrough is traipsing around pretending to be someone else."

"In order to be a spy for Nancy Musgrave," Sheriff John said. "So she would know what the po-lice were doing and how she could avoid getting arrested."

"And ifin I called Morgan's wife right now," Bubba said, "and asked, would she tell me that her soon-to-be ex-husband...stutters?"

"No," Simms said. His eyes were large and round. "Really? Him? But he's a complete wussy."

Sheriff John turned back to the computer and typed again. In another minute another driver's license showed on the screen. The man in his thirties with short, dirty, blonde hair and washed-out blue eyes regarded them.

"Look," Sheriff John said, pointing at the description information. The words under hair and eye colors said brown and brown. "That other fella was lazy. He didn't change anything exceptin' the photo."

"Let's go get him," Simms said heatedly. "Make him tell us where Gray is."

Bubba stepped back from the county car. "How long do you guess *that* will take?"

"What do you mean, Bubba?" Sheriff John asked as he logged out of the computer. "We'll get him in a room and make him sweat like a $2 whore in a church on

Sunday. I'll let Big Joe have a go at him. Hell, I'll let Miz Demetrice at him."

"You could let that kid, Brownie, have a go," Simms suggested maliciously.

That would do it but not in a timely fashion.

"It'll be days," Bubba said deliberately. "He'll lawyer up. His lips will be stitched up tighter than a corpse at the mortuary. And ifin she's still alive, no one will know where she's at, and- "

"Jesus," Sheriff John said, "you're right, Bubba. God help us."

"Morgan's worried about me," Bubba said. "Thinks I know too much. We got to do something about that. Make him think something happened to take me out of the big picture."

"Something like what?" Simms said.

Bubba rubbed his chin. "Morgan came like poop out of a goose when he thought I was gonna talk to Forrest Roquemore. What could Forrest know that would hurt Morgan?"

"The old man is a disagreeable sonuvabitch," Simms said, "but he loved his nephew. I had to come out here and work things out between him and his neighbors more than once, and he talked to me even though he didn't like me too much. Didn't think much of Matthew Roquemore's decisions, on account of him stealing money from orphans, but he said he used to visit Matthew once a month down to Huntsville. Prolly didn't think much of Nancy Musgrave murdering folks neither."

"When you go back to the Pegram County Sheriff's Department, you've all got to pretend you don't know Robert Daughtry is really Morgan Newbrough," The PSS announced. He held up the bubble wrap. "This is all used up. You think the post office clerk would give me some more?"

"I'll buy a roll of the stuff ifin you come up with something we can do," Bubba declared.

"Take Bubba to jail and tell everyone he did something to Forrest Roquemore," The PSS said. "You found him with a bloody handprint on the door and no old man anywhere to be found. That'll fool Robert, uh, Morgan, I mean."

The three men stared at The PSS.

"Then, you shadow Robert/Morgan," The PSS said. "He seems sort of the follower type. This was Nancy's plan. She was the leader, utterly completely. Without her guidance, the brother is dangling in the wind. He's probably confused, even scared half to death. It was a knee jerk reaction to come out and do harm to his great-uncle. It was likely a knee jerk reaction to take Deputy Gray, too. When Morgan got here, he might very well have confronted Forrest, and Forrest, being as contrary as you've suggested, probably got in his face. Morgan felt that he didn't have any choices.

"You've got to hurry on this before Morgan figures out that he left his bloody handprint on the door because I know you people had to have fingerprinted him. Then he'll know you're onto him.

"Finally, wherever Nancy and Morgan were planning on keeping Miz Demetrice, they wanted her to live long enough to see what was happening to the rest."

Bubba goggled at The PSS.

"They needed a place with heat, water, and enough seclusion to prevent others from hearing anything like an elderly woman screaming for help." The PSS turned the piece of bubble wrap over and tried to find a few bubbles he might have missed. "Conclusively, Morgan likely put the beautiful Deputy Gray there and consequently his great-uncle.

"Convince Morgan he has to go to that place, and you can follow him there."

Chapter Twenty-Two

Bubba Yells, "Damn the Torpedoes!"

Friday, January 6th

Bubba sat in the back seat of the official county vehicle while Sheriff John extracted his cell phone from a pocket and dialed his secretary, Patsy.

"Sheriff's office," Patsy said promptly, and Bubba heard her perky voice from the back of the SUV. He could even hear the song, "Heartlight", in the background before the music suddenly cut off.

"Patsy, it's Sheriff John," he said. "Do me a favor and call Robert Daughtry."

"But he went home sick," Patsy said.

"I know. Um, but we need him back working the lines for just a few hours, ifin he can. It's important."

"But Mary Lou is- "

"She's got...female troubles," Sheriff John said. "Yeah, female troubles. Just tell Robert I hope he's better, but it's an emergency and we need him bad."

"Mary Lou didn't say anything about female troubles," Patsy said indignantly, "and she was just in here talking about you arresting Bubba on suspicion of murdering that old man out to Nardle."

"Well, don't say nothing to the gal, Patsy," Sheriff John snapped. "Mary Lou would be embarrassed to have all and sundry knowing about her private business.

"Okay," Patsy said reluctantly. She disconnected and Sheriff John said, "Mary Lou's already spreading the word like gas on a bonfire. Dang, I need to call her and beg her not to spill the beans, don't I?"

The PSS said from the open window, "Shall I take

your truck and your dog home, Bubba?"

Sheriff John dialed another number on his cell phone while The PSS leaned in the window to listen to Bubba.

"Can you drive a stick, David?" Bubba asked.

Sheriff John spoke to Mary Lou in the background, quickly explaining what he needed and why.

"I *am* a superhero, Bubba," The PSS said with extreme confidence. "It's all in my noggin like schematics I can systematically extract. Pshaw. It's only an internal combustion device that runs on hydrocarbon materials from extinct animals. This planet needs to go to renewable fuel sources. Just like mine."

"Yes, Mary Lou," Sheriff John said into the cell phone. Bubba couldn't hear the other side of the conversation this time. "Two days off next week, and you've got to go home now because of personal stuff. You don't tell no one nothing else about that." Pause. "Talk about Bubba's arrest all you want. Go tell the janitor ifin you want about that. But on the other, I mean no one. Get it?" He listened for a few moments. "Okay, three days off next week. Swear on your mama's grave, Mary Lou. I mean it. I got to go. Remember, no one." Another pause. "Tomorrow you can talk about it all you want. Swear, Mary Lou."

"I 'spect that's a yes," Bubba said to The PSS. "Do me a favor, David. Would you take the truck back to the Snoddy place, and tell Miz Demetrice I got thrown in jail for suspicion of murder. Tell her it was bloody and awful. Po-lice brutality, too. Stuff they'd never do on your home world, which I thought was blown up, by the way."

"I'm gonna have to do dispatch myself next week," Sheriff John muttered and turned in the front seat. He replaced the cell phone in his pocket. "You know, telling

Miz Demetrice you're being arrested for suspicion of murder is going to rile her up something fierce."

"That's what Ma would do ifin it were the real deal," Bubba said. "And she cain't act worth a plug nickel."

"So don't tell Miz Demetrice anything else," The PSS confirmed.

"Don't tell her a bit of anything else," Bubba instructed. He passed his keys to The PSS. "Don't grind the second gear or Precious will bite your elbow."

The PSS sauntered back to the old, green Chevy truck. It started a minute later with a hack, a groan, and a wail. Precious howled in concert. The truck turned around in the driveway and headed back to Pegramville.

Bubba was impressed that David hadn't stalled the truck.

"Miz Demetrice is gonna be angry with you," Sheriff John said. "Hellfire and brimstone furious. Be pure perdition to live with."

"I can camp out in the new house," Bubba muttered, "and it's for a good cause."

"Bubba," Sheriff John said after an elongated minute, his voice was a study in neutrality, "it ain't really a good chance for her. Morgan Newbrough didn't have no reason to keep her alive. You know that, don't you?"

Sheriff John wasn't speaking of Miz Demetrice and Bubba knew it. The older man's voice was both sorrowful and miserable.

"I know," Bubba grated through his teeth, "but we got to try, don't we?"

"Yeah," Sheriff John agreed and turned forward. He put his seat belt on and started the county car. "I reckon we've spent enough time waiting for folks."

His cell phone rang, and he answered it gruffly.

"It's Patsy," Bubba heard the secretary say.

"Did you talk to Daughtry?" Sheriff John asked.

"Yeah, Sheriff, I called him at home. He said his stomach was doing better and said he'd come in as soon as he can," Patsy's voice echoed back to Bubba, and he nodded.

"Even Robert heard about all the excitement today," Patsy added, and Sheriff John's eyes met Bubba's in the rearview mirror.

"Patsy," Sheriff John said, "you need to go and make sure Mary Lou don't talk about nothing else. It's important. More than important. It's vital. Make damn sure she don't talk about going home because I asked her to."

"Ain't no female trouble then?" Patsy asked.

"No, it's more than that. I don't have time to explain. Just do as I asked and follow Mary Lou into the bathroom ifin you have to."

"I can do that," Patsy said firmly.

After she hung up, Bubba said, "Give David a little time to get to Ma. It'll make it look better ifin she's hollering at the front of the jail."

•

An hour later, Sheriff John parked the county car smack dab in front of the Pegram County Sheriff's Department and waited for the audience to appear. Once there, he even let the sirens keep going for a full sixty seconds. After a few minutes, he got out and Simms exited the other county car, joining him on the sidewalk. Both men conferred quietly as they eyed various people coming out from businesses and city hall. People gathered to see who was sitting in the back of the Bronco, although rumors had been rampant.

Sheriff John took his time getting Bubba to the county jail to allow everyone to percolate in a steady manner. When they thought enough people had gathered, the sheriff opened the back door for Bubba.

Bubba reluctantly climbed out with what most people would have called a frantic, criminal-like expression on his face. At least that was what he was going for.

Sheriff John held one arm and Steve Simms the other. Bubba lagged a little in their arms as if he was hesitant about being put into jail...again. Sheriff John directed Bubba toward the jail entrance so he could be locked up.

"Oh, Bubba dear," Miz Demetrice wailed from the crowd. The PSS stood beside her and patted her awkwardly on her shoulder. "Why does this keep happening to you?"

Precious, on a lead held by The PSS, bayed woefully.

Simms snorted. "Criminals go to jail, ma'am. Ain't surprising." He spoke loudly so as to be heard above Precious's noise.

The crowd shifted. Some of the reporters still hanging about had cottoned to events and were present in abundance, excitedly waiting for further developments.

"Sheriff, does that man have something to do with the disappearance of the deputy?" one reporter called.

"Oh dagnabit, no!" Miz Demetrice cried and tried to brain the reporter with a silver clutch. The reporter ducked and weaved until Bubba's mother gave up.

"We're looking into all possibilities," Sheriff John said with a grave expression. "We haven't finished our investigation."

"Does the missing man, Forrest Roquemore, have anything to do with the missing deputy?" another reporter called.

"I ain't harmed no one," Bubba said at full volume.

Simms said, "Stop struggling, Bubba. Ain't gonna do you no good."

Bubba jerked his arm out of Simms' hold. "I'm an innocent man!"

Sheriff John got a better grip on Bubba's other arm. "Stop that!"

Bubba glanced around the gathered people. They thought Mary Lou Treadwell would spread the word about Bubba and evidently she had. She must have spent twenty minutes on the phone making sure everyone knew that Bubba Snoddy was being arrested again. Sheriff John telling her she could talk about that all she wanted was akin to waving a red flag in front of a pissed-off bull.

They should install a revolving door for me in the jail.

Willodean's mother and father stood apart from the crowd. Evan Gray had an arm wrapped around Celestine's waist. Both parents were gaunt and red eyed. The previous week had been hell for them. Celestine visibly tried to figure out what the latest development had to do with Willodean while Evan attempted to contain her.

The town was well represented. Foot Johnson gawked at Bubba. Mike Holmgreen used his smart phone to make a digital recording. Doris Cambliss, owner of the Red Door Inn, stared incredulously at Bubba as he struggled. Edward Minnieweather, a process server and likely a frequent visitor to the jail, observed with aplomb. Roy and Maude Chance tussled with other reporters for the best surveillance spot. The mayor, John Leroy Jr., had unmistakably climbed out of his bottle to supervise the hullabaloo. Wilma Rabsitt walked over to Miz Demetrice and patted her back in a consolatory manner. Tom Bledsoe, the resident pickpocket, hovered over the reporter's backsides. Mary Lou Treadwell abandoned her post as dispatcher/receptionist and stood by the front door of the sheriff's department. Patsy hovered beside her as if ready to restrain Mary Lou's rapacious tongue.

Most importantly, Robert Daughtry stood next to Mary Lou and Patsy as if he had just shown up. He stared at Bubba just as all the others did.

Bubba let his eyes flutter past Robert as if he wasn't interested in the man in the least and yelled, "Hell no, I won't go!"

Miz Demetrice yelled, "Hell no, he won't go!"

The PSS yelled, "Superheroes ROCK!"

Precious bayed.

Mike Holmgreen shifted his smart phone toward The PSS for a moment.

Big Joe, Pegramville's Chief of Police, wandered over to see the ballyhoo. Two of his officers stood next to him. Haynes and Smithson, of the steel tipped boots, stared wide-eyed at the event.

Bubba jerked his arm out of Sheriff John's arm. "Ya'll are framing me!"

Should have handcuffed me. That would have looked more real.

His eyes shifted over Robert's tense form. The man appeared as if he might flee at any moment. Bubba knew that he had to make things look more realistic.

Bubba drew back a powerful arm and decked Simms. Simms fell over in a lump.

"Ya'll won't get away with it!" Bubba shouted. He danced to the left, trying to avoid the sheriff's grasping hands.

Sheriff John said a few eloquent and nasty words. Wilma Rabsitt gasped loudly. One of the reporters grinned like a Cheshire cat.

Bubba spun toward Sheriff John and ignored the fact of Big Joe and his officers pounding toward him. Four large men converged on Bubba, and all that could be seen were boots, fists, and a cloud of dust as they jumped on him and made a right proper mess on the ground, rolling about.

The only reason Bubba didn't get kicked in the head again was because Sheriff John put his large hand protectively over Bubba's head. When one of the local officers aimed a steel- toed boot at Bubba's head, it got the sheriff's hand instead and Sheriff John cursed roundly.

Miz Demetrice waded in with her silver clutch, crying, "You should be glad I don't have my purse with the brick in it, you communist poo-poo heads!" She smacked the backs of the officers' heads until The PSS hauled her back from the throng. Precious slipped her lead and tried to molest Haynes' leg in a most unsavory manner. The PSS got Miz Demetrice back and then retrieved Precious's lead before Haynes aimed his steel-toed boot at her, too.

A minute later Bubba made kissy-face with the cement of the sidewalk while he was handcuffed. He managed to get his nose out, away from the hard surface and turned his head so he could look through the men around him and on top of him. The crowd parted just enough to see Robert Daughtry smiling at the hubbub.

•

"Hey, Bubba," Tee Gearheart said. Tee was Pegram County's County Jailor and a friendly fellow. He was fair to his prisoners, and Bubba never had cause to complain about him. In fact, Tee had been instrumental in clearing up the case of Lurlene Grady/Donna Hyatt by allowing Bubba out of jail to do last minute investigating.

"Hey," Bubba said.

Tee paused to write down the date and time on a

291

scrap piece of paper. "Well hey, look at that," he said.

Sheriff John tugged Bubba a little closer to look at the sheet of paper. "Damn. I had the week of the fifteenth," he muttered. "Who won the pool for when Bubba went to jail next?"

"You have a pool on when I'm going back to jail?" Bubba asked.

"Yeah, well," Tee said, "going to Dallas County Jail didn't count. The pool's only for Pegram County Jail but next time we should just include all jails, huh? Just take those cuffs off, Sheriff, and I'll check the calendar."

Sheriff John cast a glance at the two city police officers who followed them. "You fellas can go on now. Thanks for the help." He held up the hand that had been kicked. It was red and throbbing. "But I swear to God, this better not be broken."

Smithson shrugged and Haynes scuttled away before Sheriff John could say anything else.

"Haynes was aiming for your head, Bubba," Simms said matter-of-factly. "He's still ticked about that kid biting him. Said Doc Goodjoint used a needle the size of a pitch fork's prong on his ass." Simms absently patted his buttock in commiseration.

"Good," Bubba said.

Sheriff John unlocked the cuffs, and Bubba brought his hands around to rub his wrists. "Did you have to make them so dang tight?"

"Did you have to clock me?" Simms asked belligerently. He rubbed the swollen part of his jaw. "I saw stars. Seriously. I saw stars and not the good kind with boobies."

"Well, Morgan bought it, dint he? And I cain't very well hit Sheriff John, can I?" Bubba asked.

"Why the heckfire not?"

"He's still wounded." Bubba pointed at Sheriff John's

throat. "And he's older than you. Cain't hit your elders."

"You hit Big Joe, and he's older than you," Simms protested.

"That was different," Bubba said.

Tee shuffled papers, peering at them carefully. "The person in the pool who had January 6th was- dang."

Bubba glanced at Tee and then back at Sheriff John. "When are you making the phone call?"

"Let Daughtry settle down for a bit. Get all relaxed like. Get hisself a cup of coffee. I'll say hey to him and thank him for coming in on short notice when he ain't feeling good. I'll go to my office, and he'll think he's safe," Sheriff John said. He looked sharply at Tee. "And Tee, you got to keep your mouth shut for the next couple of hours. Everything is bizness as usual. Bubba's in jail for suspected murder and ain't nothing else going on."

"Empty your pockets, Bubba," Tee said, noticeably confused.

Bubba sighed. He took everything out of his pockets and put it on the counter. Tee put the meager possessions in a small box and had Bubba sign a form.

"What *are* ya'll talking about?" Tee asked.

"It's a secret," Simms said. "Who won the pool? I had next week, and I don't reckon this should count seeing how it's not real and all."

"It's real," Sheriff John insisted. "Bubba's going to jail, ain't he?"

"Who's gonna make that call?" Bubba asked.

"My wife," Sheriff John said. "She took drama in college. And she's right fond of Gray. She'll drive over to Nardle in about an hour and pretend that she found some girl dressed in a po-liceman's uniform on the side of the road."

Tee perked up. "Ya'll are up to something serious."

"Ifin Morgan put Forrest Roquemore in with Willodean, it had to be only a couple of hours ago," Bubba said. "He ought to know whether she was able to get out or not."

The icy feeling of dread accompanying what was suggested nearly overwhelmed him.

"It can't be far from Nardle," Sheriff John said. "I looked, and Morgan Newbrough don't got property around here. Neither does Nancy. But Forrest does. He's got several pieces around Nardle. Ifin we can't follow Morgan, then I've got someone petitioning Judge Posey for a warrant for the property right now. Not that we need it on account that the old man is likely a victim of a crime and his property is a crime scene. Like to dot my i's and cross my t's just to be sure."

"Jumping to conclusions again," Bubba said. "That's a whole lot of if, and, and but with emphasis on the if."

"You said it before," Sheriff John said. "It's all we got. Patsy said she called Robert at home, *on his home phone.* So whatever he did, wherever he went, it wasn't far from Nardle. Think about it. It's a gamble, but it's worth the risk."

"Ifin Willodean is already dead," Bubba swallowed convulsively, and his eyes shut for a moment, "then Morgan will know it's a fake call. He'll run instead."

"Morgan's nervous, like the loony- ah, I mean, David Beathard said," Sheriff John stated. "We cain't lose on this roll. We shake him up and follow him. He'll check on Gray and Roquemore."

"It should be a call about Forrest Roquemore then," Bubba said. "There's a better chance that the old man is alive than Willodean." The hole in Bubba's chest seemed to grow exponentially. "That old man's gonna outlive us all. Probably come back from the dead to haunt us, too. The call should be about a bleeding elderly man on the side of the road. Unconscious, so Morgan won't run instead of going to check on them."

Sheriff John thought about it. "Yeah, that's better. But even better the call should say he's dead already and then Morgan won't feel like he's got to run right away."

"And you need to look at a map. There's two roads that go to Nardle. Make sure the call comes from the road Morgan wouldn't normally take. Ifin he's just a regular fella, he goes straight there. That's U.S. Highway 67. That call's got to say County Highway 6. Double check that on a map."

Tee looked from one man to the other. "You think you know where Deputy Gray is?"

"Not yet," Bubba said coldly. "But we're gonna know."

"Maybe you can tell her she won the pool," Tee said tentatively.

Chapter Twenty-Three

Bubba and Sheriff John Do a Thang

Friday, January 6th

"Five minutes until Robert Daughtry goes off shift," Bubba said, glancing at the clock on the wall in-between the cells. He didn't know why it was there because it was guaranteed to drive some inmates crazy with waiting for the hands to move.

Newt Durley, parked in a cell two doors down, said, "I said, I'm fine now. Can I please go home?"

Tee said, "You hit a fire hydrant, Newt. No one on that block could flush their toilets for three hours on account of it."

"I'll clean their toilets," Newt whined, "with a toothbrush even. I don't like it here. A cockroach is looking at me all friendly like and it ain't in a good way. I think it winked at me."

"Judge Posey is thinking about sending you to rehab," Tee called.

"What? Again? I was driving a golf cart. Ain't nobody said I cain't be driving a golf cart! And that fire hydrant jumped right out in front of me! It tried to molest the golf cart!"

"A motorized vehicle is a motorized vehicle," Tee advised.

"Bubba, do you need a driver's license to drive a golf cart?" Newt yelled.

"Don't rightly care," Bubba said.

A loud screech came from the end of the hall. Bubba stuck his head out of the cell while Tee meandered in the direction of the noise. Tee hadn't thought it was right for Bubba to be locked up officially because he wasn't really under arrest, so he'd left Bubba's cell door open. Through the entrance to the cellblock, Bubba could see Mary Lou Treadwell being hauled along by Sheriff John on one side and Patsy on the other.

"Ain't got no right to put me in jail!" Mary Lou wailed.

Tee got to the door and said, "We ain't got women facilities. The last time was on account that the city jail was full. That Miz Cambliss was shore a pleasant lady about it."

"Put that curtain up again," Sheriff John ordered furiously. "Mary Lou came back because she couldn't keep her mouth shut. She wanted to see what we were all up to."

"You really expect me to go home when all this excitement is happening?" Mary Lou exclaimed. "Oh holy guacamole, no. This place smells like a baby's butt and that's without the baby powder."

Tee made a face. "I use Febreze," he protested. "Hawaiian Aloha™ and Moroccan Bazaar™. Makes it smell like a luau on the Med."

"What in the name of bejesus is going on?" Mary Lou demanded.

"That call about to come in?" Bubba asked Sheriff John.

"Yeah, Darla called me a few minutes ago," Sheriff John said as he tugged Mary Lou down the row of cells. "We got two cars waiting on us. My cousin's Mercury and Simms will be driving his sister's Ford F-150. Both are a little beat up but run proper. I got the police band radios in 'em, so we can hear what's going on. But Patsy and Simms and I will keep contact by cell phone. Patsy's going up to relieve Robert in about ten minutes."

"Why couldn't ya'll just tell me you had something special going on?" Mary Lou asked in an irate tone.

"Because *you* have a big mouth," Patsy said and unceremoniously shoved the other woman into the cell. Obviously, Sheriff John had filled Patsy in on the details of the scam they were about to implement on Robert Daughtry/Morgan Newbrough.

Tee locked the door to Mary Lou's cell with economical ease.

"Who me?" Mary Lou asked. "I don't have a big mouth." She pressed her head against the bars and paused while Tee locked the cell. "I'm just silence challenged."

"Call that other gal to take over dispatch just as soon as she can," Sheriff John said to Patsy. "What's her name?"

"Arlette Formica," Bubba answered.

Sheriff John looked at Bubba oddly. "Yeah, her. Come on, Bubba, we're going out the back."

Bubba stared at Sheriff John. "I thought you'd try to make me stay here."

Sheriff John shrugged. "I figured you'd go through Tee, and Tee's got a family to support so he cain't be losing his job."

"Don't bring up the thing about the mascot no more, Bubba," Tee said with an utterly serious expression.

"Wonder what ever happened to that goat?" Bubba asked innocently.

Sheriff John looked around. "Mary Lou's all shut up. Check. Cars ready. Check. Got my cell phone and it's charged. Check. Patsy's got both numbers of the cell phones. Check." He stopped to pat his shirt pockets. "Got my gun and it's loaded. Check. Patsy be ready to call an ambulance ifin we need it."

Patsy crossed her fingers on both hands and held them in the air as she looked at Bubba. "Okay, I guess that's my cue to be in the front area when the call comes in," she said. "I'm gonna be praying."

"Me, too," Bubba muttered.

•

Bubba and Sheriff John sat in a Mercury Grand Marquis. Both men slumped down in the seats with only their eyes peering over the dashboard. Morgan Newbrough's Suzuki Samurai sat three cars down from them. A half block down, Simms sat in a blue and white Ford F-150 truck.

Sheriff John called Simms and told him, "Going now. I'll take the first lead. As soon as he gets on the highway, you'll take over."

Bubba couldn't hear what Simms said, but Sheriff John disconnected the phone without delay.

Next, Sheriff John called his wife, Darla. He said, "Hun, we're all ready for you. Remember we changed the script. Your name is Jane Stamper. The real Jane lives out there and agreed to let us use her name. Be sure to use the disposable cell phone. You just found a fella off County Highway 6 and Routen Road. He's dead because you can't feel a heartbeat and it looks like he's been beaten. You think it might be that old man who went missing from Nardle on account that it ain't too far away. Can they send the po-lice and quickly."

Darla said loudly enough that Bubba could hear it, "I got the text you sent, you durn fool!"

"Sorry, hun," Sheriff John said. "This is key. Ain't gonna get another chance like this."

"I know. I can pull it off," Darla said. "Let me talk to Bubba."

Sheriff John frowned at the cell phone and handed it to Bubba.

"Ma'am," Bubba said.

"We all want the best out of this sad situation, Bubba," Darla said. "Cain't thank you enough for saving

299

John from that awful woman, Nancy Musgrave."

"It ain't necessary, ma'am," Bubba said.

Sheriff John tapped his watch.

"Have hope, Bubba," she said. "Tell that old stick in the mud I'm making the call right now."

The call ended.

"She's doing it now," Bubba said and handed the phone to Sheriff John.

Bubba wanted to cross his fingers, knock on wood, throw salt over his shoulder, and anything else he could think of for luck. If a black cat had appeared, he would have gleefully chased it out of his path.

Sheriff John turned on the police band radio. A minute later, Robert Daughtry's voice came over the line, directing several units to a location in Pegram County for a code indicating a deceased individual. The voice stuttered several times and Bubba groaned.

"Shush," Sheriff John said with his hand on the microphone. He keyed it and responded, "Unit 1 en route to County Highway 6 and Routen Road. ETA ten minutes."

Two other officers responded. Darla would meet them and explain the situation. They would be instructed to call Sheriff John on secure lines to confirm. Furthermore, she had Lloyd Goshorn covered with ketchup lying in the ditch on the side of the road as the dead "victim."

A minute passed. One of the deputies stumbled out of the building and trotted for his cruiser. He took off in the right direction with his siren blaring and the lights revolving brightly.

"What about *your* county car?" Bubba asked.

"I parked it two blocks over so that fella wouldn't see it and get suspicious. Simms did the same."

"Come on," Bubba said with impatience as he stared

at the front door of Pegram County Sheriff's Department. "Take the bait, fella. Come on."

The cell phone rang and both men jumped.

"Yeah," Sheriff John answered.

Bubba could hear Patsy reply. "Well, Robert took the call, threw up in the trashcan and ran into the bathroom. I expect he ain't really feeling well. Sure he's the one?"

"Don't say anything else, Patsy," Sheriff John instructed.

"Okay, but he ain't rushing- " Patsy's voice trailed off. Both men heard her say, "You don't look so well, Robert."

Both Sheriff John and Bubba leaned toward the cell phone. They couldn't hear what Robert said to Patsy.

She said, "Yeah, you should go on now. I'll hold it until Arlette Formica gets here. Maybe you should get some Pepto-Bismol or something."

Bubba said, "Look."

Robert Daughtry walked out the front door. His color was as gray as a battleship's butt. He stumbled once and wiped his mouth with the back of his shirt sleeve.

"Sheriff," Patsy said, "he just left. On account of he's sick. And he *is* sick. Well, he was sick. I ain't cleaning that trashcan."

"Call me ifin Robert comes back," Sheriff John said. "And as far as anyone else is concerned, that last call was as real as rain until I say otherwise."

"Okay, Sheriff, tell Bubba my fingers are still crossed," Patsy said and disconnected.

"She said- " Sheriff John started and Bubba interrupted, "I heard."

Robert got into the Suzuki and started it. He backed out of the space and drove down the street. Sheriff John started the Mercury and followed him, allowing the other car enough space so as not to alarm the man.

"Not stopping at the convenience store," Bubba said.

"And his apartment's on the other side of town," Sheriff John said.

"And he just passed the clinic," Bubba added.

They got to the edge of Pegramville, and the Suzuki turned on U.S. Highway 67.

The Ford truck Simms drove passed them on the left and took up after the Suzuki.

Bubba clenched the oh-shit bar above the glove box. Dimly he registered that the shape of the plastic bar was contorting with the strain. He let go with a curse.

Sheriff John glanced over and said, "My cousin won't mind. This is the car he's going to give to his daughter when she turns sixteen. He wants it as disagreeable as can be so she won't be taking all kinds of other teenaged passengers with her. Runs like a top but needs a paint job and seat covers. Kids don't wanna ride in an ugly car."

Bubba couldn't see the logic, but he couldn't really concentrate on Sheriff John's words. It occurred to Bubba that Sheriff John was trying to comfort him, in his own gruff manner.

The cell phone rang and Sheriff John answered it. "Yeah?" He pulled it away and pushed the speaker button.

"Simms here. Daughtry just blasted through a stop sign," Simms said. "Reckon he's in a hurry. As far as I can tell, he ain't cottoned to me. Need to back off before we reach Nardle though."

"As soon as we get to the old church a mile out of Nardle, you turn off, and I'll take over," Sheriff John said.

Bubba took a breath and thought about the day he'd taken this trip in Willodean's official county car. He

302

hadn't been looking around that day. He'd been staring at her, trying to figure out the best way to entice her into a date. It hadn't hurt that she'd kissed him first, but he hadn't wanted to make mistakes.

There was only one bitter realization. Waiting to ask Willodean out had been a mistake.

Sheriff John adjusted the volume on the police radio and listened to the chatter about the code near Nardle. Bubba knew the other deputies would reach Darla within a few minutes, and she would convince them within seconds. Darla was anything but a priggish miss.

Sure enough, Sheriff John's cell phone rang a minute later. He spoke quickly. The setting had reverted to a regular one, and he said into the cell, "Deputy Tempchin, I know it's irregular, but we got something going on. Pretend there's a real damn dead body there." He paused, and Bubba couldn't hear the deputy's words. "Ifin the state po-lice show up, then tell them the same thing. Keep your traps shut for the next hour. You're investigating a dead body. Call a paramedic and the acting coroner like you would for any other damn dead body." Pause. "Yes, I know we've got lots of dead bodies lately. Just go with it, boy." Another pause, and Sheriff John sighed. "Lloyd Goshorn may only smell like a dead man but just go with it. I'll tell you when we can move on. Pretend, dammit."

Sheriff John shoved the phone at Bubba. "Hold that." He punched the gas on the Mercury and caught up to Simms in the Ford F-150. Simms turned off the road at a church with a steeple that was canted precariously to one side. Bubba stared at Simms as he turned around in the church's dirt lot.

"Sheriff?" a tinny voice said from the cell phone.

Sheriff John peered ahead, his head moving left and right. "Oh cheese and crackers," he muttered.

"Sheriff cain't talk right now," Bubba said into the cell phone. As he spoke he looked to see what Sheriff John was seeing. "Just do as he said. You can call Simms on his cell phone for verification. Also Patsy at the department, too. Call the President ifin you have to."

Sheriff John said a nasty word. He drove the Mercury around the gradual bend passing the 7-Eleven and the post office. Abruptly he pulled the Mercury to the shoulder of the road. He said a few more nasty words. Craning his neck frenziedly, Bubba peered around. He couldn't see the Suzuki anywhere. That was the reason Sheriff John had been cursing.

There were a few cars parked near the minimal amount of houses in Nardle, but none of them was a dark blue Samurai with a cracked cream-colored ragtop.

"He's gone," Bubba said. His voice was a hoarse pit of anguish. "*Oh no.* He's gone."

And so was any opportunity to find Willodean.

Chapter Twenty-Four

So What Happened to Willodean?

Friday, January 6th

Miz Demetrice's only beloved son was imprisoned and by Bubba's own words, falsely.

Bubba had shrieked out his innocence even while the blackguards leaped upon his blameless body. No mother should have to witness such a sordid affair. One of her hands fluttered dramatically over the area of her heart indicating the possibility of an imminent heart attack.

Quickly she called Lawyer Petrie and begged for his instantaneous attendance upon Judge Stetson Posey.

"Damn the fees, man!" she bellowed into the cell phone. "Bubba has been unjustly accused of dire, horrid actions! You must act accordingly!"

Injustice occurred and legal maneuvering must overcome!

But a mother can only do so much telephonic manipulation. She finished with calls to the governor's office, the ACLU, the newspapers, and a distant cousin once removed who attended Harvard. She followed up with an interview with the reporters who still hung about the Pegram County Sheriff's Department like flies on, well, excrement.

It was a short interview on account of the fact that Miz Demetrice had no idea of the evidence against Bubba or why he wouldn't have done deadly harm to Nancy Musgrave's great-uncle, Forrest Roquemore.

The PSS interrupted with, "Bubba Snoddy is a fine and honorable individual, just like those peoples from my home world."

The reporters spent about five minutes questioning The PSS's general sanity.

"I am THE PURPLE SINGAPORE SLING," The PSS said, as if the statement clarified any question of his mental competence.

Miz Demetrice glanced around the front area of the sheriff's department and decided she would visit with her son.

Damn the authorities.

Marching into the Pegram County Jail, Miz Demetrice dragged Precious along on her lead. The PSS followed reluctantly, flagrantly wanting to continue his fifteen minutes of fame with the reporters.

Tee Gearheart sat at the front counter. Slowly he stood and towered over the diminutive Miz Demetrice. "Ma'am," he said.

"Tee," Miz Demetrice said.

"Ain't visiting hours yet," Tee said.

"You'll let me speak to my son all the same," Miz Demetrice instructed.

Tee pulled at the collar of his shirt. "I cain't do that."

Miz Demetrice frowned.

"Ma'am- " Tee started and faltered. Then he repeated, "Cain't do that."

Miz Demetrice put her best sternest, motherist face on. "Tee Gearheart, you have eaten at my dinner table on more occasions than I can count. You have done your duty by my son in an honorable way by allowing him to investigate while being jailed in your cell. Surely, you can provide me with a sparse five minutes?"

"Don't call me Shirley," Tee said weakly.

Miz Demetrice stared at him. Her head tilted, and she looked around him. The door to the block was standing open, and she could clearly see the lines of cells. "Isn't that Newt Durley climbing out the window?"

306

"What?" Tee turned to look. By the time he figured out that Miz Demetrice had fooled him, she had slipped around him and moved swiftly down the block, looking for her son.

Tee trailed after her, at a loss for what to say. The PSS wandered in, saying, "I always wondered what the inside of a jail looked like."

"Hey," Tee protested, "no, ah, loonies or dogs in the cellblock."

Miz Demetrice stopped at Mary Lou's cell and said, "What are you doing in here, Miz Mary Lou?"

"Apparently, I gotta big mouth," Mary Lou said. Her words dripped with bitterness.

"Where's Bubba?" Miz Demetrice asked. "Is he being questioned?"

Tee said, "Uh, uh, um. You need to talk to Sheriff John."

"Bubba's gone," Mary Lou said.

"Gone?" Miz Demetrice repeated. "Gone where?"

"Sheriff John's got some kind of trap set up for the fella who's prolly the one who took Deputy Gray. It was Bubba's idea, and they said I couldn't keep my mouth shut, so Sheriff and Patsy drug me here and locked me up. I'm as mad as a bear stuck in a hornet's nest because he thought it was bees and there ain't no honey."

Miz Demetrice's mouth opened and shut. Then it opened again. "The arrest was...fake?"

"Miz Mary Lou!" Tee thundered. "Cain't you keep quiet about nothing?"

Mary Lou shook her head sadly. "No, not really, no."

"What's going on, Tee?" Miz Demetrice asked.

"Cain't tell you," Tee said forlornly.

"Bubba thinks Nancy Musgrave's brother is really Robert Daughtry," Mary Lou said immediately. "Or is it that Robert Daughtry is really Nancy's brother?"

"Oh, Christ," Tee said and straightaway added, "beg pardon."

"And they thought ifin they called in a false report about someone finding the great-uncle dead, then Robert would rush out to check on it," Newt Durley said from three cells down.

"And Sheriff John took Bubba with him?" Miz Demetrice asked.

"Sheriff thought I might let Bubba out," Tee muttered.

"Where did they go?"

"Back out to Nardle," Mary Lou said quickly.

Precious let out an anxious howl.

Newt said, "Who's the guy in the purple mask? Oh, please tell me I ain't got the DT's again. I cain't take no more of them pink spiders!"

Miz Demetrice hadn't exactly lost hope, but she was fully aware the chances of Willodean Gray being found alive were slim. However, she liked long shots, and she would do just about anything to help her son.

"Oh, Tee," Patsy said from the door of the block. She held a stack of magazines she was evidently bringing to Mary Lou Treadwell to keep the woman occupied. "Cain't you keep no one out of your jail?"

Miz Demetrice rushed out of the jail, dragging Precious with her. The PSS trotted after the Snoddy matriarch. When she plunged through the exterior doors, she saw the Grays gathered near the entrance to the sheriff's department

Ifin I was that girl's mama, I'd want to know, Miz Demetrice thought. She went ahead and told the Grays what she had discovered while she hurried to her car.

•

"Cain't have gone far," Sheriff John said.

Bubba cast his glance around frantically. It was a one-horse hitching-post town. There wasn't anywhere for the Suzuki to have disappeared. His eyes scanned a ranch house with five rusting cars parked there. Since the last time Bubba had seen it, the 64 ½ Mustang hadn't moved, but one of the front doors had fallen off. Forrest Roquemore's house was sadly empty. Tape had been left across the tiny front porch. The evidence team had come and gone, leaving only a bit of yellow streaming in the wind. The other shotgun houses were desolate and alone. The entire area was as quiet as a tomb.

People lived here, but they hid in their houses or were away.

Bubba got out of the Mercury. He couldn't just sit there. It was like accepting the specter of death knocking at the door with a scythe.

What he wanted to do was roar at the world. He wanted to scream and holler at the unfairness of life. *Why that woman? Why her? She ain't done nothing to deserve that from no one.*

Bubba wanted to bargain with God. *God, if you're listening, now's the time for a little something on your end. Flaming arrows pointin' the way. Something. Anything.*

"The Suzuki was only out of my sight for twenty seconds," Sheriff John said into the cell phone. While Bubba was trying to talk God into action, the sheriff was rallying reinforcements, and an instant of shame overcame Bubba.

"Ain't but two roads out of here. Call Deputy Tempchin." Pause. "No, I ain't got his cell number. Call Darla and have her hand the phone to Tempchin. Keep an eye out for the Suzuki Samurai. It's a 1987 with Texas plates, XJG-555. That's X-ray, Juliet, Golf, fiver,

fiver, fiver."

Bubba spun around. Then he spun around again. Sheriff John poked fingers at his cell phone again. For a solitary moment, there was silence.

But it wasn't all silent.

His head snapped to the left. Forrest Roquemore's house was the third on the left. It was merely a narrow shotgun home with a dirt yard. There was a drive way up the side that went around back.

He remembered something.

Sheriff John said Forrest had properties around Nardle. If this didn't work, they would be checking those out. The police would be searching them because Morgan and Nancy had to have a place for Miz Demetrice to be kept. That was assuming The PSS was correct about what he'd heard while heavily dosed with antipsychotic drugs.

There was something else Bubba remembered. *I looked out into the backyard and noticed the old man's property spread out significantly once it got past the typical backyard. The fences opened into pasture area with a small barn. Twin ruts twisted through the pasture toward a wall of trees in the distance. A single donkey pawed a broke-open bale of hay.*

Twin ruts led through a pasture and toward a wall of trees. Twin ruts that looked well-used and Forrest said he lost his vehicle when Hurricane Katrina caused a tree to fall on it and couldn't replace it. So ifin Forrest ain't got a car, whose car is making the ruts well used?

Bubba heard the whine of a not-so-distant motor. He knew motors. It was the strained noise of an old four-cylinder engine struggling to cross a field of grass and mud. It made sense. In the sparse seconds the Suzuki had been out of sight, it had turned into Forrest's drive and gone behind the house. Robert

Daughtry/Morgan Newbrough had taken a moment to open the gate and drive through. He'd probably taken another moment to close the gate to ensure the donkey didn't get out.

Bubba ran. Surprisingly for such a big man, he ran fast.

•

Sheriff John dialed Patsy and told her to put a BOLO out for Robert Daughtry aka Morgan Newbrough in the dark blue Suzuki Samurai. She was to use the secure lines in order to get it out to all the law enforcement in the area. He didn't know if Morgan had a police radio in his car, but it was a strong possibility considering the enormity of Nancy Musgrave's planning.

Patsy said, "Doing it right now, but Sheriff, there's something else."

"What?" Sheriff John snapped.

"Miz Demetrice forced her way into the jail and found out Bubba wasn't there," Patsy said all at once.

"Tee Gearheart weighs over 300 lbs. and he couldn't stop that little lady? Did she have a bazooka?"

"Well, he's afraid of her," Patsy explained. "But then Mary Lou told her why Bubba wasn't there. Mary Lou was desperate to tell someone something, so she did."

"Oh crap," Sheriff John said, "I mean carp."

"Miz Demetrice rushed out of here, followed by that fella in the purple get-up and Bubba's dog. And Miz D. told Deputy Gray's family as she was running past." Patsy sighed. "They all got in their cars and rode off like bats out of hell. They nearly ran Alice Mercer down in the road. Her dog, Bill Clinton, got away and bit one of the reporters who says he's suing everyone. The reporter called us all but lowdown penis wrinkles."

"Okay," Sheriff John said when Patsy paused to take a breath. He disconnected and called Simms back.

"Simms. Civilians coming into Nardle. Stop them. It's Miz Demetrice and the Grays. Stop them even ifin you have to shoot them."

"Really?" Simms sounded intrigued with the carte blanche to shoot someone with his official sidearm.

"No, dumbass. Just stop them." Sheriff John disconnected again and looked around for Bubba. The passenger door to the Mercury hung open and Bubba had vanished.

Sheriff John's head swiveled, not unlike a fourteen-year-old's head in a 70's horror movie.

Bubba was well and truly gone.

"CRAP!" Sheriff John yelled. "OH HELL, I MEAN CARP!"

•

Bubba took the gate by virtue of sailing over it. One hand hit the top rail, holding it as the rest of his body floated over to one side. His boots cleared the top by a good foot. The donkey had been ambling back over to the bale of hay when she was startled by Bubba's sudden appearance in her field. She hee-hawwwwwhed and fled for the barn, braying all the way.

He couldn't see the Suzuki, but the grass around the gate had been driven over, and recently. The tracks of tires made patterns in the soft earth of the ruts.

Bubba followed the tracks at a dead run. He peered into the woods ahead of him seeking the Suzuki, but he couldn't see any sign of the little SUV. Desperately, he made himself stop. For a long moment, all Bubba could hear was the hoarse rasp of his own breathing. The blood was thundering through his body and even it sounded as loud as church bells on Sunday.

Why else would Morgan drive back here? This has to be where he'd put Forrest and likely Willodean, too.

It would have been difficult to guess Forrest had all

312

this property behind his little shotgun house. Bubba hadn't realized it, and he wondered if anyone but the neighbors knew.

They'd probably complained about the donkey's braying, so they had to know. But why mention it to the po-lice? It wasn't like they recognized it would be important. Maybe the neighbors didn't want to mess with the irritable old man and could care less about his back property. Who knew?

Bubba held his breath and listened intently. He heard the grinding of the car's gears, and then the engine abruptly went silent. He let out the breath and loped toward the wall of forest. The Suzuki was in there. So was Morgan Newbrough. And there was where Bubba was going.

He discovered another fence and another gate, making short work of both.

He plunged into shadows and paused to let his eyes adjust. The day had sped away while they were anxiously waiting to see if their impromptu plan worked. The minutes that seemed like hours before now became like seconds instead. The sun was about to set, and the entire area would be a miasma of darkness.

Bubba made himself slow down. He made his feet make careful steps so as not to alert the man he was pursuing. It wouldn't do to let Morgan know Bubba was right behind him.

Morgan thinks he's alone. He thinks he's clear for the moment. He doesn't know I'm here. I don't want to give it away. Bubba repeatedly warned himself to be careful despite the urgent need to rush.

Bubba kept to the darkest shadows as he moved down the narrow ruts ground into the forest's floor. He rounded a towering stand of hardwoods making an almost impenetrable barrier.

An old building sat there. The Suzuki parked next to it. The engine was off. No one sat inside the vehicle.

Bubba's heart fell into his stomach. The place was secluded. It was isolated. Few people knew about it. However, Nancy had likely known about it. It could very well be a place where Miz Demetrice could be kept until all the others on Nancy's Christmas killing list had been done away with.

Morgan was nowhere to be seen which made Bubba's heart drop even lower.

He's inside with Forrest? With Willodean?

The front door of the building slammed open, and Morgan came out. Bubba no longer cared if he was standing in a shadow or not. Morgan wiped the back of his mouth with his sleeve and shifted the rifle he carried in his other hand.

Bubba's eyes focused on the rifle and only the rifle. Rage saturated his entire being.

Without hesitation, Bubba began moving forward in a direct line. In the beginning, it was a slow charge, but with each step it evolved into an increasingly faster pace, until he was a juggernaut intent on supreme destruction.

Morgan didn't realize Bubba was coming at him until he was ten feet away. Morgan's head snapped up, his eyes went as large as saucers, and he fumbled to bring the rifle up.

But it was too late. Bubba plowed into the other man with a great forceful impact. The rifle went flying into the bushes, and Bubba roared as Morgan's back smashed into the wall of the building. Planks of wood cracked in response.

Bubba took a step back and doubled up one great fist. A world-ending roundhouse punch took Morgan out. He promptly fell down on the ground and didn't move again.

Bubba spared the unconscious man only a brief glance. He turned to the building and hurtled inside.

Coming to a lumbering stop nearly ten feet inside, Bubba realized the building was part of an old cotton gin. Bits of rusting equipment littered the floor. Crates once used for transporting bales of cotton sat along one wall. He unfroze and searched left and right.

But neither Willodean nor Forrest were in the old building.

•

Steve Simms had selected a good point to block the highway into Nardle. Miz Demetrice had to admit it even while she cursed the deputy's thoroughness. The Ford F-150 blocked the middle of the road. A deep ditch prevented going around on one side. A steep embankment kept anyone from driving past on the other side. The deputy kept himself centered in front of the truck. His sidearm was out and pointed downward.

Miz Demetrice stopped the Cadillac and got out in a rush. "You'll move!" she shouted. "Damned if you won't."

"Now, I don't want to have to arrest you, Miz Demetrice," Simms said reasonably.

Miz Demetrice chomped down to keep the slew of vicious words from pouring out of her mouth. She took a breath and glanced back to see the Gray family pulling up behind her; furthermore, two news vans stopped behind them.

Reality crashed upon Miz Demetrice's head. She didn't want to admit it. Whatever Bubba and Sheriff John were doing, it was for the benefit of Willodean Gray and not for Miz Demetrice.

She would have to trust that if the worst was to happen, Bubba would manage to restrain himself from killing Nancy Musgrave's brother.

Please, God, she prayed, *don't let Bubba murder that man in hot-blooded fury. I don't believe the boy could live with himself. Amen. And if you're listening, God, it would be right nice ifin Willodean were to come out of this alive and healthy. Thank you. Don't listen to all those people that say bad things about you. You rock.*

Miz Demetrice glanced over her shoulder again. Celestine and Evan Gray climbed out of their car. Their other daughters weren't with them. Miz Demetrice suspected they'd had to go back to Dallas and return to their everyday lives as if Willodean wasn't missing at all.

The PSS clambered out of the passenger side of the Cadillac. Precious tumbled out after him, and she immediately began sniffing at the side of the road.

Simms kept a wary eye on all of them.

Celestine approached Simms and said, "Is there anything you can tell us?" Her voice cracked with anxiety. Miz Demetrice's heart warped at the sheer angst contained within the tone.

Simms' face twisted. "I ain't heard nothing yet, ma'am. I wish I could tell ya'll something else. I surely do."

Miz Demetrice had never particularly cared for Steve Simms. He liked to give tourists speeding tickets too much. He had several favored locations he used for speed traps in the county; additionally, he didn't like Bubba, and Bubba had intimated that Simms hit on Willodean.

But with that last statement to Celestine Gray, Miz Demetrice's estimation of the man rose. A little bitty notch, but it still rose.

She rubbed a tired hand over her face.

None of them could do anything.

"Hey!" The PSS said and lunged for Precious's lead.

The Basset hound darted around The PSS. She shot past Simms who said, "Dang it!"

With long ears soaring in the wind and her crooked knees nearly knocking together, Precious galloped headlong into Nardle.

•

Bubba searched the building again. He took a moment to shred his t-shirt into strips and hogtied Morgan Newbrough in a manner which would have made calf ropers proud. Unfortunately it wasn't timed; Bubba thought he might have broken a record.

Morgan didn't shoot anything just now. I didn't hear a gunshot. I didn't hear a gunshot. Bubba repeated the mantra as if it would save him. *There* wasn't *a gunshot.*

Bubba paused to call Sheriff John, but he hadn't gotten his disposable phone back from Tee. He looked slowly about and decided he could look for a freshly turned patch of earth.

Numbness began to settle in his bones.

•

Sheriff John looked in Forrest Roquemore's house and shook his head. No one had been inside. The seal from the CSI team was still on the door, unbroken, until he had broken it a minute before.

He stepped back onto the porch and thought about it. Bubba had to be around somewhere. The good ol' boy had seen something and taken off like a bullet.

Big fella like that dint fly away.

A hint of movement caught Sheriff John's eye. His eyes got big as he perceived what it was coming.

Bubba's Basset hound came bounding down the road, spared Sheriff John a brief glance, and turned down Forrest's driveway. She went right around the house. A tan leash trailed behind her as she ran.

After a moment of hesitation, the sheriff pursued the

dog. As he came around the edge of the house, he saw Precious scrambling under a gate. A donkey hee-hawwhhhed at the dog and wheeled away.

Precious ignored the braying donkey and chased ruts across the field.

Sheriff John paused to open the gate on account he couldn't squeeze under the fence. By the time he trotted across the field, the animal was out of his sight. But the other gate just inside the tree line wasn't.

•

Bubba couldn't find anything. He couldn't find any sign the earth had been recently dug up. He couldn't find Forrest Roquemore. Most importantly, he couldn't find Willodean Gray.

But he had Morgan Newbrough.

Bubba stomped to where the man lay hogtied next to the broken wall of the building. Staring down at the still-unconscious brother of a killer, Bubba couldn't decide exactly what to do next.

Or just another killer?

Bubba's hands were nearly wrapped around Morgan Newbrough's neck before he stopped himself.

She still might be- oh hell. She still might be...

His hands twitched longingly. Bubba could pick Morgan up and bash his stupid skull against the wood until the man stopped breathing. He could break Morgan's silly addlepated neck in a heartbeat. He could push Morgan's face into the mud and wait until he stopped breathing.

And oh, I want to, oh how I want to.

His hands convulsed closer to the insensible man.

Bubba stopped. His eyes closed.

Then something licked his hand in a wetly salacious manner. His eyes snapped open.

"BARRRR-OOOOOO!" Precious bayed at Bubba. She

318

danced on the ground, attempting to paw at him while her tail wagged furiously.

The air came out of Bubba's chest in a convulsion of pain. He knelt in order to pet his dog. Precious licked his hands and arms and his chest. She then put her front paws on his knees so she could lick his face. He would have held her but he didn't think he was capable.

"I lost her, Precious," he said to the dog. "I lost Willodean. We gambled and we failed. I'm the dumbest redneck in the whole county and that's saying a lot."

Precious's head perked up at the sound of Willodean's name. She bayed again. "BARRRR-OOOOOO!"

Bubba blinked at his dog.

Precious dropped to all fours on the ground and systematically sniffed. Lew Robson had trained Precious to hunt just like the other hounds he raised, but she hadn't been one of the best. That was one of the reasons she had been given to Bubba.

"Hunt, Precious?" Bubba said hoarsely. He stood up and discovered his knees felt like warmed rubber.

"BARRRR-OOOOOO!"

"Hunt. Find Willodean?" he said with a strained voice. "You know her, girl, don't you? She gave you half her sandwich from Arby's when she thought I wasn't looking."

Precious put her nose to the ground. *Silly human. Of course I remember the one with the roast beef.* She paused abruptly and bayed again. "BARRRR-OOOOOO!"

Off she went like a rocket. Precious went around the Suzuki and into the woods. A barely perceivable trail curled into the thick forest. Bubba hadn't noticed it before because it was overgrown with brush and fast growing pines. He staggered after the dog; the numbness stilling his chest was starting to fade as he moved to follow Precious.

One hundred yards into the forest was another building.

Bubba hesitated. It was falling to pieces. Wood planks lay on the ground near the walls. The roof canted to one side. The shingles were half gone. Those remaining were covered with green moss. One side had collapsed into the ground. He could see right through the walls and knew straightaway no one was there.

Precious bayed again. "BARRRR-OOOOOO!!!" She cast an impatient glance over her shoulder at Bubba. She circled the house.

Bubba stumbled after the dog. She stopped in front of a pair of doors set at a forty-five degree angle into a great hill of earth and rocks. It was about fifty feet away from an antique house at the center of a small clearing. It was an old storm cellar. This part of Texas was tornado country during the windswept spring, and shelters had been used for the better part of two centuries here.

The breath in Bubba's chest froze as he took in the sparkling-new chain and lock on the moss-covered doors of the storm cellar.

Wouldn't be a new chain and lock ifin there weren't something to hide. Morgan put the rifle in the old cotton gin building so it wouldn't be in his car. He'd stopped there to get it and was gonna come here next?

Bubba didn't bother with the chain and the lock. He simply ripped the doors off. The wood was old and the hinges rusted. They came off with an alacrity that even surprised him. An alarming thought speared through him.

If Willodean is alive, she wouldn't have been stopped by these doors. Oh no, no, no. Everyone gave up hope, but not me. I didn't. Maybe there's a little chance.

320

With swelling trepidation, Bubba descended three stone steps into the darkness. The storm cellar was larger than he would have guessed. Once people stored canned goods here, as well as used it to protect themselves from the irregularities of a thundery Texas spring.

His eyes adjusted for about three full seconds before someone shrieked loudly and slammed him on the head with something very hard.

As Bubba fell over, he saw Willodean step into the light flowing in from the wide opening he'd just made. She stared at him with a horror-filled expression on her lovely face. Black laced tightly around his awareness as he made contact with the hard-packed dirt floor. An explosion of pain rocked his face as it connected violently against the lowest step. As the darkness closed in, he registered Willodean leaning closer to him. She seemed as though she'd lost ten pounds, and a blackened bruise discolored the right side of her face.

Bubba heard a crotchety voice say, "That ain't my thrice-damned great-nephew!"

Willodean said, "Oh God, Bubba," and it was like heaven to his ears.

Before Bubba's eyes closed he saw Willodean and Forrest Roquemore staring down at him from a great distance. Both wore heavy iron shackles around their wrists and chains that trailed into the darkness. Obviously, she had used the shackles as a weapon to hit him. Obviously, the chains had prevented her from escaping. Obviously, she was well and truly alive!

Oh.

Precious stared down at them from the opening. A panting Sheriff John materialized, holding his service weapon in his hands. "Holy God," he exclaimed, "what happened here?"

Willodean knelt next to Bubba and put her hand on his forehead. Nothing had ever felt better in Bubba's entire life.

It didn't matter that the back of his head and his jaw felt as if they were about to explode. Bubba smiled as he lost the battle to stay conscious.

Epilogue

I Ain't Giving Nothing Away with the Chapter Title So
You'll Just Have to Read It

*Saturday, January 7th or maybe Sunday, January 8th or
maybe Monday, January 9th*

Bubba heard voices.

Angels?

The voices discussed him.

"It's only a little fractured skull," said one.

"But he's been unconscious for a long, long time,"
said another. That one sounded like an angel. Throaty.
Sexy. Feminine.

A saucy angel. Just the kind I like.

"The doctor said it was okay," the first voice said.
"He thinks Bubba will wake up anytime now."

"I didn't mean to- "

"Bubba *will* understand the light from the open
doors blinded you, and you had to hit whoever came
down the stairs in order to survive. After all, Morgan
said he was going to kill the both of you. It could have
just as easily been him instead of Bubba."

"If I had seen it was Bubba," the second voice nearly
wailed.

"Oh hush," a third voice said. "He's got a hard head.
One of those deputies said the local police officers tried
to kick it in on Christmas Day, and he recovered from
that, didn't he?"

"Mom," the second voice said, "what if I caused brain
damage or something?"

"Then he'll forgive you because he won't know any
better," said the first voice.

The third voice laughed.

"That's not funny," said the second voice.

Bubba wasn't certain, but he thought the first voice was his mother. The third voice was likely Celestine Gray, and the second voice sounded a lot like Willodean.

Ifin Willodean is here I have to be in heaven.

His eyes slowly opened. He wished for toothpicks because the eyelids didn't want to stay open. He forced them up and made an effort to keep them there.

It wasn't exactly heaven, but it did have one angel in it.

Dimly Bubba recognized he was lying in a bed in a hospital room. If he wasn't mistaken he'd been in this very room the last time someone bashed in his noggin. An IV was attached to his right arm, and he was covered with several blankets, one of which was his great-great-grandmother's quilt made from Civil War uniforms.

Worse yet, he was wearing one of the hospital's baby-puke colored gowns again. He could just see the sleeve of it on his arm lying on top of the quilt. It wasn't a good color for him.

But what wasn't worse was Willodean standing at the side of the bed, looking at someone beside her. His eyes keenly roamed over her. She wore a red t-shirt and tight blue jeans. Her black hair tumbled around her shoulders, and she appeared as if she hadn't slept for some time. The bruise on her face had changed to shades of blue, green, and yellow. Despite all of that, she was still incredibly beautiful.

Thank you, God, Bubba prayed briefly.

Behind Willodean, Bubba's mother sat in a straight-backed chair. Her snowy hair was scraped back into a tight bun, and her cheeks were drawn. The normally spiffy clothing she wore was rumpled, indicating she wasn't as relaxed as she presented. She didn't appear as though she'd had much more sleep than Willodean.

On the little table next to his mother sat an arrangement of sunflowers with a bouquet of balloons bouncing about in the air above it. Next to the sunflowers sat a largish box with a prominent red ribbon on it. Bubba recognized the box. It was a hat box, and he'd seen it before in Willodean's apartment.

Something warm and mushy happened to his heart kind of like what happens to chocolate when it's been sitting in the sunlight.

Bubba's glance flickered back to his mother before something started to leak from one of his eyes.

Miz Demetrice's cornflower blue eyes widened as she grasped Bubba's eyes were open. A lingering, heartfelt sigh emitted from her mouth.

Celestine Gray walked in-between Willodean and Miz Demetrice. Willodean's mother said, "I've got to get some coffee in me. Can I- " She realized Miz Demetrice's mouth gaped open and turned to look at Bubba.

Bubba saw Willodean's wrists were heavily bandaged and reached out to touch one.

Willodean's head spun back as she jumped and cried, "Bubba!"

Bubba didn't know what to say when she leaned over him and pressed her face into his chest. Awkwardly, he stroked her back and tried to talk anyway but found he couldn't open his mouth.

Miz Demetrice grinned broadly at him. "Willodean beaned your head with the manacles," his mother said. "Then you broke your jaw when you fell down. The doctors have got it wired shut."

Celestine joined Willodean at the side of the bed and patted her daughter on the back.

"Morgan Newbrough confessed to just about everything," Celestine said. "Nancy Musgrave and he were up to some severe no-good. Morgan also led police to the grave of Robert Daughtry, the real Robert Daughtry."

The PSS bounded into the room. Purple cloth whirled around him in a cloud of violet grandeur. Somewhere he'd found a properly colored sheet to use as a cape. "See! My super senses told me Bubba would soon awaken!"

The cantankerous nurse, Dee Dee Lacour, followed him. "No loonies on the ward!" she cried.

"I resent that!" The PSS cried and leaped into the hallway. "I must go and save the rest of the world!" he trumpeted as he bounced down the passage, the purple sheet flying like a flag behind him.

Dee Dee cast her sour visage upon Bubba. "Oh, he's awake," she said, sarcasm dripping from her words. "Joy abounding. I'll get the doctor." She walked out just as sharply as she'd walked in.

"Did we leave anything out?" Miz Demetrice asked Celestine.

"No. Bubba rescued my daughter, got thumped for it, and now he's awake. That stalker guy didn't have anything to do with Willodean's disappearance, and Bubba pretty much came out smelling like a rose. Although he looks like something a mad cat dragged in, and his head probably hurts like a bitch." Celestine shrugged. She looked at Bubba again. "Thank you, Bubba," she added sincerely. "You're okay for a big rednecked goober." She stepped away.

Bubba's head did hurt. His jaw ached, and so did everything else. However, it was getting better considering Willodean was draped over him with her chin tucked into his chest.

"They'll give you something for the pain," Miz Demetrice said. She approached the bed from the side

326

opposite Willodean and carefully kissed his forehead. It seemed about the only place not damaged in some form. "Good to see your eyes open, Bubba dearest."

Willodean pulled away and stepped back. The expression on her face was curiously flushed. Bubba couldn't recollect a moment when Deputy Willodean Gray had such rosy cheeks and self-conscious eyes.

"Coffee, Miz Demetrice?" Celestine asked knowingly.

"Oh yes," Miz Demetrice agreed.

The pair left quickly.

Bubba stared at Willodean, soaking her in. Her face was on the gaunt side, and her green eyes were ringed with black, but she didn't look bad at all.

On the contrary.

Bubba motioned with his hand, a circular motion as if writing.

Willodean said, "Oh, the nurse brought in one of these magnetic writing boards for kids." She handed it to him and helped him to adjust his bed so that he was sitting at a forty-five degree angle. His head pounded like a drummer on meth, but he couldn't be too unhappy about it.

The writing board was in the shape of a frog's head and had an attached stylus. He blinked at it, picked it up, and wrote, "Did he hurt you?"

Bubba watched Willodean swallow at the words. "No, Morgan backed into my county car on the road. Knocked me out. Took me to that storm cellar and chained me to the supports. The manacles rubbed my wrists raw, but nothing else is wrong with me. Morgan was angry Miz Demetrice wasn't with me. His sister had told him to get your mother, but when it came down to it, he thought Miz Demetrice would be with me since the other officers were talking about Big Joe releasing her from jail. He was mad she wasn't. He was also confused. I think he needed a lot of guidance from Nancy Musgrave. Once she was arrested, he wasn't exactly sure what to do."

She took a breath and went on, "There were blankets in the storm cellar and a portable heater. He left bottled water and some packaged food. I had just about managed to pry the chains free of the cement supports when he brought Forrest Roquemore in and chained him, too. The old man's got seven stitches on his head, but he's okay." She paused. "I'm okay, too. Better than you."

Willodean's face crumpled. "I didn't mean to bash *your* skull in."

Bubba sighed. The air whistled between his wired jaws. He gingerly took her hand and caressed it lightly. It was the softest flesh he'd ever held and he didn't want to let go. But after a moment he did, erased the previous words on the pad, and wrote, "I know. It's okay. I'll be okay."

Her breath hitched once. Her exquisite face was expectant. "We still have a date to go on, don't we, Bubba?"

Bubba nodded and instantly wished he hadn't moved his head. He wrote, "Might have to puree that steak."

She chuckled.

"Is he awake?" Brownie stuck his head into the door. "Bubba!" he cried happily. He trotted over to the bed. An odd clicking noise followed him, and Bubba wearily figured Precious snuck in after the ten-year-old. "You look like heck warmed over, Bubba. I brought your dog. I got to go on television. You know they have funny kinds of shops in Times Square? I think folks in New York City were a mite tetchy with me. That fella on the news show sent a lawyer to see me with a piece of paper that said I cain't come within a hundred yards of him no more."

A dog's nose appeared at the side of the bed as Precious leaned up. Bubba let his hand droop so she could sniff it. She licked once, whined, and went under the bed to hide.

"No dogs in the hospital!" Dee Dee Lacour yelled from the hallway and tromped off.

Janie peeked in. "Is Bubba awake?" She smiled brightly. The typically dour eight-year-old seemed to be a completely different person when she smiled. "Bubba! Thank you so much for finding my auntie! She didn't mean to crack your melon!"

The girl came around on the other side of the bed and touched his hand. "I guess you're not really a perp after all. You're really a good guy. That investigator in Dallas was really bothered you found that stalker guy first. Also, I called Judge Perez and told her personally what a hero you are, and I'm pretty sure that made her drop the charges against you."

Janie stopped suddenly and stared intently at Bubba's face. "What happened to his- ?" she asked Willodean.

Willodean bit her lip.

Brownie stared at Janie and said, "'*Sup,* ba-bee." He bobbed his head and stuck his chest out in a way that was similar to The PSS.

Janie critically surveyed Brownie as if she had just sighted a criminal of the worst type. After a lengthy examination, she said, "You're the one who shocked the Christmas Killer with a Taser, and Matt Lauer, too."

"I'm Bubba's second cousin," Brownie said lasciviously. "Do you want to see my stun gun?"

"Yeah," Janie agreed and they fled the room.

"Does that kid know I'll kill him if he touches my

niece?" Willodean wondered. "Seriously, age does not matter when it comes to Janie's well-being."

"Janie can whup him," Bubba wrote. He dragged the strip across the magnetic board and erased the words. He wrote, "What's wrong with my face?"

"Um," Willodean wavered. "You remember what happened when Brownie got hold of some Sharpies before?"

Bubba nodded slowly. Visions of flowers, cat's whiskers, purple stars, and assorted pithy phrases danced in his head, not unlike sugar plums.

"Well, your cousins brought him yesterday, and plainly, Brownie thought you needed some...decoration."

Bubba would have sworn, but he really couldn't open his mouth. He thought several virulent words and phrases instead. He finally wrote, "Do I want to know what Brownie did?"

Willodean smiled slowly. "No, you really don't, big guy. Let's just say he used every color in the 24-pack assortment he brought. But don't worry. It won't stop me from kissing every part that doesn't hurt."

Bubba blushed, although he was aware Willodean couldn't tell on account of all the drawings on his face. He started to write something on the magnetic board but Willodean gently took it away.

Willodean leaned in and started with his cheek, carefully pressing her lips there. She softly pecked the end of his nose. And very tenderly she brushed his lips so as not to bother his jaw.

By the time Willodean had finished, Bubba had forgotten about any pain. He'd also forgotten about the Sharpie markers, which was just as well considering what Brownie had done.

The End

~

Author's Notes

Thanks to Mary E. Bates, freelance proofreader of ebooks, printed material, and websites. Contact her at mbates16@columbus.rr.com. She cleaned it up nicely. Anything that's left is just my "Bubba style."

I took liberties with the setup of Dallas and the organizational structure of the Dallas Police Department as well as with the Dallas Parole Office and the Dallas County Jail. I also messed with the prison systems of Texas and possibly some other stuff to suit my story. And I made it so that a Texas driver's license says the hair and eye color when in truth it only lists height and eye color. (Maybe they used to list hair color until everyone starting dyeing and bleaching.) Please forgive me for my literary initiative.

Thanks to R. Mac Wheeler for reading the manuscript and making it all pretty with all the colors he used to highlight it. He needs a 24-pack assortment of Sharpies! Read about Mac and his writing at http://home.roadrunner.com/~macwheeler/.

It was my sister's idea to have Miz Demetrice "kill" Elgin Snoddy in various manners. Originally I was going to stick with poison. Now I'm going to have to come up with an endless list of methods for killing off Bubba's father in perpetuity. Thanks, Cat. I love ya dearly.

There's a little something I have to confess. (No, I didn't murder anyone.) In *Bubba and the 12 Deadly Days of Christmas* I named one of my characters after an aunt. In later reworking's of the manuscript it ended up that this character became the murderer. (It was not so originally.) So basically, I named the murderer after my aunt. In a purely "duh" moment I thought my aunt would probably never read the book and it wouldn't be even marginally successful and it didn't matter. That's where the "duh" comes in. In any case, my aunt is a very good person and has always been supportive of her family. She is *not*, do I really need to say this, a murderer and never has been. *Sorry, dear.*

So in order to make a little amends, I named characters in the third book after the rest of my aunts and uncles. They're the hunting hounds that belong to Lewis Robson. Do I really need to say that I don't think of my aunts and uncles as dogs? Well, they're not, but I thought it was funny. I expect they'll think it's funny, too. If not, well, they'll never speak with me again.

I truly appreciate my husband and daughter putting up with my weirdness while I'm writing. I know I'm a complete goop when I'm into a book. Love you both!

A note to Matt Lauer. Please don't sue me. It was meant in a wholly good way and not defamatory to you in the least. Plus, it was funny. Also, I changed the arrangement of *The Today Show*'s set so that Brownie could sit next to Matt as prelude to you-know-what. That isn't the way the show is, but it is in my imagination.

And thanks to all those wonderful fans on Facebook, on my blog, and from my website who are endlessly supportive, especially when I gripe about bad reviews. Love ya!

If I left anyone out, I sincerely apologize, but thanks all the same.

Caren L. Bevill

About the Author

C.L. Bevill has lived in Texas, Arizona, and Oregon. She once was in the U.S. Army and a graphic illustrator. She holds degrees in social psychology and counseling. She is the author of *Bubba and the Dead Woman*, *Bubba and the 12 Deadly Days of Christmas*, *Bayou Moon*, and *Shadow People*, among others. Presently she lives with her husband and her daughter in Virginia and continues to constantly write. She can be reached at www.clbevill.com or you can read her blog at www.carwoo.blogspot.com

Other Novels by C.L. Bevill

~

Mysteries:
Bubba and the Dead Woman
Bubba and the 12 Deadly Days of Christmas
Bubba and the Missing Woman
Bubba and the Mysterious Murder Note

Bayou Moon

Paranormal Romance:
Veiled Eyes (Lake People 1)
Disembodied Bones (Lake People 2)
Arcanorum (Lake People 3)

The Moon Trilogy:
Black Moon (The Moon Trilogy 1)
Amber Moon (The Moon Trilogy 2)
Silver Moon (The Moon Trilogy 3)

Cat Clan Novellas:
Harvest Moon
Blood Moon
Crescent Moon (Coming Soon)

Shadow People

Sea of Dreams

Suspense:
The Flight of the Scarlet Tanager

Black Comedy:
The Life and Death of Bayou Billy
Missile Rats

Chicklet:
Dial 'M' For Mascara

~

CPSIA information can be obtained
at www.ICGtesting.com
Printed in the USA
BVHW041259120521
607177BV00012B/269